LOOKING FOR MR BIG

MAGGIE HUDSON

LOOKING FOR MR BIG

HarperCollins*Publishers*

This novel is entirely a work of fiction. The names,
characters and incidents portrayed in it are the work of the
author's imagination. Any resemblance to actual persons,
living or dead, events or localities is entirely coincidental.

HarperCollins*Publishers*
77–85 Fulham Palace Road,
Hammersmith, London W6 8JB

www.**fireandwater**.com

Published by HarperCollins*Publishers* 2001

1 3 5 7 9 8 6 4 2

ISBN 0-00-226137-5

Typeset in Sabon by Palimpsest Book Production Limited,
Polmont, Stirlingshire

Printed in Great Britain by
Omnia Books Ltd, Glasgow

For Sheila Flight.
A brilliant sister-in-law and a good friend.

ACKNOWLEDGEMENTS

Again, many thanks to my agent Caroline Sheldon, and my editors, Rachel Hore and Anne O'Brien.

For all the help, stories and laughter, my thanks to Hannah Bownes-Smith, Linda Britter, Natasha Pemberton, Don Rumbelow and Jock Steven.

Chapter One

There was an air of tense expectancy in the courtroom. Somewhere in the distance thunder rumbled. Though no windows looked out towards nearby St Paul's, Deena King knew that the cathedral's dome would be silhouetted by rain-heavy cloud. She also knew that the case she was presenting was a case she was about to lose.

Her eyes locked with those of the man whose testimony she had been so sure of.

'Five minutes, Mr Graveney?' she queried, her voice studiedly neutral in order to give him room to admit to a slip of the tongue. 'You are quite certain?'

In his statement Mr Graveney, a retired policeman, had been quite categorical about the time. 'Forty-five minutes,' he had said. 'That's how long the van was parked outside the house with a man seated in the front passenger-seat and with the house door shut. I was clearing out my garage. My driveway slopes down from the road so steeply that when they drew up the driver and his passenger wouldn't have seen me. I saw the driver get out of the van and go in the house and then someone – who, I couldn't say – closed the door. I was opening my garage doors and was listening in to the England–Ireland match on my tranny. It had just kicked off when they arrived and it was when I was going back into the kitchen, at half-time, that the van moved off. So I'm quite sure of the time that the driver of the van was in the house. It was forty-five minutes.'

Coming from so reliable a source it had been vital testimony in a case that rested entirely on the plaintiff's unsubstantiated allegation that, for over thirty minutes, she had been prevented from leaving her home and during that time had been subjected to unwanted sexual advances and, finally, a sexual assault. It was an assault the defendant, twenty-three-year-old Malcolm Porritt, denied. He had, he said, been in the Mustafa home for no more than five minutes and the friend who had accompanied him to the house had been with him throughout.

It was a statement his friend had corroborated. 'We'd just popped in to see old man Musty about a plumbing job he wanted doing. He wasn't in, so we said we'd come back another time. That was all there was to it. In and out, we were. Five minutes at the most, and the door was open the whole time. If she says any different, she's a nutter.'

Throughout the previous day eighteen-year-old Naheed Mustafa, the plaintiff, had been seated in court with her father and sister, a black scarf swathing her head and shoulders so that only her eyes were visible. A Bosnian Muslim, her testimony had been spoken in such a low, hesitant voice that Deena had been well aware of the Judge beginning to lose patience.

She had not lost patience, though. What she had been – and still was – was angry. Furiously, monumentally angry. Five years ago in her home village of Sjeverin, Naheed Mustafa had, together with her mother and her sister and other women from Sjeverin, been rounded up by Serb soldiers who had fire-bombed their homes and, as their homes had burned, gang-raped them.

Her mother, who had been unable to live with what she perceived as her shame, had committed suicide. The rest of the family had eventually been granted refugee status in Britain. After the horrors they had known, Deena could only imagine how safe a sanctuary Britain must have seemed to the Mustafa family.

And then, in Britain, men she did not know had again entered Naheed's home. Not soldiers this time, but young, casually dressed Londoners. And one of them, watched by the other, had forced her into a sexual act that Deena knew would have ripped wide the years, bringing back unspeakable memories, robbing her of all sense of newly regained safety.

'Five minutes,' Mr Graveney repeated. Deena, seeing how white his knuckles were clenched, knew that nothing was going to budge him. He'd been got at, either by bribery or intimidation.

She hitched her gown a little higher on her shoulders, struggling to maintain her air of outward calm. Usually, if there was the remotest chance of a witness being got at, she was at least aware of it – and prepared.

This time, though, the possibility hadn't even crossed her mind. And she wasn't prepared, not in the slightest. In a case which rested almost entirely on who was speaking the truth – the plaintiff or the defendant and his friend – she had been so sure Graveney's evidence would clinch things in Naheed Mustafa's favour that she had left herself with no fall-back position.

For someone whose case preparation was usually so very thorough it was an unforgivable error. As Mr Graveney apologetically explained to the Court that he was epileptic, that he had suffered a *petit mal* whilst listening to the rugby and therefore been totally disorientated about time, she knew it was an error that was irrecoverable. Five minutes may have been long enough for a forced act of fellatio to have taken place, but no jury would now be convinced that it had done so.

As speedily as possible she brought her disastrous

3

examination-in-chief to a close, knowing quite well why she'd been so negligent. Her mind had been on other things – had been ever since Hugh had failed to register at college after his summer holiday in Turkey. That, at twenty, her son was a more than capable adult hadn't lessened her anxieties – and in succumbing to them she had failed Naheed Mustafa in a way she would not soon forget.

'We ran into bad luck there,' her junior counsel whispered to her as the case was dismissed and they gathered up their papers and rose to their feet. 'Graveney was nobbled, wasn't he?'

Deena nodded, privately determined to find out exactly how he'd been nobbled. Malcolm Porritt hadn't looked as if he would have had either the nous or the wherewithal to coerce a witness, but appearances, as she well knew, were often deceptive.

Twenty minutes later as she left the lady barristers' robing-room and began walking along the busy concourse towards the main staircase she saw Porritt, standing in conversation with his solicitor. And she saw something else. She saw a metal badge of two scarlet amalgamated letters in his lapel. A badge that had most certainly not been on display when he had been in court. NF. National Front.

Her jaw tightened. So that was who had intimidated Graveney. It hadn't been Porritt alone; it had been the ugly organisation of which he was a member.

Sensing her eyes on him, Porritt turned his head, met her gaze and, with a look of triumph that made her flesh crawl, winked.

Trembling with anger, she strode on to the end of the concourse and then hurried down the broad sweep of

4

the stairs. It wasn't the first time she'd been treated with such leering contempt by men she'd faced across a courtroom. Usually, though, as they were found guilty and their sentences handed down, the final triumph was hers. That hadn't happened in this instance and the failure anguished her.

She stepped out on to the pavement, her junior scurrying at her heels.

'Are you going straight back to chambers, Ms King?' he asked as, instead of heading into Fleet Street on foot as she usually did, she crossed to the kerb and began flagging down a cab.

'No. I have some other business to take care of.'

As a cab slewed to a halt she didn't trouble to explain that the business in question was personal. Just yards away the Mustafa family were also getting into a taxi-cab and she was too acutely aware of them to be in the mood for speech of any kind.

'Whitehall,' she said tersely to the driver, stepping inside the cab and sinking back against the cracked leather seating, her fingers pressed against her temples in an attempt to relieve the pain fast building up there.

'You don't look very well, Deena dear.' Rupert Pembury-Smythe, a Foreign Office official with so many years' service behind him that retirement was seductively beckoning, cocked his head slightly to one side, eyeing her with concern.

She stood at a window near his desk, looking down at a magnificent view of the Cenotaph. 'I've had a bad day in court,' she said bleakly. 'All my own fault, and all because I've been so worried about Hugh that I didn't give the case sufficient thought and attention.'

'Were you prosecuting or defending?' As he poured

out two glasses of dry sherry, there was real interest in his voice. She was the daughter of a long-deceased friend and, though their relationship wasn't very close, he had always followed her career with interest.

'Prosecuting,' she said, and something in her voice told him that, whatever it was that had gone so disastrously wrong, it wasn't up for discussion.

He handed her the sherry, reflecting that her father, who at his death had been one of the youngest High Court judges in the country, had been similarly unforthcoming about any case in which he was involved.

'Hugh is missing,' she said, coming straight to the point of her visit. Her fingers tightened around the stem of the sherry-glass. 'He went to Turkey during the summer vac, backpacking with a friend. He's at Oxford, as I think you know. Term started two weeks ago and he hasn't returned, hasn't been in touch with me in any way.'

'Two weeks?' He raised silvered eyebrows. 'Two weeks isn't very long, Deena. Not when the young person in question is male and . . . how old? Eighteen? Nineteen?'

'Twenty.' She turned away from the window to face him, jaw-length black hair swinging glossily. 'But I know my son, and his not being back for the start of term is totally out of character. I wondered if you would help, Rupert. If you would ask the British Embassy in Istanbul if they could contact him for me . . .'

He took an old-maidish sip of his sherry, surprised at the depth of her anxiety. Remembering the circumstances – that there was no husband on the scene and hadn't been since she had returned from St Hilda's at twenty-two, married and with a child – he said: 'I could certainly ensure that the Embassy is informed Hugh is travelling in Turkey and that there are concerns as to his exact whereabouts – I take it that once you know where he is, your anxiety will be alleviated whether he then does, or doesn't, contact you?'

'Yes,' she said, setting her sherry-glass down on the corner of his Biedermeier desk, well understanding his reluctance to put Foreign Office officials into the nannying position of asking a twenty-year-old man to telephone home for no urgently valid reason. 'I know how neurotic this sounds, Rupert, but I keep thinking of the two hundred and fifty or so tourists who have vanished in Turkey over the last few years. I know the Foreign Office plays down passport theft, but it *is* rife and, all in all, Hugh has now been out of contact for six weeks.'

She gave an expressive lift of her shoulder, amethyst eyes meeting his. 'He's all the family I have, Rupert. You're in a position to have my fears either eased or verified, so I had to come and I had to ask.'

He wasn't a man who went in for much physical contact but he stepped towards her, putting a comforting hand on her Armani-jacketed shoulder. 'My dear Deena, though I certainly don't share your fears as to Hugh's safety – and have to admit that I find them excessive – I shall most certainly make enquiries regarding his whereabouts. Now, let me recap. He is a young academic who is backpacking in Turkey because . . . ?'

'Because he's interested in Islamic art. He intended visiting Iznik, Edirne and Istanbul, returning to Britain the first week in October so as to be back in Oxford for the start of term. I contacted the police yesterday and reported him missing. They said they would put a passport-check in hand.'

He suppressed any surprise he felt at that last bit of information and, his voice full of reassurance, said: 'Then as well as seeing to it that the strongest representations regarding Hugh are made to our Embassy in Istanbul I will chivvy up the results of that check. Stop worrying, my dear. Leave things with me.'

'Thank you, Rupert,' she said gratefully and, having kissed him on the cheek, walked across to the door, not wanting to take up any more of his time.

Now that they were no longer in eye contact, his facial expression changed, becoming so sombre it would have scared the life out of her if she had seen it.

As the door closed behind her he was profoundly thankful that she'd had no way of knowing how expected her visit had been. He gave a heavy sigh. There were now many telephone calls to be made. None of which would be to Istanbul.

Deena stepped out into Whitehall and began walking in the direction of Trafalgar Square, well aware that she should be going straight back to chambers. She was in court again tomorrow and as it was already late afternoon, Cheryl, her clerk, would by now know which court she would be appearing in and would have an updated brief awaiting her attention.

She paid no heed to the busy traffic, thick with taxi-cabs. It would only take her twenty minutes or so to walk to Lincoln's Inn and it was a walk she needed in order to clear her head. Had she been idiotically premature in asking for Rupert's help? In her experience all Foreign Office mandarins were ascetic pricks who hadn't a clue about real life and Rupert was no exception to the rule.

Instead of curving right, into the Strand, she embarked on a detour by walking briskly down Northumberland Avenue to the Embankment. It was a warm day for mid October and the sun was bright. She dipped into her shoulder-bag for her sunglasses, aware of how gilded her picture of Hugh had been. 'I know my son,' she had said in categorical tones. The truth was, of course, that like many other mothers of twenty-year-olds, she was only too aware of how little she knew her child.

Still deep in thought she began to walk through the soothing green swathe of the Embankment Gardens. Hugh's self-containment was something she had long become accustomed to and, if he kept his thoughts to himself, it wasn't so surprising when she tended to do so, too.

She turned left, walking through the narrow alleys and courtyards of two of London's Inns of Court, the Middle Temple and the Inner Temple. As a member of Lincoln's Inn, the Temple wasn't home to her, but she had always found its atmosphere particularly peaceful.

In Middle Temple Gardens she sat down on a considerately placed bench seat.

Did it matter that she had perhaps misled Rupert into thinking that Hugh had been far more precise about his arrangements than, in fact, he had been?

'Hi Mum,' he'd said with typical teenage nonchalance. 'I'm taking off to Turkey for the rest of the summer vac. Iznik, Edirne, all those ancient pottery and tile places. I'll send a postcard.'

He hadn't, of course, but then, like most backpacking teenagers, he wasn't in the habit of sending postcards; not unless he was asking for money to be wired to him.

She foraged in her bag for cigarettes and lighter, darkly reflecting that, on far too many occasions, bringing up a son single-handed was no joke. Pleasant and well-mannered though he was, Hugh never talked to her in the way she was sure a daughter would have talked. After an evening out he never came into her study, or bedroom, to chat. No confidences were ever shared. His

Oxford friends were mere names to her; any girlfriends a complete mystery.

'Boys are like that,' Cheryl had once said with comfortable ease. And Cheryl, who at fifty-eight was twenty years her senior, and whose job it was to organise her day for her, accepting solicitors' instructions, arranging client conferences, making sure papers that had to be seen before advising were with her in time, had the domestic experience to know what she was talking about for she was married with five teenage children, three girls and two boys. 'My two boys never chat like the girls do,' she had said, checking the court list for the following day. 'Getting info about their private lives is like getting blood out of a stone.'

It had been comfort of a sort, but not much. Cheryl had, after all, a husband to help share domestic worries. She had only a well-heeled lover, heir to an earldom, who had so far breezed through his thirty-two years without any domestic shackles whatsoever.

She dropped her barely smoked cigarette to the ground and crushed it into extinction. Benedict had warned her that Rupert would be reluctant to cause waves on behalf of an adult male who had merely dropped out of sight for a couple of weeks whilst backpacking abroad. 'Christ, Deena!' he'd said exasperatedly, triggering off an almighty row between the two of them. 'If Hugh is old enough to get married, die for his country and vote, he's old enough to do without this level of maternal angst!' That he'd been proven right was not something she wanted to dwell on. Wishing she'd never mentioned her intentions to him, she rose to her feet.

Evening was drawing in. The October sun had lost its Indian-summer warmth and, as she still had to be apprised about tomorrow, she needed to make tracks pretty briskly if Cheryl wasn't to be late leaving for home.

'Get hold of Teddy for me, will you, Cheryl?' Deena said the instant she set foot in her office.

Teddy was the young private investigator who did all of her unofficial ferreting. 'To do with this morning, is it?' Cheryl asked, dumping a sheaf of faxes down on Deena's already crowded desk.

Deena nodded, accustomed to Cheryl knowing the results of cases almost as soon as judgement was handed down. 'It was a disaster,' she said bluntly, flicking through the faxes, 'and not because Naheed Mustafa was unable to stand up to cross-examination – she did, hard for her though it obviously was.'

'Well, whatever it was that went wrong,' Cheryl said, knowing exactly what had gone wrong because Deena's junior counsel had told her the instant he had returned to chambers, 'there's nothing that can be done now, is there? The verdict's been given and it's history. So why the need for Teddy?'

Deena pushed the faxes to one side. 'Because the bastard was National Front. He flaunted the badge as he left court. So, either Graveney backed down because the Front told him that if he didn't he'd face unpleasant consequences, or he did so because he's a sympathiser. I'd like to know which. And I'd like to know why Graveney took early retirement from the Police Force. Was it voluntary or was it a way for the police to be rid of a rotten apple?'

Cheryl opened her mouth to say something and then changed her mind. It was pointless telling Deena she took her cases too much to heart. She always did. It was what made her such an exceptional barrister. Instead she said:

'I've put an early edition of this evening's *Standard* in your in-tray. Thought you might like to know what kind of shenanigans have been going on in Court One whilst you'd been doing your stuff in Court Two.'

'Court One? The Virtue case?' Despite having so much else on her mind, Deena reached towards her in-tray. The Virtues were not so much a family as a criminal clan. Years ago she had appeared for the Prosecution when Al Virtue, the eldest of the four Virtue brothers, had received a sentence of ten years for handling stolen bullion. It had been her first major case and, because the Virtues' ability to escape guilty verdicts by dint of bribery and corruption was legendary, winning it had been the making of her reputation.

She looked down at the *Standard*'s front page. The headline 'Judge Rules Virtue Evidence Unsound' surmounted a photograph of twenty-five-year-old Tommy Virtue leaving the Old Bailey, his brothers and various hangers-on ranged jubilantly around him. All were either brandishing bottles of champagne or giving triumphant victory signs; all except one were shouting with laughter.

The exception was the tall beefy figure standing with an arm draped around Tommy's shoulders. Al Virtue merely had a negligently amused smile on his face. She wondered who he had bribed to lose or corrupt evidence this time and, so strongly reminded of Malcolm Porritt that a spasm of revulsion shook her shoulders, dropped the newspaper into the waste-paper basket.

'Tomorrow's case is being heard at ten o'clock at Snaresbrook,' Cheryl continued as the fax machine bleeped into life again. 'And Mr Deakin would like a word with you, when you have a moment.'

Deena made a non-committal noise deep in her throat.

Snaresbrook Crown Court was only a half a dozen or so stops away on the Central line and if she left in the morning at eight-thirty she would be there in plenty of time. Mungo Deakin, her Head of Chambers, probably wanted her agreement on a piece of chambers' business.

None of the faxes she'd flicked through were of importance and, after she'd spoken on the phone to Teddy, giving him a full briefing of what she wanted from him, her thoughts reverted to Hugh.

Looking at the situation objectively she was, of course, over-reacting. Rupert had certainly thought so, but Rupert wasn't a parent; if he had been, his true feelings might have been a little different.

'There are some new briefs to be looked at,' Cheryl reminded her as she emerged from the small ante-room wearing her coat and clutching a carrier-bag full of the groceries she had bought in her lunch-hour. 'You don't need me for anything else this evening, do you?'

Deena looked towards a small table on which two briefs tied with white ribbon were waiting for her attention. 'No, that's fine Cheryl, thank you,' she said appreciatively. 'Goodnight.'

As Cheryl let herself out of the building, Deena put the briefs in her large shoulder-bag, her thoughts still on Rupert. Would he pull as many Foreign Office strings as possible for her? He had said he would, but saying and doing were two different things.

She walked from the room, locking the door behind her, reflecting that the main problem was Rupert's total lack of any sixth sense, coupled with her own – where Hugh was concerned – too highly developed one. Her fingers tightened on the key-ring. She had always trusted her instincts both in and outside the courtroom and, trusting them now, she was certain Hugh was in trouble.

She dropped the keys into her bag, knowing that the first priority had to be finding him. Not until she had located him could wheels be set in motion to sort out whatever trouble he was in.

'How did things go?' Benedict asked, removing the cork from the bottle of Beaujolais he had brought with him.

Deena, who hours ago had wished she'd made no arrangement to cook dinner at her home that evening – and who now had no intention of doing any cooking at all – slid a pack of Marks & Spencer's lamb chasseur into the microwave.

'So-so,' she said, turning away from the microwave to face him. 'Rupert didn't share my urgency about the situation but he's going to ask the British Ambassador in Istanbul to give Hugh's disappearance his personal attention. You were right, though, when you said he would think my anxiety excessive. When I mentioned the possibility of Hugh having been the victim of passport theft his eyes practically glazed over.'

Irritated as he was at once again finding himself discussing Hugh – sure that if he had been the one who'd gone AWOL in Turkey she would barely have noticed – he suppressed a flare of amusement. 'Yes,' he said wryly, his suede-booted feet crossed at the ankle as he leaned against her breakfast bar, his arms folded. 'I can imagine.'

'No, you can't.' Tiredness made her voice sharp. 'You think all this maternal anxiety is comic, don't you? Well, it isn't.'

As he curbed his now rising irritation she folded her arms tightly across her chest.

'Have you any idea of the demand for new identities that exists in countries like Turkey?' she demanded, making him feel as if she were a school-teacher and he a not very bright small boy. 'Violent passport theft has rocketed and the only reason the figures aren't more widely known is because of the knock-on effect it would have on the tourist industry.'

She was wearing what he thought of as her 'work' clothes. An Armani jacket, a tailored skirt, a silk blouse and court shoes. Today the jacket was silver-grey, the skirt black, and the blouse white. It was an uncompromising fashion statement, though he had to admit that as today's skirt had a decently high centre split and the grey suede shoes were stiletto-heeled and worn with shiny sheer stockings, the overall effect was surprisingly sexy.

The pinger went on the microwave. Deena ignored it. 'What the tourist industry should be doing,' she continued relentlessly, wanting him to see the situation as she saw it, 'is abandoning its head-in-the-sand approach to identity crime and using its profits to lobby governments into taking action in preventing it.'

His irritation was threatening to become full-blown. As far as he was concerned, her being dressed as if she were still in court was one thing; her speaking to him as if she were was quite another.

He flashed a look across to the cork wallboard where a reminder list, a shopping list, two dry-cleaning tickets and a shoe-repair ticket were pinned next to a recent photograph of Hugh. Dark-haired like Deena, Hugh was also, unlike Deena, so dark-eyed as to look more Spanish or Italian than English. The friend who had photographed him had caught him standing against a backdrop of trees, a can of Coke in one hand, the other hooked by a thumb into the front pocket of his jeans. Even to Benedict's critical eyes he was an extremely personable young man – tall and slenderly built, with a whippiness about him that suggested he was tougher than he looked.

Not for the first time he reflected on the oddity of having a girlfriend whose son was a mere twelve years his junior. If they married, he would be Hugh's stepfather. As he couldn't even imagine an elder brother/younger brother kind of relationship with Hugh, the prospect was bizarre.

'I hate the complacency that is shown to this kind of crime,' Deena was saying as she finally took the lamb chasseur out of the microwave. 'It means that all victims of identity thefts are simply listed as missing persons . . . and that's only if and when they *get* listed.'

Where the subject of identity crime was concerned, he'd had enough. 'How long will you leave things before informing Hugh's father?' he asked, genuinely interested and knowing the question would stop her in her tracks.

She was sliding the meal from its microwave container into a serving dish and her hand jerked so abruptly that sauce spilled on to the immaculate surface of flecked granite. 'What the hell kind of a question is that?' All the emotions she'd kept such a tight rein on all day – her anger at her performance in court, her growing anxiety over Hugh – surged to the surface as she spun to face him. 'Have I ever said anything to indicate that Hugh's father is even alive, let alone that I'm in contact with him?'

'No,' he said equably, reaching for the bottle of Beaujolais. 'You've never said anything about him, period. Which is why I was interested and why I asked.' He poured out two glasses of wine and proffered her one of them, still waiting for an answer to his question.

'Informing anyone other than the police and the Foreign Office isn't an issue,' she said stiffly, accepting the glass of wine and leaving him no wiser than he'd been before.

'But surely . . .' he began persistently, about to make an issue of it and then stopped short, appalled. She was holding the stem of the wine glass so tightly that her knuckles were white.

'Deena . . . I'm sorry.' He put his glass of wine down so swiftly it spilt. 'I shouldn't have brought up a subject you can't bear speaking about. Not at a time like this.' He took her glass and set it down, deeply concerned at seeing her so near to losing control.

Putting his arms round her, he drew her away from the kitchen units, his mouth against her hair. Despite his concern, a smile touched his lips. No matter how severely she dressed for court, her hair never looked severe. Thick, shiny as satin and Cleopatra-black, it had been the first thing he had noticed about her. The second thing had been her eyes. Light and clear and full of intelligence, they were the most amazing shade of amethyst. He was a sculptor, not a painter, but he'd wanted to paint her. And to make love to her. Neither objective had been easily achieved.

They'd dated for three months before he finally got her in his bed. By then he'd been beginning to wonder if the outcome would be worth the effort. It had, but not quite in the way he'd been hoping for. The reticence he found so tantalising hadn't been shed with her clothes. Though their lovemaking was satisfying to both of them, he'd always been aware that, where truly deep emotion was concerned, Deena never gave one hundred per cent.

It was a glitch in their relationship that never ceased to bug him. Though it wasn't something he brooded over, he did sometimes wonder about her relationships with previous lovers – the lovers her bedroom expertise told him she must have had, but whom, like Hugh's father, she never spoke about.

'Let's forget the meal,' he said gently, knowing neither of them now wanted it. 'Let's go to bed.'

His hands had moved to her shoulders and he was

looking down into her face. As he saw heat darken her eyes until they were violet, he knew he'd made the right suggestion.

'Let's not go to bed.' Her voice was taut. Sex, if it was urgent enough, would enable her to forget her anxiety and fear, at least for a little while. Her hands were against his chest, her eyes meeting his. 'Let's make love now. Here. In the kitchen.'

He sucked in his breath, his hands slipping down over her skirted bottom, his reaction, as he realised she was wearing stockings, not tights, immediate. Exultant that an evening that had seemed so doomed was, at last, proving enjoyable, his mouth came down on hers in swift unfumbled contact and, kissing her deeply, he pulled up her skirt, his fingers caressing the smooth warm flesh above her stocking-tops.

Later, much later, they had continued their lovemaking in the bedroom. Much later still, when they had both finally fallen asleep, the ringing of her bedside phone had brutally woken them.

'Yes? Who?' he heard her say as, still naked, she silenced it and pushed herself up against the pillows. And then, a few seconds later: 'But that's impossible! It just can't be!'

Violently she swung her legs out of bed, standing up, pushing her tumbled hair away from her face. 'Are you sure? Are you *quite* sure?'

Aware that the evening was now well and truly over and that it was time he started making tracks towards his studio in Camden, he, too, swung his feet to the mahogany wood-blocked floor.

'I'm in court tomorrow until four o'clock,' she was saying, her voice tense. 'Yes, afterwards. Of course.'

She dropped the receiver with a clatter. 'It was the

police,' she said starkly, facing him from the far side of the rumpled bed. 'Hugh isn't in Turkey. He can't be. His passport expired six months ago and he's made no application to have it renewed.'

She stared across at him, her pupils so dilated her eyes looked black. 'At the time he phoned me he can't have realised, but when he discovered he wasn't going to be able to get it renewed in time for his Turkey trip, why didn't he tell me he was going to have to change his plans? And if he isn't in Turkey, Benedict, where is he? *Where in God's name is he?*'

Chapter Two

'Where the hell is she?' Al Virtue shouted across the crowded pub to the brother nearest him in age.

Several yards away forty-year-old Stuart Virtue shrugged massive shoulders. 'Dunno, Al,' he shouted back over a sea of smoke-wreathed heads. 'Her mobile is turned off. I left a message on it and another one for her at the university. Obviously she ain't got 'em yet.'

'Shit!' Al's expletive was for no one's benefit but his own. He drained his glass of brandy in a deep swallow, knowing he shouldn't have asked Stuart to make the telephone call, knowing he should have made it himself. With everything else he'd had to take care of that day, though, it had seemed only reasonable to have delegated the phone call telling Fleur of her uncle's acquittal and asking her to get herself to London for the celebration party.

'Blimey, mate! What yer doing with an empty glass in yer 'and?' someone said as they squeezed past him.

Grappling with intense disappointment, Al didn't trouble to answer. Why the hell hadn't he made sure Fleur had received the message? He shot the cuff of his Italian hand-tailored suit, looking down at his Rolex. It was nearly nine. Even without a message she would know by now what had happened at the Bailey. The early evening news programmes had been full of nothing else. And she would know where they'd be partying. So why wasn't she with them? Oxford was an hour away – it wasn't the ends of the earth.

'Here you are, AV,' a barmaid who looked as if she should still be in a school-room said, as, having fought her way through the crush, she took possession of the empty brandy-glass, replacing it with a generously full one. 'It's a smashing party. Will we be carrying on after hours?'

'Better ask Max, Lulu,' he said, his smile taking any sting out of his words. 'He's the landlord.'

'Oh! Yes.' She blushed furiously. 'Sorry, AV. I forgot.' It was an easy mistake to have made. Where Al was concerned, there were certain things that, though fairly widely known, were never openly referred to – and The Maid being his pub, though his name was not above the door, was one of them.

Al made a mental note to check whether Lulu was old enough to be served drinks, let alone be serving them, and went back to pondering his gross act of carelessness where his precious only child was concerned.

It wasn't as if he'd spoken to Fleur recently. Well over a month ago, during the summer holidays, she'd gone abroad for a couple of weeks with a university friend. It had been a cheap package deal to Tenerife or Tuscany or some other place beginning with 'T'. He'd had other phone calls coming through when she'd rung him and – a rare event for him when talking to Fleur – his attention had been diverted. Wherever it was, though, that she and her girlfriend had gone, he'd expected to see her before she returned to Oxford for the start of the autumn term.

He hadn't done so. Tonight would have been the first time he'd seen her in weeks, and he, like the rest of the family and the host of friends who had known her since the cradle and who were all now whooping it up at his expense, had been looking forward to her joining them.

He looked around him. All three of his brothers were

there. Tommy, the baby of the family and the brother for whom the party was being held, was nearly so senseless with champagne that only the number of people pressing round him was keeping him upright. Kevin, seated nearby on a bar-stool, had the neck of his shirt undone, his tie dragged loose. He was cracking a joke, his wife and daughter at his side, his girlfriend only a few feet away.

Al's eyebrows pulled into a slight frown. Lol didn't yet know Max's ex-girlfriend was now her husband's mistress, but she soon would and then – as always – it would be time for everyone to take cover. Hoping the shit wasn't going to hit the fan this particular evening, his eyes flicked across to where Stuart was centre of a throng containing not only his two sons, but also his twin stepsons. Stuart took family life seriously and his wife, Ginny, had very few causes for complaint. Other wives were in the bar, of course, and other girlfriends and aspiring girlfriends along with aunts, uncles, cousins, a near army of mates and a heavy sprinkling of business acquaintances.

Some of the businesses were straight, as were a couple of the friends. 'Rule number one,' their old man had always said: 'make sure you've got a few trustworthy straight mates who'll be willing to front things for you.'

The straight mate category was the one Max fell into and, when it came to property that really mattered to him, such as The Maid, the name on the title deeds was Max's.

'No Fleur?' Max now said as, leaving the bar in the hands of the bar staff, he eased a way through the crush towards him.

'Nope. Stuart didn't manage to contact her. Not that I'd have thought it would have been necessary, considering the press coverage.'

'Have you tried yourself?'

'Yeah.' Al tapped the bulge in the breast of his jacket occasioned, by way of a change, by his own mobile and not a rather different piece of hardware. 'I tried a second or so ago.'

'Nothing much you can do then,' Max said, almost as gloomy as Al at the prospect of not having Fleur at the party. 'Maybe she's got a lot of work on . . . studying and all that.'

'Yeah. Maybe.' Despite the intense pride Al took in his daughter's university life the finer details of it were as much of a mystery to him as they were to Max. What he did know, though, was that Fleur's Oxford college was world-class premier league. If Fleur had to be there, even though a family celebration was on, then she had to be there and that was all there was to it. It didn't, however, alter the fact that she could have phoned. Even if she hadn't been able to reach him on his mobile, she could have rung the pub.

'No use brooding about it, Al,' Max said, remembering the reason he'd deserted the bar. 'Bazza's left a message. He says the number you talked about will be parked up tomorrow in the NCP at Hanover Square and he wants to know if he should try and make the eleven-thirty ferry in the morning?'

'Yeah.' Al dragged his thoughts back to business matters. 'Tell him Harwich, not Dover. Dover's been done to death this last few weeks.'

Max nodded, uncaring of what the messages meant, far more interested in the knot of people clustered close to Kevin. 'D'yer think Lol will do a re-run of her air-rifle routine when she finds out Kev's playing away from home again?' he asked suddenly, his voice queerly abrupt.

'Hell! I hope not!' Al shot Max a hard look. 'You're

not thinking of dropping her a word, are you? Because if you are, don't. Anyway, I thought you weren't that bothered?'

'I'm not.' It was a lie that wouldn't have convinced a three-year-old. 'She's a gold-digger.' His eyes remained fixed on the young redhead standing dangerously close to Lol. 'When she realised my pockets weren't deep, she moved on to someone whose were.' He shrugged. 'It's an old story. I should be used to it by now.'

This was so true, Al didn't bother to comment. Max's trouble was that he wanted the kind of streetwise glamorous girlfriends that the Virtues were always knee-deep in. As these were generally gangster-groupies who liked to be seen out and about with heavy villains, the disappointments Max met with were legion.

He drank his brandy and then, as the noise level in the pub grew even more deafening, said: 'I'm shooting off, Max. Keep an eye on Tommy for me. He'd be better staying here the night than going home.'

'Yeah. Right. I'll do my best. What do I tell Sharlene if she shows?'

'She won't.' Al didn't bother explaining why. Explanations weren't his scene.

He began to make his way out of the pub, the crush of family, friends and hangers-on making way for him as automatically as the Red Sea parting for Moses.

'Wotcha, Al.' 'Nice ter see yer, AV.' 'Is your Tommy a lucky bastard, AV, or what?' was said to him time and time again as he made steady progress towards the door.

With a nod of acknowledgement here and throwing a friendly punch on a shoulder or a slap on the back there, he finally reached his objective. As he stepped out into the fresh air and the darkness of the car park he took his mobile out of his pocket, punching in Fleur's number. It was still unavailable.

'Sod it,' he said, walking across to his Shogun jeep, half tempted to drive off in the direction of the M40 and Oxford. He glanced down at his watch. It was nearly half-nine. Ashworth would be waiting for him and, even if Ashworth weren't in the equation, driving to Oxford so late when Fleur wasn't expecting him would be a waste of time. Her halls of residence rules were antiquated. After eleven o'clock no visitors were allowed unless they logged their names at the lodge – and he wasn't going to arse around doing that. Even more exasperating was the fact that she wouldn't be allowed out, at least not without a fuss – and he never caused fuss and trouble for Fleur.

He gunned the thirty-grand jeep into life, turning east out of the car park. Fifteen minutes later he was tooling around Greenwich's one-way system in the direction of Woolwich. Traffic was light and he didn't trouble to hurry. He liked the thought of Detective Inspector Ashworth kicking his heels in the dark and the cold.

Musingly he turned the hi-fi on and the sound of Tina Turner at full belt blasted his eardrums. He glanced at his dashboard. It was nine forty-five. Sharlene would just be taking off from Linate Airport. Not for the first time he wondered why fashion models were always booked on to either crack-of-dawn flights or middle-of-the-night flights, especially after an arduous booking – and according to Sharlene, doing a stint for Versace in Milan was harder work than hacking coal down a mine.

He turned left off the main road at the far side of Charlton, negotiating the small maze of streets leading down to the Thames Barrier. The only other vehicle near the Barrier car park was Ashworth's Peugeot and, as Ashworth wasn't in it, the first thing Al did after parking up was to reach into the back seat for the anorak that always lay there.

It wasn't his preferred fashion style, but for meets like this, where a bloke wearing a Vicuna overcoat would be more out of place and noticeable than one dressed as if taking a dog for a walk, it served its purpose.

Standing in the dark beside the jeep he zipped the anorak to his throat and set off along the bleak river walkway. Once on it, Ashworth's bulky figure was discernible beneath the orange glow of the river walk's lighting, twenty yards or so away. He strolled down-river towards him, enjoying, as he always did, the slick black sight of the Thames at night.

'Christ, but it's enough to freeze the balls off a brass monkey,' Ashworth said, as he approached. 'There'll be no more of this weather for me, thank God. Not after the New Year. Once I'm retired it'll be all sun and sangria.'

'Spain is for retired crims, Sid, not retired coppers. They aren't going to want you sunning yourself beside them. Do the world a favour, retire to Florida instead.'

'Can't oblige.' Ashworth turned his overcoat collar up against the chill breeze blowing off the river. 'The wife doesn't like flying. Marbella's as far as she'll go.' He grinned, tombstone teeth gleaming. 'And this last little bonus had better add considerably to my pension fund, AV. What I pulled off for Tommy was nothing short of a miracle, and you know it.'

'Yeah. Well. It was a miracle that didn't come cheap.' Al unzipped his anorak, reaching into the inside pocket of his suit jacket. The envelope he withdrew was bulky. 'With only a couple of months till you ride into the sunset this'll probably be our last transaction,' he said drily as he handed it over. 'Don't spend it all at once.'

Ashworth flicked open the envelope. 'You're going to

miss me,' he said, running a stubby thumb over the wads of notes and assessing the amount. Happy with the conclusion he came to, he stuffed the envelope deep in the pocket of his overcoat. 'You're going to miss me so much that, if I were you, AV, I'd do what I'm doing – retire.'

Al's mouth quirked in amusement. 'You know better than to think you'll be hard to replace, Sid. Your friends are lining up, believe you me.'

'Not like in the old days, matey,' Ashworth said flatly. 'The world's changed. The Met's on its way to becoming squeaky clean.'

'Yeah. Well. One day soon, maybe. Not yet, though. Take it from one who knows.'

Ashworth shrugged, well aware of the name of the officer who would be stepping into his shoes and Al's pocket, and pretty damn sure the new arrangement wouldn't have the mileage in it his own arrangement had had.

'Whichever one of us is right, you should still be thinking about retiring,' he said again, moving his weight from one foot to the other in an effort to keep warm. 'Crime's moved on since your old man had you and Stuart vaulting over bank counters as if they were sweetie counters. It's all white-collar fraud now, or drugs. Neither's your bag, so what's left? Bullion hauls aren't exactly thick on the ground and even though the last one wasn't pinned on you, the little bit of stuff who did the prosecuting managed to make the charge you did cop for stick. You get done for anything in future and you can bet your life the Crown will use her again. What was her name? Prince? Duke?'

'King,' Al said, and spat.

Ashworth grinned. He'd got Al rattled and the pleasure was enormous. 'One ten-year sentence in a lifetime is enough, AV,' he said, as aware as Al that this was probably going to be their last meet and in no particular hurry to bring it to a conclusion. 'Cop for another and, even with parole, how old will you be when you get out? Fifty-three? Fifty-four?'

'Stop the gloating, Sid. It isn't going to happen.'

Ashworth's grin deepened. 'If I had a tenner for every ex-con who's said that, I'd be a millionaire.'

'You mean you're not?'

Ignoring the sarcasm, Ashworth hugged his coat collar a little tighter at his throat. 'Sadly, no,' he said blandly. 'Though I must confess I've often wondered about you, AV. You must have a nice little nest-egg stashed away, considering all those bank robberies you pulled off through the eighties. They were lovely little earners, weren't they? Shame technology and supergrasses put an end to most of them.'

'Yeah, tear-jerking.' Al had no intention of being lured into a trip down memory lane for Sid's benefit. Ashworth knew quite enough about some of his activities, without him knowing more.

'And then there were the security van raids.' Ashworth, knowing how much he was annoying Al, was beginning to enjoy himself. 'What was it you always said, Al? Why put yourself out robbing one bank when you can get the cash from ten banks in the back of a Ford van? High living may have made inroads into it all, but there must be a hell of a lot left. If I were you, I'd settle for that hell of a lot – otherwise, trust me, it's going to be another courtroom, another judge, and another long, long sentence.'

'You're a right little ray of sunshine, Sid. Anyone ever tell you?'

There was now an edge to Al's sarcasm and Ashworth decided he'd pushed as far as it was wise to push. He was going to miss his verbal sparring sessions with AV, though. In all the long years of his professional life he'd never come across a villain he'd really liked, but AV came nearer than most.

'Right, I'm off,' he said, following the pattern for all their meets over the last twenty years by being the first to leave. 'Just don't keep pushing your luck, AV. Tommy was lucky this time. Next time will be different. Bribery and corruption isn't the merry-go-round it once was.'

'Sod off,' Al said equably, refusing to let Ashworth know just how deeply riled he was.

As Ashworth walked away from him down the otherwise deserted pathway, he watched his retreating back, hands tucked in his anorak pockets. Just as the bulky figure turned off the path towards the car park, he called out: 'Yer know your monicker's goin' to be El Sid once you go to Spain, don't yer, Sid?' He cracked up with laughter and, slightly muffled by the trees surrounding the car park, an answering guffaw rumbled back to him.

He made no attempt to follow in Ashworth's wake. Instead he looked out over the dark river as Ashworth's car door slammed and, seconds later, the engine revved.

Why was he feeling so bloody rattled? Was it because of Ashworth rabbiting on about the changing face of crime, making out he'd have to look to his laurels if he wanted to remain a major league crim? Was it because he was still narked at Tommy's carelessness on his last job – a job no one else in the family had been involved in – and all the wheeling and dealing he'd had to do to ensure an acquittal? Was it the mention of drugs and the inevitable memories of young Billy that had come with it? Or was it Ashworth's taunting reference to his own trial? A trial that had not had as happy an outcome as Tommy's; a trial that had resulted in his serving seven years in one of the hardest nicks in the country.

The sound of the Peugeot's engine faded into the distance and still he didn't move. Deena King. God, but the mere mention of the name was enough to have him spitting fire. He and his silk had thought they were on to a winner when they'd been given the name of the barrister for the Crown. 'She's a babe in arms, AV,' Brian Vault, a bear of a man who had defended him with great success on previous occasions, had said confidently. 'This is her first really heavy case. It's going to be a walk-over.'

It hadn't been a walk-over. It had been a nightmare.

He stared broodingly across the still surface of the water to where, a little way to the right on the opposite bank, the dark sprawl of a factory sent a constant stream of smoke puffs into the night air. The same Tate & Lyle sugar factory where, thirty-five years or so ago, when he'd been a snotty-nosed kid in ragged-arse trousers, his mum had done shift-work.

His eyes narrowed. Deena King's mother had never stood long hours at a factory conveyer-belt. He knew all about Deena King's mother – a lady of leisure who had never done a day's paid work in her life – and her father. He had made it his business to know. His mistake had been in making it his business too late in the day for the knowledge to be any good.

With his hands still in his anorak pockets he turned his gaze westwards, to the sodium-lit flood barrier.

Neither his solicitor nor his silk had realised that Deena King was the daughter of the late Mr Justice Frensham. If they had, they might have realised there would be more to her than met the eye.

God, but she'd been sharp – and completely impossible to rattle. By the time of her summing-up he'd hated her voice more than he'd ever hated any woman's voice. He'd hated the way she'd dressed for court, as well. The white silk blouses and dark straight skirts she'd worn beneath her gown were innocuous enough, but the sheer dark stockings and high-heeled black court shoes she favoured were, in his opinion, completely and provocatively out of place.

In the beginning, of course, when he'd been carelessly confident of an acquittal, he hadn't minded. When the Prosecution had first begun the case for the Crown he'd quite enjoyed trying to unsettle her by leering at her from the dock. Beneath her wig her hair had been stylishly jaw-length and, as her features were classically sculpted, viewing her as little more than a sex object had been easy.

By the time the last witnesses were being called his attitude towards her had undergone a radical change.

'For Christ's sake!' he'd shouted at Brian Vault. 'She may be young, but she's a blinder! She's sewing the case up tighter than a teddy-bear's arse!'

Despite attempts to placate and reassure him, he'd known what the outcome was going to be. For the first time since his teens, he was going to go down. And he did. Ten years, he'd copped for. It had meant the end of his second marriage and the end of being any kind of a father to Fleur. She was nine years old when he'd been hustled down the back stairs in handcuffs to wait for the Brixton run and, except for a handful of agonising prison visits, he hadn't seen her again until she was sixteen.

Bitterness choked his throat. Ashworth was wrong if he thought he'd ever live through that scenario again – and he was equally wrong in thinking he was going to settle for a life of crucifying boredom.

He swung round, striding away from the river towards his parked jeep. He was forty-five, for Christ's sake.

Nowhere near retirement age. Despite Ashworth's insinuations, his best years weren't over. He had plenty of mileage yet. Plenty.

He yanked open the Shogun's door. The high-class stolen car market was proving to be both steady and lucrative. There were plenty of people who, for a generous tip, would phone him with word of where a suitable motor was regularly parked and then the rest was easy. He would have someone away with it and across to the Continent before the theft was even reported. Most of the Rolls and Bentleys went to a dealer in Antwerp, while the Ferraris and Jensons were disposed of in Lille.

He slid the jeep into gear. It was profitable but it wasn't the sort of scam to get the adrenaline going. Ashworth had been right: opportunities for his kind of crime were getting rarer and rarer. It wasn't as if he could pull off any City of London fun and games. Guinness-style insider dealing and the multi-million-pound antics of Lloyds brokers were the preserve of Old Etonians – and he'd gone to a secondary modern in Bermondsey.

He began tooling the jeep through the near-deserted streets of Greenwich, aware that if high-tech fraud was out, so, too, was the drug scene.

Little Billy had seen to that.

He replaced the Tina Turner CD with The Verve, his mouth tightening to a thin line. Billy had been Stuart and Ginny's first kiddie together and, when he'd been twelve, he'd been fed crack cocaine at his school gates. By the time he was thirteen, he was very, very dead.

The family had sorted the murdering bastard responsible. No one had kicked up too much of a fuss when word got out he was missing. The Bill were too well aware someone had done them, and the world, a favour. Besides, no body was ever found – and no body, no case.

By the time he'd stopped remembering young Billy he was on the A20 and speeding towards Kent. Bermondsey and its immediate surrounds were still the area he and his brothers thought of as home, but though they spent most of their time there, only Stuart had carried on living there. Tommy had an upmarket flat over the water in Canary Wharf and Kevin lived out past Erith, on the Thames estuary.

His own home was perched high on a wooded shelf of the North Downs. Low and sprawling and white-walled, it went by the name of Ponderosa.

'Naming a house after an ancient TV western is just too naff for words, Dad,' Fleur had said when he formally christened it.

'Ponderosa wasn't the name of the series,' he had said, uncaring. 'It was *Bonanza*. Personally, I thought that a bit cheeky for a bank robber, but if you want me to change it . . .'

There had been squeals of horror followed by convulsive giggles. It was a good memory and, after all the shit he'd had in his head for the last half-hour or so, a welcome one. Taking a hand from the wheel he took out his mobile again and punched her number. It was nearly one o'clock and her phone was only taking messages. 'It's Al,' he said, though Fleur never called him Al. It was always Dad or Daddy. 'Where the hell are you, kitten? Give me a bell before I really start to worry. Love you.'

Certain she would be returning his call next morning before he even got out of bed, he swerved off the A20 on to the A223. Reducing his speed, he made another phone call, this time to The Maid.

'Hi, Al,' Max said, knowing very well what his query was going to be. 'Everything's sweet. The cozzers didn't show.' He sounded more than a little drunk. 'Lulu's stayed behind to help clear and most everyone's gone. Speak to you tomorrow, mate. Ciao.'

Satisfied that he'd nothing to worry about, Al dropped the mobile into his anorak pocket and turned left off the main road. Like all the minor roads fringing the steep chalky slopes of the North Downs it was narrow and winding, edged in by dense woodland.

After a mile or so he turned left again, the stretch of road now so narrow the trees on either side met overhead. Another left turn and for a couple of hundred yards he was on an untarmacked track. White gates gleamed in his headlights and seconds later, as they electronically opened, he was swooping down the steep driveway of his home. As he stepped out of the jeep there were no nearby lights visible. Ponderosa was as isolated as any house a bare twenty miles from the centre of London could be.

'Don't all this countryside give you the willies?' Tommy had asked the first time he'd visited. 'Where's the nearest Indian? And what do you do when you run out of ciggies?'

'There's a whole host of Indian restaurants a handful of miles away in Bromley,' he had said, wondering what the hell his baby brother would do if he ever found himself in the wilds of Wales or Scotland. 'And I never run out of ciggies. Or anything else, come to that.'

It had been Ponderosa's lonely situation which had first attracted him to it. With no cheek-by-jowl neighbours, there was no one to take a nosy interest in his comings and goings – and he couldn't be taken by surprise. Any car turning off the lane on to the track had to be heading for Ponderosa – there was nowhere else it could possibly be going – and as sound travelled with clarity on the high wooded ridge he always had ample warning when visitors, welcome or otherwise, were on their way.

He entered the house knowing immediately as his Rottweiler bounded to greet him in frenzied delight, that Sharlene wasn't yet home. It didn't matter. By the time he'd let Blitz out and made himself a nightcap, she would be. And she wouldn't be tired – or at least, not too tired for sex.

His mouth tugged into a smile as he walked into the vast drawing-room, taking off his anorak as he did so and throwing it on to a sofa. One of the merits a twenty-two-year-old girlfriend came with was stamina. Not, he reflected as he slid open a plate-glass patio door allowing Blitz to lope out into the darkness, that he'd ever known any other type of girlfriend.

Carol had been eighteen when he'd married her. He'd been a twenty-five-year-old Jack-the-Lad, totally unsuited to any sort of steady relationship. Fleur had been born six months later. Divorce had followed as night the day. When Carol had left him she hadn't taken Fleur with her. She hadn't wanted to. She hadn't wanted any part of him. Not even their child.

As Blitz ensured no wildlife from the woods was encroaching on Ponderosa territory, Al lit up a cigarette. For most of the time he'd looked after Fleur on his own. When he'd been away on a job – and a large number of the banks he'd robbed had been in the North and North-East – either Ginny or Lol, or the girlfriend of the moment, had looked after her. By the time he'd gone down for handling the bullion he'd been married to Marsha and she had looked after Fleur – until he'd given her her marching orders.

Twenty-one when they'd married, she'd been twenty-five when, on a prison visit, he'd told her it was over.

She'd refused to believe him, of course, but her sobbing and pleading had cut no ice with him. He hadn't wanted a woman on the outside waiting for him. He hadn't wanted to lie awake at night wondering if she was being faithful and, if she wasn't, wondering who the current boyfriend was. Cutting all ties with life outside the boob made it easier to hack the hell of being inside it – apart from Fleur, of course. Never for a moment had he wanted to break the ties that bound him to his daughter.

Fleur had gone to live with his mum and then, when he'd been in Parkhurst six years and his mum had died, she'd gone to live with Stuart and his family.

He glanced down at his watch, not wanting to think about the funeral he hadn't been allowed out of prison to attend. It was just after one o'clock and he wondered whether to leave another message on Fleur's mobile. Aware that there wasn't much point, he decided against it. He'd speak to her first thing in the morning. She'd have her phone turned on by then and he knew she'd have a good reason for not having phoned that evening and for not being at Tommy's acquittal party. More to the point, that it would be genuine.

He whistled Blitz in, and, as he did so, heard the sound of a car turning into the track above the house. He closed the glass doors and dragged his tie undone. Sharlene was back. Six feet tall, beautiful, as feline as a cat and with legs so long they seemed to go up to her armpits, Sharlene was class – as, with the exception of Carol, had been all the many women in his life.

He re-crossed the room, tossing his tie on to a pale cream armchair. Some of the circles he moved in weren't the most liberal-minded and there'd been several raised eyebrows when it was known his live-in girlfriend was black. He hadn't given a stuff. The only person whose

36

opinion he remotely cared about was Fleur's – and Fleur and Sharlene got on just great.

He grinned wryly as he dragged his shirt over his head. There was no reason for them not to, considering how small the age difference was between them. As her car door slammed he kicked off his shoes. The only person in his family still hostile to the relationship was Ginny, and that was on account of the age thing. 'Strings of dolly-birds at your age are a sign of immaturity, Al,' she had said scathingly. 'What on earth do you find to talk about?'

'We don't talk, Gin,' he'd said, knowing her real concern was that Stuart might one day follow his example. 'But we do shag a lot.'

He'd thought it funny. She hadn't. It had been two long months before she'd even spoken to him again.

Sharlene's key turned in the lock and Blitz raced into the rotunda-sized hall to greet her. Seconds later she was kicking the door shut behind her, dropping her travel-bags to the floor, calling out throatily: 'Hi, sugar! I'm home!'

Naked apart from his trousers and Rolex he strolled out of the drawing-room in Blitz's wake. 'About time,' he said laconically, making no attempt to greet her as ecstatically as Blitz was doing. Instead he leaned against the drawing-room's door-jamb, his hands in his pockets, one foot crossing the other at the ankle.

Sharlene was unfazed. His being such a cool dude was part of the attraction. His heavy reputation was another. No one messed with Al. Not even professional enforcers. Just being seen out and about on his arm gave her a thrill of excitement nothing else came close to.

He was also a man who spent freely and, for a man in his mid-forties, he was in prime physical condition and criminally handsome. His near-black hair was barely flecked with grey and was still thick and curly as a ram's fleece. His eyes were the colour of splintered slate and there was a cleft in his chin to die for.

He wasn't faithful, of course, and apart from her decorative usefulness she was well aware she played no part in his life. Al's real life centred on his daughter, his extended family, the jobs he pulled and the reputation those jobs gave him. Anything else – and anything else was a category girlfriends fell into – was window-dressing.

For the moment, though, she didn't care. Being Al's live-in lady suited her just fine. It gave her status both amongst Al's friends and within her own fast-lane set. Her cliquy, druggy, bitchy, up-all-night friends loved the *frisson* of rubbing shoulders with a high-profile villain. Being known as a moll was fun. It set her apart.

Coolly aware of all the reasons he so turned her on, she flashed him a blinding smile, shrugged herself out of an ankle-length coat – a gift from an Italian admirer – and catapulted towards him.

His hands flew out of his pockets to catch hold of her, and as her hands slid up over the bulging muscles of his chest, around his neck and into his hair, she heard the faint bleep of his mobile phone.

The sound was coming from the drawing-room and was muffled, as if the phone was deep in a coat pocket or buried beneath a cushion. As his mouth came down on hers in hard unfumbled contact, she was sure she knew who was calling. Fleur. Fleur had been out of contact, which, in her book, meant only one thing – she was having personal problems. A phone call at this hour was no doubt a plea for her dad to zoom up to Oxford in the morning to see her. Well, he wasn't going to.

'Fleur rang me,' she whispered against his ear. 'She'll be down tomorrow,' and then, as she felt relief surge through him, she said, 'Let's make love, sugar. Right here, baby. *Now*.'

As his hands moved from her buttocks to his trouser-belt and she slid to her knees in front of him, she permitted herself a smile of satisfaction.

For all of tomorrow she was going to have him to herself – and when Fleur didn't arrive, she'd tell him the line had been so bad perhaps she'd got the message wrong.

Chapter Three

Benedict wasn't sure if, after the pre-dawn phone call from the police, Deena had gone back to sleep, but he doubted it. At seven-thirty, when he woke, disturbed by her moving about the room, she was already showered and dressed. He had enough sensitivity not to complain at being disturbed. By his standards it was cripplingly early, but even under normal circumstances Deena enjoyed working out in a gym by eight o'clock.

There was going to be no gym this morning, though. She was dressed for the day in a navy pin-stripe suit, cream silk blouse, dark tights and court shoes. 'Inspector Rose,' he heard her say queryingly as she sat at her dressing-table, the telephone in one hand and a cup of black coffee in the other. 'It's Deena King.'

He pushed himself up against the pillows, knowing what short shrift he'd be given if he'd attempted to contact a police inspector at that hour in the morning. Deena, though, was a Queen's Counsel. It carried clout.

'That's correct,' he heard her say as the conversation continued and then, a few moments later: 'No. Hugh's father is dead.'

Her back was towards him and his eyebrows shot high. It was what she'd always hinted at, of course, but this was the first time he'd known for sure.

He heaved himself from the bed, mystified as to why she'd always been so unforthcoming about it. Was it because talking about it would have been painful for her? Yet if she were still carrying emotional baggage for Hugh's father, surely there would have been a photograph of him on display somewhere? And there wasn't. Even when he'd first visited the house – before the two of them had become lovers – he'd hadn't seen one.

Aware that if he wanted a coffee he was going to have to get it for himself, he dragged on his jeans and padded barefoot in the direction of the kitchen. Initially he'd found Deena's reticence where previous personal relationships were concerned intriguing. Lately, however, he'd begun to find it annoying. It wasn't as if their relationship was carelessly casual. They'd been a heavy item for nearly two years now. However odd her early marriage, it would, surely, have been natural for her to have talked about it with him – and she never had.

He pushed the kitchen door open, making a beeline for the steaming coffee-pot.

That there'd been something bizarre about Deena's marriage had been obvious to him ever since he'd realised how young she'd been when Hugh had been born. Girls from Deena's background didn't, by choice, marry and start a family whilst still at university. The Deena he knew was always so coolly in control of her life that it was hard for him to imagine her facing a situation where abortion, adoption, single motherhood or marriage had been her only options. He'd long assumed, though, that that had been the scenario – which would certainly explain why she never talked about it.

He poured coffee into a breakfast mug and searched the fridge for some cream. By the time he had met Deena her father had been long dead. He hadn't, however, been dead when Hugh had been born. As he poured cream into his coffee he wondered how Mr Justice Frensham had reacted to the news of his only daughter's teenage pregnancy – and was pretty sure it had been none too happily.

The wall phone gave a click and, aware that Deena's conversation had ended, he walked back upstairs, curious what her next course of action was going to be.

'Rose and Rupert are clones,' she said crossly, dragging a Louis Vuitton overnight bag from the depths of her wardrobe. 'In Rose's opinion, as Hugh is over eighteen there is no cause for concern. Like Rupert, he thinks there's nothing too surprising about Hugh not being back at Latimer for the start of term.'

She swung the bag on to the still unmade bed. 'He did stop short of telling me I was an over-anxious mother wasting police time, but if I'd been an ordinary member of the public he wouldn't have.'

She began opening drawers, taking out a change of lingerie, a pair of silk pyjamas, a travel hairdryer, a toilet-bag. 'He thinks Hugh found the academic going too tough and has dropped out and gone walkabout.' She stuffed everything into the travel-bag. 'If he knew Hugh, he'd know it was a ridiculous idea. Nothing stresses or fazes Hugh.'

It was true. Listening to her, he realised it was one of the reasons he'd never taken to Hugh. Deena's son had ice water in his veins, and it wasn't endearing.

'And so,' Deena continued, her voice fraught with frustration, 'as I can't convince the police that something is gravely amiss, I'm going to speak to Hugh's dean.' She zipped up the bag. 'And I'm going to speak to him face to face.'

'I thought you were at Snaresbrook this morning?'

'I am.' Her eyes met his. 'And despite Inspector Rose's unhelpfulness I'm still having a meeting with him when Court finishes. Then I'm driving to Oxford.' She glanced down at her watch. 'It's too early to phone Cheryl but I will in half an hour or so. She'll arrange that someone deputises for me tomorrow.'

He frowned slightly, aware that he should be volunteering to accompany her. He didn't want to. It had been hard enough yesterday evening tearing himself away from the sculpture he was working on without knowing that, when he re-started work again this morning, he'd have to down tools by late afternoon. When a project was going well he often worked far into the night and his current project, a giant male head and torso in tin, was going very well. Though it sounded naff, it didn't look it – at least not so far. Even thinking about it made his fingertips burn.

'OK,' he said laconically. 'You'll give me a bell when you get back?'

'Mmm.' Her eyes had narrowed slightly and he knew that whatever her thoughts, he wasn't in them.

He felt an irrational spurt of annoyance, not liking the feeling of being unnecessary to her.

He sat down on the edge of the bed and bad-temperedly slipped his feet into his shoes, wondering if her self-sufficiency was the reason why, though he'd let her know he was happy for marriage to be on the cards, he'd never done so in a way that needed a categorical yes or no from her.

Even to someone as ignorant of marriage as he was – and he'd been brought up by a bachelor uncle whilst his playboy father and socialite mother indulged in love affairs the length and breadth of Europe – marriage summoned up a vision of two people needing each other and being necessary to one another. He didn't feel needed by Deena, or necessary to her.

He continued to sit on the edge of the bed, watching her, brooding on thoughts that rarely surfaced. Was she necessary to him? As their relationship had lasted longer than any he'd ever had, he could only suppose that the answer was yes. Just watching her read through her case notes, as she was doing now, made his prick stir. Certainly he loved her conventionality. His titled family was eccentric to the point of being near-certifiable and, artistically haphazard himself, it was the very opposite characteristics in Deena that so attracted him.

Deena, especially when resplendent in wig and gown, was responsibility and respectability personified. He had once asked her if he could make love to her whilst she was robed for court and her outraged indignation had amused him because it had been so predictable. Deena very rarely surprised him. Her present anxiety was the only time she'd ever behaved in a way that had even mildly astonished him.

A wry smile touched his mouth. Whatever it was he'd been asking himself, he knew the answer. Deena might irritate him beyond belief at times, but, when it came down to it, he couldn't imagine a committed relationship elsewhere.

'I'll make some toast,' he said, rising to his feet, knowing she rarely ate breakfast and that he was making the offer for his own benefit.

'Mmm,' she said again, not bothering to look up, skimming the page she was reading so fast that he didn't know how she managed to make sense of the words. 'One slice with honey, Benedict, please.'

He mooched out of the room and back down to the kitchen, reluctantly aware that he and Deena were creatures who, for very different reasons, needed their own space. As the present set-up suited both of them, what was the sense of changing it?

'If it ain't broke, don't mend it,' he said aloud to himself and as he rummaged in the bread-bin he began to whistle, his thoughts again centred on his Tin Man.

Forty-five minutes later, seated on a crowded tube-train on the way to Snaresbrook, Deena was in a far-from-whistling frame of mind. Though she hadn't said so to Benedict, since being told that Hugh was still in the country her anxiety level had fallen. His disappearing off the map in England was less nerve-racking than his disappearing in Turkey. It didn't, however, alter the fact that she didn't know where he was.

As yet more commuters pushed their way on to the train at Queensway she tried to focus her thoughts on her day's workload. Within seconds she was thinking about Hugh again. Six weeks ago he'd told her he was going to spend the next three or four weeks travelling in Turkey with a friend. At that point he obviously hadn't realised that his passport, issued six years ago for a school skiing trip, was out of date – and when he had realised, he had equally obviously changed his plans. Why, though, hadn't he telephoned to tell her what his new plans were? Why hadn't he telephoned her again, period? Even more disturbing, why hadn't he returned to Latimer two weeks ago for the start of the Michaelmas term?

She lifted her bulky briefcase from the floor and on to her lap as a barrage of people struggled past her to get off the train at Mile End. Seen in the cold light of day, neither fact was cause for serious concern – as Rupert and Inspector Rose had been at great pains to tell her. It wasn't the facts, though, that were disturbing her. It was her intuition.

Even in courtroom situations her intuition rarely let her down. When it came to her only child it never let her down – or at least it hadn't yet. Whenever she thought of Hugh she felt a catch in her throat. He was the most wonderful thing that had ever happened to her, though she hadn't thought so in the beginning. Aware that her thoughts were about to go down a road she never allowed them access to, she put a sharp brake on them. She was nearly at Snaresbrook and she had a case to concentrate on. It had priority even over Hugh.

'Have you read about the latest Virtue acquittal?' a colleague asked her in the robing-room, handing her a copy of the previous night's *Evening Standard*. 'Slippery bastards, aren't they?'

'Thanks, but I've already seen it.' She handed the newspaper back without looking at it, saying as she hitched her gown more firmly on her shoulders: 'I've got more on my mind than South London scum. Mad Mike is sitting in Court 2.'

All judges had nicknames, some more unkind than others.

'Could be worse,' her fellow barrister said sympathetically, 'though not much.' She was again looking at the *Standard*'s photograph of the Virtue brothers, apparently as intrigued by it as Cheryl had been. 'Good-looking brutes, aren't they? And they look reasonably intelligent. Why they choose to live the way they do beats me.'

Deena made a sound of exasperation. 'Why you're even giving the time of day to speculating about them beats me. They're career criminals, scum – and, in the case of the Virtues, scum of mega proportions.'

'They haven't chosen scummy names for their children,' her colleague continued undeterred as they walked out of the robing-room together. 'Or at least Al Virtue hasn't. According to an article on one of the inside pages his

46

teenage daughter is called Fleur, which is amusingly *Forsyte Saga*-ish for a gangster's daughter.'

'Is it?' Deena put a hand up to her wig, making sure that it was straight.

'And what about his girlfriend's name?' her fellow barrister persisted. 'Sharlene. It's rather pretty, don't you think?'

Deena paused as they came to a point in the corridor where their ways divided. 'No, I don't. It's a stripper's name – and if she's Al Virtue's girlfriend, that's most likely what she is.'

Her colleague shifted her bulky case notes a little higher in her arms. 'They're not called strippers now. The preferred terminology is exotic dancers. And good luck with Mike,' she added. 'Hopefully his haemorrhoids won't be troubling him.'

'Thanks.' Nothing in Deena's voice, as they walked off in different directions towards their designated court-rooms, revealed how devoutly she was hoping the same thing.

It was a long day and throughout it she was plagued by an atrociously bad conscience. The situation in her personal life didn't warrant her being absent on the second day of trial, yet that was what she had arranged. It was a day when the prosecution would be continuing to outline its case and her absence wouldn't be dire – she had, after all, highly competent junior counsel – but her client deserved better of her.

Despite her pangs of guilt, as the jury were empanelled she began mentally listing the things she wanted to do whilst in Oxford. She wanted to have a thorough search of Hugh's room; most particularly she wanted to know if his out-of-date passport was still in it. She also wanted to speak to the friend he had intended going to Turkey with. With typical off-handedness, Hugh hadn't told her his friend's name but one of his other friends would surely know.

Her thoughts were interrupted by the sound of her client clearing his throat and she flashed a look towards the dock, wondering if he was trying to attract her attention. He wasn't. He was leaning forward slightly, concentrating with burning intensity on the proceedings taking place in the well of the court.

Aware that her own concentration had unforgivably wandered, she jettisoned Hugh from her thoughts and, until court rose at four o'clock, dutifully allowed nothing else to impinge on her consciousness but her client's best interests.

'And then what happened?'

Benedict was speaking to her on the mobile as she drove her Mercedes 500 SEL westwards, out of London.

'Inspector Rose said that Hugh is now officially listed as being a missing person,' she said as yet another halt in the slow-moving traffic forced her to bring the Mercedes to a standstill. 'His description has been circulated, but because he's an adult male and there are no suspicious circumstances that, at the moment, is as far as the police are prepared to go.'

It was already growing dark and with a sinking heart she saw that the nose-to-tail traffic ahead of her stretched into seeming infinity.

'So . . .' she added, wishing that she hadn't bothered with the not-very-helpful meeting, knowing that without it she would have been free of London before the early-evening traffic had built to its present hellish grind, '. . . no investigation is being put in hand.'

'If the friend he intended going to Turkey with is also AWOL, perhaps they'll think differently.'

Benedict didn't truly believe it would make the slightest bit of difference, but he was shattered after a long session of welding and telling her what he thought she'd like to hear was the easiest way to keep the conversation going.

'Or then again,' he said as there was stony silence from the other end of the line, 'if the two of them have gone walkabout together, perhaps it means that there's absolutely nothing for you to worry about.'

'Sod off, Benedict.' There was no rancour in her voice, only exasperation. She could put up with a lot, but woolly-minded thinking always drove her wild. 'I'll see you late tomorrow. Bye.'

She clicked the mobile off without waiting for his response. The traffic ahead of her was now edging on to the beginning of the M40. She would be in Oxford in under an hour. She wondered if she'd be able to locate any of Hugh's friends that evening, aware that, as she didn't have any names to go on, it might prove difficult. Pulling ahead of a van, she eased on to the motorway, picking up speed, unhappily aware of how little she knew about her son.

'Of course I know nothing about Hugh's private life,' the dean said, well aware that Deena King would have been greatly surprised to hear otherwise. 'His Head of Faculty is the person you need to speak to and an arrangement has been made for you to meet with him tomorrow morning.'

He toyed with his glass of sherry, aware that Deena's glass was, as yet, quite untouched.

'I have, of course, already discussed the situation with him,' he continued, 'and he is quite in the dark as to the reason for Hugh's current absence from college. The Students' Union may be of more help – the Union is often the first port of call for any student in difficulties, personal or otherwise – and I suggest that tomorrow you speak with one of its officers.'

'Thank you. I shall.' Despite the dutiful concern in the dean's voice, Deena was almost certain that if it hadn't been for the letters after her name he wouldn't, when she had spoken to him on the telephone earlier in the day, have granted her such a speedy interview.

'I'd like to speak with whomever it is Hugh rooms with,' she said, aware of Latimer's antiquated residency arrangements and also aware that, like Rupert and Inspector Rose, the dean didn't yet think the situation sinisterly alarming. 'His room-mate will most likely know the name of the friend Hugh intended travelling to Turkey with. If anyone knows where he is, and why he isn't back at college, I imagine that particular friend will.'

'Yes. Absolutely. Quite so.' The dean was annoyed with himself for not having already furnished himself with such information. He had, however, ensured he had Hugh King's room details to hand. 'Hugh shares with a third-year English student, Tim Grant, on Staircase J, Shelley Quad,' he said, resolving to summon Grant to an interview first thing in the morning and to speak again with Hugh's Head of Faculty and with the House Matron. If anything *was* seriously amiss, it wouldn't do for there to be accusations of negligent pastoral care. 'As I mentioned earlier, if you would like to stay in House overnight, we have a guest room available.'

'Thank you. That would be very convenient.' Deena flashed him a coolly polite smile and fifteen minutes later, buried deep in an ankle-length navy wool coat, was making purposeful strides across Great Quad in the direction of Shelley Quad.

'Mrs King?' Tim Grant stood at the open door of his room, repeating in incredulous parrot-fashion the name she had introduced herself with. 'You're . . . excuse me . . . you're Hugh's *mother?*'

He was an attractive young man, his black jeans looking as if he'd been poured into them, shining-clean hair tied in a ponytail.

'Yes,' she said, stepping into the room as he gathered his wits and ushered her in. 'And it's *Ms* King.'

'Really?' His emotions were so mixed it was hard for Deena to know which was uppermost. He was obviously delighted at being disturbed, incredulous at the idea of her being anyone's mother, and more than a little anxious as to her reason for being there. 'Is this about Hugh not being back from Turkey?' he asked, assuming an expression of due concern as he plumped up tired-looking cushions on an even more tired-looking sofa and motioned her to sit down.

Deena didn't move. She couldn't. The realisation that Tim Grant was unaware that Hugh *hadn't* gone to Turkey was just too unexpected.

'Hugh didn't go,' she said when she could trust herself to speak. 'He didn't know at the time he was making his plans, but his passport is out of date.'

His jaw dropped and he looked endearingly young as he struggled to decide what response would, in the circumstances, be the most correct. 'Then where is he?' he floundered. 'I mean, if he didn't go to Turkey, Mrs King – sorry, *Ms* King – where did he go?'

'I don't know. I was hoping *you* would be able to tell *me*.'

'But I can't. I haven't a clue. Honest.'

Deena believed him. 'Perhaps some of Hugh's other friends will know. I'd like to speak to them. Is there a particular pub where they all meet up?'

Tim's face, which had been respectfully anxious, brightened. 'The Corn Dolly in Cornmarket is a good bet. Phyllis is usually in there on a Tuesday night – Tuesday nights are Jazz Club nights – and he's as close to Hugh as anyone.'

'Phyllis?' Deena wondered if she hadn't quite heard right.

Tim grinned, looking even more attractive. 'Phyllis is Phil Swayles' nickname. He isn't gay, if that's what you're thinking. It's just that he can be a bit of an old woman at times.'

Deena gave a nod of understanding. Even if Phil Swayles had been gay, it wouldn't have disturbed her. As long as he was happy, she would have gone along with it.

She looked around at the room. It was typical undergraduate accommodation: shabby, but adequate. There was a three-seater leather settee, two fabric armchairs, two desks. In the centre of the room was a coffee-table, its surface obliterated by a variety of magazines, books, empty beer cans, drained coffee mugs and a half-empty packet of fig biscuits. One wall was lined floor-to-ceiling with shelving crammed full of hardbacks and paperbacks. The other walls were decorated with posters, a couple of pinboards and an eclectic selection of knick-knacks. She wondered which of the posters and knick-knacks were Hugh's. And which desk was his.

Following her gaze and reading her thoughts, Tim said: 'Do you want to look through Hugh's things?'

She nodded and he crossed the room to the tidier of the two desks. 'This is Hugh's. He's a pretty private sort of person and usually . . . well . . . usually this wouldn't be on. You are his mother, though . . .' His voice tailed off and it was quite clear he would have found it easier to believe that she was Hugh's sister.

Well aware of how furious Hugh would be at having his desk drawers rifled through, Deena carefully and systematically rifled through them. His childhood passport was tucked in a folder in the bottom left drawer together with his medical card and his Student Union card.

Well aware of Tim's discomfiture and none too happy herself about what she was doing, Deena looked through Hugh's clothes drawers and rail. The search wasn't helpful. There were too many clothes for it to look as if he'd left college with no intention of returning, and too few to rule out the possibility of his merely having overstayed on a holiday.

She glanced at her wristwatch. It was eight-thirty and Cornmarket was a twenty-minute walk away.

'I'll come with you, if you like,' Tim said as she made signs of leaving. He grabbed a jacket from the back of one of the armchairs. 'Do you know Oxford? Cornmarket is central and easy to find . . .'

'Yes,' she said in a voice of neutral disinterest, battening down on memories she never allowed herself. 'I know Oxford.'

Eagerly he loped along at her side as she walked back down the staircase and out into the Quad. 'I'm from Hampshire,' he said chattily. 'Not the rural part – though I can't convince Hugh of that.'

'Was Phil the friend Hugh had intended travelling with to Turkey?' she asked as they walked briskly out into the Quad.

'Christ, no!' Tim's surprise was so great that he stumbled slightly. 'He went with Flo . . . or rather, if he'd gone he would have gone with Flo. I thought you knew that? I mean, I didn't realise that you didn't . . .'

He was floundering again to such an embarrassing extent that she cut him short. 'No,' she said, wondering if all Hugh's friends had feminine nicknames and, if so, was Hugh similarly burdened? 'Is Flo likely to be at the Corn Dolly tonight?'

'Well . . . um . . . I don't know . . . hard to tell, really. I mean, as Hugh isn't around . . .'

They were out of Latimer now, in The High, and as they walked up to Carfax she held memories at bay only with difficulty. She had never wanted Hugh to come to Oxford. 'Cambridge,' she had said to him over and over again when he'd been doing his A-levels. 'Sit for Cambridge.'

He hadn't, though. As stubborn as she could be herself, he had sat the Oxford University entrance exam and gone up to Latimer. Her one relief had been that he wasn't going to be at Trinity. Trinity would have been more than she could have borne.

The night air was cold and she dug her hands deep in her coat pockets, feeling an imperceptible tightening in the frozen region of her heart. God, but she could do without the pain of trekking around Oxford!

'Hugh's father was an Oxford graduate, wasn't he?' Tim said suddenly as they turned right into Cornmarket. 'Nice that – perpetuating a bit of family history. I wish my father had been an Oxford grad.'

The shock was so great she was beyond speech. Hugh never talked about his father. And she had never told him about his father. Not only did she refuse to talk about him, under normal circumstances, she tried never to think about him. If Hugh had wanted to mention he'd had a parent who'd been to Oxford, why hadn't he cited her? For what God-awful, God-mysterious reason had he cited his father?

'Here we are,' Tim was saying cheerfully as they approached the door of a pub. 'Mind the steps, *Ms* King.'

With her chest feeling as if it had been sledge-hammered, she stepped with him over a threshold that topped a short flight of steep steps.

The interior was noisy, crowded and smoke-filled. 'I don't see Flo,' he shouted across to her as they began threading their way towards the bar, 'but Phyllis is over there by the cigarette machine. What would you like to drink, Ms King?'

She fought the temptation to ask for a double brandy, saying, 'Half a Guinness, Tim. Thank you.'

As he began pushing his way through the crush at the bar, she looked towards the cigarette machine, aware that the Corn Dolly's customers were a very mixed bag. There were large groups of what were clearly locals, smaller groups so obviously American tourists they might as well have worn labels around their necks and, standing in the vicinity of the cigarette machine, three rowdy T-shirted and bejeaned undergraduates.

Aware that, as Tim had had the courtesy to accompany her to the pub, it would be out of order not to allow him to make the introductions, she didn't walk immediately over to them. Instead, as she waited for Tim to rejoin her, she concentrated on bringing her breathing back to a normal level. It wasn't too difficult. Where iron self-control was concerned, she'd had years of practice.

Looking across at the grouping by the cigarette machine she wondered which of the undergraduates was Phyllis. None of them looked as if it was a name they would happily answer to. One was ginger-haired and bearded, one had a Zapata moustache. All three were built like rugby players.

'Christ, it's as crowded as a football pub, isn't it?' Tim said as he battled back to her side. He handed her a foaming glass of Guinness. 'This isn't my usual haunt. I tend to favour the Black Dog in St Aldates.'

Deena wasn't interested, nor was she interested in the male heads that swivelled in her direction as she and Tim made their way across the crowded pub. Admiring glances were something she took for granted. Even when she was conservatively dressed as now, something in the way she moved, coupled with the drama of her swinging black hair, creamy skin and cameo-like features, always attracted attention.

'Don't bother struggling with Ms,' she said as they neared the group by the cigarette machine. 'Just introduce me as Hugh's mother, Deena King. OK?'

'OK,' Tim said, hoping that some people in the pub would think he and she were an item. If word went round he was dating a sophisticated older woman, his reputation as a Lothario would rocket sky-high.

'Y-e-s?' The ginger-bearded undergraduate said with interest as they approached. 'And who have we here, Tim? Your sister? Or are St Hilda's and Lady Margaret Hall brightening their ideas up where their dons are concerned?' He made an exaggeratedly courtly bow. 'Whoever you are, fair lady, we are all exceedingly pleased to make your acquaintance.'

There was laughter at his foolery from the friend standing next to him, but not from Tim. 'Stuff it, Ralph,' he said, deeply embarrassed. 'Deena, Ralph Donaldson. Ralph, Deena King, Hugh's mother. She's here to try to find out where the hell Hugh is. Phil Swayles,' he continued as the moustached Zapata look-alike inclined his head in her direction. 'And Giles Gargrave,' he said, introducing the clean-shaven member of the group. 'Giles rooms on the same staircase as Hugh. The person who can probably help you best is Phil.'

'Hey, steady on!' Swayles' alarm was obvious as Tim, his clumsy introductions over, took a step or two backwards. 'I've already had the Prof *and* Administration on my back wanting to know where Hugh is, and I don't know.'

He looked towards Deena, acutely uncomfortable. 'All I know, Mrs King, is that Hugh talked of going off to Turkey with Flo some time during the long vac. He didn't say for how long, but obviously I thought he only meant for a few weeks. And that's it, I'm afraid. That's all I know.'

Deena didn't allow her disappointment to show. There was a *frisson* of tension in the group; not the tension that came when outright lies were being told, but tension nevertheless.

'Hugh isn't the most communicative person in the world,' Ralph Donaldson proffered in his affected drawl. 'He always has some private agenda on the go. It's typical of him to keep his plans to himself – and not to give a toss about being late for the start of term. I was under the impression that he and Flo were off rock-climbing. I suppose Turkey might fit the bill – Mount Ararat and all that.'

'And where might I find Flo?'

'Flo?' Phil Swayles sounded bewildered. 'I don't know. This early in term a lot of people aren't frequenting their usual haunts yet. Besides, Flo is usually to be found wherever Hugh is. Your best bet is to have a word with St Clemence's Admin.'

'St Clem—' For the second time in twenty minutes

Deena felt as if she'd been pole-axed. St Clemence's was a women's college. It hadn't occurred to her that the friend Hugh had spoken of could have been a girlfriend.

Aware of new curiosity in Phil Swayles' eyes, not wanting him to know that she hadn't realised Flo was a girl in case he, and Hugh's other friends, then clammed up altogether, she flashed him a cool, unrevealing smile. 'Thanks. I'll do that. What is Flo's surname? Hugh never bothered to tell me.'

Phil shrugged. 'I don't think I've ever been told it either. I do know that Flo isn't a diminutive for Florence. Her name is Fleur.'

'It's an unusual name for an English girl, isn't it?' Tim said, suddenly springing to life with puppy-dog eagerness. 'There can't be too many Fleurs around, can there?'

'No.' Deena was suddenly very still. Tim was quite right in saying that it was an unusual name, but it was a name she'd heard quite recently. Where, though? On the radio, on the drive up to Oxford? Or had it been in conversation?

'I know her surname,' Giles Gargrave said, an odd expression in his eyes. 'It's Virtue. I think that's why she and Hugh don't bandy it around. Apparently it's quite well known in some of London's less salubrious circles. Would you like another drink, Mrs King? A short this time? You look as if you could do with one.'

Chapter Four

Though all next day Fleur remained uncontactable on her mobile, Al didn't worry – or he didn't until the evening grew late.

'Where the hell is she?' he said time and again to Sharlene. 'Didn't she give you any idea of when she was going to arrive?'

Sharlene squirmed, knowing that the moment of truth – her fictionalised version of it, anyway – had come.

'It was a very bad line, babe,' she said, with what she hoped was such a sexy pout he would be unable to be seriously angry with her. 'It was so bad, it may not even have been Fleur . . .'

He'd been flicking through a pile of CDs. Now he stopped. 'Run that past me again, would you?' he said in a voice under-shot with steel.

Seated on the sofa across the room from him, Sharlene forced a pussy-cat smile, fear beginning to stir deep in the pit of her stomach. Al's temper was legendary, but so far she'd never experienced it – nor did she want to.

'The line was breaking up, but it was a young woman's voice and it sounded like Fleur . . .'

'Jesus Christ, Sharlene! You could have told me you weren't sure who the fuck you were speaking to!'

His fury as he realised he'd wasted an entire day waiting for Fleur to show when there'd never been any real chance she would do so was so great he was a flicker away from laying violent hands on her.

Well aware of the depth of his fury, knowing that a wrong word now would precipitate the kind of scene their relationship might never survive, Sharlene kept quiet.

Al looked down at his Rolex. It was ten-forty. Haring off to Oxford now would be pointless. He would go tomorrow, after two long-arranged business meetings – one at the Dorchester and one in the City – were over.

And now, in order to avoid a full-scale ruck with Sharlene, he was going to take Blitz for a long late-night walk.

The next morning, even though he'd been asleep for only a little over five hours, Al was wide awake by six-thirty. Half-an-hour later he was behind the wheel of the Shogun, heading for London and his early-morning breakfast meeting with a Swiss banker who was going to give him the low-down on government bonds.

Not that he was thinking of investing in any – at least not in the accepted sense. He did, though, want to know everything possible about them. Where bonds were concerned he had plans – big plans. Plans so big he hadn't even talked about them with Stuart. And when those plans came to fruition he intended to follow Ashworth's example and retire.

His second scheduled meeting was with a representative from the company that was fitting out the love of his life, his yacht, *The Mallard II*. Berthed for the winter in Marseilles, *The Mallard II* was so special to him, just thinking about her made his scalp tingle. He had always loved being on water. It was his earliest memory. The Thames estuary at early light, sitting cross-legged atop the coiled stern rope on his dad's barge, *The Mallard,* while his dad made a brew-up and seagulls dipped and soared.

His old man had been a lighterman, as had many Bermondsey men in the days before container ships had put an end to the Thames as a great port. When it had been school holidays, or when he'd wangled being off sick or had played hookey, he'd spend the day on the river with his dad and think himself in heaven. Looking back, he still thought those days on the river were as near to heaven as he was ever likely to get.

Despite his on-going anxiety where Fleur was concerned, he grinned as he left the steep narrow lanes of the Downs behind him and tooled the Shogun on to the A223.

The time he and his dad had spent together when Stuart had been too young for such jaunts, Kevin had been a toddler and Tommy hadn't been born, had forged a special bond. It was a period when his dad had taught him a lot. Even now, thirty-five years later, he still retained a map of the river in his head and names such as Barking Reach, Maplin Sands, Barrow Deep, Mucking Flats, Condemned Hole, Cuckold's Point, were as familiar to him as Bermondsey street names.

His grin deepened as he continued to reminisce. The old man had taught him more than river lore. He'd taught him how to walk home from the docks with stolen goodies secreted about his person and, in his later years, how to be an ace bellman when it came to breaking and entering and a careful gellyman when it came to safe-blowing.

Not, he reflected as he approached the turn-off for the A20, that there was much call for either talent these days. When Ashworth had said crime had moved into an era all high-tech or drug-related, he hadn't been kidding. For crims like himself it meant the old skills were no longer rated, which was the reason he was about to have breakfast with his Swiss friend. A mammoth bonds theft was the way he should be going – he could feel it in his water.

As he slid into the outside lane his mobile rang. 'A bit early, mate, but a piece of info you should know.' The speaker was Sid. 'One of The Maid's barmaids didn't go home last night. Apparently she's little more than a kid – you should get Max to start asking ages when he takes staff on – and her dad's rung his local police station asking for hospitals to be checked. Normally it wouldn't cause a ripple, but you can imagine the glee when the name of the pub was mentioned. There'll be as much mileage made out of it as possible.'

'Which barmaid is it?'

'The name logged in is Beryl Keene, though there's a rider that she's also known as Lulu.'

'OK, mate. I'll give Max a bell. Ciao.'

He severed the connection, hoping to God Lulu was eighteen or over. If she wasn't, the Bill would be sure to give Max grief over it. Even though they didn't know the precise details, they knew he had strong links with the pub and that it was a favourite haunt for many villains. If they could make a case for Max losing his licence, they would. Christ, they'd probably even start checking if the bar staff's National Insurance contributions were being paid!

Rattled at the annoyances he could see coming all because Lulu had been a naughty girl and gone off with a boyfriend for the night, he turned into the Old Kent Road, his thoughts on the meeting ahead of him.

Thieving government bonds was nothing new, of course. Instantly negotiable bearer bonds had always been a prize – if they could be successfully disposed of. Way back in the sixties the Kray twins had helped the Mafia dispose of stolen Canadian securities – or rather the men who were the financial brains behind them had arranged that they do so.

The Krays had never been too strong in the brain-box department. If they had been they'd never have gunned down Cornell in broad daylight or left it to henchmen to dispose of McVitie's body. Both acts had been the works of imbeciles – in the case of Ronnie, quite literally. The thinking – if any – had been that their terrorising techniques were so well honed no one would dare to grass or testify against them.

They'd been wrong, though. The gutsy barmaid who had witnessed Ronnie's shooting of Cornell in the Blind Beggar *had* testified. And when the Krays were safely off the streets and in prison on remand, their henchmen, eager to save their own skins, had turned Queen's evidence and been major witnesses for the police.

He'd only been thirteen years old at the time but he hadn't been too young to learn a valuable lesson: only family could be trusted absolutely. A few years later, when he'd become a full-blown rascal, that was the way he'd kept things – within the family.

As commuter traffic into London began building up, forcing him to reduce speed, his thoughts drifted back to the Krays. Their swan-song days had come just as his dad's days as a lighterman had ended. Always at home in a shady environment, his dad had embarked on a new career, running a little drinker in Soho – and it was then he'd crossed swords with Jack-the-Hat McVitie.

'The drinker was going great guns,' was the way his old man always told the story. 'That was 'cos I had the Old Bill straight. They'd raid it every four weeks with the arrangement there'd be a bloke they could arrest and charge – a different one every month.

'The regular way things were run, I'd be on the door.

Punters would just ring the bell and in. I had a big ashtray for silver and the notes went straight in my pocket.

'One night things are buzzing along nicely and in walks the Hat, five-handed. Orders a drink. Doesn't pay for it. Everyone's relaxing. Slashing a bit down their necks. Then Jack says to me, "What help have you got? Who's looking after you?" I tell him no one and that I don't need no one. He says, "Yes, you do. What if there's a right row or something?"

'I tell him to fuck off – that there's no chance of me paying protection. Next thing he turns on a customer with a razor and begins opening him up, knowing for a cert that it's as good as closing me down. The Bill can turn a blind eye to a lot, but not to punters being razored.

'Course, everyone's breaking their necks to get out and there's bollocks-all I can do because my back's to the wall and one of Jack's mates is bringing a blade down somewhere behind my ear. I thought I was done for, but I wasn't left in as bad a shape as the punter. Jack razored his backside to ribbons – the place was like an abattoir.

'When the Hat and his sidekicks have finished their party pieces and strolled off into the night, I grab as many towels as I can lay my hands on. I've got 'em round my neck and packing the punter's arse and I'm scaring the shit out of a taxi-driver and offering him the moon to drive us to a hospital way out of the area.

'He gets us to one Barnet way and there's the usual questioning about what the hell happened and we say we was just walking down the street and someone hit us. Leastways, it's what I said. The punter wasn't up to saying anything. He had to have five hundred stitches and I copped for thirty-two. The police showed up, of course, but it's OK because I'm miles from the West End, see?

'Anyways, a few days later I tool up and go over

the river to the Regency, the Kray hang-out in Stoke Newington. Tommy Flanagan's on the door. "Is he here?" I say, meaning the Hat. "No," he says, so I say, "I want to see Reg." "Upstairs," he says, and up I go. Christ, but it was like something out of a film. Very intimidating. Everyone suited and booted. Lots of mohair. Course, Reggie knows why I'm there. "What do you want done about it?" he asks. "Nothing," I said. "I want to do it myself."

'"Fine by us," Reggie says and so I've got the all clear, see? He and Ronnie aren't going to be on my tail when I do for McVitie. So . . . I'm looking for him when I get pulled by the Bill in a betting shop in the West End. They want to know who did the punter. "We either nick them for it," they said. "Or we nick you." Next thing, I'm in the van to West End Central. "Have you decided what you're going to do?" they say. I'm keeping shtum. I ain't grassing. Not even on McVitie. "Charge him," they say. "What with?" I ask. "Trying to obtain money from a police officer by false pretences."

'I do twelve months and while I'm in prison, festering about it all, a con comes up to me and asks if I'm still after Jack. I say yes and he tells me I'm too late. "He's dead," he says. "Don't say fuck all, but he's dead."

'So there you are. That's how come it was nearly me who did for Jack-the-Hat and not the Krays. They had their own reasons for doing him, of course. It weren't done as a favour to me. The Krays were always ironing out their own. Anyways, by the time I'm back on the streets, Ronnie and Reggie are off 'em, starting life for double murder – one of the murders being the Hat's. Funny old world, ain't it?'

Al cruised over Westminster Bridge, a smile touching his mouth. His old man was right, it *was* a funny old world. Ronnie and Reggie were now six feet under in Chingford cemetery and the old man was swanning about the Costa del Sol with a host of other ageing rascals – though in his case he had a permanent young lady in tow. A year ago, at the grand old age of seventy-five, he had become a father again.

As he turned right into Whitehall, en route for Park Lane and The Dorchester, it occurred to him that by the time his half-sister was of age, he'd be sixty-two and old enough to be her grandfather. His grin deepened. With his reputation people would probably think she was his latest girlfriend. Whatever the future, when the old man finally popped his clogs, she'd be looked after – as would her mother. Blood ties constituted family and when it came to family, the Virtue clan went by the same motto as the three musketeers – all for one and one for all.

He sped past the Cenotaph, unaware of being watched. The watcher, from a window high above Whitehall, was Rupert Pembury-Smythe. Happily ignorant as to the identity of the Shogun's driver, he was charting its progress for no other reason than that it was the most distinctive vehicle currently in view.

'Yes,' he said to his telephone caller as Al exited into Trafalgar Square. 'The main player has entered the game, but whether things will move in the way optimistically predicted is impossible to tell. Even if the other participant is successfully brought into play, I cannot imagine the two of them joining forces. The ingredients for the cake may be there, but as for it ever rising . . .'

He left the sentence unfinished, too scrupulously polite to spell out that it would be a miracle on par with Christ walking on water.

His caller went off on a long spiel about how such set-ups were commonplace in drugs intelligence work and how it was absolutely essential that they be co-operative with their American counterparts.

Rupert had heard it all before. He hadn't been convinced then and he wasn't convinced now. He thought longingly of retirement and the house being built for him in Grand Cayman. He would do some sailing, of course. He wasn't too creaky in the joints for what had always been his favourite leisure activity. Once, years ago, he and Wilfred Frensham had circumnavigated the Isle of Wight. Deena had been only a small child at the time, six years old, maybe seven. Inevitably, the memory brought his attention back to the subject under discussion.

His unhappiness deepened.

If his old friend knew what was now in hand, he'd be spinning in his grave like a top.

A surge of satisfaction swept over Al as, his meeting at The Dorchester concluded, he waited for the Shogun to be driven up from the hotel's underground car park. His banking friend from Lugano had told him exactly what it was he wanted to hear and, as a consequence, he had a new job to plan – and planning a job always gave him a very special kind of buzz.

Minutes later, as he drove down to Hyde Park Corner he took his mobile from his breast pocket and flicked through the electronic listing for St Clemence's Administration number.

'Al Virtue,' he was saying a couple of moments later as he drove one-handed around Hyde Park Corner. 'My daughter, Fleur, is a second-year undergraduate reading English. Since her return to college I've not heard from her or been able to contact her. Can a call be put through to her, or a message passed on?'

There was the waffling he'd expected, but he'd no

intention of being deterred by it. 'Yes, I do know how many students there are at St Clemence's,' he lied glibly, 'and I'll hold.'

Very faintly in the background he could hear a woman in the Admin office saying to the person he had been speaking to, 'Fleur Virtue's father? Here, let me . . .'

There was sharp interest in the voice and, fearing it might be for the wrong reasons, Al's mouth tightened.

'Mr Virtue?' the voice queried. 'I'm afraid we're unable to help you. Fleur did not return to college at the start of the Michaelmas Term. Administration has had no communication from her and so we are as much in the dark as –'

'*What?*'

The Shogun veered so sharply it nearly mounted the pavement.

'For Christ's sake!' Bringing the jeep under control he slewed round a corner into Parliament Square. 'What the fuck do you mean she hasn't returned to college?'

'I'll put you through to the Bursar.' If the voice had been ice-cool originally, it was glacier-like now.

Al didn't care. He couldn't believe what he was hearing. Fleur hadn't returned to college since her summer holiday? How many weeks was that, for Christ's sake? One? Two? *And the college hadn't informed anyone that she was missing?* It was incredible. Totally fucking unbelievable.

He sliced past a bus, looking for somewhere he could pull over and give the phone call total concentration. How long ago was it since he'd last spoken to Fleur? He couldn't remember exactly, but he did know that it was before she'd gone to Tenerife or wherever, because that was what she'd been talking about.

The next thought came roaring at him with such dread-ful implications he thought he was going to have a heart attack. *What if she hadn't returned to college because she'd never returned to England?* He screeched to a halt within yards of Winston Churchill's statue, uncaring of the strict no-parking regulations. His daughter was missing and was probably missing abroad. *And he didn't even know in which fucking country!*

'Mr Virtue?' This time the speaker's voice was more authoritative. 'I'm afraid we appear to have a serious situation on our hands. It hadn't been realised that Fleur was missing from home as well as from college. Naturally, with your permission, we shall inform the police. If you would like an interview with the dean, she will be available at your convenience.'

An open-topped London tour bus, full of camera-clicking Japanese, was passing dangerously near to him. Big Ben was deafeningly chiming the hour and an army of cabbies was hooting at him.

He was oblivious. The police! Christ Almighty – how come he was looking a situation in the face where he might voluntarily tangle with cozzers?

'Do nothing,' he said tersely, 'until I get to Oxford. Understand?'

'And when will that be, Mr Virtue?'

'In an hour. Probably less.'

He threw the phone down on to the passenger seat and gunned the engine into life, racking his brains to remember every detail of his last conversation with Fleur. It had been five or six weeks ago. She'd said she was going away with a university friend. A cheap package deal, she'd said. But where to? His attention had been on something else at the time and, for the life of him, he couldn't remember.

69

As he re-circled Parliament Square, leaving it, not as he had originally intended by the route leading over Westminster Bridge, but by St Margaret's Street so that he could speed westwards out of town through Chelsea and Hammersmith, he pondered names, praying to God that one of them would click. Tuscany, Trieste, Torremolinos, Tangiers?

No, not Tangiers. He cut in front of a Volvo and slewed into Millbank. The destination had definitely been Europe – or as near to Europe as made no difference. If she'd been going to Tangiers he'd have clocked it as being dicey at once. He drove one-handed as fast as the traffic would allow and with his free hand picked up his mobile, punching Stuart's number.

In personal situations it was always Stuart he contacted first. Max was for the straight – or near straight – business side of his life. More to the point, Max wasn't family.

'Stuart?' he said tersely. 'I've got a problem.' He overtook a Peugeot and, taking advantage of a clear bit of road, careened down it, only to be brought to a standstill by red lights on Chelsea Embankment. 'Fleur's missing,' he said without preamble as he brought the Shogun to a jarring halt. 'She's not at college. Hasn't been since term started two weeks ago.'

'Christ, Al!' Stuart's alarm was instant and deep. He'd been about to drive over to The Maid, intending to pull Tommy out of bed and have a few hair-of-the-dog drinks with him. Now he said, 'Where are you? What are you going to do? What can I do?'

'I'm on the Embankment. I'll be in Oxford in under an hour. First thing I'm going to do is to find out why the hell no one got in touch the instant she didn't appear after the holidays. Can you *believe* that, Stu? Can you fucking *believe* it?'

With the lights at amber he screeched away from them.

'Then I'm going to find out the name of the friend she said she was going on holiday with. If *she's* back at St Clemence's . . .'

He left the sentence unfinished. If the girl in question was back, what would it mean? Everything would depend on whether the two of them had gone away together as planned. If they hadn't . . . if Fleur had gone alone . . . But at least the girl she'd been going to travel with would know where it was Fleur had gone.

'Do you want me to follow you up there?' Stuart asked, breaking in on his thoughts. 'I can be right behind you in twenty mins or so.'

'No point. Sit tight and keep your mobile switched on.'

'OK. The club Paulie's girlfriend runs, the one he stayed at last night, is smack on the King's Road. You'll be driving right past the door. Shall I give him a bell and tell him to get his arse on to the pavement so's you can pick him up?'

'Do that. Tell him he's got two minutes.'

Al severed the connection. If he was going to be hunting out Fleur's friends, two pairs of legs would make shorter work of the job than one, and Paulie always made a reliable sidekick. Paulie hadn't been christened Paulie. His given name was Paul; it was only when little Billy died that Stuart and Ginny had made Paul and Richard's names as like their dead half-brother's as possible.

As Chelsea Embankment gave way to Cheyne Walk he reflected that Stuart knew all about losing a child. The very thought of losing Fleur brought beads of perspiration out on his forehead.

But he wasn't going to lose her, he reassured himself as

a figure with his shirt hanging out of his trousers and a tie hung loose round his neck waved frantically to him from the crowded pavement. Not in the way Stuart had lost Billy. Fleur wasn't dead. She wasn't missing permanently. She'd just been careless about letting him know where she was.

He veered to a halt to allow Paulie to scramble aboard. Twenty years old, dark-haired, blue-eyed and with inborn swagger, Paulie was the son he'd never had.

'What gives?' Paulie asked, buttoning his shirt as Al drove away at a speed usually reserved for high-tailing it after a job. 'Dad just said I'd got thirty seconds to get myself on to the pavement. Is it a bit of business?'

'It's Fleur.' In vast relief Al saw that the traffic was thinning. Another few minutes and they'd be on the motorway. 'I haven't heard from her since she belled me six weeks ago saying she was off on holiday with a friend. Term started two weeks ago and she hasn't showed.'

'Shit,' Paulie said expressively, knowing it was the reaction his uncle would expect. He looked across at him with curiosity. How was it that a guy who was so sharp in every other aspect of his life was so unknowing about his daughter? Perhaps all fathers were the same when it came to girls – not having a sister, he didn't know. He did know, though, that his dad wouldn't be flapping if he'd dropped out of sight for two weeks – and that when they caught up with Fleur she would be exasperated by Al's over-anxious concern.

'It's easier, sometimes, not to let him know what's happening in my life,' she had once said to him smoothly when he'd pointed out to her that if Al knew about the bloke she'd then been going around with – a bloke who was twice her age – there'd be ructions of mega proportions.

Knowing that his uncle wouldn't even begin to believe him if he told him how street-wise his butter-wouldn't-melt-in-her-mouth, demure-looking daughter really was, Paulie said again, insincerely, 'Shit – that's not like Fleur, is it? I mean, she's not in the habit of being out of touch, is she?' He fastened his tie, leaving the knot rakishly loose and the top button of his shirt undone. 'So where are we off to? Oxford?'

'Yep. First I'm going to have a word with the dean. Then I want to check out the girl Fleur said she was going on holiday with. If she's missing as well . . .'

He sped on to the motorway and pulled immediately into the fast lane, putting his foot down hard on the accelerator.

'If she's missing as well, then we're going to have to check out everyone she and Fleur hang out with. It'll probably take time. There must be hundreds of girls in an all-girl college.'

In any other situation Paulie would have fisted the air at the prospect of so much talent, conveniently corralled. As it was, mindful of the mood his uncle was obviously in, he merely said, 'Yeah. Well. Whatever it takes, eh?'

'Yep.' Al's mouth was set in a grim line. That they'd do whatever it took was a massive understatement. The speedometer needle moved from 100 to 105 as he pressed his foot to the floor, an angry man prepared to go to the limit – no matter what that limit should prove to be.

Chapter Five

Deena strode purposefully down the High on her way to St Clemence's. The sky was a clear, brassy blue and the leaves beginning to turn colour on the trees were a riot of gold and amber and rose-red.

Their beauty was totally lost on her. She'd just spent the most sleepless night of her life and even now her mind was churning nearly as feverishly as her stomach. The moment, the previous evening, when she had learned that Hugh's girlfriend's name was Fleur Virtue, was one that would live with her for a long, long time. Even without being told that the girl didn't bandy her surname about, she'd guessed whose daughter she was. How many Fleur Virtues could there be? It wasn't exactly the commonest name on the planet.

A gaggle of undergraduates cycled past her, college scarves streaming in the breeze. A frown puckered her brow. Did Hugh know that she had once acted for the prosecution in a trial that had resulted in a ten-year sentence for his girlfriend's father? It was nearly impossible to believe that he didn't. The Al Virtue trial had been the making of her professional reputation. People meeting her for the first time invariably referred to it.

Hugh, however, wasn't someone meeting her for the first time. He was her son and, in what she believed to be fairly typical behaviour in a child, had never shown interest in her working life. At the time of the trial he had been only ten and so it was within the bounds of probability that he knew nothing whatsoever about it. He would, though, know the kind of family Fleur Virtue came from. If his friend knew the reason she was so reticent about her surname, then so did Hugh. He'd known she came from a family of professional criminals and, knowing it, he'd still gone ahead and formed a relationship with her.

She came to a halt in the middle of the busy pavement. 'Professional criminals' was a kind description of the Virtues. Notorious villains or premier league gangsters suited them better. Once again, as she had when she'd first been told Fleur's surname, she felt sickly giddy. How could Hugh have done such a thing? How could he have even contemplated doing such a thing? Surely it went against every single aspect of his upbringing.

As fellow pedestrians streamed past her, she remained as stationary as a pillar of salt. Hugh wasn't stupid. He would have known the potential damage to her reputation if it became known she had a son who was on bedding terms with a Virtue. He would also have known the shame, embarrassment and pain such an association would cause her. And he hadn't cared. The realisation was so hurtful she could barely breathe.

A mother with a toddler in tow narrowly avoided walking smack into the back of her and with great difficulty she forced herself again into movement, her clenched hands buried deep in the pockets of her coat. No wonder he had misled her into thinking the friend he intended backpacking with was male. No wonder he hadn't told her there was a girlfriend on the scene.

She was at the end of the High Street now and crossing Magdalen Bridge. The views of the meadows edging the Cherwell's banks were stunning, as were the spires of the colleges that backed on to them. On the right-hand side was Merton, on the left Magdalen and in front of her, on the Cherwell's far bank, lay St Hilda's and, a little further away, St Clemence's. None of the anciently tranquil buildings registered on her consciousness. Her thoughts were far too dark and turbulent. Hugh's awareness – or lack of awareness – as to just how gravely ill-judged his relationship with Fleur Virtue was, had been fairly easy to assess. Fleur Virtue's level of awareness was another matter entirely.

Did she know the kind of judicial family Hugh came from? It was quite possible that Hugh, knowing her background, had been shrewd enough not to tell her. Secretiveness was an integral part of his character. Even as a little boy the old saying, 'Still waters run deep,' could have been coined for him.

Now well beyond the bridge she kept up her brisk pace, not looking right towards St Hilda's. St Hilda's held too many memories; memories she didn't want burdening with when she had so much else on her mind.

Dominating her thoughts was the possibility that Fleur Virtue hadn't needed Hugh to tell her anything about his family background. That when she had met him, she had known exactly who he was; that she had known because her father had told her.

It was a horrendous thought and other horrendous thoughts followed fast. Had Fleur Virtue's first meeting with Hugh not been one of chance? Had it been connived at? Had his family background been her motivation in establishing an intimate relationship with him? And had she done so at her father's behest?

She came to a halt at the kerb, waiting for the road to clear before crossing it. St Clemence's lay set apart from the noise and bustle of the city and the traffic was light. A couple of cars cruised past and another convoy of bicycles. She remained immobile.

On the surface, her latest speculation bordered on paranoia – or would have, if she hadn't had so much experience of the often bizarre workings of the criminal mind. Al Virtue would know the harm that would be done to her professional reputation if it became known her son and his daughter were romantically involved. Even if it didn't become known, there would still be mileage in it for him. In the event of her prosecuting a case in which he, or a member of his family featured, he would be able to attempt blackmail to influence the outcome. And even if the opportunity for blackmail never arose, the distress the situation would cause her would amuse him vastly.

She remembered the sardonic mockery with which he had observed her on the first day of his trial. She had soon wiped the amusement off his face. Deep in her coat pockets her hands once more balled into fists. If her assumption as to the present situation was correct, she'd put paid to the glee he was deriving from it just as fast as she'd put paid to it ten years ago. It was a pleasure that would, however, have to wait. The first priority was to find Hugh and, as the person likeliest to know his whereabouts was Fleur Virtue, she needed to speak to Fleur Virtue's dean as quickly as possible.

'Ah, Miss King. You telephoned earlier this morning, didn't you?' the dean's secretary said to her when she made herself known. 'The dean did say she could see you at ten-thirty, but I'm afraid she has an unexpected crisis on her hands. If you wouldn't mind waiting . . . ?'

'I'll wait. It's no problem.'

Well aware she was fortunate in having obtained an appointment so speedily when she didn't have a daughter at St Clemence's, Deena suppressed her impatience and seated herself on one of the chairs outside the dean's room.

It gave her yet more time to think, but for once her thoughts weren't constructive. She was wondering just how any child born into the Virtue clan could have survived their school years so intact that they'd gained a place at Oxford. That was, of course, assuming Fleur Virtue had gained her place there on scholastic merit. If Al Virtue could corrupt the judicial system for his own ends, the educational system would have presented no problems to him.

'Miss King?' The secretary said, attracting her attention. 'The dean will see you now.'

Deena rose to her feet.

The woman waiting to speak with her was breathtakingly elegant, possessing the kind of bone-deep beauty that age hardly touches. Her skin was pale and clear and expertly made-up, her brows delicately drawn and arched, her hair sculptured silver. It was a surprise, but one that Deena rode easily. The days when high-flying female academics could be referred to as old trouts was long gone.

'I very much appreciate your giving time to see me,' she said, seating herself at the near side of an inspiringly uncluttered desk. 'My son is a third-year undergraduate at Latimer. He was last in contact with me six weeks ago when he informed me he intended spending the remainder of the long vac backpacking in Turkey with a friend. When term started, he didn't register for it. I am naturally concerned as to why he didn't do so and anxious to know his present whereabouts. The police, to whom I have reported him as a missing person, have informed me that his passport is out of date. Consequently his Turkey trip cannot have taken place, but I would very much like to speak with the friend he had intended travelling with.'

'And her name is?' the dean queried with business-like brevity.

'Fleur Virtue. I would appreciate it if I could speak with her. It's highly likely she will know what alternative plans Hugh made when their trip had to be abandoned . . .'

'I'm sorry, Ms King. There is no way I can facilitate such a meeting. Forty minutes or so ago I –'

'I obviously haven't made clear the urgency of the situation.' Deena smiled with sweet reason, but it was reason under-shot with steel. 'Hugh is officially listed as being a missing person. When the police are informed that Fleur Virtue was to have been my son's travelling companion, they, too, will wish to speak with her. My speaking to her first may well mean they never have to.'

'I'm afraid you are putting me in a very difficult pos-ition, Ms King. Normally only a parent would be privy to this kind of information, but under the circumstances . . .' She made a small dismissive gesture. 'Fleur Virtue has not returned to college this term. The number of undergradu-ates who drop out is always higher than we would like,' she continued, ignoring Deena's intake of breath, 'and her absence, until her father telephoned the college a little less than an hour ago, aroused no great alarm. Mr Virtue telephoned because Fleur has not been in contact with him for some weeks. He was perturbed, but believing her to be at college, not overly so. Now, of course, the situation is very different and he is, as we speak, on his way here from London.'

At the realisation that not only were Hugh and the Virtue girl missing together, but that she risked a face-to-face meeting with Al Virtue at any moment, Deena's composure nearly deserted her.

'If I could be given the name of Fleur Virtue's room-mate in college,' she continued, her mind racing. 'Fleur might well have spoken to friends about her and Hugh's revised travel plans. Perhaps if her head of studies was approached . . .'

'I think the best thing would be for me to put this meeting on hold until after I have spoken to Mr Virtue,' the dean said decisively. 'That his daughter is missing in the company of a male friend will put rather a different complexion on matters for him. It does, I think, make the situation a little less sinister.'

'Not to me!' Deena wanted to shriek. But what she said, as she rose to her feet, was: 'I shall be in Oxford all day. My mobile number is on my card.'

The dean's eyes flew wide. 'But surely you are going to stay here until Fleur's father arrives? He will no doubt want to talk with you, and it might help if you were to discuss the situation with him.'

'If Mr Virtue is driving here hot-foot after realising his daughter is missing, finding himself facing the mother of the young man she has apparently disappeared with might complicate rather than help the situation,' she said, moving to the door, not wanting to waste time on anything other than a brisk goodbye. If Al Virtue had left London for Oxford before her interview with the dean had begun, he would, if she was any judge of the kind of car he drove and the kind of driver he was, be on the outskirts of Oxford, or even in Oxford, by now.

She left St Clemence's swiftly, anxious to avoid a head-on meeting with a man who hated her to the depths of his being and whom she despised to the depth of hers.

A pub that she knew from her student days to be shabby and quiet lay on the far side of the road. She stepped off the pavement, only to have to jump smartly back on it again as a Shogun jeep nearly ran her down.

The near-accident didn't interrupt her thoughts. They were far too deep. What if her fear that Al Virtue had engineered the relationship between Hugh and his daughter for his own ends was justified? What if Hugh was missing because Al Virtue had wanted to cause her distress?

It was a thought to freeze the blood and, pushing open the pub door, she knew her fears wouldn't need spelling out to Inspector Rose. The minute he realised Al Virtue was Fleur's father, he would be way, way ahead of her.

She ordered herself a brandy and took her mobile phone out of her shoulder-bag. Then, sitting at a quiet corner table, she pulled up Rose's number and, as she waited for him to respond, drank the brandy in one deep, needy swallow.

'Careful, Al! You nearly did for that poor cow!' Paulie said as Al sped out of the High Street and on to a bridge. 'It would've been a crying shame. She was a real good looker.'

Al, who'd barely noticed the woman he'd almost mown down, didn't trouble to comment. Now he was virtually on St Clemence's doorstep he was too busy battling with the problem of whether to report Fleur's disappearance to the police. To do so would mean he was seeking help from them, and seeking help from the Bill was anathema of such proportion he gagged even thinking about it.

The unwritten law, 'Thou shalt have no congress with cozzers' – unless, of course, the congress was bribery – was one that had been bred into him at his mother's knee. Under normal circumstances nothing would have made him walk voluntarily into a police station.

Fleur being missing wasn't normal circumstances, though.

He swerved to a halt as near to St Clemence's as he could get. If the situation remained unchanged after he'd spoken to the college's dean and everyone he could lay hands on who knew Fleur and there were still no leads as to where she was, then he might very well have to report her to the police as being missing. Certainly the dean would be expecting the police to be informed.

As they walked through an archway to the porter's lodge, Paulie gave a long low whistle. 'Quite a pile, ain't it?' he said, looking beyond the lodge to the college's ivy-clad, ancient walls. 'Beats the hell out of Jamaica Road Juniors.'

Al grunted, in no mood for chit-chat. He had to find out the name of the girlfriend Fleur had gone on holiday with. He had to find out where it was they had gone and, even more importantly, if they had returned. If they hadn't, it would have to be a police job. Hell, it would have to be an Interpol job!

'Al Virtue,' he said brusquely to the porter. 'I'm expected.'

A few minutes later he was striding down a long corridor, Paulie at his side, oblivious of the many book-carrying girls casting appreciative glances in his and Paulie's direction.

If Fleur and her friend *had* returned to England and been seen since their return, then it was just possible that Fleur was simply being a naughty – and thought-less – girl. It would be out of character, but he'd lived long enough to know that there was a first time for everything.

'Al Virtue,' he snapped at the middle-aged woman who suddenly stepped in front of him on the threshold of the door marked DEAN.

'Ah, yes,' the dean's secretary said brightly. 'Just one

moment, Mr Virtue. I'll see if the dean is ready to see you.'

She turned her back to him, opening the door, about to step into the room unaccompanied. Al shouldered past her, Paulie hard on his heels.

The secretary's cry of alarm and the dean's exclamation of indignation merged and, as far as Al and Paulie were concerned, were ignored.

'Al Virtue,' Al said unnecessarily as he stood full square in front of the dean's desk and she rose hastily to her feet. 'I want to know why you didn't contact me when my daughter failed to register for the autumn term.'

'For the *Michaelmas* term . . .'

'And as she hasn't showed for school since the beginning of term I want to know –'

'This is a *college*, Mr Virtue!'

'– why the hell,' Al continued furiously, not giving a damn what it was, 'no one bothered to tell me!'

The dean sucked in her breath, inwardly debated whether to ask her secretary to summon the porter and decided against it. Clearly the porter's presence would be totally ineffectual. Moreover a situation in which a student was missing from both college and home was deeply perturbing and Fleur Virtue's father had every reason to be agitated. That being the case, allowances for his objectionable manner had to be made.

She struggled to make them. 'I quite understand your concern,' she said placatingly. 'It had, of course, been assumed that Fleur was . . .'

Al didn't give a flying fuck what had been assumed. 'I want the name of the friend she went on holiday with,' he said explosively. 'I want to know if the two of them came back to England. I want to know . . .'

Faced with Al Virtue in a temper, most people sprang

to do his bidding. The dean, though unaware of just who he was, was no exception. Her reasoning was that the sooner she off-loaded the information she had, the sooner he would be gone; and the sooner he was gone, the better she would like it.

'The friend in question is also missing,' she said with brutal curtness, feeling an unworthy stab of satisfaction at the way this stopped him dead in his tracks.

The halt was only temporary.

'Christ Almighty! Have you informed her father that his daughter is missing? Or are you waiting for him to cotton on to the fact in his own time?'

He clamped his hands down on her desktop, leaning his weight towards her, permeating the room with an atmosphere of barely controlled violence.

She flinched, but did not back away. 'I have done nothing with regard to the second missing student,' she said icily. 'And that, Mr Virtue, is because this is an all-girls' college. The student in question, Hugh King, is a third-year undergraduate at Latimer.'

'Shit!' they both heard Paulie say.

For a split second Al said nothing. He simply wasn't capable of it.

A bloke! Incredibly, it had never crossed his mind! Fleur had said she was going away with a friend and he had simply assumed . . . He'd kill him. When he got his hands on the pair of them, he'd kill both of them. But even as he made the vow, he knew it was meaningless. He'd be so bleedin' relieved to set eyes on Fleur again he'd probably buy her a Rolls Royce convertible.

'Hugh's mother's information is that Hugh intended going to Turkey with a friend – since identified as Fleur – for the last few weeks of the long vacation. Since then she has heard nothing from him.'

Turkey! Al felt sweat break out on his forehead. Wasn't Turkey considered unsafe for young women?

'However,' the dean continued, 'as Hugh's passport had run out and not been renewed, it is quite obvious that Hugh, at least, didn't go ahead with the plan. The question now is whether Fleur did so, either alone or with a substitute travelling companion. I have given instructions for all Fleur's known friends at St Clemence's to be interviewed and asked when they last saw her, what her plans were, etcetera . . .'

'If both of them are missing, then they're missing together!' Al's relief that he could forget about trawling Turkey from end to end was vast, but he now had fresh anxieties. Why would Fleur and a boyfriend – if she'd been planning to go away with him, that was, presumably, what the bloke was – have dropped out of sight together? No answer that he liked came to mind.

'Hugh's mother has already reported his disappearance to the police,' the dean was saying. 'With your permission, I would now like to inform the police that Fleur, too, is missing.'

'Not yet,' he said swiftly. 'First I want to see Fleur's room and I want to speak to whoever she roomed with and all the people she was friendly with.'

'The correct procedure, Mr Virtue, would be to . . .'

'And I want to do all those things *now.*' There was barely reined-in menace in his voice.

'Very well, but I cannot possibly countenance a delay of more than a few hours. St Clemence's has its reputation for pastoral care to consider.'

'It's a pity it didn't consider it two weeks ago when my daughter failed to register!' Al exploded as, with commendable composure, the dean began dialling a three-digit internal extension number.

*   *   *

'Who does that mare think she is?' Paulie said, referring to the dean as the dean's secretary led the way across a great grassed square, scurrying as far ahead of them as she could get. 'The Queen?'

They were on their way to another part of the building to meet with Dr Sheila Golightly, the woman the dean had spoken to on the phone. Al didn't bother answering him and Paulie chewed the corner of his lip, aware that his uncle was in a dangerously contrary mood. What the fuss was about, he still didn't know. So Fleur had dropped out of a sight for a few weeks. So what? Dropping out of sight was something he did all the time.

As they neared an ivy-covered doorway that looked as if it had come straight out of a Hammer Horror film, Al's mobile rang.

He glanced at the number of the person ringing him and then answered it, saying tersely: 'I think I know what this is about – I tried to reach you earlier but you weren't around. There's no need to get stressed out. If the girl lied about her age when you took her on, it isn't your fault . . .'

Paulie was near enough to recognise the caller's voice. It was Max. He was also near enough to hear him say in absolute panic: 'There's every need for fucking stress! She's dead, Al! She's been found dead down by the railway line! What the hell am I to do? The police are going to be round here six-deep any minute!'

Al sucked his breath between his teeth. 'Put Stuart in the picture,' he snapped, a nerve beginning to throb at the corner of his jaw, hoping to God that whoever Max's informant had been, he'd got it wrong. 'He'll check whether it's for real or not. And don't phone anyone else. Understand?'

A yard or so ahead of them, just inside the doorway and at the foot of a stone spiral-staircase, the dean's secretary had come to a halt, waiting for them to catch up with her.

Paulie didn't bother to pretend that he hadn't heard every word. 'This is going to be real trouble, ain't it?' he said as Al thrust the mobile back into his breast pocket. 'Every punter the pub has is going to be roped in for questioning. Which barmaid is it? When did she last work a shift?'

'It was young Lulu,' Al said, registering that Paulie looked as if someone had just socked him in the gut. 'Now, let's get on with what we came here to do.'

As he strode across the stone threshold into deep shadow, every nerve and muscle he possessed was taut with tension. Lulu had been missing from home for only one night and had been found dead. Fleur had been missing for at least two, possibly six, weeks.

Never in his life had he experienced real fear – the kind that came without an accompanying buzz of highly charged adrenaline – but as he walked towards the doorway where the dean's secretary was waiting for them, fear rose in his throat as thick as bile.

Chapter Six

Sharlene woke and, without opening her eyes, stretched out a hand in the expectation of making contact with a hard-muscled body. All she met with was empty space. The shock to her system was profound.

She catapulted upright, tawny eyes shooting wide. Despite his anger of a few hours ago, it hadn't occurred to her that she'd be waking up alone. Where the hell was he? He'd known she wasn't working today, and it wasn't as if he had to show his face anywhere at the crack of dawn. Al's day rarely got into gear until it was time for lunchtime drinking to begin.

Knowing just by the feel of the house that it was empty except for herself, she turned her head to look at the clock. It was ten-fifteen. So . . . not quite the crack of dawn, but if he'd had to shoot off somewhere he could at least have woken her and told her where he was going and when and where to meet up with him.

She ran a hand over her scalp-short hair. She was now in desperate need of a cigarette and a cup of tea, and the only way she was going to get the cup of tea was if she hauled her ass down to the kitchen and made it herself. Not, of course, that it would have been any different if Al had been home. Bringing his lady a morning cuppa was not Al's style. Fetching and carrying wasn't in his repertoire.

In Italy, of course, with Giorgio, things were different. Giorgio had staff. Unobtrusive Thai girls who picked up clothes dropped on the floor, laundered and ironed them and hung them in closets, their pleasantly smiling attitude implying that it was a privilege for them to do so.

To want a drink was to have a drink. The same went for having a bath run and for a thousand and one other little personal chores. For a girl brought up in a family of seven in a council flat in Brixton, being waited on in such a way was a delightful novelty. With the money he had, Al could have had staff too, of course, but Al didn't like his privacy being invaded. The only resident help at Ponderosa was a young Bermondsey-born ex-con who took care of the house and garden and looked after Blitz.

The only visitors were family and even their visits, Fleur apart, were few and far between. Mostly Al and his brothers met up at The Maid, doing so on an almost daily basis. A host of south-east London and West End pubs and clubs were used for other kinds of socialising and for business meets. Weekends were for wives and the regular girlfriends of men who didn't have wives. Weekday afternoons and nights were for the girlfriends of the married – and in crim circles, a girlfriend was just as obligatory as wearing the right clothes, driving the right car and being seen in the right places.

She wrapped a scarlet silk dressing-gown around her rake-slender body, her mouth tightening. Much to her displeasure, the weekday category was still one she was confined to. But protesting about it would mean she couldn't see him during the week, and she didn't want that. Nor did she want the tedium of nights out with only Al's brothers' wives for company. If that became a habit, he might just start treating her as a wife and, much as she would have liked the status it would bring her – she'd seen the way wives were expected to behave and it wasn't for her.

She padded barefoot into the kitchen, opening the patio doors so that Blitz could do a recce of the garden all the way down to the trees on the escarpment, then she plugged the kettle in.

Once she'd had a cup of tea she would make some phone calls. First to her agent and Al – and then to Giorgio. She lit her first cigarette of the day, wondering if she was being wise or rash in maintaining what she'd begun thinking of as her Italian connection.

Count Giorgio d'Argenio was tubby and balding and didn't possess a whiff of the dangerous excitement Al generated. As well as being rich and single he was, however, seriously obsessed with her, and his proposing marriage wasn't totally beyond the realms of possibility. Italians with titles weren't quite as hung-up about marrying black girls as their British counterparts, and the prospect of becoming a countess was a definite sexual turn-on.

She poured boiling water into a mug containing a Tetley's tea-bag and added a slice of lemon to it, still wondering what she would do if faced with the choice of becoming Countess d'Argenio or continuing as Al Virtue's live-in moll. On the face of it, of course, there was no choice to make. Giorgio was by far the best bet.

She carried the mug of tea over to the wall telephone, not sure if she'd have the willpower to opt for him. Set against Al's swagger and attitude and throat-tightening sexuality, Giorgio wasn't even in the running.

Just thinking about Al sent desire flooding through her and, instead of ringing her agent first, she rang Al's mobile number. Only a recorded message answered. 'Sharlene,' she said, fighting down her disappointment. 'It's ten-forty. I'll try you again later, sugar.'

When she'd safely severed the connection she said, 'Shit, shit, shit!' The trouble with Al was that there was no

90

keeping tabs on him. He wasn't answerable to anyone. If Al didn't choose to come home he never explained why, not even if he'd been absent for days on end. 'It's something you just have to accept,' Lol had said to her the first time Al had dropped out of sight without a word of warning. 'When men like Al and Kevin go out of the front door you never know when you'll see 'em again. Could be hours, could be days, could be weeks. Christ, if they get nicked, it could be years!'

She finished her mug of tea, stubbed her cigarette out and came to a decision. She would drive up to Bermondsey and The Maid. It was the likeliest place to find Al and, even if he wasn't there, other members of his family would be. At least she'd be in the thick of things, and she might get a whisper of how long he was going to be gone. Hours, she could cope with. Days or weeks would be a different matter entirely.

Benedict leaned back on his heels, surveying his handiwork. Tin was not a well-regarded medium, but he had an inexhaustible appetite for new materials and he hated predictability. The figure he had created was so gigantic in size, it looked as if it was trying to wrest itself free from a force of nature. The sea perhaps? Or cleaved rock?

He ran a hand through his sun-bleached hair and stood up. He'd been welding and soldering since late the previous evening and was sweaty as a pig and absolutely knackered. He'd got movement into the bastard, though. By God, he had! He continued to survey it, this time with eyes half-closed. Could it be Poseidon? No, Poseidon was too trite, and he hated triteness. Prometheus would be better. Prometheus as a prisoner of Zeus, struggling in chains at the edge of the world.

He wondered what time it was, aware only that it was

daylight and had been for some time. He was aware of something else as well. He was ravenously hungry. Rising to his feet, he reluctantly turned his back on his creation and, leaving the integral garage that served as a foundry-cum-studio, headed in the direction of the kitchen.

Twenty minutes later, a mug of tea in one hand and a doorstep-sized bacon butty in the other, he remembered Deena and that she was in Oxford. He looked at the wall clock. It was twelve-thirty.

He took another bite of his butty. Should he ring her, find out how her day was going? He looked around for his mobile but couldn't see it, which meant he'd probably left it in the foundry. Or in the car. Anyway, she wouldn't appreciate his ringing her if she were in deep confab with Hugh's dean, or his head of studies, or whatever. Plus, he was having a good day and he didn't want it spoilt by Deena's pointless maternal anxieties.

He finished his butty, drained his tea, and wandered over to the sink to rinse the mug under the tap, certain that if *he*'d disappeared from sight Deena's cool self-composure would have barely been dented.

He looked at the clock again. He couldn't work any more, he was too drained. Anything he did now would be far from his best. Yet despite having been up all night, he didn't feel as if he could sleep. So . . . what was it to be? More coffee, but this time in the Four Ways Café? The Four Ways was one of the perks of living in Camden. The other was the High Street, where he could easily buy whatever work materials he needed.

He dragged his mind back to the problem of what he was going to do until he was tired enough to sleep. In such a situation he generally opted for visiting a gallery, usually the Whitechapel or the White Cube. There was an

Op Art exhibition on at the Whitechapel Gallery which, as it included some Sedgleys, was definitely not to be missed. He'd been intending to take Deena on Saturday morning. Op Art wasn't her bag, but the lunch he had planned afterwards at Le Caprice was.

He strolled out of the kitchen in the direction of the bathroom, pulling his sweater over his head, aware that, wherever he went, he'd have to take a shower first – he was as grimy as a navvy. He dropped the sweater to the floor en route and unzipped his jeans. His trolling down to the Whitechapel today didn't mean he and Deena couldn't do Le Caprice on Saturday. They could always go to the White Cube to view the Katherina Fritsch exhibition – though la Fritsch was probably even less to Deena's taste than Sedgley. Still, he'd spent enough time indulging her preference for fourteenth-century Italian artists. Where gallery-going was concerned, she owed him one. They would have a pleasant, relaxing day together. By Saturday, her silly anxiety about Hugh would be over. Indeed, it was probably already over, if his judgement of the situation – that Hugh was simply taking time out and being an idle bastard – was proved correct.

He walked into his billiard-sized bathroom quite certain that Deena would, by now, have tracked down some of Hugh's friends; equally certain that there would be precious few of them to track. Though Hugh had devilishly dark good looks he was too much of a cold fish to be likeable. What friends he had would, however, know where he was. The crisis over, Deena was probably already on her way back to town.

He stepped out of his jeans and turned on the shower. She'd be cross, of course. She'd be cross with Hugh; cross at having her time wasted; cross with herself for having so over-reacted. He kicked his boxer shorts to one side. Deena cross would be infinitely preferable to Deena frenetic with maternal angst. She would probably refuse to speak Hugh's name for weeks.

He was whistling as he stepped beneath the needle-like jets of almost unbearably hot water. If God was very good, the weeks might even last into months.

Max forced himself to carry out his normal pre-lunch opening routine. Under the circumstances, it wasn't easy. He was bottling up, counting the spirits and wines that needed re-stocking when, for the third time, he came to a halt, having forgotten the number that he'd got to.

Lulu dead. He struggled to absorb the reality of it and couldn't. Christ, she was only a kid. Had been, he corrected himself. Had been only a kid. He took a firm grip on the bar, feeling giddy.

'You all right, Mr Collett?' the elderly woman who came in as a daily cleaner asked, pausing in her task of wiping out ashtrays she had emptied earlier. 'Yer don't look too lively, if yer don't mind me sayin'. What is it? Kidney stone trouble again?'

Max looked across at her with loathing. He couldn't stand old women. They always reminded him of his mother. 'You're running behind time again, Nellie,' he said curtly, wishing to God Al would stop using the pub as a help-out for the wives of old lags. Nellie's husband had once been a crony of Al's dad and was presently inside, as per usual, serving time for petty theft.

'Oh, aye?' Nellie pressed a hand into the middle of her creaking back. 'I didn't know I was in a race. AV be in this lunch-time, will he?'

It was a not very subtle hint that her real guv'nor was Al, not him, and that if he began giving her aggravation she'd have a word in Al's shell-like.

94

'An' maybe I wouldn't be behind time if I 'ad all my tackle. Where are my rubber washing-up gloves, that's what I want to know. They were 'ere Monday morning, 'cos I was using 'em. I always use 'em. They ain't 'ere now, though. They've bleedin' walked.'

Trying to control the pressure building up behind his eyes, Max ignored her and again began counting the bar stock, frantically trying to remember what he'd done with the gloves. He hadn't left them with Lulu's body, he knew that. And rubber gloves wouldn't retain fingerprints – not when they were always in and out of hot water.

How had it all happened? Sweat beaded his forehead and began to drip into his eyes. How the *fuck* had it all happened? One minute The Maid had at last been empty of Tommy's friends, Tommy had been tucked up, senseless, in one of The Maid's spare bedrooms, and Max had been about to go to bed. The next . . .

He unlocked his storage fridge and with shaking hands began stocking up from it. The next thing there'd been a knocking at the door and he'd opened it to find Lulu on the threshold. 'Sorry, Mr Collett,' she'd said sheepishly, 'But one of Mr Virtue's friends, Barney, was following me and being a nuisance. Is it all right if I stay here for a while? Just till he's gone?'

Naturally he'd said yes. What else could he have said?

Trouble was, he, like everyone else, had had far too much to drink. And he'd suffered torments all evening seeing Marilyn with Kevin. He clamped down hard on the thought of Marilyn. If it hadn't been for her, none of this would have happened. It was all her fault. Christ, how he hated her for the way she'd so publicly mortified him! Everyone had known she and he were an item. Everyone.

Nauseously he realised there wasn't enough stock in

the fridge to finish bottling up and so, on legs that felt like jelly, he walked over to the hatch leading down to the cellar and pulled it open. Al had told him to contact Stuart and not to phone anyone else. Well, he'd followed the sparse instructions to the letter and Stuart was on his way over, but it wasn't Stuart he needed as back-up when the police arrived. It was Al. But only as long as Al had no idea of what had really happened.

He climbed down the steps. If Al knew, he'd stand no chance. Al would kill him. Al would imagine the same kind of thing happening to Fleur and tear him apart with his bare hands.

He dragged an empty crate towards him. Al was right to have fears for Fleur. Young girls were all alike. They wore see-through blouses and skirts so short they barely skimmed their bottoms and then, when a man reacted to the signals being given, instead of playing ball they shut up shop.

He began filling the crate with bottles of spirits, aware that if Lulu hadn't shut up shop, she wouldn't now be on a morgue slab. He'd only wanted a bit of a kiss and a cuddle. He'd only wanted not to feel so bad about Marilyn.

She'd reacted as if he were a dirty old man – and he'd known that she wouldn't have reacted that way if it had been Stuart or Kevin or Tommy who'd been coming on strong with her. It had just been more than he could take. He'd thought of Marilyn letting Kevin do whatever the hell he wanted with her, and he'd lost his rag. He'd lost it completely. He'd pulled the silly chiffon scarf she was wearing tight around her throat and, seeing only Marilyn, had kept on pulling until he'd thought his wrists had been going to break.

With trembling hands he lit a cigarette, inhaling deeply

and closing his eyes. Christ, but it had been a nightmare. He hadn't known what to do with her. He'd been in a state of such blind panic he'd soiled his pants. What he had done, though, had been quite cute. Wearing Nellie's washing-up gloves, Max had carried Lulu's body out of the pub and loaded it into the boot of Ritchie Virtue's red Volvo. It was a stroke of luck that Ritchie had gone off with a crowd of Tommy's friends, leaving his car at The Maid. Though they'd never advertised the fact, Lulu and Ritchie had been seeing quite a bit of each other. The cozzers were bound to check out Lulu's boyfriends, and if they thought Ritchie was in the frame it would take the heat well away from him.

Still wearing gloves, he'd driven to the railway embankment, hoisted her body over the fencing and rolled it downhill until it lay beneath scrub. Then he'd driven the car back to the car park and, from then on, had tried to act normally so no one would realise anything was amiss.

He hadn't expected the body to be found so quickly, though. Christ, he hadn't even expected her to be reported missing yet. That she had been was down to her age and the fact that she still lived at home.

He finished filling the crate and made no move to begin carrying it up the steps. No one would suspect him. Why should they? There'd still been a handful of people around when Lulu had left for home. Who was to know she had come back? Who, in any case, would suspect *him* of an act of violence? Unlike the majority of his punters, he wasn't a criminal. He didn't have a record. He'd never even committed a driving offence. Remembering all the snide remarks he came in for, about him being gutless, he felt a kind of grim satisfaction. He wasn't being gutless now. All he had to do was to keep shtum and go on playing the concerned employer. Which wouldn't be hard, because he was concerned. He was so concerned he was nearly out of his mind.

He heard the pub door open again and, seconds later as it closed, Stuart's deep baritone called out, 'Hiya, everyone. Nellie! How ya doin'? You look as sexy as ever, darlin'.'

As Nellie cackled with laughter, Max yelled: 'I'm in the cellar, Stu. Come down!'

Seconds later Stuart, suited and booted, came down the cellar steps, drinking from a bottle of lager.

'Hi, Max. What's the panic?' he asked, wiping his mouth with the back of his hand. 'You were like a demented parrot on the phone. I couldn't understand a word.'

Max dropped his cigarette to the stone floor, crushing it out beneath his foot. 'It's one of the barmaids . . .' he began tersely.

'Aw, for Christ's sake!' Stuart's exasperation was total. 'Are you tellin' me you've got your knickers in a twist because you're having staffing problems? You're becoming a real Jessie, you know that? Where's Tommy? Is he still crashed out?'

As he asked after Tommy he turned, about to climb back up the steps.

'The barmaid is Lulu – Al's regular tip-off down the cop-shop says she's been murdered.'

The way he was feeling he wouldn't have believed anything could have given him satisfaction, but as Stuart stopped dead in his tracks he felt a surge of something very close to it.

'Lulu? Little Lulu?' Stuart had the kind of big-featured face that looked as if it had been carved from stone. There was nothing impassively stone-like about it now, though. He looked absolutely appalled.

Max's demeanour gave him his answer. Stuart ran a hand through his hair. 'Christ,' he said unsteadily. 'Sweet Christ. Poor little cow.' He shook his head as if to clear it. 'Does Al know?' he asked, suddenly sharp again. 'Did he tell you to get me over here?'

'Yep. He's out of town.' Even as he said the words, Max realised that Stuart would already know that Al was out of town – and where. He suppressed a shaft of emotion not far removed from jealousy.

'As the cozzers already know she worked here they're going to be round any minute,' he said, hardly able to believe the pub wasn't awash with Old Bill already. 'Point is, she was behind the bar last night and, thanks to Tommy's party, the place was even thicker than normal with villains. So . . . what do I do when the cozzers start asking for names? I have to know how Al will want it handling.'

Stuart took another swig from the bottle of Skol, wiped the top of it and said, 'There ain't nothing to handle, Max. Leastways, not where the cozzers are concerned. As far as I know, Lulu wasn't knocking around with anyone in the family and, besides, we're all covered for last night. Paulie went over to his tart's place on the King's Road. Ritchie went off with mates of Tommy's. Kevin was deep in the bosom of his family. Tommy crashed out here. The only thing that needs handling is finding the bastard responsible before the cozzers do.'

There was the sound of more activity from above their heads as lunch-time regulars began drifting in, and then a laugh that Max recognised. Lol was in. With a police presence imminent, that was all he needed. Kevin's wife was a drama queen who could turn a bad situation into

99

a nightmare at the drop of a hat. She also possessed vocabulary that would do a navvy proud. He needed Lol, mouthing off at the police at full throttle, like he needed a hole in the head.

'So I just tell it as it is?' he said, wanting to get his script right before he went back upstairs. 'Tell them who was in, who spoke to who . . .'

Stuart clapped a hand on his shoulder. 'Wouldn't surprise me if you didn't have to tell it at all,' he said reassuringly. 'It'll have been a boyfriend who did for Lulu, and London's finest will probably have pulled him in by now – though it'll be cryin' shame if they have.'

Max stared at him in blank incomprehension.

'Lulu was one helluva lovely girl,' Stuart said, ferocity in his voice. 'And none of us is goin' to want to see whoever did for her bein' handed a cosy little sentence. For real justice to be done, me and Al need to get to the bastard first, understand?'

Max swallowed hard. He understood all right. He bent down to the heavy crate, knowing his feelings would be showing on his face and not wanting Stuart to read them.

Looking as ill as he felt, he hoisted the crate off the floor and began manhandling it up the cellar steps and into the bar.

Sharlene parked her Morgan in The Maid's car park, noting that Lol's car was also parked up but Ginny's wasn't. Thank God. She found Lol a laugh. Ginny, however, was a pain in the neck. Why Al regarded her so highly and why her husband was so besotted with her, she couldn't imagine. The woman was a middle-aged frump.

Comfortably aware that she was as far from a frump as it was possible to get, she sashayed into the pub wearing her ankle-length Italian coat over a knee-skimming red jersey dress. With her extraordinary height, willow-slim figure, black skin and white-blonde hair, she would have stopped traffic even without the way she moved. With it, she was pay-money-to-watch sensational.

The instant she made her entrance she knew being pay-money-to-watch-sensational was a waste of time. Al wasn't there. His Shogun hadn't been in the car park, of course, but that hadn't necessarily meant he wasn't at the pub. There were times when Al didn't publicly announce his presence anywhere.

'Hello, Sharly,' Lol said from her favourite bar-stool. 'You missed a great party last night. Where were you? Strutting your stuff in New York?'

'Milan.' Sharlene hated having her name shortened to one only suitable for a dog or a small child, but Lol did it to everyone. Max was Maxie. Stuart was Stuie. Her husband was Kevie. Tommy she had to content herself with not changing. The only other name she didn't tamper with was Al's.

Lol nodded as though she was as familiar with the fashion modelling circuit as Sharlene. 'Have you brought any samples back with you?' she asked hopefully. 'I can always get great prices for things. You know that.'

Sharlene did. Lol specialised in off-loading high-quality clothing that had come from dodgy sources.

'I'm empty-handed, Lol. Sorry.' She slid on to a bar-stool. 'Where is everyone? It's like a tomb in here.'

'Yeah,' Lol said drily. 'I reckon most people must have gone on somewhere after we left here last night. My Kevie's still in bed, snoring like a pig. Stuie's here, though. I haven't seen him yet, but his car is round the back.'

Sharlene's interest stirred. If Stuart's car was round the

back and not in the car park, Al's jeep might be parked alongside it.

'So where is Stuart?' she asked as the barmaid slid her usual tipple, a glass of mineral water with a slice of lemon, towards her.

Lol pushed shoulder-length red hair away from her face. 'He's down in the cellar, helping Maxie re-stock. Are you on your own?' She looked away from Sharlene towards the doorway as if expecting Al to make an appearance.

Sharlene hesitated. Admitting she didn't know where the hell Al was wouldn't exactly reinforce the image she was always at such pains to project: that Al was lucky to have her, knew he was lucky to have her, and would no more treat her off-handedly than fly to the moon.

Her hesitation was only a pulse beat, but Lol picked up on it. 'The bastard hasn't shot off somewhere, has he? It's like keeping tabs on Batman!'

'Yeah. Ain't it?' Sharlene gave an easy smile, but inwardly resentment was rising fast. This time Monday she'd been on a catwalk in Milan, the eyes of the fashion world on her, an Italian count in servile attendance. Now here she was, sitting in a near-empty pub in Bermondsey, her only companions a pseudo-glam middle-aged woman and a handful of pensioners who'd been using the pub as their local ever since the war. And why was she here? Because she was trying to track down a man who hadn't even bothered to wake her to tell her he was leaving the house, let alone where the hell he was off to. Was she mad, or what?

'Al home last night, was he?' Lol asked, trying to keep prurient curiosity out of her voice. 'I mean, you haven't just this minute flown in from Milan? You have been down to Ponderosa since you got back?'

For a brief second Sharlene wondered whether to lie but decided it wasn't worth the effort. 'I got home in the early hours – just after Al,' she said, deciding she wasn't about to hang around The Maid any longer. She would drive up to Mayfair, call in at the agency and see if she could rustle up any more work in Italy, ring a few friends in the fashion world and meet a couple of them for lunch somewhere smart like San Lorenzo or Le Caprice. When Al woke up to the fact that she wasn't around, *he* would have to look for *her*.

As she finished her drink and slid from the bar-stool, Lol said, 'Have you seen this morning's papers? There's something about Tommy in nearly every one of them. Some geezer in the *Guardian* has written a whole page about his acquittal with the headline "The Not-So-Sweet Whiff of Corruption". It's more about Al than Tommy, though. Look, there's photos of the boys, but none of me or Ginny or any of Tommy's girlfriends . . .'

Sharlene clocked that there wasn't a picture of her, either, and didn't know whether to be relieved or miffed. She was just about to tell Lol that she was shooting off when the door banged back on its hinges and a long-standing friend of Al's strolled in, his hands in his pockets, a trilby at a jaunty angle on the back of his head.

'Hi, girls,' he said to her and Lol as she looked beyond him, wondering if Al was about to walk in after him. 'Quiet in 'ere this mornin', ain't it? Where's the guv'nor?'

Not for one minute did anyone imagine he was referring to Max.

'Out and about, Barney,' Lol said, perking up now there was a personable male in her orbit. 'Enjoy last night's party, did you? I saw you making eyes at Max's new little barmaid. Did you get anywhere?'

'Leave it out, Lol! I'm fifty, not fifteen. Gawd knows where Max gets his bar staff. A kindergarten by the look of some of 'em.'

He was still speaking as Max climbed up out of the cellar, Stuart behind him. For the second time Sharlene paused before leaving. If anyone knew where Al was, it would be Stuart. It made sense to hang around for a few minutes longer.

'Seen this, Barney?' Lol asked, retrieving the *Guardian* from the depths of an imitation leopard-skin shoulder-bag. 'There's a smashing photo of the boys in it.'

As she handed him the newspaper she looked across at Sharlene, saying with a throaty chuckle: 'Al may be a tosser at times, Sharly, but living with him ain't dull, is it?'

Sharlene was just about to say sourly that, at this precise moment, it was so dull it would make a cem-etery seem a rave, when the door crashed open again and three men it would be impossible to mistake for anything other than plain-clothes police officers strode in.

'You're late, fellas,' Lol said, crossing still shapely legs so that, seated as she was on a high bar-stool, her short straight skirt rode higher than ever. 'The party was last night. But if you want me to give Tommy your best wishes . . .'

'Mr Collett?' Ignoring Lol's mocking sarcasm, the sen-ior of the three policemen addressed Max: 'I understand you employ Miss Beryl Keene?'

'*Beryl?*' Lol nearly choked laughing. 'If he does, I don't know her. Max only has babes working in The Maid. If you're looking for any frumpy Beryls you'll have to go to the Conservative Club.'

No one laughed. Not even Barney. The plain-clothes

men had brought an atmosphere into the pub with them – and it wasn't a pleasant one.

Stuart was leaning against the rear of the bar, his arms folded across his chest, one foot nonchalantly crossing the other. He looked completely at ease, but even Sharlene could see how watchful his eyes were. Max looked anything but at ease. Barney seemed puzzled. The clique of regulars, seated round a table at the far end of the bar, had settled back, ready for a bit of entertainment. Nellie, who had been washing the floor by the darts board, was leaning on the handle of her floor-mop, her wrinkled face avid with curiosity.

Sharlene knew exactly how she must look to them. Out of place and bored. The police were probably on Max's back for violating the licensing laws or some such rubbish. Whatever the reason for them being there, it was nothing to do with her.

'I'm off,' she said to Lol.

Lol, not averse to having Barney to herself, nodded.

Max said in a strangled voice. 'Beryl worked here under the name Lulu. Everyone knew her as Lulu. No one ever called her Beryl.'

'She won't be working for you any more, Collett,' the senior officer said brutally. 'Her father identified her body an hour or so ago.'

There was a stunned silence.

'She's dead?' It was Lol who broke it. 'Little Lulu? The barmaid who was working here last night? She's *dead*?'

There was total incredulity in her voice.

Over at the far table the regulars were rising clumsily to their feet, not sure if they'd overheard right.

Nellie's jaw had dropped wide enough to garage a car.

Sharlene, halfway to the door, came to an abrupt halt.

Which of the barmaids was Lulu, for God's sake? And if she was dead, what kind of dead? Dead as in a road accident? Dead as in she'd killed herself? Dead as in . . .

'She's been murdered,' the senior officer said to Max. 'And one of the people we want to speak to in relation to her death, is your guv'nor.'

Sharlene whirled round. The tableaux at the bar hadn't moved. Stuart stood rooted to the spot. Lol's eyes were the size of gob-stoppers. Nellie looked as if she was about to have her first orgasm in thirty years.

'I don't have a guv'nor.' Max's voice was brittle as glass as he tried to field the remark. 'I'm the guv'nor here, and you bastards damn well know I am.'

'Oh aye, we know you're the landlord,' the officer continued, one foot resting on the rail of the bar as if he'd just called in for a pint. 'Which is why, in a minute, we're going to ask you to help us with our enquiries. But before that – and before we begin talking to everyone who was in here last night – we want to know where AV is.'

'Why?' The taut question came from Stuart.

'*Why?*' The officer turned towards him. 'Because, according to her father, Beryl had a crush on AV. We know he was here last night, we know she was here. And this morning she's dead and he's evading us to the best of his not inconsiderable ability. So we're interested. Get my drift?'

Chapter Seven

Seated alone in the rather gloomy, inaptly named snug bar, Deena clicked her mobile off and ordered another coffee. Rose's voice had been as carefully ironed of expression as, under certain professional circumstances, her own often was. Nevertheless, to say there had been a quickening of interest was a mammoth understatement. He hadn't wasted time debating what it could mean. He'd had no need to. He'd simply said: 'This matter is now likely to come under Thames Valley jurisdiction, Ms King. Their HQ is at Kidlington. By the time you get there, they'll be expecting you.'

'I bet they will,' she'd thought grimly, knowing it was essential Kidlington CID were told that she had been responsible for Al Virtue's spell in Parkhurst.

'As Hugh's last-known whereabouts was Oxford, it makes sense having his disappearance investigated by people who know the ground,' Rose had added. 'And can I forewarn you of something without your taking offence? The first thing that is going to spring to mind at Kidlington is that there's a drugs connection. Oxford is awash with drugs. The public relations people try to minimise the problem, but the general word is, it's worse than Tangiers.'

'Thank you,' she'd said crisply. 'I'm quite aware of Oxford's reputation for drugs, but where Hugh is concerned it is not an issue.'

'I'm glad to hear it,' Rose had said drily. 'But remember that he's now involved with a Virtue.'

When she had put down the phone her hand had been shaking.

It was still shaking as she drank the last of her coffee. Incredibly, amongst all the many possibilities she'd so far conjured up, a drugs-related scenario hadn't featured.

And still didn't, she said to herself five minutes later, after taking the time to ring Teddy and ask how his investigation into Graveney's background was going. All he said in reply was 'interestingly', so she left him to it, her thoughts reverting to Hugh as she drove out of Oxford towards Kidlington. The explanation for his relationship with Fleur, and for them both being absent from college, was in all likelihood quite simple. He'd probably had no idea who Fleur's father was and, when he discovered the anxiety he'd put her through by not letting her know his whereabouts, he would be horrified. He might even, at this very minute, be back home in London, playing ghastly modern music on her stereo.

She negotiated a busy roundabout, picked up her phone and tried Benedict's mobile again. This time he answered.

'Have you called in at the house today?' she asked abruptly. 'My house?'

'Nope.' He sounded bemused. 'I've had no reason to, Deena. I'm down at the Whitechapel Gallery. There's some stunning Sedgleys and –'

'I'm not interested in Sedgleys!' Deena struggled to keep her temper in check. 'I'm interested in Hugh. I thought he might have come back whilst I've been away.'

'No, he hasn't. Still . . . it's good to know you're expecting him to show at any minute and the crisis is over. I don't think I'll be around when you get home. I worked all night and haven't been to bed yet. The minute

I leave here I'm going back to the studio to crash out. I don't suppose I'll surface until tomorrow . . .'

'The crisis isn't over.' Deena allowed a lorry to overtake her, knowing very well she shouldn't be continuing the conversation whilst she was driving, and not caring. 'The crisis has got bloody worse. The so-called friend Hugh intended travelling to Turkey with was a girl, Fleur Virtue.'

She paused, wondering if Benedict would make the connection for himself. He didn't.

'Her father is Al Virtue,' she continued acidly. 'That's Al Virtue as in high-profile criminal and "Hey, Deena, didn't you once act as prosecuting counsel when he went down for ten years and wasn't his photograph splashed all over the *Evening Standard*?"'

'There's no need for the sarcasm.' Benedict's voice was nearly as taut as her own. Did she think he could work nothing out for himself? And what did it mean? Had Hugh been kidnapped in some gangland revenge scam? Or was he playing at being Al Pacino in *Scarface*? Either way, there was to be no quick return to normality for himself and Deena.

'What are the Oxford City Police saying about it all?' he asked, falling back on a question that couldn't be rubbished. 'Are they in touch with the Met inspector you were talking to early this morning?'

'I haven't been to the Oxford City Police. Inspector Rose is contacting the Thames Valley Police for me and I'm on my way to their headquarters now. Benedict, I'm . . .'

She had been in Kidlington for the last few minutes and now she saw the sign, blue with white lettering, that she'd been looking for. She'd been about to tell Benedict that she was scared, but as she drove into the forecourt of the brick and concrete building, the words wouldn't come. After all, what could Benedict do? He could hardly materialise at her side and, even if he could, his presence wouldn't change anything.

'I'm there,' she finished brusquely, wishing she were anywhere but. 'I'll ring you later.'

'I'll go back to your place to sleep,' he said, 'then we can talk the instant you get back.'

It was as much comfort as he could give. It fell on deaf ears. As usual, Deena had severed the connection before he had finished speaking.

'Our normal procedure would be to log your son as a missing person,' a young detective inspector by the name of Fallon said to her, telling her nothing she didn't already know. 'However, under the circumstances . . .'

The circumstances – that Hugh's girlfriend was also missing and that her father was a villain Deena had once faced across a courtroom, to his detriment, were gone over in minute detail.

'It means a revenge element is possible, though not likely,' DI Fallon said at last. 'It's a decade since his trial. Would he have waited all this time to try and avenge himself? He's served his time, is out on the streets and, if the fiasco of his brother's acquittal is anything to go by, is busy making fools of us all again. Quite honestly, Ms King, these are all good reasons for not thinking the revenge card likely.'

Deena drew in a deep breath and with an effort switched from thinking subjectively to objectively. 'Al Virtue is a chancer,' she said. 'It would have been out of character for him to have put a price on my head, or on the head of a member of my family, in the immediate aftermath of his being sent down. He's not the type.

However, if he discovered that his daughter and my son were at Oxford together . . .'

She thought back to the man she had confronted in Court 2 at Knightsbridge Crown Court. Even though the charge he was on was not one of murder or manslaughter, she had been sure she was fencing with a man capable of almost anything. She had sensed a ruthlessness hidden under that dangerously attractive exterior. There'd been a nonchalant ease about him, even in the dock, which had been hard to ignore. He hadn't been nonchalant when the foreman of the jury had declared the jury's verdict, though. He'd been blindingly angry.

'If he discovered that my son and his daughter were at Oxford together,' she said again, 'then yes, I think it's not beyond the realms of possibility that he would see the situation as a heaven-sent opportunity for revenge of some kind.'

'Even though he's not a man known for heavy violence or intimidation?'

She sucked in her breath sharply. 'We're discussing an *armed robber*,' she said when she could trust herself to speak. 'A man who has walked into banks and held up security vans at gunpoint!'

'I know. I'm not saying Virtue is a teddy-bear. I'm just saying that I don't see him as a kidnapper. If he'd ever been into the darker side of crime, protection and extortion, then yes, it would be a possibility. I haven't had time to access his records as yet, but if memory serves me right any crime with the Al Virtue stamp on it was always one carried out with military precision and a certain flair. Months of surveillance with escape routes planned, vehicles assembled, safe houses arranged. You know the kind of thing.'

'Yes, Detective Inspector Fallon, I do.' Deena's voice

was as icy as the Arctic. 'But I'm not here to discuss Al Virtue's working methods – and even if I were, I would not, as you apparently are, be admiring of them. I'm here because my son is missing. Has been missing for six weeks. Until now there were – as far as the police were concerned – no suspicious circumstances. Now, because of the Virtue connection, there are. So what action are you now going to take? *When is something going to be done?*'

DI Fallon forced himself to remember that he wasn't talking to just any member of the public and that high-handedness would not only be out of order, but could possibly rebound to his detriment. His telephone rang and, for one brief moment as he answered it, he was grateful for the interruption. Only immense self-discipline prevented him betraying any reaction when he was told that Al Virtue had walked voluntarily into the station and was demanding to speak with a senior officer.

'Put him in an interview room,' he said tersely, debating whether to tell Deena King of Virtue's arrival. Under the circumstances, it would be premature. Who knew what Virtue was up to? He might even be about to deliver some kind of ransom demand.

'I'll be in daily contact with you until such time as your son is located,' he said, rising to his feet and concluding their conversation. 'If there's anything you're not happy with . . .'

Deena flashed him a look that would have slain a lesser man. There was a lot that she wasn't happy with, but to detail everything now would be a waste of breath. She would speak to Inspector Rose. And even though she now knew Hugh had never gone to Turkey, she would speak to Rupert again. Rupert had connections in high places. He, surely to God, would be able to ensure that the investigation was imbued with urgency.

She strode from the room, letting the door swing heavily on its hinges behind her. There were a handful of people in reception. A sulky-faced girl and a harassed-looking woman were seated beneath a Neighbourhood Watch poster. At the front desk a broad-shouldered, expensively dressed man had his back to her as he entered his name in the Visitors' Log. A much younger man, equally immaculately suited, was standing alongside with his hands in his pockets.

For a brief second, as she swept towards the exit, their eyes met and his widened, as if in recognition. As she registered his reaction his white teeth flashed in a grin and he gave her an impudent wink. It was a wink that jarred a chord in her memory, but she couldn't place who she was reminded of. It didn't matter. She didn't know him. Dismissing him from her thoughts she continued on her way out of the building, intent on returning immediately to London and a long, face-to-face discussion with Inspector Rose.

Al signed his name in the Visitors' Log with pin-neat exactitude. It was a first. Previously in such surroundings he'd only ever signed statements. Just what had propelled him to Thames Valley HQ with such speed was something he would have to ponder on later. It had been far from the top of his agenda a couple of hours ago. Then, his intention had been to sort things out as he always did – by himself. That, though, had been before his meeting with Dr Sheila Golightly, Fleur's head of studies and, even more importantly, before his brief telephone conversation with Sid Ashworth.

Sid had been bluntly to the point. 'There's bugger-all I

can do, AV. Your best bet is to report her missing to the local CID. The HQ you want will be Kidlington, a few miles north of Oxford on the A423. Just the fact that she's a student at St Clemence's will ensure the report is given serious attention. Too many MPs' daughters are students at Oxford for the local CID to be cavalier about any who go AWOL.'

If Sid had said no more he might still have put off going to the police. But Sid's voice had changed tone as he'd added: 'I'm assuming someone's got word to you about your barmaid, have they? It'll be the boyfriend – it smells of that kind of a case – but you're wanted to help with enquiries, seeing as how it's known you're the real guv'nor at The Maid.'

He'd felt as if a fist had been slammed hard into his gut. Not because the cozzers wanted a word with him about Lulu – he'd known that would happen from the word go – but because he'd been fighting down thinking about Lulu's death and could do so no longer. It had certainly concentrated his mind with regard to Fleur's disappearance. When young girls went missing they often ended up dead. If the cozzers could find Fleur before anything terrible happened to her, then he was going to go to them. No question.

He gunned the Shogun's engine into life, taking other things into account. There would, for instance, have been no problem if he and Paulie had been trying to track down a scummy liberty-taker in south-east London. They'd have found the geezer in question before the sun was over the yard-arm. But Oxford wasn't south-east London. It wasn't his manor – one he knew inside-out and upside-down. And he wasn't trying to track down a scummy liberty-taker. He was trying to find his precious daughter.

It was a measure of just how precious she was to him that when he reached Oxford's ring road he headed unhesitatingly north, towards Kidlington. Paulie was going to think him demented, but he'd never yet worried about Paulie's opinion and wasn't about to start now. Not after the bomb Dr Sheila Golightly had dropped.

'There was a drugs death in Oxford at the end of the Trinity term,' she had said, puffing on a small pipe. 'The girl in question wasn't a St Clemence's undergraduate, but Fleur knew her. If I were in your shoes, Mr Virtue, I would make sure the police knew of the connection. Amabel Lyndhurst's death may have disturbed Fleur more than had been realised.'

It had been a ridiculous insinuation, of course. Fleur wasn't likely to have taken off into the blue because one of the many people she knew in Oxford had died of a drug overdose. All the same, he hadn't liked it. He hadn't liked it at all.

'Remind me not to let anyone know we've done this,' Paulie had said to him as, after parking the jeep, they'd taken the long gradient to Thames Valley's HQ at a fast pace.

He'd ignored the remark, deep in thoughts of Hugh King. Had Fleur's boyfriend known Amabel Lyndhurst? One thing was certain, he and Paulie were going to be trawling the city's pubs that evening, searching out Hugh King's friends. And when they found them, they were going to get hard information out of them. Or else.

'I don't think Thames Valley's ever had the pleasure, AV,' a cocky young DI said, breaking into his thoughts as he sauntered across reception towards him, his hands in his pockets. 'Got lost and asking your way, are you?'

'You can cut the comedy. I'm here to report a missing person. My daughter. And it's Mr Virtue to you. Got it?'

The DI shrugged, looking beyond Al to the constable manning the front desk. 'I'm taking this particular member of the public to my office,' he said, and then, glancing towards Paulie: 'Just the two of us – unless Mr Virtue's friend wants to hold his hand.'

Al's eyes glittered but he had no intention of being provoked into the kind of response so obviously hoped for. His reason for being there was too important. Leaving Paulie to kick his heels surrounded by wanted posters, he strode off in the DI's wake.

'Name? Address? Nature of complaint?' Fallon said the instant they were both seated.

'Cut the crap. You know who I am. And I've told you why I'm here. My daughter is a student at St Clemence's and I haven't seen her or heard from her for six weeks. Neither has anyone else.'

Fallon regarded Al impassively, careful not to let his thoughts show. If Virtue was trying to cast a smokescreen over Hugh King's disappearance by making out his daughter was also missing, he was doing a good job. Simulating fierce concern wasn't as easy as most villains seemed to think and, though he hated to admit it, Virtue's concern came across as genuine.

Deciding to play along with him, he set up a file on his PC, saying as he did so, 'Give me your daughter's details,' reflecting that either way he had an interesting situation on his hands. If Virtue really was ignorant as to Hugh King's whereabouts, then it was very likely he was also unaware as to the identity of King's mother.

'The boyfriend's name is King. Hugh King,' Al said tightly a few minutes later, having snapped out Fleur's name, home and college address, date of birth and the date and circumstances he'd last been in contact with her. 'And I fucking know he's already been reported missing. His mother told Fleur's dean earlier this morning.'

There wasn't the merest hint that he knew the mother in question was Deena King, QC, and Fallon chewed the corner of his lip. If Virtue was acting, then he'd missed his way in life. He should have been on the stage.

'OK,' he said. 'You're telling me your daughter's missing, and I'm going to be obliging and go along with it. When you've given me all the info possible, her particulars will be circulated and everything that should be done will be done. That's because, where the safety of young women is concerned, I'm a scrupulous copper. It's one area of policing where over-zealousness is never a waste of time. We'll need a photograph of her. As near passport-type as possible. That said . . .' he leaned back in his chair, settling in for the real nitty-gritty, '. . . your being here, telling me she's missing, isn't quite as clear-cut as it seems, is it? There are more than a few suspicious circumstances. Particularly where you and your daughter's missing boyfriend are concerned.'

'What the *fuck* do you mean?'

Before the slate-blue eyes turned black with rage, Fallon saw Al's pupils dilate in a split-second of utter bewilderment. He wasn't in the habit of putting bets on anything where villains were concerned, but at that moment he'd have staked his pension that Virtue knew zilch about Hugh King.

A knot of pleasure so intense as to be almost sexual began forming in his gut. There weren't many moments of unalloyed joy in police work, but he knew he was working towards one now.

'Hugh King is also missing,' he said, picking up a pen

and beginning to swivel it between his fingers. 'And that causes me a great deal of concern . . .'

'And so it fucking should!' Al was so incensed at Fallon's laid-back manner that he nearly lost his self-control. 'The silly bitch of a dean thought King being missing made Fleur's disappearance *less* reason for concern, but not in my book it doesn't! If King is –'

'. . . it causes me a great deal of concern where *you're* concerned, Virtue,' Fallon continued, cutting across him, his voice thick with innuendo. 'You've no reason to be pleased about your daughter's relationship with Hugh King, have you? In fact, people of an unpleasant turn of mind might say you have so little reason for being pleased you might well have wished, or be wishing him, actual bodily harm . . .'

'From today, they'd be right!' There was no bewilderment in Al's eyes now. He'd had too vast an experience of coppers to be surprised at Fallon's inane attempt to turn the situation on its head and to somehow stitch him up. 'Unfortunately, at the time he disappeared I'd never met him. I didn't know he was Fleur's boyfriend. I didn't even know of his existence. Making out I had reason to be after him with a shotgun won't wash.'

'I'm not sure you're right,' Fallon's voice was silky smooth. 'It would be hard for you to prove that you didn't know of your daughter's relationship with him – and if you did, you certainly wouldn't be happy about it, would you? Not under the circumstances.'

It was the moment when everything changed. The moment that Al knew Fallon was enjoying himself. And in his book, coppers only ever enjoyed themselves when someone was about to slip on a very nasty banana-skin. The nerves in his stomach coiled spring-tight.

'What circumstances?' he asked menacingly.

There was a beat of silence.

Their eyes held.

Fallon smiled.

'The circumstances being that Hugh King is the son of Deena King, QC,' he said.

Chapter Eight _

Al erupted out of the interview room at such speed and with a face so contorted with passion that Paulie's instantaneous reaction was that his uncle had done for the copper he'd been closeted with. His simultaneous reaction was that the only way they were going to leave was if they made a violent break for it.

He took a swift step backwards, towards the doors, his weight on the balls of his toes, his fists bunched.

The expected eruption didn't come. No alarm bells sounded. No officers rushed towards them. The copper at the front desk didn't vault it. Al didn't yell out the kind of action he wanted him to take. Instead he careened past him, storming out of the building, his rage so intense sparks seemed to be flying from him.

Paulie spun round, following hard on Al's heels. As Al charged down the long ramp to where the jeep was parked, he shouted across to him: 'What the hell happened, Al? Where's the fire?'

'Fleur's the fucking fire!' Al yanked open the driver's door. 'She's missing, all right! She's bleedin' missing because she's scared to death of fucking facing me!'

With only a couple of rare exceptions everyone Paulie knew swore every other word. Al was one of the exceptions – or was usually.

He sprang up into the passenger seat as Al flung himself behind the wheel and turned the key in the ignition. 'She's only shacked up with the son of the bitch who did for me ten years ago!' He gunned the engine into life. 'Can you believe it? *Can you fucking believe it?'*

It wasn't a question waiting for any kind of an answer and Paulie had the sense to realise that questions were also out. As his uncle slewed the jeep out of the parking area and on to the road he scrabbled in his memory for a clue who was being referred to. No one had ever done for Al in the sense of having maimed or mutilated him and, to the best of his knowledge, no one had ever double-crossed him on a job or cheated him out of dosh. Ten years ago Paulie had only been a kid, of course, and all sorts of things could have been going on that he knew nothing about. It was ten years ago, for instance, when Al had gone down for receiving stolen bullion.

'She knows who he is! I don't believe for one minute she doesn't know who he is!' Al was heading back to Oxford at speed, holding the wheel with one hand as he took his mobile from his inside breast pocket with the other.

Paulie's mind continued to race. Had anyone grassed Al up when he'd gone down for the bullion job? Surely he'd have known about it if they had? From everything he could remember the verdict had all been down to chance. The prosecuting QC had been a knife-sharp bitch who . . .

Comprehension dawned.

'King!' Al said, punching a number on his mobile. 'The dean told me Fleur's boyfriend's name was King – and it never registered! It never bleedin' registered!'

Paulie could hear the person at the other end of the line answering. It was his dad.

'Fleur's with a bloke – and his mother is the bitch who did for me ten years ago,' Al repeated tersely. 'I don't know where, but I soon will!'

'What? The QC?' Paulie could hear his dad saying in

the kind of stunned, disbelieving voice he'd have used if he'd been asking if they were talking about the Queen Mother. 'You can't be serious!'

'I'm serious, all right – I'm so serious I'm going to seriously kill someone.'

The way he was driving, Paulie reckoned he'd do so before they reached Oxford.

'Al, I don't like putting this on you just now, mate, but you have other problems as well.' Even at one remove Paulie could hear the tension in his dad's voice. 'The Bill have only just left The Maid over the matter Max has already filled you in on. They're looking for you high and low . . .'

'They should try looking for me in cop-shops. I've been in the Thames Valley HQ for the last bleedin' hour. There's a couple of things I want you to do.' He itemised them at staccato-like speed. 'Check up on Bazza. He's on the alternative run. Make sure Max treads carefully with the cozzers. Put feelers out as to what the hell happened. I want a meet with the cunt responsible.'

'Will do, Al. Bye, mate.'

The line cleared and Al punched in another number.

Paulie remained silent as a new kind of tension licked his nerve endings. Not being expansive on the phone, even when the phone was a mobile, was in-built habit with Al, but what he'd said had been clear enough. He wanted to get to whoever had killed Lulu before the police did, and he could have only one reason – to personally make the bastard pay for what he'd done.

'Detective Inspector Ashworth,' Al was saying, the phone wedged between his chin and shoulder as, with both hands on the wheel, he negotiated a busy round-about.

Remembering what had happened to the person responsible for Billy's death, Paulie wondered how far down the retribution line his uncle would go. Lulu hadn't been family or a close friend, but indirectly she'd been one of Al's employees. And Al had liked her. Hell. Everyone had liked her.

'No. I'll try again later,' Al snapped on being informed that DI Ashworth wasn't available and would he like to leave his number.

As he veered off the A4260 on to the A4165, he tried another number. It was engaged. The next number wasn't. 'Kev?' he snapped. 'I've got problems. A barrow-load. I want my friend Sid to come back to me with gen on a girl by the name of Amabel Lyndhurst. He's not where he should be, so keep hard at it. I'm on the mobile and it's urgent.'

'Aw, for fuck's sake, Al,' Paulie heard his Uncle Kevin moan none-too-seriously. 'Lol's buggered off back to The Maid and I'm halfway to Sheppey with Marilyn.'

'I don't care if you're halfway to canonisation. *Do it!*'

Paulie suppressed a grin. Lol was a fierce wife where Kevin's mistresses were concerned. A year or so ago when, after a violent row, he'd stormed out of their high-rise block of flats to go and meet one of them, she'd fired down on him with an air-rifle as he'd crossed the forecourt to his car. Being a pretty mean markswoman, she'd hit him and, if the weapon had been a shot-gun, would have seriously injured him. If Kevin was being cautious where his present relationship with Max's ex-girlfriend was concerned, then he, for one, didn't blame him one little bit.

As Al dialled yet another number, surging on to Oxford's ring road as he did so, Paulie wondered why his uncle wanted info on Amabel Lyndhurst. Was he just following up on what the Golightly woman had said, or had the Lyndhurst girl been mentioned again in the Kidlington interview room? Come to that, what had been discussed in the interview room, period? Apart from telling him that Fleur's boyfriend was the son of the QC who had done for him, Al still hadn't put him in the picture.

'What's the plan?' he asked as whoever Al was ringing failed to answer the call. 'Are we going back into Oxford or heading for the M40?'

'Oxford.' Al spat. 'We're going to hunt down every friend Hugh King has!' His rage was still so white-hot he didn't trust himself to say more. Sharlene wasn't at the house. Tommy wasn't answering his mobile. As for Fleur . . . When he next laid hands on his daughter he was going to throttle her. It was nothing, though, to what he was going to do to Hugh King. Hugh King he was going to kill.

Deena drove straight from Kidlington towards the M40, her every instinct screaming that whatever the trouble Hugh was in, it was deep trouble.

DI Fallon may have been dismissive about the possibility of Al Virtue being involved in Hugh's disappearance, but Inspector Rose's response to the news made it clear that *he* wasn't. What she wanted now was an in-depth, face-to-face discussion with Rose. And with Rupert. Even though there now seemed no need for any Foreign Office string-pulling, Rupert had the kind of Whitehall connections that, if he chose to exercise them, could catapult any enquiry into the urgent bracket.

She circumnavigated Oxford, leaving the A4165 for the A40. She hadn't enjoyed her visit one little bit – and not just because of her reason for being there. Oxford held memories she'd spent the last twenty years trying to obliterate. The meadows by the Cherwell. The walk down St Giles's, past Balliol College, past St John's College, past the Lamb and Flag. Blackwells bookshop. The medieval cobbled lane that was St Helen's Passage near New College. The Grapes in George Street. The White Horse in the Broad. The Turf Tavern. All were places she had walked or bicycled or visited, time and time again, with Jimmy.

Her hands tightened on the wheel. Why, after all these years, was she thinking of him by name? Why wasn't she thinking of him as she had schooled herself to think: JN? Initials only.

She sped past signs informing her that the M40 was half a mile ahead and pressed her foot down even harder on the accelerator. Her lack of emotion where Jimmy was concerned wasn't genuine, of course. She had plenty of emotions, all of them bottled tight and deep; so deep that no emotion since had ever done more than struggle for life.

She remembered the information she'd given to Rose. 'He's dead,' she had said, quite categorically. Well, so he was. To her. Had lying to Rose been a mistake? It was a stupid question. Any lie to the police was always a mistake. It wasn't important to the situation, though. Jimmy had nothing to do with her life, or with Hugh's. And surviving the prurient interest Hugh's relationship with Fleur Virtue was going to occasion would be bad enough without the truth about Hugh's birth tarnishing her reputation even further.

She signalled left, moving on to the motorway slip-road. So far in life she had succeeded in doing what many people tried to do, or would like to do. She'd rewritten her history. She swooped on to the motorway. And even under the present circumstances, the way she had rewritten it was the way it was going to stay.

'It's no use getting into a tizzy just because Rose isn't prepared to drop everything and make time to see you at a moment's notice,' Benedict said to her reasonably, an hour and a half later. 'If you've spoken to him on the phone, then he's *au fait* with the situation, OK? And if he told you to report it to Thames Valley CID, then surely it means it's now their baby, not his?'

She'd been using the telephone that sat on her hall table, her back towards him. Now she whirled to face him, the skin drawn tight across her cheekbones. 'This isn't slight concern over a piece of lost property! It's my *son* who's missing, Benedict, not my umbrella! And if Kidlington CID are going to treat the matter as you are apparently treating it – as though it's something of not very much consequence – then I don't want them handling it! I want Rose in charge!'

'Christ Almighty! Don't lose your rag with me as well!' Benedict had had enough. He hadn't caught up on his missed sleep yet. He'd only been in her bed a couple of hours when, a mere ten minutes or so earlier, she'd arrived home. The whole idea of his being there, waiting for her, was that she would be grateful for his supportiveness. And she quite clearly didn't give a stuff about it.

'I'm off,' he said, well aware Deena was going to be no pleasure to be with until she'd got her present bees out of her bonnet. Wearing only jeans, his hair still tousled from sleep, he looked around for his loafers and located them under the hall table. 'Some faxes have come through for you from Cheryl or Charmian or whatever her name is,' he said as he slid his feet into them, 'and there are a

126

couple of calls on the answer-machine. When you're back to being your sane self, ring me.'

He looked around for his T-shirt, realised he'd left it upstairs on the bed and couldn't be bothered traipsing after it. Instead he scooped his bomber-jacket from a nearby chair and slipped it on, tugging the zip high over his naked chest. 'And for what it's worth, Deena,' he said as he reached the door, 'I don't think for one minute there's anything sinister about Hugh's girlfriend being Tommy Virtue's daughter. It's just sheer chance, that's all.'

'Al Virtue!' she hurled after him. 'Not Tommy! Al, Al, *Al!*'

The door rocked on its hinges and she sucked in her breath, knowing she was behaving like a fishwife and hating herself for it. The problem was, of course, that Benedict didn't understand just how complex a person Hugh was. From out of nowhere came the thought: like his father. She thrust the thought to where it had come from – the back of her mind. She wasn't going to start thinking about Jimmy again. Not now. Not ever. She looked down at the telephone, no longer thinking about Benedict either.

The person she was thinking about was Rupert.

She hadn't spoken with him since Inspector Rose's telephone call informing her that Hugh wasn't in possession of a current passport. For the first time it occurred to her that, if the police had ferreted out the information so quickly, so should Rupert. Yet if he had, he hadn't come back to her with it – which was distinctly odd.

Frowning, she pressed the playback button on her answerphone.

There was a message from Cheryl, informing her that Milton Darcus, who was standing in for her at

Snaresbrook, could, if necessary, stand in for her again tomorrow. There was a message from an old schoolfriend saying she was going to be in town the first two weeks of November and asking if they could make a date to meet up for supper one evening. There was no message from Rupert.

She looked down at her watch. It was a quarter to six. She reached for the phone and dialled his Whitehall number. There was no reply.

For a long time after she replaced the receiver she stood, thinking. Then, wearing the coat she still hadn't taken off, she left the house and, ignoring her parked car, flagged a cab. Twenty minutes later she was in her office in chambers, standing before a bookcase filled with law books and statutes and shelf after shelf of barristers' blue notebooks. She ran a forefinger along their spines, looking for one particular year: 1990. And one particular case: *Crown vs Virtue*.

Rupert Pembury-Smythe climbed the crimson-carpeted, ornately decorated central staircase at the Reform Club, Pall Mall. It was five to six and he was looking forward to his first dry Martini of the evening. Though he didn't trouble to acknowledge him, he could see that the Whitehall mandarin he was to meet was already *in situ* at one of the discreet leather-chaired tables for two overlooking the classically pillared atrium.

At the top of the open staircase he turned left, strolling beneath life-size portraits of fearsome nineteenth-century liberal luminaries.

'Ah, Rupert!' Sir Monty Gargrave said at his approach. 'What a man you are for being precisely on time. If only our friends, the Americans, were more like you.'

'The Americans aren't like anyone,' Rupert said drily,

seating himself in a chair of dark red cracked leather. 'I assume this meeting has been arranged because they want to know if I have more information on how things are progressing?'

Sir Monty nodded.

A waiter approached.

'A Martini,' Rupert said, and then, returning his attention to the matter in hand: 'Such impatience is really quite tiresome. So tiresome it verges on the childlike.'

'Ah, but then so does their naivety,' his companion said, dismissing all Americans, but especially their opposite numbers in Washington, with a disdainful wave of his hand. 'This time, though, my personal interest is such that I, too, am curious to know if their little scenario is running as forecast. Has contact finally been made between the two main protagonists? My sprog has been well primed, as you know. He won't be leaking any critical information until there is a pairing.'

Rupert lifted a brimming, frosted Martini-glass from a proffered tray. 'My perception is that events are in motion,' he said, the cigar-laden air reminding him that his second pleasure of the evening still awaited him. He reached into his inside pocket, withdrawing a silver-cased Bolivar Royal Corona. 'More than that I can't say. For me to harry for information would be exceedingly tactless. The DEA,' he added, finality in his voice, 'are simply going to have to hold their horses.'

Al's entrance into the Corn Dolly, Paulie in his wake, was one that turned heads. Though he'd never been an enforcer, the type of London underworld hyena who got a sexual buzz knowing his presence aroused fear, he could still project an awesome sense of menace if, and when, he wanted. And he wanted to now.

'So where's Giles Gargrave?' he said to the barman, hard-faced and hard-voiced.

The barman hesitated. The Dolly wasn't a pub that saw much trouble, but then men like the massively shouldered, Crombie-coated one he was now facing didn't usually patronise it. As he was inwardly debating which would be the safest option – to point Gargrave out or to say he didn't know him from Adam – he was saved the problem.

'He's over there, mate,' a youth in grubby overalls, tool-bag at his feet, said. 'The clean-shaven pillock standing with his snobby uni mates near the jukebox.'

Al looked, registered who was being pointed out, and turned back to the barman. 'Two Black Labels with Highland Spring,' he said as Paulie eased in beside him at the bar, 'and another of whatever my friend here is drinking.'

'Ta, mate,' the youth said. 'And I hope I've just fucked him up. Those posh-speaking uni wankers get on my tits, know what I mean?'

With his thoughts centred fast on Hugh King, Al knew exactly what he meant.

'What now?' Paulie asked as the barman slid two glasses of whisky and a small bottle of Highland Spring towards them. 'Do we go in heavy-handed or sweet and reasonable?'

Al splashed water into his whisky. 'Reasonable,' he said, 'for starters.'

'Yah,' Giles Gargrave was saying laconically, five minutes later. 'I'm Giles Gargrave.' His light-coloured eyes were speculative. 'And you are?'

'Al Virtue,' Al said, his voice dangerously expressionless. 'Fleur Virtue's father. And I'm looking for Hugh King.'

'And I'm experiencing a sense of déjà vu.' Giles reached on top of the jukebox and retrieved a pint of beer. 'I played this little scenario out yesterday evening, with Hugh's mother.'

As Al breathed in hard through his nose, one of Giles Gargrave's companions, red-headed and bearded, cleared his throat. 'Steady on, Gy. Remember why Flo didn't bandy her surname around.'

It was obvious that everyone else in the group remembered. The tension could have been cut with a knife.

'Who put you on to me?' Giles continued, ignoring his friend's warning with a coolness even Paulie grudgingly admired.

'Your dean.' Al kept his temper tightly leashed. 'I've just left him.'

Gargrave shrugged. 'Well, even if I wanted to help you – and unlike old Peeble I don't go around giving out personal info willy-nilly – I can't. I may room on the same staircase as Hugh, but I'm not a close friend.'

He moved to replace his pint glass on top of the jukebox. With great economy of movement, Al knocked it from his hand.

It crashed to the floor. Everyone, apart from Al and Paulie, was sprayed with best bitter and flying slivers of glass. Giles Gargrave and the blond, ponytailed friend standing next to him were drenched.

'What the fuck . . . !' the red-headed youth roared as he leapt out of the way.

A moustached Zapata look-alike shouted: 'For Christ's sake!'

The blond, ponytailed youth stepped swiftly backwards, calling in alarm for the barman.

The barman, struck conveniently blind and deaf, ignored him and retreated to the far end of the bar.

Only Giles Gargrave betrayed no consternation, seemingly uncaring of the beer saturating his jacket and dripping down on to his trainers. 'Playing the hard man is going to get you nowhere, Virtue,' he said, a note of something very like satisfaction in his voice. 'The person who'll know by now where Hugh and Flo are is Hugh's mother. So try the London phone-book, why don't you?'

Al regarded him through narrowed eyes. He didn't take lip from anyone – and Giles Gargrave was dangerously near to giving it. Neither did he go a bundle on hearing Fleur called Flo. He moved towards him, forcing Gargrave to step swiftly backwards.

The wall was only inches away and as Gargrave banged into it, alarm finally crossing his face, Al fought the temptation to grab him round the throat with one hand and punch his lights out with the other.

Instead he seized hold of the lapels of Gargrave's jacket and said through his teeth as he half-lifted him off his feet: 'I don't like liberty-takers, sonny. And where information is concerned, violence always works. Trust me. I want you and your friends to understand that. And I want you to understand this: my daughter is missing and I'm going to find her. I'm going to find her fast. And I would not want to be you, or one of your friends, if I discover you could have helped me find her even a beat quicker, and didn't. Is that understood?'

He'd been concentrating so totally on keeping his temper tightly reined – on going only so far with Gargrave and no further – he was oblivious of how much commotion his near-throttling, tête-à-tête technique was occasioning.

Accidentally broken beer glasses were a common enough occurrence in the Corn Dolly and, with a high preponderance of students and young working-men amongst its habitués, even glasses smashed in anger didn't arouse too much consternation. The present disturbance was, though, quite clearly not a run-of-the-mill, youthful hot-headed fracas.

The barman, forced to intervene in some way or other, had phoned for police assistance. From a safe distance a handful of elderly regulars were shouting at Al to let Gargrave go. His three friends were being deterred from pitching in on his side by the street-fighter glint in Paulie's eyes and, more especially, by the lethal-looking knuckle-duster now gracing his right hand.

Well aware that Gargrave wasn't going to risk throwing a punch at him, Al released him and, as a police siren was distantly heard, turned his back on the students and began walking towards the door.

Paulie followed him, sliding the knuckle-duster off his hand and back into his pocket. 'So where now?' he asked as they stepped, unhindered, out on to the pavement.

'Chancery Lane,' Al said tautly, 'Or somewhere damn near it.'

A police car slid to a halt at the kerb only feet away from them. Neither of them gave it a glance.

'That lot in the pub aren't going to run away,' Al continued as a couple of police officers stepped from the car. 'And they were all useless wankers.' The officers, one of them with his radio still crackling, brushed shoulders with them as they hurried towards the pub. 'No use wasting time with small fry when there's a big fish in the picture.'

'The King woman?'

'The King woman,' Al said, the nerve at the corner of his jaw once again beginning to throb. He opened the Shogun's driver's door, adding an epithet Paulie had rarely heard him use about a woman. Any woman.

As he slid behind the wheel, Paulie jumped into the passenger seat. If Al was going to search out and confront the woman he held responsible for his seven years in the boob, life was going to become very interesting. He cracked his knuckles, wondering what kind of a battle-axe she was; wondering if she had any idea of the trouble heading her way.

Chapter Nine

Deena re-entered the elegant Georgian townhouse that was her home, locked the door behind her, dropped the blue notebook she had retrieved from her chambers on to the hall table and slid her arms out of her coat. She could have read through the notebook in her office, but hadn't wanted to. She'd wanted to be at home, just in case Hugh should telephone or return.

She draped her coat over the carved newel at the foot of the stairs and glanced down at her watch. It was seven-fifteen. There was plenty of time for her to do all she needed to do.

Picking up the notebook, she carried it into her high-ceilinged sitting-room, dropping it on to a massive coffee-table. She never worked at a desk at home. All her reading of briefs and note-taking was done from the comfort of her deeply cushioned sofa.

She kicked off her shoes, switched on lamps, lit her simulated coal fire and padded into the kitchen, returning a few minutes later with a mug of coffee. Still not reaching out for the notebook, she turned on the laptop lying next to it. First she sent an e-mail to her Head of Chambers, Mungo Deakin. Then she sent e-mails to Cheryl and to Milton Darcus.

Only when her professional workload for the next day was satisfactorily taken care of did she reach for her barrister's blue book.

*   *   *

Half an hour later nothing was any clearer to her. Venomous though the looks he had shot across the courtroom at her had been, during the entire length of the trial Al Virtue had uttered no threats as to her or her family's future safety.

She took a drink of her now cold coffee, thinking back to the man she had faced ten years ago. He had been thirty-five, a top echelon criminal who, thanks to the casual corruption then rife at the Yard, had never been successfully prosecuted. Nor was he prosecuted for the theft of the bullion. After a classic rooftop chase he was, though, charged with handling it.

And she had been the prosecuting barrister.

She finished her coffee.

It had been an exceptionally high-profile case for a young female barrister and she had put every ounce of her very considerable talent and energy into it. The result had been the making of her reputation and the loss, for seven years with parole, of Al Virtue's freedom.

She had never felt, at the time, that she had put herself at risk. There was no wild talk of his having put a bounty on her head. Once she had left the courtroom she had put him out of her mind as, after every case no matter whether it was won or lost, she put every defendant out of her mind.

Or she had done until the last twenty-four hours.

The headache she had been trying to block grew more persistent.

Re-reading her trial notes hadn't been as helpful as she had hoped. Of the many crimes he was suspected of but had never been charged with, none had been 'rope-ups'. No petrol had been poured over security guards whilst sick games were played with lighted matches. No bludgeonings had been laid at his door. There was nothing to hint that he might, if the opportunity were thrown across his path, seek revenge of a particularly sadistic type, ten years down the line.

Her fingers tightened around her now empty coffee mug.

None, except that he was a lifelong criminal.

A lifelong criminal who, she was sure, thought nothing of walking the streets with a pistol rammed down his trouser waistband.

'Are you tooled up?' Paulie asked Al as they flashed past the turn-off for Aylesbury in the outside lane, the speedometer needle above the hundred mark.

'Nope.' Al shot him a sharp glance. 'Why?'

'Nothing.' Paulie was hugging a knee as his foot rested on the Shogun's dashboard. 'I just wondered, that's all.'

'Don't,' Al said succinctly, knowing damn well that if he had been carrying a piece, and if he'd admitted it, Paulie would have wanted to emulate him. Which was the last thing he needed.

For years, even before the old man had headed off to the sun on the Costa del Crime, he had been the godfather figure of the family, the acknowledged leader. He was the one who decided what jobs they went on and how they carried them out. He was the one who decided where money should be stashed, how it should be laundered, when it was safe to begin using it. His word – even where his father and his sisters-in-law were concerned – went. When there was trouble of any kind, professional, marital or financial, everyone came to him. And he sorted it. It was a responsibility that had always sat easily with him – until recently.

There was a Merc ahead of him and his eyes narrowed as he pressed his foot even harder on the accelerator, forcing its driver to pull over into the middle lane.

The trouble lately wasn't with his brothers – or at least not with two of his brothers – it was with their offspring. Being a tight-knit family, it had been taken for granted by everyone that when the boys reached their late teens they would, if they wanted, be incorporated as part of the family team. Kevin's two boys were still only thirteen and fifteen, but Stuart's twin stepsons were twenty-two, Paulie was twenty, Ritchie was eighteen, and all four of them regularly made themselves useful. So far, there'd been no problems, but with the changed face of crime – and the fact that the youngsters in his family were easy with it – one was looming.

He sped over the M25 junction, steamrollering everything in front of him out of his way. When he'd been Paulie's age and going out with the old man on jobs, the criminal scenario had been relatively straightforward. There'd been thieves – like his dad and his dad's friends – and there'd been thieves' ponces – gangsters who lived off their reputation for no-holds violence, extorting money from anyone and everyone who had pulled off a successful 'tickle'. That had been the dark side of crime, inhabited by the likes of the Krays; the side old-fashioned thieves, like his dad, steered well clear off.

He eased his foot off the accelerator, allowing his speed to drop from a hundred miles an hour to ninety.

The days of the Krays were, of course, long over. They had been over so long he knew that Paulie and Ritchie, if they thought of that period at all, thought of it as history. Which it was. The age of the gangster had effectively ended when the Krays had received sentences that had put them away for good.

The trouble was, in the decades that followed, other old-style crimes had also gone to the wall, making many of the skills he had learned from his father – the art of the ace bellman and gellyman – defunct.

The 'jump-up' for instance, a method of robbery his father had always favoured, had become as obsolete as the dodo. His own speciality, bank robbery, had also been wiped out. At least as far as he was concerned. His way of working had always entailed detailed planning and had only ever been undertaken if the rewards had been guaranteed to be great.

The drug-high gangs robbing banks now took chances no self-respecting old-style robber would have been prepared to take – and they did so for much smaller rewards. Essentially street muggers who reckoned they'd graduated, their method of operation was to burst into a bank – any bank – wave guns at customers and cashiers alike, and grab what was available.

His mouth tightened. With the age of the traditional bank robber having gone the way of the old-fashioned gangster, the only game in town now was drugs. In one way or another drugs had become the highway and conduit for all other crimes. It was a situation that was threatening to leave him high and dry, because he wouldn't touch them. He couldn't, not after what had happened to Billy.

He flashed a quick glance at Paulie. He had been eight when Billy had OD'd on crack cocaine and Al knew that, to Paulie, his older brother's death was ancient history. As Ritchie thought the same, and as their step-brothers Zac and Clint had no reason to feel strongly about Billy's death, it was obvious that the differing attitudes between himself and the younger members of his family were soon going to cause real problems.

A problem not looming, but in the here and now, was the trouble he was experiencing with Tommy. His other brothers rarely ran with anyone other than family – and if they did, they always put him in the picture so he could yea it or nay it. Generally, whatever jobs they did, they did together. Not all the family was involved in every job, though all of them would know what was going off. It was a near-exclusivity he had nurtured hard and believed in profoundly.

In a gang comprised entirely of family there wasn't the remotest possibility of anyone grassing a job up, or of one member letting another down. Aside from his own organisational skills and impudent nerve, if any one thing accounted for their long run of success as career criminals it was their never taking on board outsiders and seldom hiring themselves out.

It was a track record Tommy, with near-disastrous consequences for himself, had well and truly blotted. The job he'd been collared for had been one Al had known nothing about. Even more disturbing, he'd known nothing about the people who'd been caught with Tommy, or who had set the job up.

Furious as he'd been, he'd turned things around, though it had cost an arm and a leg. Sid Ashworth had done his stuff, ensuring that the evidence brought against Tommy was, when re-scrutinised, deemed inadmissible. All through the afternoon and evening of the day of the acquittal he hadn't let his fury with his kid brother show. He'd hugged Tommy's shoulders, cracked open bottles of champagne, roared with laughter – all the time knowing that next day or the day after, when Tommy sobered up, he was going to give him the bollocking of his life.

He hadn't, though. Not yet. His concern for Fleur had put everything else on a back-burner.

Fleur.

The muscles around his heart contracted. Where in the

name of God was she? He'd been pretty sure none of the university wankers in the Corn Dolly had known – which was why he hadn't wasted precious time on them. When he wanted to see them again, he knew where to find them. The supercilious git he'd had to fight hard not to throttle had shown him who it was he should really be grilling.

Deena King.

Unless she'd moved chambers over the last ten years, he knew where to find her. It had been part of the picture he'd gone to great pains to build up of her at the time of his trial.

He couldn't depend on finding her at her chambers now, though. Not when it was getting on for eight o'clock. Slowing down a tad further, he swooped the Shogun off the motorway, heading for West London. As he did so, he took his mobile out of his breast pocket. He'd always gone through life making sure people owed him favours – even silks.

'Brian?' he said, seconds after he'd punched in a London number. 'It's AV. I'm calling in the favour you owe. I want a home address – Deena King's.'

There'd come the sound of someone having a near heart attack. Al remained indifferent. Paulie grinned. Brian Vault had been Al's barrister on the bullion trial and on several other, happier occasions. Once, when Al had been about to go on an identification line-up and everyone on it, apart from himself, was togged in anoraks and caps, Vault, a big lump of a man who, naturally enough, was also city-suited, had insisted that in order for the line-up to be even halfway to fair, he should take part in it too. The joke had been, of course, that it had been Vault who'd been picked out. Al always cracked with laughter when he told the story.

'No,' Al was responding to something Brian Vault had

said. 'Why? Do you think I'm brain-dead? I'd sooner lay hands on a leper.'

Half a minute later he tossed the mobile down between his seat and Paulie's.

'Got what you wanted?' Paulie asked.

Al sliced out of one lane of traffic and into another.

'I always get what I want.' Tension emanated from him in waves. 'As a certain bitch is about to find out.'

Tommy Virtue swaggered into Caspars, a club within spitting distance of Soho Square that the rest of his family never put their noses near.

'Tommy, old mate, congrats on the result!' someone he barely knew shouted over the blare of a Tom Jones number. 'What a turn-up for the books, eh?' Having darted across to him, he was slapping him on the back. 'Christ, that judge must've been spittin' feathers when 'e 'ad to let you walk! What you havin'? Whatever it is, make it a double and 'ave it on me.'

'Armagnac,' Tommy said, taking the effusive greeting as his due and acknowledging many other shouted congratulations. The person he was meeting wasn't in yet, but it was early. He tapped out a Sub Rosa and lit it. Back in The Maid, fat expensive Turkish cigarettes were viewed as laughably posy, but he liked them. They were different. Just as, where his family was concerned, he was.

He slid on to a bar-stool, his blue shirt undone at the neck, a thumb hooking a black linen jacket over one shoulder. Families were a fucker. All day he'd been expecting to be collared by Al and to have the living daylights blasted out of him for having involved himself with a team from the Essex heartlands. True, the job had gone pear-shaped, and true, it was Al who'd ensured he hadn't gone down for it, as the others on it had gone down.

He picked up the glass of Armagnac that the barman slid towards him and raised it in the direction of his well-wisher. The sentences those with him on the job had copped for hadn't been mammoth, but even four- and five-year sentences were sentences no one wanted to serve and, being a Virtue, his sentence would probably have been even longer. He took a deep swallow of brandy. If Al hadn't done his stuff, even with parole he could have been looking at being inside when it was thirtieth birthday time.

It didn't alter the fact that Al came the eldest brother lark too heavy-handedly. Christ, he wasn't a kid anymore. It was Paulie and Ritchie who were the kids – and he didn't reckon they'd be happy kow-towing to Al's party line for much longer. Zac and Clint certainly weren't, though Al hadn't cottoned on to it yet. The trouble with Al was that he was old school. Forty-five going on sixty-six. Granted, when he pulled a job, it was always a job worth pulling with plenty of funds all round, but how often did such pay-days come along? Most of the really big ones had been years ago, when he had been too young to get involved.

As Tom Jones gave way to Sonique, another Armagnac came his way, unasked, and he accepted it with a nod, still deep in thought. The bullion job, for instance. He hadn't been in on that. He'd still been a schoolkid when Al, Stuart, Kevin and the old man had creamed off a cool half-mill with only Al going down for it – and then only for the handling.

Since then the old man had buggered off to the sun, only to be seen on high days and holidays, and too many of the present jobs were like the specialised stolen-car tickle – lucrative, but with an adrenaline-charge that was fuck-all zero. Which was why he'd cast his eyes elsewhere.

He took another deep swallow of Armagnac, well aware of just how close a call he'd had. Not because he'd so nearly gone down for it, but because the job itself had been absolutely peripheral to what had really been going on. Which, as far as the geezer he was now waiting for was concerned, was just fine and dandy.

The problem was, the only game worth playing for now was drugs. That was where the ceaseless flow of mega-money was and, whether Al liked it or not, Tommy was out for big money. As were Zac and Clint. It was an area of operations the twins had had no trouble infiltrating. The organising force behind the on-going drugs set-up they were all now in on was his sister-in-law Ginny's first husband – Zac and Clint's dad.

What would happen when Al found out who'd been behind the job he'd so nearly gone down for, Tommy didn't know. Nor did he care. By the time that day dawned he'd be rolling in squillions and wouldn't give a flying fuck. Not that he wasn't relieved there'd been no confrontation today, because he was. And he had little Lulu's death to thank for that. The plain-clothes boys had descended on The Maid in fighting form and Al, obviously tipped off, had given the place a wide berth.

If anyone had known where he was kicking his heels, no one had been saying. Sharlene had been in The Maid for most of the day with Lol and hadn't had a clue. Max had been in such a pathetic state of nerves because of the police presence and questioning that if he'd known where Al was, he'd have been begging Stuart to go get him. Kevin hadn't shown all day. Till two o'clock, Lol had been unperturbed, believing him to be where she'd left him: sleeping off the excesses of the night before at home in bed. But after two o'clock, when he still hadn't shown at The Maid and was unobtainable on his mobile, she'd known he'd conned her and that, if he was still in bed, it wasn't their bed he was in.

From then on there'd been ructions – ructions not helped by the fact that everyone there knew whose bed Kev was in. Max's ex-girlfriend's.

That Max had taken Marilyn's defection to heart was common knowledge. Under normal circumstances he'd have been bleating on about it ad infinitum, but mercifully the hoo-ha over his barmaid's murder had ensured he'd had other things on his mind and they'd been spared his belly-aching about Kevin nicking his bird.

Their old family friend Barney had been in The Maid all day, none too happy at having to submit to police questioning over who he had been with and where he had gone after leaving The Maid the previous evening. It was no secret that he'd fancied Lulu something rotten and, what with Barney crying grief-stricken into pints of Guinness, Max having a nervous breakdown about the cozzers being in, Lol ranting about Kev not being able to keep his pecker in his pants, the atmosphere had been the pits.

If Paulie or Ritchie had been there it would have livened things up a bit, but no one seemed to know where they were. Knowing more about his nephews' private lives than the rest of the family, he wondered how Ritchie would react when he heard about Lulu. He didn't think they'd been a heavy number, but that wouldn't make any difference to the cozzers. Once they knew of the Ritchie–Lulu connection, young Ritchie would be in the frame – or he would be until Al got him out of it.

As Sonique was replaced by an ear-shattering Britney Spears number, he wondered whether he should have said something to Stuart but satisfied himself that nothing could have been gained by it. There'd been too many other people around. He'd have a word with him later – or he would if Ritchie didn't do so first. Then Ritchie or Stuart could put Al in the picture.

He was just wondering who the pervert was who'd really killed Lulu when a hand like a bunch of bananas clapped him heavily on the back.

'How ya doin?' Ginny's ex-husband wheezed, sliding his vast bulk on to a neighbouring bar-stool. 'This music is murder, ain't it? I'll throttle a brandy, then what say we mosey somewhere quieter to talk business?'

Sharlene drove as fast as the mid-evening traffic would allow into Notting Hill. God, but it had been a pig of a day. Al hadn't shown and hadn't even had the decency to telephone her to tell her where he was. The police had corralled everyone who'd been in The Maid when they'd arrived there, taking names and addresses. Wanting to know if they had been drinking in the pub the previous evening, who else they had seen there, if they had spoken to Lulu, if they had seen anyone else speaking to her.

'She was a barmaid, for God's sake,' Max had said explosively at one point. 'Everyone spoke to her – or they did if they wanted a drink!'

'So where's the guv'nor?' the police had kept saying, reducing Max to a state of near-apoplexy. 'And we don't mean the bloke whose name's above the door. We mean Virtue.'

'Which one?' Stuart had interjected. 'There's four of us. You can take your pick.'

'We want the organ-grinder,' the plain-clothes copper had said tauntingly, 'not the monkeys.'

It had all been very tedious. She didn't believe for a minute that Al had had anything to do with the barmaid's death, but the way the coppers had hammered on about not being able to lay hands on him because he had deliberately gone to ground had been disturbing to say the least.

She veered out of Kensington Park Road into Colville Terrace, using side streets to cut the corner into Westbourne Park Road. As if being questioned by the coppers hadn't been bad enough, there'd been Lol bashing number after number into her phone as she tried to track Kevin down, and a whole army of old regulars gawping at them as if they were a free show. Which in a way, she supposed they were.

She turned into All Saints Road, slowing to a crawl as she looked for somewhere to park. By the time the coppers had cleared the premises and the air had been fit to breathe again, Tommy had come in, driving her demented by insinuating that Al was nowhere to be found because he and she had had a ruck and he'd gone off on a drinking binge.

It had all been too much and she'd stormed out. Then, in an imitation of Lol, she'd run through her mobile's memory, pushing number after number on the speed dial, trying to hunt down fashion-world friends to spend the evening with.

The result had been a speedy drive to Westminster Bridge and then a haul north of the river towards the Sugar Club in Notting Hill, a favourite watering-hole for her photographer and model friends – and for Mick Jagger and Robbie Williams too.

She parked up, enjoying the sensation of being in an environment suited to her professional status. South London was fun when she was out and about on Al's arm. Without him, it was the pits.

As she slid out of the Morgan, she wondered if she would eat and if so, what. Despite its name, the Sugar

Club was a restaurant not a club, and the food, Pacific Rim cooking with a slight Middle Eastern influence, was sensational. Normally, to keep her figure racehorse-thin, she existed on not much more than salad leaves and mineral water. Tonight, though, she was so pissed off with life she needed something a little more comforting. Sautéed scallops with sweet chilli sauce and crème fraîche, perhaps. Or grilled squid with sweet-and-sour pepper.

She was so busy thinking about food that as she walked hip-swingingly across the pavement to the restaurant's doors, she didn't see the lethal crack between the paving-stones. Her stiletto heel went down hard, and wedged, wrenching her ankle and sending her crashing, one shoe on and one shoe off, into the casually dressed male who, like herself, had been heading for the Sugar Club's doors.

Benedict's reaction was swift. He caught hold of her, the momentum of her fall throwing him off balance too. Together they tottered for a moment and then fell.

As Benedict purposely took the brunt of their fall, all he was aware of was black skin, close-cropped kinky ash-blonde hair, and a pair of legs that went on for ever.

All Sharlene was aware of was the excruciating pain screaming through her ankle and the hideous knowledge that, if she'd fractured it, it would mean weeks away from any catwalk.

Rather reluctantly, Benedict disentangled himself from the best pair of legs it had ever been his pleasure to tangle with and stood upright, taking her by the hand to help her back to her feet.

'Are you hurt?' he asked anxiously as, leaning against him for balance, she hopped on one leg, rubbing her injured ankle exploratively.

'Of course I'm hurt!' Her attention was still focused on

whether she'd done herself real damage. She had a show in Dublin at the end of the week and a three-day slot in Amsterdam immediately after it.

'Can I help you inside? Get you a drink?'

'You can pull my shoe free,' she said, certain the heel was broken and, even if wasn't, having no intention of putting it on again, 'but before you do . . .'

She leaned even more heavily against him as she lowered her injured foot to the ground and cautiously put weight on it.

'You've sprained it, not fractured it,' he said as she slid her other foot out of its shoe.

Her feet were bare. Strong, straight feet with mulberry-varnished nails.

Sharlene looked him full on for the first time. If she'd had to crash so spectacularly into someone she could have done a lot worse. He was thirtyish, good-looking in a clean-cut, fair-haired, Harvey Keitel kind of way. And if he was casually dressed, he was also expensively dressed. And she was mad at Al. Spitting mad.

'About that drink,' she said. 'You're on.'

'Is this her pad, then?' Paulie said as they swerved into a row of tall, distinguished-looking Georgian houses. 'She's not without a few bob, is she?'

It was gone eight o'clock but, although it was deep twilight, it was still possible to see that the front doors were glossily painted and the window-boxes carefully tended.

Al, well aware of the sort of money that Deena King would be on, merely grunted. He knew, from what he'd been told at St Clemence's, that Deena King was aware her son's girlfriend's name was Fleur Virtue. Had she put two and two together? Would she be expecting him?

Was she really concerned about her son's whereabouts, or was she more concerned about the fact that her son was romantically involved with his daughter? It was quite possible she knew damn well where her son was and was just trying to cause waves at Fleur's college in order to break up the relationship. Certainly she would have some idea of the kind of places her son would go if he wanted to drop out of sight for a while.

He found the house number and slewed into the kerb. He wasn't going to take any high-handed patronising nonsense from her. They weren't defendant and prosecuting barrister now. She could cry intimidation until the cows came home, but nothing was going to stop him from what he was about to do. And what he was about to do was to get a handle on where Fleur could be.

'Wait here,' he said to Paulie, springing out of the Shogun, slamming the driver's door behind him. Her sitting-room curtains weren't drawn. He could see apricot-coloured paintwork, the subdued lighting of elegantly shaded lamps, a glimpse of a book-lined wall.

He strode to the door and, not bothering with the bell, knocked hard, twice.

Deena frowned, put down the legal pad she'd been making notes on, and rose to her feet. It wasn't a familiar knock. It sounded more like a policeman's knock. Suddenly, certain that it *was* a policeman and that he was bringing news of Hugh, she exited the room fast. There was only one terrible reason why police officers came house-calling on respectable homes after dark. With her heart racing, convinced she was about to be confronted with dreadful news, she ran down the hall and yanked the door open.

Al didn't give her the chance to slam it in his face. He

crashed into the house so fast she didn't even have time to scream.

'Right,' he said between clenched teeth as she fell back against the wall and he kicked the door closed. 'Your son. He's with my daughter. *And I want to know the fuck where!*'

Chapter Ten

Deena's reaction was fast. Without wasting time in useless panic or in trying to flee, she hurled herself towards her hall table, her hand shooting for the telephone.

Al's reaction was even faster. 'I don't think so!' He knocked the phone to the floor, kicking it across the polished surface, keeping his hands off her only with the greatest difficulty, knowing if he didn't she'd have him on an assault charge quicker than it took to spit. 'You and I need to talk! After we've talked, you can phone who the hell you want!'

His face was blazing with a rage she utterly identified with. It was the mirror-image of her own scorching rage. A rage so intense she thought she was going to choke on it.

Making the split-second decision not to jettison all dignity by scrabbling on hands and knees after the phone, she shouted: 'Get out of my home!' and then, as he quite obviously wasn't going to budge: 'Where did you get my address? WHO GAVE IT YOU!'

He stood between her and the door, ignoring her questions, saying in a voice that cracked like a whip: 'My daughter's missing! Everyone I've spoken to believes her to be with your son. What I want to know from you is where that might be!'

Deena sucked in her breath. This wasn't what she had expected. It wasn't behaviour that tied in with her fear of Al Virtue being personally responsible for Hugh's disappearance. Quite possibly it was a smoke-screen, but why would he bother? The answer was that he would bother so as to enjoy witnessing the anxiety Hugh's disappearance was causing her; he would bother so that he could gloat.

She checked herself. If he *was* gloating, he was doing a damned good job of hiding it. All that was readable in his handsome face was deep, almost frantic concern. A concern she fully empathised with.

'I have no idea where Hugh is.' Her voice was flat. Her statement categorical. Not only was her rage now firmly under control, so were all her other turbulent emotions.

To Al, she seemed as chillily unconcerned as a block of marble.

'Neither,' she continued, 'until yesterday evening, was I aware of any involvement between my son and your daughter.' She paused, eyeballing him as she would a recalcitrant witness. 'Were you?'

He clenched his jaw, hating her plummy upper-class vowels, her composure and the way she had regained it so swiftly; the vivid memories that facing her brought back to him. He could almost smell the odour of the courtroom again – and the odour inside the Black Maria as, handcuffed, he was transported to Brixton for the first night of his ten-year sentence.

'Get real!' he roared explosively. 'Do you think I'd have allowed it to continue if I'd known?'

'Why not?' Her voice was now as brittle as glass. 'It's a situation a man of your morals could turn to advantage . . . so much so, that it beggars speculation as to whether or not it was a situation you engineered.'

This time the force of his anger drained his lips, as well as the lines around them, white. With teeth clenched he said in a voice that was near a snarl: 'If you think that for over ten years I've had you on my mind, you flatter yourself!'

Beneath the exquisite tailoring of his suit jacket she could tell that his arm and shoulder muscles were bulging with tension and barely controlled violence. Suddenly his height and breadth seemed not only big but massive. Equally suddenly her hallway seemed very small. It took all her considerable nerve not to take a step backwards towards the open door of the sitting-room.

'I'm thinking it's a situation with too many coincidences!' she snapped back. 'Out of the entire population of Oxford your daughter and my son not only meet, but form a relationship? Do me a favour, Virtue. It's unlikely to the point of disbelief.'

His eyes narrowed to near slits. 'Why? Because it's too fucking unlikely any son of yours would even pass the time of day with a girl who comes from my neck of south-east London?'

'Because it's unbelievable he would form even a passing acquaintanceship with a girl whose entire family have criminal convictions!'

'You're out on your reckoning.' If his voice had been vicious before, it was ferocious now. 'Apart from your little piece of luck, we don't go in for being sentenced – as you would know if you'd read any of this week's papers.'

The hatred in his eyes was nothing to the contempt she knew was in her own. 'I don't give a damn about what might be in the tabloids,' she spat. 'All I want to know is if Hugh's meeting your daughter was stage-managed – and if the relationship that followed was one you manipulated.'

'And if I'm now responsible for your son's disappearance and Fleur's supposed disappearance? That's the line you've fed the cozzers, isn't it? And because you've put that idea in their brains, it's the one they'll follow instead of getting off their arses and finding out where Fleur is!'

As he spoke his daughter's name, anxiety swamped his rage. 'You wouldn't want your son in a relationship with my daughter, would you,' he said. It was a statement, not a question. 'You'd go to any lengths to break it up. Is that what this is all about? Have the two of them gone off without telling anyone because of something you've done or threatened to do? Because if that's it . . .'

He took a step towards her and she backed away fast, her foot knocking against the telephone as she gained what felt to be the comparative safety of the sitting-room's open doorway. 'My God, Virtue! If I'd known about this relationship, you're damned right I'd have set about breaking it up! What is more, I'd have succeeded! I'd have succeeded if it was the last thing I ever did!'

He wrenched his tie loose at the throat, about to say savagely that at least they now knew where they stood. It was a movement she utterly misconstrued. Certain he was about to lay violent hands on her, she made a lightning-swift lunge for the phone and, hugging it to her chest, slammed the sitting-room door in his face.

In the beat of time it took her to ram a chair under the door-knob, he could easily have stormed in on her – and could have done so almost as easily, afterwards. He didn't bother. It wasn't worth his while.

He stood for a few seconds, regaining control of his breathing as he heard her frantically punching in numbers on the phone. She could call the police – and the Lord High Chancellor too, for all he cared. He didn't give a toss. He'd found out what he needed. Deena King was as in the dark as he was. Even if the ding-dong between them had continued, there would have been nothing to gain from it.

He turned on his heel, striding out of the house, leaving the door gaping wide behind him. A drastic re-think was necessary – as was a long personal telephone call to Sid Ashworth.

The number Deena had been frantically punching in as Al exited the house wasn't the emergency services – it was Benedict's mobile number.

'Benedict,' he responded laconically when she made the connection – or that was what she thought he said. The noise level of the restaurant or club he was in made it hard to be sure.

'Benedict? It's Deena.' Try as she might, she couldn't prevent her voice from shaking. Al Virtue had left the house. She'd felt the reverberation of his footsteps as he'd walked swiftly away down the hall. Even so, she still continued the phone call leaning her full weight against the sitting-room door.

'Al Virtue's been here.' She strove to steady her voice, wondering how long it was going to take Benedict to get back from wherever he was. 'God only knows how he got hold of my address . . .'

'What was that, Deena? Can't quite hear. There's a twenty-first birthday party going on at the next table . . .'

Above the general racket of laughter and loud conversation she could hear the clink of silver and crockery.

'This is great bubbly, Benny baby,' she heard a young-sounding woman say in a voice that sounded as if it had been steeped in honeyed molasses, and then Benedict was laughing, saying something so indistinct that she knew he must be speaking to the husky-throated female, not to her.

'Al Virtue!' she yelled, trying to get through to him that she wasn't just ringing to find out where he was and whether he was having a good time. 'Remember Al Virtue? Thug. Gangster. Villain par excellence! He's been *here*, for Christ's sake. At the *house* . . .'

'Yeah, well, a night in is probably a good idea, Deena. You've been haring around too much lately.' His voice was thick with pseudo-understanding and alcohol. 'This line's so bad I can hardly hear a word. I'll ring you tomorrow and . . . what was that you said, Deena?'

It was something so rude that, furious as she was, she severed the connection rather than repeat it.

Benedict slid his phone back into his jacket pocket. Deena was quite obviously still in the same ratty mood she'd been in earlier that evening – which was fine by him, so long as he wasn't around to bear the brunt of it.

'Was that your wife?' Sharlene asked.

'Nope.' Benedict reached towards the ice-bucket, secure in the knowledge that it wasn't a lie. For a brief second he wondered whether to mention that the call had been from his long-term girlfriend, but decided against it. It would only complicate things and what was the point? When push came to shove, he was a free man. It was a good feeling, especially as the demeanour of the ringless, amazing-looking girl seated next to him was that of a spirit as free as a bird.

He pushed a lock of hair away from his eyes and, in happy belief that he was enjoying a dalliance that could have no comebacks – least of all grossly unpleasant ones – refilled their glasses from a second bottle of Benedick Grande Réserve.

Al sped away from the general area of Bloomsbury, down

through the City and towards Tower Bridge wondering if, when he reached The Maid in another fifteen minutes or so, he would find Sharlene there.

With traffic light as he crossed the river, he punched in the number for The Maid. 'I'll be with you in ten mins,' he said unceremoniously when Max answered the call. 'Is Sharlene with you?'

'No, and thank Christ!' Paulie heard Max say in a voice thick with panic, and then: 'I don't mean thank Christ Sharlene isn't here, Al . . . She has been here, but she went off hours ago to meet up with a friend or a photographer or someone . . . I mean, thank Christ you're on your way. It's been a hell of a day. The plain-clothes boys have been in asking all the punters when they last saw Lulu, taking statements, wanting to know everyone's movements after closing time last night, behaving as if you'd gone on the run, insinuating all sorts of . . .'

'OK, Max. When I get in, eh?' Not wanting to suffer another second of Max's old-maidish panic, Al abruptly cut the call. He'd known, right from the off, that the cozzers would make difficulties for him and his where Lulu's murder was concerned – difficulties that he would sort. He wasn't going to start sorting them right now, though. For the moment he had other, even more urgent, priorities. The run-down on Fleur's friend's death, for instance. Why the fuck hadn't Ashworth got back to him with info on it? He sped out of Tooley Street and into Jamaica Road, hitting in Sid's number as he did so.

'So what happened back at the silk's house, then?' Paulie had been panting to know ever since they'd careened away from the kerb. Max's conversation with Al about what had been going on at The Maid wasn't such a teaser – not when they'd be there in another few minutes. He was, though, avid to know what had happened when his uncle had burst in on Deena King. 'Did she shit herself when she saw who'd come calling?'

'Nah.' Al snorted derisively. If Deena King had been afraid on that scale, it had been fear she had hidden well. 'Women of her class,' he said as a recorded message told him Sid wasn't available, 'women who speak as if they have a cucumber up their arse, are women who don't go in for bodily functions, Paulie. I thought you'd know that.'

Paulie was just about to say that it wasn't too surprising – not if the cucumbers were taken into account – but Al was snarling a message into the phone and, even before he had finished giving it, the Shogun was slewing off the road into The Maid's car park, its headlights illuminating Max as he stepped out of the pub's rear door flanked by what were clearly two plain-clothes cozzers.

Max was so glad to see Al he almost wet himself. Being questioned in the pub in an above-board manner was one thing. Being taken outside to be questioned in a dark car park was quite another. Not that it was being done in a manner that indicated a hammering was in the offing. Quite the reverse. They were being so friendly anyone would think he was a snout or a grass. It wasn't a comfortable thought – but then he hadn't had a comfortable thought since the moment he'd accepted that Lulu was dead.

He'd been helpful when being questioned earlier in the day, but as the questions had all been about who'd been in the pub the previous night and who had spoken to whom, it had been relatively easy to give straight answers.

He'd admitted that there had been a party to celebrate Tommy's acquittal, and he'd also made an effort at remembering who'd been there, whether Lulu had served them and if she had been seen to speak to them more than was usual, and what time everyone had left.

When it had come to mentioning members of the Virtue family, he'd been as vague as they would have expected him to be. There'd been a sea of questions about the vehicles that had been in the car park that night – and those that had still been there next morning. 'I wouldn't know,' he had said. 'My place at night is behind the bar, not roaming the car park – and in the morning I'm in bed until it's time to do a re-stock and open up.'

They'd taken note of the half-dozen cars currently parked up. His own, of course, Stuart's, Lol's, Sharlene's, Ritchie's. All of the regulars who'd been in when the police descended were locals who never bothered to drive to The Maid. Apart from Barney, of course. Barney's car had been parked alongside Stuart's and, when Barney had been questioned as to whether it had also been there the previous evening, he had become so defensively aggressive it had been little short of a miracle that he hadn't been arrested then and there.

When it had come to queries about Ritchie's car – and the fact that Ritchie wasn't around – he hadn't gone overboard about it. He'd simply said that Ritchie must have gone off somewhere in a cab.

That had been a mistake. 'What cab firm?' they'd asked. 'Who rang for the cab? What time did it arrive?' It had made him near dizzy and it hadn't even been proper questioning. Not the sort of questioning Al and the others were accustomed to. At the thought of being questioned as a suspect his stomach had twisted into knots. He wouldn't be able to front it out. The best thing would be for suspicion to fall on Barney – or on Ritchie.

It was the thought of how he would handle things

if questioned as a suspect that was causing him loss-of-bladder-control anxiety as he stepped out into the car park with the plain-clothes cozzers. He was finding things difficult enough just answering straight questions and trying to keep everyone's backs covered, but if the tone of things changed . . .

Then the Shogun had erupted into the car park, its headlights nearly blinding him, and his relief had been enormous. Al was back and Al would sort things. He affected a casual stance so that it wouldn't look as if the cozzers were unnerving him, and almost immediately lost it as Paulie vaulted from the Shogun in Al's wake. For a heart-palpitating second he wondered if Ritchie was also with Al, if Ritchie had been with him since the previous night and had a cast-iron alibi. Then Al was striding towards him, with no one tagging behind but Paulie, saying to the cozzers: 'Do you boys have a problem, or did you just bring Mr Collett out here for a pally Jimmy-riddle?'

'Watch your mouth, AV,' one of the cozzers said, his attention immediately and undividedly on him. 'There's a young girl dead. Jokes are out, got it?'

In the happy knowledge that the focus of attention had now moved away from him, Max stepped back a couple of steps so that he was no longer hemmed in upfront. As he did so the other cozzer said sarcastically to AV: 'Bit unfortunate for you, this. Running bang into us when you've been avoiding us like the plague all day.'

Max eased backwards a bit further, edging towards the pub's still open rear door.

'Avoiding you as in having been in an Oxford cop-shop all afternoon?' Al was saying sarcastically. 'That's really being under cover! That's being so under cover I should be in the fucking SAS.'

Max reached the door and seconds later was on the other side of it, knowing that, for the present moment at least, he was off the hook; knowing, too, that Al would want him to go back into the bar.

As he took up his familiar stance behind the pumps, a regular said: 'It's a bit grim in here tonight guv, ain't it? Perhaps you should've closed as a mark of respect.'

Max chewed the corner of his bottom lip. It was a thought that hadn't occurred to him. He wondered if he should remain closed on the day of the funeral. The problem with that, of course, was that many of The Maid's regulars would be attending the funeral and they'd be expecting to congregate in The Maid both before and after.

From the far side of the bar Stuart caught his eye and raised an eyebrow queryingly. Knowing what was being asked, he leaned towards him. 'Al's just arrived,' he said, keeping his voice low, 'but he's been waylaid.'

'Was my Paulie with him?'

Max nodded. 'I thought Ritchie might have been as well, for a minute,' he said, fishing to find out if Stuart knew where Ritchie was.

It was a remark Stuart, anxious as to what was going on in the car park, made no response to.

Knowing the conversation was at an end, Max reluctantly transferred his attention to his clientele. Lulu's murder had made the front page of that evening's *Standard* and, as The Maid had been mentioned, there were punters in the pub he'd never seen before.

'Ghouls,' Zac, one of Stuart's step-sons, had said about them when, still a little hungover from the previous night, he'd strolled in and been put in the picture. 'Where's Al, Max? He's going to want to find the bastard responsible. You know that, don't you?'

Max did – and it wasn't a pleasant thought.

At the present moment Zac was playing snooker. His twin, Clint, was also in the pub, which as Tommy wasn't, was a bit of a surprise. Max often wondered what Al thought about the Tommy, Zac and Clint alliance. But where family business was concerned, he knew better than to put his speculation into words.

His eyes continued to flick over the many different groups and cliques. Kevin wasn't in, which was a relief of mammoth proportions. Had Kevin been in, Marilyn would most likely have been with him. At the thought of Marilyn, his hand tightened on the pump so that the veins stood out like cords. She'd been the girl he'd thought he'd finally scored with. The girl he'd bought an engagement ring for, hiding it in his sock-drawer ready to surprise her with it on her birthday. It was still there and it occurred to him that he should get rid of it – fast – before there was any kind of a search and it was found and questions asked.

Sheer terror at the situation he was in roared through him with such crippling intensity he began to shake.

'You all right, Mr Collett?' one of his barmaids, looking far from right herself, asked.

'Yes. Delayed shock, I think,' he said, speaking God's honest truth.

The barmaid, still in shock herself over Lulu's death, flashed him a look of understanding and got on with her task of pulling pints of Guinness.

Max breathed in and out deeply, wondering how much longer Al's confab with the cozzers was going to take; wondering what was being said. There was a whole host of people panting to speak to him. Bazza was in, probably wanting to be paid for the bit of business he'd done for Al a couple of nights ago. Barney was in, desperate to off-load on to Al the anxieties he'd already confided to him and Stuart.

'It's the police, see? The way they're questioning us all,' he had said when, mid afternoon, the first lot of plain-clothes men had left The Maid. 'I sort of had a thing for Lulu, see? Kept asking her out. In the end, I suppose I might have come on a bit too strong . . . got a bit too fresh, know what I mean? And she didn't like it. She got a bit upset about it. Not last night, though. I swear to God I didn't see her on her own last night. Thing is, if the cozzers find out I fancied her and that I'd chanced my arm once or twice . . . well, they're goin' to put me in the frame, ain't they? I mean, they will, won't they?'

'Highly likely,' Stuart had said, not helping matters in the slightest.

Barney had tottered out of the pub ashen-faced, only to return early evening in the hope of waylaying Al.

Stuart, too, was waiting to talk to Al – and would certainly get to do so before Barney did.

Max, like Barney, would have to wait until Stuart had had his say.

The thing was, what was he going to say to Al when he did get his ear? Did he tell him about Ritchie and Lulu and try to prepare the ground for the suspicion that Ritchie had killed her? Or did he just sit tight and see if Barney would end up taking the fall for it?

'Hi, AV!' Barney suddenly shouted, erupting eagerly from his bar-stool. 'Have you got a minute, mate? It's real urgent . . .'

Max spun round as Al and Paulie entered the bar from the rear entrance.

'Al, a word . . .' Stuart was saying, shouldering a way swiftly towards his brother, blocking access to the many other people who wanted to speak to him.

Max moved fast, following hard on Stuart's heels. 'Where's Tommy?' he heard Al say to Stuart and then, before Stuart could reply, the saloon door crashed open and Ritchie fell inside, so wrecked it was impossible for him to stand unaided. With a half-full bottle of Johnnie Walker in one hand and a giant box of chocolates in the other, he swayed into the first table he came to, sending bottles and glasses crashing to the floor.

'Oops, sorry,' he said, grinning blearily across at his dad and uncle. Rocking back on his heels, he looked across to the bar. 'Where is she, then?' he asked as the already subdued noise level deteriorated into stunned silence. 'Where's my girl, Max? Have you given her the night off? Where's Lulu?'

Chapter Eleven

'I could do without all this!' Al said explosively. It was two o'clock in the morning and he was still at The Maid. Paulie was long gone, leaving only Al, Max, Stuart and Ritchie on the premises.

'Fleur's missing!' he continued angrily, pacing the sitting-room above the public bar. 'Do you realise that? I'm so fucking concerned I've spent the afternoon voluntarily in a cop-shop – an experience I could have well done without. And then I get back to this! Ritchie letting the whole world know that he and Lulu were an item!'

He ran a hand through his hair, knowing exactly what would happen when word got back to the cozzers – and knowing it was only a matter of hours until it did so.

'I didn't know it was going to matter.' Ritchie was slumped in a battered easy-chair, one leg slung over the arm, a hand across his eyes. He was wearing snakeskin loafers, a crumpled pale blue suit and a pink shirt open at the throat. If his face hadn't been chalk-white, he'd have looked like a tired kid after a party.

'I'd just got sick of keeping quiet about it,' he continued dazedly, as if he still didn't truly believe everything he'd been told. 'Lulu said if her dad knew about me, he wouldn't let her work at the pub any more. I told her she was old enough to tell him to stuff it. We had a real row about it . . .' He broke off, too choked with emotion to continue.

'So where did you go last night after the two of

you'd had a ruck and you'd left The Maid?' Stuart asked urgently, knowing that once the cozzers learned of Ritchie's involvement with Lulu, they'd have him in the frame fast as light. 'Who were you with, son? Will it stand up?'

'I don't know, Dad!' Ritchie took his hand away from his eyes, revealing a face strained with shock and grief. 'I loved her and now she's dead and I can't think of anything else . . .'

'You have to.' Al's voice was brutal.

Ritchie took a deep breath and closed his eyes for a second. When he opened them, he said: 'By the time I left The Maid I was pretty well oiled. I went off with some friends of Tommy's. I can't even remember their names. We went to someone's gaff to carry on the drinking, and I got absolutely rat-arsed and crashed out on the floor. I wasn't the only geezer who kipped down there. This morning, round about lunch-time, we all went over to the other side of the river for a hair of the dog at some pub somebody's sister ran. I got into a card game that lasted a fair while. Then I came back here – to see Lulu. To make things up with her.'

Everyone's eyes went to the forlorn box of chocolates on a nearby coffee-table.

It was Stuart who broke the silence. 'Mates of Tommy's?' he said heavily. 'The filth are going to love that. As far as alibis go, you haven't fucking got any.'

'It's OK,' Al said abruptly. 'It can be sorted.' He took a long hit on a can of Stella, mentally running through a list of people whose statements, if they said they'd been with Ritchie at Tommy's mate's gaff all night, would be far harder to rubbish than Tommy's mates' would be. There was an ex-copper who owed him a favour. Now, quite obviously, was the time to call it in.

'Where did this row you had with Lulu take place?' he demanded, crushing the now empty can of Stella. 'Who overheard it? Who *could* have overheard it?'

'No one. We were on our own in the kitchen.'

Al tossed the Stella can on to the nearest available surface. So far, so good. Now came the difficult bit.

'Leave us,' he said to Stuart, taking hold of a dining chair and positioning it a foot or so away from Ritchie's armchair.

'Christ, Al! I'm his dad . . .'

'*Leave us.*'

Stuart shot a glance at his son, who was now looking terrified, and another at Max. 'OK,' he said at last.

Max didn't have to be asked to leave, but when he did so, it was with great reluctance.

Al straddled the chair, back-to-front. 'Right,' he said. 'It's 'fess-up time, Ritchie. Don't even *think* about playing games on this one. If you did it, accident or whatever, I have to know. No one else need know. Not even your Dad. *But I have to!* Have you got that?'

'Yes, Al. But it ain't a problem . . . Christ . . . I *loved* Lulu . . . I would never have hurt her in a million years . . . I . . .'

Al eyeballed him. 'Yes or no, Ritchie. Did you kill her?'

'No!' Ritchie erupted from the armchair like a person demented. 'No, Uncle Al! No, I didn't kill her!' Tears poured down his face. '*No! No! NO!*'

Al rose to his feet. He'd got the reaction he expected – and the reaction he believed. He looked down at his Rolex. It was two-thirty in the morning. 'I don't want to do this now, Ritchie,' he said truthfully, 'but leaving it till later is dodgy. There could have been a plain-clothes cozzer still hanging around in The Maid when you announced that Lulu was your girl, and if there was, you'll be hauled in for questioning p.d.q.'

'So what is it you want to do?' There was panic on Ritchie's face now, as well as grief.

'I want to take you through everything as a cozzer will take you through it. Let's go from the moment you arrived at The Maid with Tommy. That way we'll soon see where the problems are. When it comes to the point where you and Lulu were by yourselves in the kitchen, mention that you walked through looking for Max and that she was there and you had a passing word. It's safest . . . just in case anyone did glimpse the two of you together. So . . .' he stretched his back out, craving a mug of tea. 'It's Monday and you're leaving the Old Bailey with Tommy and the rest of the family . . .'

By the time he finally drove the Shogun away from The Maid it was four in the morning and he was knackered. Ritchie had gone home with Stuart. Max had put him in the picture about Barney. And the person on his mind was Tommy.

He drove fast towards Kent on near-deserted roads. Where *was* Tommy – and what was he up to? He thought back to the moment when he'd walked into The Maid and asked Stuart where Tommy was. Before Stuart had been able to make any kind of a reply, Ritchie had burst in, becoming the focus of all their attention, but not before he'd seen the look that had flashed between young Zac and Clint. They'd known where Tommy was – and they hadn't been about to tell.

It had confirmed his long-held suspicion that Stuart's stepsons had been in on the bit of business that Tommy had nearly gone down for. What he wanted now was the name of the geezer pulling their strings.

He threw the jeep around Swanley roundabout, eager to be home. Tommy was a problem, as was Ritchie, but they were nothing compared to his anxiety over Fleur. Tomorrow morning he'd begin an all-out search for her. He'd speak to Sid Ashworth and get the low-down on Amabel Lyndhurst's death. He'd go back to Oxford and this time he'd question Hugh King's friends in a way they wouldn't forget in a hurry. He'd chase Thames Valley Police too. For the moment, though, he needed some kip. So tired his eyes hurt, he swung off the main road, diving into the narrow, steeply wooded lanes that climbed to Ponderosa.

Rupert Pembury-Smythe was in need of sleep too, but it wasn't forthcoming. He was being kept awake by what was, for him, a rare occurrence. He was suffering from an unquiet conscience. Deena King had come to him for help and he wasn't providing it – at least, not in the way that would best serve her.

As a government mandarin, his credo had always been the greatest good for the greatest number. This time, though, he had doubts. What would happen if, and when, this particular pot came to the boil? The old adage 'needs must, when the devil drives' sprang to mind, but as he had very little time for the devil in question, it was of little comfort. He didn't rate Americans. They were too brash. Too confident. Too prepared to take risks. Too fond of games. Games like the present one, which he had no desire to be part of.

Wearing crisply ironed pyjamas, he lay between pristine Irish-linen sheets, staring into the darkness. Did he or did he not owe it to his old friend Mr Justice Frensham, to telephone Deena? If the boot had been on the other foot, he knew what Wilfred would have done. But Wilfred had been a High Court Judge. Morality had been his *raison d'être*.

He switched his bedside light on, almost overwhelmed by the temptation to reach for the telephone. Almost, but not quite. There would be consequences to his career if he did so. He thought of those consequences and, having thought of them, switched off the light. Morality may have been Wilfred's *raison d'être*, but expediency had always been his, and he was too long in the tooth for a *volte-face* now.

The decision made, he closed his eyes, emptied his mind of all troubling thoughts, and slept.

Deena felt as if she had forgotten how to sleep. Al Virtue's invasion of her home had unnerved her more than she would ever admit. How had he found out her address? She wasn't in the telephone directory. Only her number at chambers was listed. In all her years as a barrister nothing like it had ever happened to her before. For the first time, she was acutely conscious of the vulnerability of living alone.

Not that it would have been any different if Benedict had been living with her. He would still have been out that evening, doing his own thing. She remembered his half-drunken idiocy on the telephone and disappointment in him flooded through her. She'd been in shock and she had needed him. And what had been his reaction? He hadn't taken on board a word she'd said. Even now, he still didn't know that Al Virtue had paid her a personal visit.

She gave up all attempts at sleeping and swung her legs from the bed. Who had been with him when she'd phoned him? As she padded downstairs and into the kitchen, she ran through a mental inventory of their mutual female friends. None of them had a voice so sultry.

She plugged the kettle in and dropped an Earl Grey tea-bag into a breakfast mug. The more she thought about it, the more certain she was that the voice had been a black voice. It made the girl's identity even more puzzling. Benedict didn't know anyone black – or at least not well enough that he'd be out on the town with them.

She shrugged, dismissing the mystery as not being worth her time and attention. She had a full day in court tomorrow and somehow, as well as dealing with that, she had to have conversations with Rose and with Fallon. Both of them needed putting in the picture about her visit from Al Virtue. And she had to make headway of her own in finding Hugh. There was his bank to contact and, once she'd obtained details of his credit cards – and she'd get an injunction if necessary – there were his current transactions to follow up.

The kettle was boiling and she poured water on top of the tea-bag. Tomorrow was going to be a busy day. She only hoped, for her client's sake, that when she picked up the reins at Snaresbrook, she would do so seamlessly.

'Constable Stebbings, these questions and answers, are they accurate? Can you remember them so precisely?' Deena hitched her silk robe a little higher on her shoulders as, in her capacity as defending QC, she drew to a close in her examination of the Crown's key witness.

Stebbings eyed her stonily. 'Yes,' he affirmed, his intonation inferring she was wasting both his time and the Court's time. 'Everything I have recounted under oath is accurate. My memory of what was said to and by the defendant is crystal clear.'

Deena smiled pleasantly. 'Allow me to congratulate you on your memory, Officer. I wish my own could be depended upon with such certainty.'

As she made a movement indicative that she had come to the end of her cross-examination, a smirk of satisfaction crossed the police officer's face.

'Just one more thing, Constable Stebbings . . .' It was said as an after-thought: 'With such an excellent memory, I'm sure it will be no problem at all for you to remember the first question I asked you when you stood up.'

Her victim sucked in his breath, his eyes widening as he realised the pit yawning at his feet.

It wasn't often Deena derived pleasure from a witness's discomfiture, but then it wasn't often that her feelings towards the police were so ambivalent. DI Fallon's off-hand attitude about Hugh's disappearance had angered her. It had angered her deeply.

'Would you please repeat the question, Constable?' she asked sweetly.

He hadn't been able to, of course, and from then on, with their key witness scuppered, the prosecution hadn't had a leg to stand on.

As she journeyed home on the tube late that afternoon, Deena was satisfied that no matter how deep her personal anxieties, they hadn't affected her performance in court.

'Hello, darling,' Benedict said, strolling away from his parked car as she walked briskly up to her front door. 'How did things go yesterday? Did visiting Oxford sort things out a bit?'

Deena took her key out of her handbag and eyed him witheringly. He was wearing jeans and his leather bomber jacket and, with his wheat-gold hair flopping boyishly low across his forehead, looked nearer his twenties than his thirties.

'No,' she said, unlocking the door. 'It only confirmed what my gut feeling has been all along. Hugh has vanished because something has happened to him. Something sinister. Something deeply serious.'

As he stepped into the house after her, Benedict drew on fast-diminishing reserves of patience. He'd been hoping her trip to Oxford would have put paid to her over-reaction where the mystery of Hugh's whereabouts was concerned. Apparently it hadn't. It had made her worse.

'What makes you think that?' he asked, trying to sound interested. 'What was said?'

Deena set her handbag and bulky briefcase down on her hall table and checked her answerphone messages. They were all unimportant, social ones. When she had finished listening to them, she said: 'Nothing specific. The situation speaks for itself.'

She began walking up the stairs, taking off her suit jacket as she did so, unbuttoning her skirt. For a startled moment, he wondered if sex was on the agenda.

'Not only is Hugh missing,' she continued, entering her bedroom and making straight for its en-suite bathroom, 'so is his girlfriend. And his girlfriend just happens to be the daughter of one of London's nastier career criminals.'

She turned on the shower, took off the rest of her clothes, and stepped beneath it.

Nonplussed, he rested his weight against the washbasin, saying over the sound of the gushing water: 'And you've officially reported Hugh as a missing person?'

'Yes.'

She didn't speak again until the shower was turned off and she was towelling her hair dry. 'I had a visitor last night. I rang you to tell you. Remember?'

'It was a bad line,' he said irritably. 'All I heard you say was that you were having an early night.'

She dropped the towel to the floor. 'What I said was that Al Virtue had barged his way into my house and had tried to scare the hell out of me!'

His jaw sagged. 'Virtue? He came *here*?'

Still naked, she swung away from him, walking into the bedroom, taking a bra and a pair of panties from a drawer. 'Yes. And don't bother being concerned now.' As she put on the bra, she didn't attempt to hide her anger. 'Last night was when I needed you to show concern. When I needed you here pretty damn quick.'

She stepped into the panties and began pulling on a pair of tailored black trousers.

'Christ, Deena! How was I to know?' His concern was instant and genuine. 'I was at the Sugar Club. There was a twenty-first birthday party going on at the next table. I could hardly hear a thing. Also, I'd been on the go for nearly twenty-four hours, working on the Tin Man. I was tired, I was . . .'

'Drunk?' She was pulling a black cashmere sweater over her head. 'Don't start protesting or apologising, Benedict. However unsupportive you were to me last night, it really doesn't matter. On the scale of things that are important at the moment, it doesn't even register.'

She slipped her feet into a pair of Gucci loafers and slung a grey, Shetland-wool cardigan around her shoulders.

'So what do you plan to do now?' he asked, only too happy to let the whole subject of the previous evening drop, uncomfortably aware of the exorbitant restaurant bill in his back pocket. The bill that had Sharlene's modelling agency telephone number scrawled across its top.

'What I plan to do now is to give Al Virtue a dose of

his own medicine,' she said, walking out of the room with purposeful intent.

He followed hard on her heels.

She paused at the top of the stairs, turning to face him. 'If he can invade my home turf, then I can invade his. I'm going south of the river to the pub he owns. If his daughter is with Hugh, then I want to know everything possible about her. She's the only direct link to Hugh that I have.' Her eyes held his. 'So . . . are you coming with me?' she said, indifferent to his horror. 'Or are you going to spend the evening with whoever it was you were with last night?'

If he hadn't gone with her, it would, he knew, have been the end of their relationship. They'd gone in his car rather than waste time getting hers out of its nearby garage. Holding on to his patience tightly, he'd told her his companion of the previous evening had been a girl who'd fallen over him outside the Sugar Club, almost crippling herself in the process.

'We had a drink together and then, as it was late and I hadn't eaten for God only knows how many hours, we had a meal. It wasn't anything I wouldn't have told you about anyway.' He'd shrugged, knowing he was lying, insulted by the fact that she probably knew he was lying and didn't care.

'How do we get to this pub?' he asked as he rounded the Elephant and Castle roundabout. 'Do we go down the Old Kent Road or down Jamaica Road?'

Deena looked at the address she had made a note of when reading through her old trial notes, and then at the *A to Z* open on her knee. 'Jamaica Road,' she said, aware that the old saying about North Londoners needing a passport when travelling south of the Thames wasn't far off the mark.

'Do the Met know we're doing this?' he asked nervously as she continued to give him street directions.

'No, Benedict. Why would they?'

He flashed her a swift look. 'Because you hardly seem to have been off the phone to them these last few days. And because walking into a pub full of villains – especially when one of them has a grudge against you the size of Everest – isn't exactly my idea of a fun night out.'

She didn't respond. Instead she said simply: 'We're here.'

The dusk was quickly turning into darkness, but the sign above The Maid was easily distinguishable. Unusually for an inner London pub, there was a largish car park to one side of it and Benedict drew into it, parking next to a red Volvo.

'Sounds quiet,' he said as they began walking towards the saloon bar entrance.

'There's no reason it shouldn't be.' She knew she was hitting unfairly on every single remark he made, but she couldn't help herself. She had never before turned to him in real need – she was far too independent – but yesterday evening she had needed him and he had let her down big time.

Not giving him a chance to reach the door before her, she pushed it open, stepping inside with every appearance of ice-cool confidence. Whatever she had been expecting, it wasn't the sight that met her eyes.

The bar was nearly empty of people and as full of flowers as a funeral parlour.

'Well, at least you're dressed for it,' he said drily, reading her thoughts.

A group of elderly people, seated around a corner table, looked across at them curiously.

'Not exactly typical hard-nosed villains, are they?'

Benedict continued beneath his breath as they walked up to the bar. 'They look as if they've been here since VE Day.'

At any other time she would probably have giggled. Instead, she said: 'Someone's died. That's what the flowers are about. They're the kind of cellophane-wrapped bouquets people leave at the site of fatal road accidents.'

Even without stopping to look closely at the cards accompanying the flowers on the tables, some of the messages could be clearly read. 'IN LOVING MEMORY OF THE PRETTIEST MAID TO HAVE GRACED THE MAID' read one. On another was written: 'GOODNIGHT, GOD BLESS, DEAR LITTLE LULU.'

'Crikey,' Benedict said, the amusement wiped from his face. 'Do you think it was a child?'

'I don't know.' They were at the bar now. 'Ask.'

'What's happened?' Benedict said to the homely looking middle-aged man tending the bar. 'Who died?'

'One of my barmaids,' Max said expressionlessly, wondering who the hell Benedict was. The most obvious bet was a plain-clothes cozzer, but the Old Bill had a style about them that was easy to pick out – and it was a style his questioner lacked. 'What'll it be?' he asked, standing with a hand resting on one of the pumps.

'A tomato juice,' Deena said.

'And a vodka and tonic,' Benedict added, his curiosity still not satisfied. 'I can understand why there are so many flowers,' he said as Max turned away towards the optics. 'But where are the people who brought them? Why is the pub so empty?'

'She was murdered,' one of the elderly women in the corner called across. 'Poor little cow was only eighteen. When AV gets 'old of the bastard who did it, 'e'll cut 'is privates off and choke 'im with 'em.'

178

'Is it known who killed her?'

'No.' Max's hand was unsteady as he pushed their drinks across to them. 'The police have been in and out of here non-stop since it happened. Which is why there's hardly anyone in here tonight. You police, too, are you?'

'Me?' Benedict looked startled. 'God, no.'

There was a meaningful pause as Max waited to be told just who the hell they were. The Maid wasn't a pub that attracted casual passing trade. It was a pub where people were known to each other, a pub in which strangers were suspect.

'We were hoping to run into AV,' Deena said, grateful for the elderly lady having introduced AV's name into the general conversation, aware that if that was how the locals referred to him, it was how she would have to refer to him. 'Is he likely to be in here this evening?'

Max regarded her for a long, considering moment. Who was she? And would Al want her to run into him, or not?

'They're all dahn The Drum.' The old lady who had proffered the information that Lulu had been murdered said helpfully. 'It's only five minutes away. First left, first right, second left. Wouldn't like to buy me a port and lemon, dearie, would you?'

'I'm not keen on the way they seem to take murder in their stride around here,' Benedict said as they walked back to his car. 'What say we call this jaunt off, Deena? Any information about Al Virtue's daughter can be got for you by the police, surely?'

'The police aren't interested. Not on a serious level. And I can't imagine Virtue would be co-operative with them, can you?'

179

It had been a question he'd had no answer for. Heartily wishing he was back in Camden, he slid behind the wheel and, instead of returning to Jamaica Road, turned left, heading towards the dark, narrow cobbled streets that fronted the river.

The Drum was as full as The Maid had been empty, its décor so shabby as to look pre-war. Like The Maid, it was quite obviously a pub passing trade passed by. Despite the inconspicuous way they were dressed, the minute they stepped across the threshold they attracted instant attention – and this time not from a group of amiably harmless pensioners.

As they negotiated their way between cluster-after cluster of unnervingly fit-looking men, conversation ceased and the looks they received were both guarded and hostile. Not for the first time it occurred to Benedict that if Deena's venture ended in tears, he would be the one doing the crying because he was the one who would be beaten up.

'A tomato juice and a vodka and tonic,' he said, when after a seeming eternity they reached the bar.

'So is he here, then?' he asked in as low a voice as was feasible, considering the overall noise.

Deena nodded. 'Oh yes,' she said grimly. 'He's here.'

Benedict waited for enlightenment. He'd seen photographs of Al Virtue in newspapers, but had never had cause to take much notice of them. The place was crammed with hard-looking types standing around with drinks in their hands, looking sharp and talking out of the sides of their mouths. Which one was Virtue, though, he hadn't a clue.

'The group that's taken over the far right-hand corner,' Deena said, keeping her back to the corner in question, her voice so low he could barely hear her over the general din. 'Virtue is the one wearing the gold-coloured polo neck.'

As casually as possible, Benedict adjusted his stance at the bar so that he had a good view to his right. The group in the corner, some seated and some standing, looked almost like a family gathering. There were as many women in it as men, and nearly all of them were middle-aged – though trying not to look it.

There was a woman in her late thirties with shoulder-length red hair and an embarrassingly short skirt, and another woman whose stylish suit was marred by a fussy amount of gold necklaces. There were a couple of youths in their early twenties, both sharply dressed, and three men who were instantly identifiable as brothers. All were the same height, easily six foot; all had the same build: deep-chested and broad-shouldered.

Two of them were wearing jackets, open-necked shirts and chinos; both were displaying almost as many gold chains as the stylish-suited woman. The other man, who was listening intently to whatever was being said and had his eyebrows pulled together in a deep frown, was wearing a black lightweight wool suit that must have cost two-and-a-half grand from Savile Row and a gold polo neck that bore, at a guess, an Italian designer label. His hair was grazed with silver and cut keenly above his ears. He was ringless, the only perceivable gold, his Rolex.

He didn't look like a gangster. He looked like a very tough, very high-powered businessman.

'Whatever the subject under discussion, it must be interesting,' Benedict said, returning his attention to his drink. 'They're the only clique in here who haven't cottoned on to our presence.'

'The two men with him are his brothers.' Deena still had her back to the right-hand corner of the pub. 'One of them, Kevin, is the acknowledged heavy-man in the family. The other, Stuart, is a gellyman.'

Deena's head was almost touching his, she was keeping her voice so low.

'And what the devil is that?'

'He's an expert at blowing safes. Gelignite. Gelly. Get it?'

Someone squeezed past them and they stopped talking.

'There's another brother,' Deena continued a few moments later. 'Much younger. He's the one who made a fool out of the judiciary a couple of days ago when he walked from the Old Bailey a free man.'

'Well, now you've seen Virtue on his home ground and in the bosom of his family, I'm assuming you've thought better about confronting him.' Benedict drained his glass. 'Let's get the hell out of here, Deena. I've never felt so unsafe in all my life.'

'I'm not leaving.'

As she was speaking, Benedict saw a slightly built man begin weaving his way towards the Virtues. Seconds later he was having a word with Al Virtue – and Benedict instinctively knew what the few words were about.

'Oh Christ!' he said devoutly as Al Virtue turned and looked towards them.

'What is it?' Deena saw the expression on his face and swung round to see what it was that had so appalled him.

Her eyes and Al Virtue's locked.

Benedict made a swift movement away from the bar and towards the door, certain Deena was behind him.

She wasn't.

She was walking towards the corner the Virtues had made their own.

It was an act of such stupidity that the temptation to leave her to face the consequences was nearly overwhelming. Fighting it down, he watched Al Virtue stride to meet her.

He wasn't the only one watching them. Everyone was looking their way. He saw Deena speak to Virtue. Saw Virtue's furious reaction. And then, with feet like lead, he began walking towards them, knowing he had no option but to intervene.

Chapter Twelve

'We need to talk,' Deena was saying in clipped, curt tones to her quarry.

'We need to leave.' As far as Benedict was concerned it was the biggest understatement he'd ever made. He cupped her elbow, carefully avoiding all eye contact with Al Virtue. He might as well have saved himself the trouble. She simply ignored him, not acknowledging his presence or interruption by so much as a glance.

'Give me one reason why,' Virtue rasped.

To Benedict's intense relief, Virtue, too, ignored him, speaking across him as if he wasn't there.

'Because if I'm to find my son, I need to know every-thing about his movements in the days preceding his disappearance – and everything about those of the person he disappeared with,' Deena continued, showing absol-utely no sign of back-pedalling. 'And if your concern about your daughter is even halfway to being genuine, you're in the same position.'

Benedict took a deep breath. 'You should be doing this through the police, Deena.' Even to his own ears he sounded a prat, but having walked over to intervene – and with everyone in the pub watching to see exactly *how* he was going to intervene – he had to say something.

'Who's the wanker?' Virtue said to Deena, still not troubling to look at him.

Benedict clenched his fists, knowing he'd have to retali-ate, wondering how the fuck he was going to get himself out of the mess he'd been landed in. Kevin and Stuart Virtue were standing only three or four yards away. Both of them were watching their brother's confrontation with Deena intently. Both of them were built like brick shit-houses. And they weren't the only muscle in the Virtue corner.

There were two youths, both of them bearing the Virtue stamp. His sons perhaps, or nephews. One was dressed in a pale linen suit, open-necked shirt and snakeskin loafers. The other was wearing a sky-blue polo neck and black jeans. Though slenderer in build than the older men, they looked as if they'd be nasty customers in a fight – and as if they'd be fast as light into any fight going.

Just as he was about to make a retort he was sure would be his last, Deena said: 'He's my partner,' and then, finally looking towards him: 'I think you'd better go, Benedict.'

'Christ, Deena! I can't leave you here!'

He looked vainly round the pub, seeking help he knew wasn't there. The landlord had adroitly disappeared. His bar staff were keeping themselves busy at the far end of the bar. The blowsy redhead was sitting on the edge of her seat, as interested as if she was at the theatre. The pleasant-faced woman was looking deeply distressed, but then she'd been looking distressed long before the present confrontation had begun. The youth wearing jeans was looking amused. The other looked to have his mind on other things. The two older Virtues simply looked dangerous.

'Quid pro quo?' Virtue was saying to Deena, his eyes narrowed.

Deena nodded.

'OK.' Benedict was so awash with fury he could barely get the words past his teeth. 'You're on your own, Deena. I'm off.'

He spun away from them, hearing Virtue hiss to Deena: 'Not here. Somewhere quieter.' And then, in a louder voice and to one, or perhaps all, of his family members: 'When Sharlene comes in, tell her I'll be back before closing.'

Benedict didn't pause as he made tracks for the door. If Deena was so reckless as to go off 'somewhere quiet' with a notorious villain, then she only had herself to blame if she subsequently regretted it. He'd done all that he could to protect her from her own rashness – and just *why* she was being so rash, he couldn't for the life of him fathom. It wasn't as if Hugh was a small child, for God's sake.

As he circumnavigated knots of drinkers, all of whom were eyeing him with great interest, he allowed himself a flash of amusement at the fact that Al Virtue's girlfriend – if she was his girlfriend – had the same unusual name as the girl he had spent last night with at the Sugar Club. Until now he'd been under the impression that Sharlene was a typical black name, but perhaps he'd been wrong.

From not far behind him he heard Deena saying to Virtue: 'No, I don't have my car with me.'

Even though he knew they were on his heels he still didn't turn round. What was the point? Deena had made up her mind what it was she was going to do and he'd no intention of getting himself beaten to a bloody pulp trying to prevent her from doing it.

He was just about to put his hand out to push the door open, when it was pushed open from the street.

As she stepped over the threshold, Sharlene came to a halt almost as suddenly as Benedict. Recognition flooded her face and then, as her eyes flew to the person only feet behind him, instant alarm.

'Sorry about this, Shar,' Al said, moving past Benedict

towards the open door. 'I'll be back in an hour or two. OK?'

Sharlene nodded, her eyes flying back to Benedict's, the message in them unmistakable: *Don't acknowledge me! Don't speak to me! Don't use my name!*

He didn't. Speech was beyond him.

She moved first, blanking him as she sashayed past him into the pub. Al Virtue stepped out on to the pavement. Deena followed, saying as she squeezed past him: 'Please don't worry, Benedict. I know what I'm doing.'

He nodded, wishing to God he could say the same. He knew what it was he should be doing. He should be tearing the bill with Sharlene's telephone number on it into tiny, tiny pieces and flushing them down the nearest loo. He remembered the first split-second as their eyes had held and knew that in any other set of circumstances, she'd have been as pleased to see him as he would have been to see her.

As he stepped out of the pub, he made a decision as reckless as any that Deena had made. He wasn't going to destroy Sharlene's telephone number. He was going to put it in a very safe place and, casting self-preservation to the winds, he was going to ring her on it. He was going to ring her on it tomorrow.

'There's an Indian restaurant a street away. It's near enough to walk,' Al said tersely, his hands in his pockets as he led the way from the pub.

Deena said nothing. Hell would have to freeze over before she indulged in anything that could be construed as a pleasantry with Al Virtue.

Obviously feeling the same way, he didn't speak again until they were seated in an otherwise empty, dingy little restaurant no bigger than someone's front room.

'So . . .' he said finally when they both had a stiff drink in front of them. 'You think we can be useful to each other?'

There was cynical disbelief in his voice. Facing him across a table so small they were uncomfortably close, Deena didn't blame him. Now that push had come to shove, she wasn't sure how likely she thought it, either.

'I don't trust you, Virtue,' she said bluntly. 'I'm not convinced you're innocent where my son's disappearance is concerned. I'm not convinced your daughter is genuinely missing. I think it's quite possible that in talking to you like this, I'm playing right into your hands. But there is an alternative.'

'And that is?'

'That you are as bewildered and concerned as I am. And on the faint chance you are, I'm willing to risk a great deal.'

The waiter came to take their order. Al waved him away. 'Why?' he asked, slate-coloured eyes holding hers.

'Because if your situation with Fleur is the same as mine with Hugh, we need to pool information. The police aren't going to do it for us. Over two hundred and fifty thousand people a year go missing in Britain and, as far as the police are concerned, if they're over eighteen and there are no obviously suspicious circumstances – which is the category Hugh and Fleur at present fall into – it's no big deal. Consequently we need to share what little we know. When we last saw or spoke to Hugh and Fleur, what the circumstances were. What was said. What their plans were. What the situation with their friends was, and if anything was happening that could have had a knock-on effect where one, or both of them, was concerned.'

An expression flicked through his eyes that she couldn't

read. He was interested, though, she knew that. And she also knew that he hadn't wanted to be.

'Let's order,' he said abruptly.

Without his signalling the waiter or even looking towards him, the waiter was back at their table.

'A chicken tikka and pilau rice,' she said, not interested in the menu or with making a choice.

'Make that two,' Al said. 'Plus a Bombay aloo and a vegetable curry in a Madras sauce.' And then, returning his attention to her: 'When did you last speak to your son? And when did you find out about his relationship with my daughter?'

She slid the Shetland-wool cardigan off her shoulders and hooked it over the back of her chair.

'He phoned me from Oxford six weeks ago. He said he was going to spend the rest of his summer vacation backpacking in Turkey with a friend. At the time I assumed the friend was male. I only discovered differently when I went to Oxford two days ago and spoke to some of his college friends.'

'You can't have been very pleased when you realised who the "friend" was.' Al's voice was heavy with irony.

'I was appalled,' she said, not sliding her eyes away from his. 'I still am.'

'That makes two of us.'

Mutual animosity and contempt lay so thick between them it could have been cut with a knife.

With immense self-control, Deena forced herself to say neutrally: 'Do you think that the reaction they knew they would meet with when we learned of their relationship could be a reason for their having disappeared together? Could Fleur have been scared? What, for instance, would you have done if she'd told you who her boyfriend was?'

'I'd have killed her.'

It was the response she had expected and, coming from Al Virtue, was not necessarily a mere figure of speech. The possibility that his daughter was terrified of him was one that had already occurred to her. The snag was, though it offered an explanation why Fleur Virtue had dropped from sight, it didn't explain why Hugh had done so. Hugh wouldn't have been frightened of Al Virtue – or at least, not so frightened that he would go into hiding. Hiding wasn't Hugh's style.

'So you went to Oxford when? Two days ago?' he asked as she kept her thoughts to herself.

'Yes.'

'And who did you speak to?'

'I spoke to Hugh's dean. I spoke to half a dozen of his friends. And when I was told who his girlfriend was, and that she was also missing, I went to St Clemence's and spoke to Fleur's dean as well.'

His eyes had narrowed and she knew he was seething at the thought that Fleur's dean had discussed his daughter with her. She didn't blame him. She wouldn't have been ecstatic at the thought of Hugh's dean having discussed Hugh with Al Virtue.

For the next hour, as their meal was served and as they ate, they exchanged information. It came as a shock to her to realise how close she had come to running into him at Kidlington CID – and that he had spoken to exactly the same set of Hugh's friends as she had. The sum total of his information, though, added not a jot to her own.

'So we're no nearer,' she said wearily as the waiter cleared their plates. 'They intended going to Turkey and, when Hugh discovered his passport was out of date, changed their plans and didn't confide those plans to the people they roomed with. There are no suspicious circumstances, no –'

'Not true.'

It was an interruption she was totally unprepared for.

Al swirled his fourth whisky of the evening around in his glass. 'I didn't only speak with Fleur's dean. I spoke with her head of studies as well. She told me that a couple of months ago a girl at a different college to Fleur's had died of a drug overdose. She said that Fleur had known her. It seemed an odd bit of information for her to have passed on and so I took the liberty of asking a contact of mine in the Met to come back to me with details.'

'And?'

Deena was no longer weary. She was very, very tense.

'He said that the girl in question, Amabel Lyndhurst, hadn't died from a drug overdose. At least not officially. Officially she'd died from an asthma attack.'

Deena frowned. 'Then why . . .'

'The asthma attack story was a cover-up. Amabel was Sir Nicholas Lyndhurst's daughter. He's a government minister. Her uncle is Sir Monty Gargrave. According to my contact, Gargrave is a mover and a shaker in the Foreign Office – and when it comes to keeping things under wraps, power talks.'

He took a swallow of his whisky. 'Because of the cover-up there's no official investigation, but you can bet your life there's a fucking big unofficial one going on.'

He could see her thinking – and thinking fast. She still hadn't got to where he was going to take her, though. 'What I want to know,' he said, 'is if the investigation is one your son is running scared from. And if he's taken my daughter with him.'

'Hugh, running scared from a drugs investigation?' If he'd hit her with a sledgehammer the shock to her system couldn't have been greater. 'Absolutely not!' She was on her feet so fast coffee slopped across the tablecloth and a vase of flowers went toppling. 'Never! Not in a million years!'

At the lack of any horrified realisation dawning in her eyes, he didn't know whether to feel disappointed or relieved. If she'd suspected her son capable of drug-dealing, his concern for Fleur would have rocketed. On the other hand, it would at least have been a clue that could have been followed.

'My son isn't the one who's likely to be doing any dealing!' she spat, sweeping her cardigan from off the back of her chair, scooping her shoulder-bag from the floor. 'Your daughter's the one with the criminal background!'

He made no move to rise to his feet. 'My daughter doesn't touch drugs,' he said steadily. 'If she did, I'd know.'

She'd been about to make whirlwind-like for the door. The certainty in his voice halted her.

'I'm going to Oxford tomorrow to speak to Fleur's head of studies again,' he said, righting the toppled vase. 'She might be even more forthcoming with you than she was with me.'

It was true. He could see her mentally assessing the advantages of questioning Sheila Golightly about Fleur, with Fleur's father present.

'All right,' she said at last. 'But I'm not travelling up there with you.'

'I wouldn't want you to.'

'What time will you be there?'

'Ten.'

She breathed in deeply, 'Just for the record,' she said. 'I think you're scum.'

'Just for the record,' he said without missing a beat, 'I think you're a cunt.'

With a stab of satisfaction he saw the impact the word

had on her, and then she was walking away from him at speed, the restaurant door banging shut behind her.

He drained his glass and took a wad of notes from his back pocket. Peeling off half a dozen, he laid them on the table and rose to his feet. It had been a hell of a day. He'd had to sort a couple of alibis for Ritchie and do the same for Barney. He'd had to put all thoughts of the bond job on a back-burner and conduct business to do with *The Mallard II*'s refitting over the phone when he'd wanted to do it in person. He'd had to try and track Tommy down – knowing the kind of blazing row there'd be when he did so. He'd had to contend with Ritchie's grief over Lulu – and his demented demands that he find out who it was that had killed her. And now, last but by no means least, he had a piqued girlfriend to pacify.

'I've every reason to be pissed off, babe!' Sharlene said, breaking a long and sulky silence as they entered Ponderosa a little under an hour later and Blitz bounded to greet them. 'I've apologised about my thinking Fleur had phoned when she hadn't, but you're still taking it out on me.'

She followed him as he strode, tight-lipped, into the bedroom.

'All yesterday afternoon I was holed up in The Maid with Lol,' she persisted as he took off his suit jacket and hung it up. 'And then the coppers came in about that girl's murder, doing their Gestapo bit and questioning us all.'

She didn't follow on with an account of where she had gone and what had happened when she had left The Maid. The shock she had received in The Drum, when she'd walked smack into the good-looking sculptor she'd got so high on champagne with, was one she still hadn't fully recovered from.

'And today you've been out and about without me,'

she continued as he sat down on the edge of the bed, unfastening the laces of his black Prada brogues. 'And then tonight, when we were supposed to be meeting up, I find myself sitting with Lol again – and Ginny.'

He slipped his feet out of his shoes, still not speaking to her. She sat down beside him, wrapping her arms around his waist. 'You know how I feel about Ginny, babe,' she said conciliatorily. 'She does my head in. All she talked about tonight was how worried she was that the coppers would give her Ritchie a pull, seeing as how he'd been dating the Lulu girl.'

'She's every right to be worried.' Al shook her arms away and stood up. 'What do you think I've been spending my time doing today, Shar?' He hauled his polo neck over his head, throwing it in the general direction of a linen-basket. 'I've been covering Ritchie's arse for him and sorting things for that other priceless prick, Barney.' Bare-footed and bare-chested he walked across to the dressing-table, picking up a carton of Marlboros and tapping one out. 'And I've been running in circles trying to find where the fuck Fleur is.'

He lit the cigarette, inhaling deeply. Christ knew why he was explaining things. Anyone with a mite of sense would know why he'd had no time all day.

Sharlene opened her mouth to say something, then thought better of it. Fleur was hallowed ground. Telling him he was stressing over nothing and that Fleur had obviously gone off to do her own thing for a few weeks, would not go down very well.

Sometimes she wondered if he appreciated how close she and Fleur were in age. It never seemed to occur to him that if her dad behaved towards her as he behaved towards Fleur, she wouldn't have been able to become his girlfriend, let alone move in with him.

He turned towards her, his trousers low and snug on his hips. She felt a familiar tightening in her vagina. Even though he was in his mid-forties, his hard-muscled body still moved with an athlete's co-ordination and grace. Aware that, for a man who rang all the right bells, allowances had to be made, she abandoned every trace of sulky peevishness.

'Come on, sugar,' she said, swaying seductively against him, her hands on the buckle of his belt, her eyes dark with heat. 'Let's forget my silly mistake about the phone call. Let's make love.'

He had obliged, but afterwards, her sweat-sheened body still entwined with his, she'd known he'd been more motivated by his need of exhaustion, if he was to sleep, than by desire.

Her resentment, as he rolled away from her, was intense. So she'd fibbed to him about a telephone call. So what? There was no need for him to be so insultingly off-hand with her. She wasn't just anyone. She was a supermodel. She was special. And if Al didn't appreciate that, there were others who would. In the morning she would telephone Italy. And if Count Giorgio d'Argenio didn't demand she immediately fly out to join him, she would contact the blond, tousle-haired sculptor she'd had such a good time with at the Sugar Club.

Deena lay as far away from Benedict as she could possibly get. He'd been waiting outside the house for her when she'd returned from The Drum and, even as she'd been paying off her cab, she'd known that he was drunk. It wasn't a condition she had much patience with at the best of times. That night, with all she had on her mind, she had none.

Gargrave. The name had been resounding in her brain all the way home. Sir Monty Gargrave at the Foreign Office. Giles Gargrave at Latimer College. Al Virtue hadn't picked up on it, but she had.

If it wasn't a coincidence – if Hugh's friend Giles was related to Amabel Lyndhurst's uncle – what conclusions could be drawn? It would mean that Giles had possibly been Amabel's cousin, but that didn't get her much further where the mystery of Hugh's whereabouts was concerned. It was Fleur who had been friends with Amabel, not Hugh. The Fleur–Amabel link was, however, something the police needed apprising of, and as well as speaking to Rose and Fallon, she also needed to speak to Rupert again.

Rupert would be able to tell her whether Sir Monty and Giles Gargrave were related. Any conversation they had over it, though, was one that needed to be conducted face to face rather than over the telephone. And she couldn't see Rupert tomorrow if she was meeting Al Virtue in Oxford.

As Benedict snored heavily by her side, she focused all her thoughts on what it was she hoped to achieve when she met Fleur Virtue's head of studies. The most important thing was to find out what sort of a girl Fleur Virtue was. The likelihood, of course, was that she was trouble. How could Al Virtue's daughter be anything else? If she was also *in* some kind of trouble, it could be the reason she had disappeared. She would certainly be aware that disappearing was a way of solving problems. One or other of her relations was always disappearing, usually in order to avoid arrest.

And Hugh? She stared into the darkness, too tense for sleep. As all the Virtue brothers were exceptionally good-looking, it made sense to suppose that Fleur, too, was extraordinarily attractive and that Hugh had become besotted with her – so besotted that when she had chosen to disappear, he, concerned for her safety, had disappeared with her.

There was only one flaw to such a scenario and as she acknowledged it, a migraine began to beat behind her eyes. Hugh was far too self-interested ever to put his academic record voluntarily at risk. Selflessness of any sort was as alien to him as emotional involvement. Which was why she knew he wasn't besottedly in love with Fleur Virtue.

Hugh wasn't capable of loving her.

He wasn't capable of loving anyone.

Chapter Thirteen

After her near-sleepless night, the drive to Oxford next morning wasn't much fun. She'd tried to get away as early as possible to beat the traffic leaving town, but there had been the necessity of long, involved telephone calls to her Head of Chambers, Cheryl and Teddy.

Her phone call to Teddy had been the one that had caused her the most concern.

'You were quite right in being suspicious as to the circumstances of Graveney's early retirement,' he'd said, sounding as if he was rubbing sleep from his eyes. 'His record is spattered with racial harassment complaints. What do you want me to do now?'

'Nothing,' she'd said, knowing there was nothing further that could be done. At least, not officially. Instead she spoke to Cheryl again, dictating a letter to be sent to the Mustafa family.

By the time she had finished, it had been almost eight o'clock and there had been a further delay as Benedict had surfaced into defensively grumpy consciousness.

She'd had neither the time nor the patience to listen to him, but his insistence on making some sort of inadequate apology had taken up a further fifteen minutes or so. Then he'd discovered she was leaving the house to rendezvous with Al Virtue in Oxford and the row that had followed had meant she hadn't walked out of the house till well after eight-thirty.

As she finally swooped on to the M40 she dismissed

Benedict from her mind, wondering if she was being sensible in deferring her telephone calls to Rose and Fallon until after her meeting with Fleur Virtue's head of studies. The way they reacted to the news that Fleur Virtue was Amabel Lyndhurst's friend and that her head of studies had indicated to Al Virtue that Amabel had died from a drug overdose – and that he'd had that information confirmed by his hookey contact in the Met – was, after all, of vital importance.

What if they were only interested in who his contact had been? What if they pooh-poohed the information he had been given? Who was she going to believe? Until she'd got the measure of the woman she and Al Virtue were about to meet, it was hard to know. Why would a woman in such a responsible position have said as much as she had to Al Virtue? It was, after all, a scandalous breach of trust. And the only obvious reason for her having committed it was because she felt the information was somehow pertinent to Fleur's disappearance. Which meant it was also pertinent to Hugh's disappearance.

As she neared Oxford the word drugs resounded in her brain with tom-tom-like insistence. Al Virtue had said his daughter didn't do drugs, but he could have been lying. The criminal background she came from would, after all, stand Fleur Virtue in good stead for a bit of drug-dealing amongst her friends.

She turned off the motorway, her thoughts grim. She could even have got the drugs in question through her father. Though there was nothing on Al Virtue's record to show he'd ever been involved in drug-linked crime, it would be an absolute miracle if he hadn't been. All major crime these days was drug-linked, and the Virtues were major criminals. Was the passing on of Dr Golightly's remarks some kind of complicated double-bluff on his part? It was possible. He was, after all, a man who liked playing games.

Her mouth tightened as she began negotiating Oxford itself. If he thought he was playing a game with her, he was in for a big, big shock.

She drove through the streets towards the city's heart, resolutely ignoring the colleges and pubs that held personal memories from her own student days. Starting to see Jimmy everywhere she looked was the very last thing she needed.

There was a rare-as-gold parking place near to the Ashmolean and she nipped into it. Seconds later she was walking past the narrow frontage of the White Horse and past Blackwells bookshop.

Considering how hard she was trying not to think about Hugh's father, it was unfortunate.

Blackwells had been one of her and Jimmy's regular meeting-places. Clamping down firmly on the surge of feelings that threatened to overwhelm her, she walked briskly from Broad Street into Catte Street, making for the High and Magdalen Bridge.

He was standing at the far side of it, distinguishable amongst thick clusters of pedestrians even from a distance. It was a relatively warm day for October and, though she was wearing a coat, he wasn't. As she drew nearer, she saw that his expensive-looking lightweight wool suit was black, as had been the suit he'd been wearing yesterday evening. This time, though, it was single-rather than double-breasted, and the polo neck he was wearing with it was also black. She wondered if he deliberately dressed as though he had just stepped from a Quentin Tarantino film, or if the effect was unintentional.

'I haven't told Dr Golightly who you are,' he said

abruptly as, not greeting her just as she pointedly didn't greet him, they began walking as far apart as was possible past St Hilda's and towards St Clemence's. 'I thought she might clam up if she knew you were a QC.'

She turned her head towards him so swiftly that her hair swung. 'If she thinks I've no personal involvement, she isn't likely to be forthcoming in front of me at all!'

'Don't worry on that score.' They were at the porter's lodge now and he said to the porter, still not having looked directly towards her: 'Al Virtue and partner for Dr Sheila Golightly. We're expected.'

Deena couldn't remember any other occasion in her life when she had so very nearly choked.

'It's simpler like this,' he said as she fought for breath. 'Trust me.'

She didn't – but knowing there was a faint chance his assumption was correct, neither did she set the record straight.

Five minutes later she was glad she hadn't.

'My partner, Deena,' Al Virtue said tersely, and as Sheila Golightly took a small clay pipe out of her mouth and shook hands with her, Deena knew that Fleur Virtue's head of studies was an anarchist who would never in a million years fraternise in any way, shape or form with the forces of law and order.

'I know we're talking off the record, Sheila,' Al said in a manner so offensively intimate Deena's body stiffened into shocked rigidity. 'But I need more gen about the drugs scene here. Is it so rife that the cover-up is to protect the university's reputation, or is the cover-up over Fleur's friend's death just down to the fact that her old man is a government minister and her uncle is a big cheese at the Foreign Office?'

'Is he?' Sheila Golightly's voice was admiring. 'You've

been busy, Al. I knew about her father, of course, but I didn't know there were other family ramifications. It explains a lot.'

With fascinated horror Deena realised that Dr Golightly was flirting with him. It was a nauseating sight, especially as he was so obviously playing up to it, but it did at least explain why this morning's meeting had been so easy for him to set up.

'Whether drug-taking is any more rife now than it has been since the mid-seventies when I was a student, I don't know,' Sheila Golightly continued, toying with her pipe. 'The main difference is that in the old days it was nearly all marijuana with occasional forays into LSD, and now it's nearly all cocaine with forays into crack and heroin.'

'And who are the dealers? What's the general set-up?'

Watching him, Deena could only conclude that if he already knew the answers to the questions he was asking, he wasn't an expert when it came to bluffing, he was master-class.

'If you mean, who are the major players, I have no idea.' She shrugged. 'There'll be a Mr Big somewhere, but I doubt his name is known in Oxford.'

'But is the name of the person who supplied Amabel Lyndhurst known?' Deena interjected, trying to keep the questioning on track.

With obvious reluctance Sheila Golightly transferred her attention from Al and, as her eyes held hers, Deena was gripped by the kind of fierce certainty she often experienced in the courtroom. Sheila Golightly knew. Whether she would say, though, was another matter entirely.

Not caring that Al Virtue was only feet away from her, wanting only to see the reaction in Sheila Golightly's eyes, she said ingenuously: 'Would Fleur have known?'

The result was better than anything she had hoped for. Sheila Golightly's eyes widened. 'But of course she would,' she said, and then, looking from her to Al. 'How could she not? It was her boyfriend who was Amabel's supplier. There wasn't enough proof for criminal charges, but he was about to be rusticated. Didn't you know?'

It wasn't the first pole-axing shock she'd sustained over the last forty-eight hours, but it was by far the most vicious. Only her instant, utter rejection of what Sheila Golightly had said enabled her to retain any degree of composure. She would believe many things of Hugh, but not that he was dealing drugs amongst Fleur Virtue's friends. Not when Fleur Virtue was by far the more obvious, far more likely candidate.

She didn't have to ask Al Virtue for his reaction.

'Jesus Christ!' he shouted, erupting to his feet, eyes blazing, fists clenched. 'No wonder your fucking son has fucking scarpered!'

As his chair toppled, she scrambled to her feet, certain she was about to be punched into extinction.

'Hugh had nothing whatever to do with Amabel Lyndhurst's death!' she shouted in retaliation, uncaring of their interested audience. 'If he had, don't you think I would have been told? If he'd been about to be rusticated for *anything*, his dean would have told me when we discussed Hugh's disappearance! If there'd been even a *whisper* of a suspicion he'd supplied a Class A drug to someone who had subsequently died, the police would be as eager to trace his present whereabouts as I am. And they aren't. If it wasn't for the fact that you're his girlfriend's father, they wouldn't be interested at all!'

'I'm interested,' Sheila Golightly said, looking from one

to the other and back again. 'If you're Fleur's boyfriend's mother, why did Al say you were his partner?'

Under the circumstances it was a reasonable enough question, but neither Deena nor Al was in a reasonable enough mood to answer it.

When Deena spoke to Sheila Golightly it was to say in icy fury: 'You're guilty of slander, Dr Golightly, and it will be dealt with as such!' To Al, she said: 'I'm going to Latimer to speak to Hugh's dean and have Dr Golightly's allegations refuted – and I'm going alone!'

As she crossed the room to the door she half expected him to be there before her.

He wasn't.

The door slammed shut behind her and she descended the stone spiral staircase propelled by rage and relief; rage at the sheer viciousness of the allegations made, relief because she at least no longer had Al Virtue by her side.

By the time she was crossing the quad, the sensation of relief was fast evaporating. Al Virtue with her – so she knew where he was, who he was speaking with and what he was saying – would have been preferable to Al Virtue careening around Oxford on his own, repeating Sheila Golightly's criminal allegations to God alone knew whom.

Knowing she had made a grave error of judgement and that there was nothing whatever she could now do about it, she strode across Magdalen Bridge. The sooner she met with Hugh's dean, the sooner she would be extracting every kind of apology possible from Sheila Golightly.

'But this is most . . . awkward.' Hugh's dean said forty-five minutes later, looking beyond Deena to the door she had closed behind her when she had entered the room. The expression in his eyes was that of a man yearning for escape. 'I naturally assumed, when we spoke a couple of days ago, that . . . that . . .'

'That what?' Deena was beyond caring whether she sounded rude or not. She had entered the room certain that the interview would take no more than a few minutes and now, instead of refuting Dr Golightly's allegations with crisp contempt, the dean was flailing around as if facing a problem.

'That you were *au fait* with the situation,' he said in obvious embarrassment. 'That as the police had decided to drop all thoughts of prosecution and been adamant that the matter be taken no further . . .'

Time hung suspended. She could hear her own breathing; hear her heart slamming.

'No,' she heard herself say in a calm voice, knowing that if she allowed alarm into it he might be panicked into silence. 'No, I am not completely *au fait*. There are, I think, some gaps in the information given to me by the police. If you could take me through events yourself . . .'

She gave a small encouraging smile.

The dean, reassured as she had intended him to be, eased out a sigh of relief. 'The Proctors, as you know, are always on the alert for names of students suspected of drug-dealing. They will act on privately received information, sometimes in tandem with the police – and that is what happened in Hugh's case. There was a tragic death earlier in the summer – not at Latimer, I hasten to add – and there were rumours that it had been occasioned by a drug overdose.'

He paused.

Deena waited.

'Hugh was one of several students questioned,' he said at last, 'and it did look as if he would have to be rusticated whilst enquiries continued. However, I was informed by the police during the summer vacation that their enquiries were at an end and that no further mention of the affair should be made.'

His eyes, which had been avoiding hers all the time he had been speaking, finally made contact. 'So you see,' he continued apologetically, 'I thought it would be most inappropriate if I were to infer that Hugh's disappearance was even remotely connected with the unfortunate events of last term.'

'Yes,' Deena said, the breath in her chest so tight it was a miracle she could speak at all. 'Of course. And the police force in question – was it Oxford City Police or Thames Valley?'

If it was the City Police, then it was possible it was simply an instance of bad communications. It wouldn't be the first time a name hadn't been run as a matter of course through the computers. But if it had been Thames Valley Police, DI Fallon's failure to mention that Hugh had been questioned some weeks earlier in connection with a suspected drugs death was more than sloppy. It was sinister.

'Thames Valley,' the dean said. 'Which was unusual. Anything to do with the University is generally dealt with by St Aldates. Still . . . under the circumstances . . .'

'The circumstances being the high-profile connections of the dead student?'

'Ah, yes. You know? I wasn't sure. So confusing when the police ask one to be circumspect. Yes. It was most unfortunate. Reminiscent of young Joshua Macmillan's death from a drug overdose. He was Prime Minister Harold Macmillan's grandson . . . Balliol, of course, not Latimer. It's a long time ago now, but it caused a great kerfuffle.'

Deena remembered Joshua Macmillan's death. He'd

been a friend of Jimmy's. Considering the lifestyle Jimmy had led, it had been a miracle he hadn't been involved in the subsequent 'kerfuffle'. Slipping away from difficult situations had, though, always been something Jimmy had been good at. As she knew to her cost.

'So the loose talk you've met with at St Clemence's is regrettable . . . quite unpardonable,' the dean was saying as he escorted her to the door. 'And more than a little mystifying, too, don't you think?'

It hadn't been a question he had seriously wanted a reply to, and she hadn't proffered one. She needed to be alone so that she could think. And she needed fresh air.

Once outside the college she leaned against mellowed stone, drawing great gulpfuls of air into her lungs. Whatever she had expected when she had begun asking questions, it hadn't been for there to have been a drugs connection to Hugh's disappearance.

She forced herself away from the stone, beginning to walk with no thought of a destination. If Hugh had been questioned in the aftermath of Amabel Lyndhurst's death, why hadn't she been informed of it when she had reported him missing? Was it, despite the dean's belief to the contrary, because Hugh was still under investigation and, aware of being so, had disappeared on purpose? Were the police being even more devious than usual and hoping she would lead them to him?

She was nearly back at the bridge and, having no desire now to return to St Clemence's, she turned to the right, heading down the slope that led from the High Street towards the Botanical Gardens and the river.

The sensible course of action would have been to drive out to Kidlington and to ask DI Fallon straight out what the hell was going on.

And she didn't want to do that. Not one little bit.

She stared out across the river towards the Meadows and St Hilda's, knowing that the reason for her reluctance was instinctive, not logical. Jimmy's presence had been unwelcomely near all afternoon and liaising with the police over anything concerning Jimmy would never have been in Hugh's best interests. And Hugh was very like his father – and not only in looks.

A punt glided from beneath the bridge, its occupants looking none too warm. A couple of squabbling birds erupted from a nearby bush. Somewhere a church clock struck the hour.

She pulled the collar of her coat up close around her neck. If giving the police her implicit trust was not necessarily in Hugh's best interests, who could she turn to for help? She needed information about the drugs scene in Oxford. She needed to know if Hugh was, or wasn't, involved in it. And if he was, she needed to know who his contacts were, because they were probably the people he was with.

What she needed was someone familiar with, and at ease in, a very murky world.

Right on cue, the person fitting the job description strode up behind her.

'So what are you going to do now you've found out your son is a drug-dealer?' he rasped. 'Thinking of throwing yourself in the soddin' river, are you?'

Chapter Fourteen

'Al?' Stuart gave a sigh of relief as Al answered his mobile. 'Whereabouts are you, mate?'

'Oxford.'

Stuart winced. It had been a damn fool question. Al was going to be in Oxford until he'd tracked Fleur down. 'Course,' he said apologetically, moving outside The Maid to get better reception. 'I should have realised. How are things going? Are you any nearer finding out where she is?'

'No. Look, Stuart, unless this is important, can we cut it short? Deena King is with me and things are tense . . .'

'I bet they bloody are!' Stuart's mind was boggling, but he'd no intention of getting side-tracked by asking Al what the hell he and Deena King were doing together. 'Problem is, Al, they're bleedin' tense here as well.'

All his life he'd off-loaded his anxieties on to Al's capable shoulders, and the habit was one he wasn't about to break.

'I know you're worried sick about Fleur,' he said, speaking fast. 'Jesus, we're *all* sick with worry about Fleur! But there are things happening this end you need to know about.'

'OK.' There was clear impatience in Al's voice. 'Shoot.'

'Barney's been arrested,' he said, starting off with what he considered to be the least dire of his problems. 'He hasn't been charged – and if the hookey alibi you fixed for him stands, he probably won't be. Thing is, Max isn't too happy about it being taken for granted that Barney's innocent. According to him, Barney had been out-of-order where Lulu was concerned.'

'Then he should have fucking spoken up about it. But however out-of-order the stupid prick's been, he didn't kill her. He couldn't kill a spider. Anything else?'

'Stacks. Now Ritchie's got over the shock of Lulu being dead, he can't understand why we ain't doing anything to find and sort the bastard responsible. And he's got a point, Al. She was his girl, after all. That makes her family. And she worked at The Maid. The general feeling is that we should all be out and about leaving no stone unturned. Know what I mean?'

'Yep, but Fleur takes precedence and I can't be in two places at once. Calm Ritchie down. It's my bet Barney'll be released before the day's out and it's Ritchie who'll then be helping the cozzers with their enquiries. If he's raging off at half-cock when they take him in the cop-shop, it won't help things. You and Kevin make a start where Lulu's concerned. Find out if she was two-timing Ritchie. Find out who the boyfriend before him was. Rope Tommy in.'

'Yeah, well. That brings me to problem number three,' Stuart said unhappily, his eyes meeting Paulie's as Paulie stepped out of the pub into the car park and began walking across to him. 'I've just been talking to Paulie, Al. He's with me now.'

He took a deep breath.

'It seems like Tommy's being a real stupid fucker,' he said, wondering what the outcome of Tommy's stupidity was going to be; wondering whether their family would ever be the same again. 'The geezer behind the job he nearly went down for is Ginny's ex. And you know the kind of trade Fat Pat deals in. It's drugs. Tommy may have been nabbed for hijacking lorries and off-loading their contents, but that isn't what he and his mates are really into. They're dealing drugs for Pat . . . and doing it in a big way.' He paused again and then added, 'And Tommy isn't the only one in the family running round for Pat.'

The continued silence from the other end of the phone was so electric Stuart could practically hear it crackling.

'He's got to the boys, Al. He's got to Zac and Clint. I suppose, as he's their real dad, it was bound to happen . . . but it's going to break Ginny's heart . . .'

He broke off, unable to continue. He'd reared Ginny's twin sons since they'd been nippers – and for nearly all of that time Fat Pat Docherty had ignored their existence. Which had been fine by him and Ginny. Docherty was scum of mega proportions and Ginny hadn't wanted the kids having any contact with him. They'd had kids of their own, Billy, Paulie and Ritchie, and become one big, united family. Or they had been united until Billy had died because the kind of low-life who worked for Docherty had fed him crack cocaine at his school-gates.

And now Zac and Clint were working for Fat Pat. As was Tommy. Stuart wondered who had encouraged who. Whichever way round it had been, he couldn't envisage a day when he'd forgive Tommy.

'*I knew it!*' The savagery in Al's voice was such that Stuart thought the mobile was going to jump from his hand. 'I knew Tommy and the twins were keeping secrets!' He broke off, breathing hard.

Stuart didn't blame him. He, too, had been nearly beyond speech when Paulie had put him in the picture as to what was going on. One thing was for sure: if Al had had this info earlier, he'd never have paid a fortune to get Tommy's case dismissed. He'd have let the trial run its course and if it had resulted in Tommy going down, he wouldn't have shed a tear.

'Leave it with me, Stuart,' Al was saying now. 'I'll be in touch.'

The line went dead. Stuart clicked the mobile off and looked at Paulie. 'Well, he knows,' he said unnecessarily.

'Did you fill him in on everything? Did you tell him about Barney and Ritchie and Kevin and Max?'

Stuart rested a hand on his son's shoulder. 'I told him about Barney and Ritchie,' he said as they began walking together towards The Maid's rear door. 'The fact that your Uncle Kevin is about to blow his marriage for Max's ex-bit-of-stuff is news that will keep.'

With his free hand he pushed open the pub door.

'And that the cozzers never being out of The Maid is shooting Max's nerves to pieces, will be no news to Al. He knows his best mate. Max is a straight goer, and like all straight goers, too much police attention does his head in.'

As they stepped into the saloon bar they fell silent. There was a hefty sprinkling of early lunch-time regulars in – and the now familiar faces of a couple of plain-clothes cozzers. Personal chat of any sort was out of the question.

As Paulie strolled off to join a haggard-looking Ritchie, Stuart remained on the periphery of the bar. He was forty years old and felt fifty. The buzz had gone out of life and he had a sick feeling it was never going to come back. How could it, when the family team was disintegrating so fast? No way would he touch the drug trade – and he knew Al wouldn't, either. And Al was the one who called the shots where jobs were concerned.

He took a swallow of the Guinness he'd left standing on the bar when he'd gone out into the car park to make his phone call. The problem was that drugs were piss-easy money – and piss-easy money was what young geezers were after. Tommy was only twenty-five. He'd still been a kid when he, Al, Kevin and the old man had been pulling the really big numbers back in the late eighties and early nineties. He felt he'd missed out on things, and in a way he had. It was no excuse for what he was doing now, though. There could be no excuse for that.

When he thought of the task that lay ahead of him – breaking the news to Ginny that Zac and Clint were in cahoots with their dad – he felt sick to his stomach. As far as Ginny was concerned Stuart was their real dad. And that was the way he'd always felt, too. Until now. He knew he would never be able to come to terms with the affront to young Billy's memory – that and the fact his kid brother and his stepsons had chosen to run with vermin.

He knew that if the old man got to know of it in Spain, he'd go ballistic. His heyday had been the sixties, when gangland really had been gangland and the Krays had been kings. The Krays' kind of crime had never been to their dad's taste and, whenever he had mentioned their name, he had followed it with a spit. Never in a million years would his dad have run with the scum of his day – and it had never occurred to him, or to Al and Kevin, to run with the scum of their day, either.

He finished his Guinness. Ever since the old man had moved out to Marbella, Ginny had been hankering for him to do the same. 'We could buy a beach-bar,' she had said, time and again. 'The boys might even come with us. They could set up a jet-ski business or a scuba-diving school.'

It hadn't been a scenario he'd thought likely, but he

knew Ginny would feel that if they'd made such a move, Zac and Clint wouldn't now be dealing drugs.

'Another Guinness,' he said wooden-faced to Max's barman. Perhaps the time had come for a change of lifestyle. His kind of criminal expertise was now as defunct as the dodo. Who needed ace gellymen these days? Thanks to new technology, even *getting* to a worthwhile safe had become tricky to the point of near impossibility.

Unsmilingly, he slipped his hand around the foamingly-full pint-glass the barman pushed towards him. If he was a dodo at forty, then Al, at forty-five, was a dinosaur. He wondered when his elder brother would realise it – and what he would do when he did. And he wondered why Al was in the company of a woman who had once trashed his defence counsel so utterly he'd spent seven years in the boob as a result.

'So . . . where were we?' Al clicked his phone shut and tucked it into the back pocket of his pants.

'We'd come to the agreement that, as we are the only people truly concerned about finding our children, we should put our personal antipathy on hold and pool our resources,' Deena said crisply, her inner turmoil as superbly camouflaged as ever.

There was pure venom in the look he shot her.

'Antipathy had better mean gross, monumental, God-almighty hatred,' he said tightly, 'or it's the understatement of all time.'

'Don't worry.' She pulled her collar closer around her throat. 'It does.'

Their eyes locked. It was an impasse and it was one that, for different reasons, both wanted to overcome. Now that her suspicions of police behaviour towards Hugh had taken hold, Deena knew she needed Al Virtue to conduct investigations in a world it would otherwise be hard for her to infiltrate. Oxford's drug dealers would, with luck, talk with relative freedom to a man of Al's criminal pedigree. Whereas even in the unlikely event of her tracking any of them down, they weren't likely to say a damn thing to her. And if Al Virtue was on the level about knowing sweet f.a. about his daughter's disappearance, he needed her in order to be hard on Hugh's heels.

'So, was your son under police investigation for drug dealing?' he asked brutally, confirming her assumption. 'Was that pipe-smoking bird spot on?'

Her eyes held his. 'No,' she lied, having no intention of relaying information that she'd neither come to terms with nor fathomed. 'There were some general investigations amongst student acquaintances of Amabel Lyndhurst after she died. Nothing came of them.'

'And I'm to believe you?' His face was so hard-boned it looked as if it had been carved from granite. Even the cleft in his chin looked sculpted.

'You can please yourself.' She shivered. The sun had clouded over and it was suddenly quite cold. 'I need a coffee and something to eat. Then I'm going to make a phone call. I want corroboration that the Lyndhurst girl died from a drug overdose. So far, all I have is rumour and the word of your pet bent copper.'

She turned away from him, walking back across the grass towards the gravelled pathways of the Botanical Gardens.

'My bent copper is an unimpeachable source,' he said grimly, falling into step a yard or so away from her.

Deena didn't deign to answer him. Prior to her conversation with Hugh's dean, the obvious person to go to for corroboration would have been Inspector Rose. Not now, though. If the dean's account of events was correct, she didn't want the police knowing she was aware they'd had Hugh under investigation. Not when she had no idea why they were keeping so quiet about it.

'So where will you go for your corroboration?' he asked as they climbed the steps leading from the gardens back into the High Street. 'A pet cozzer of your own?'

'No. A civil servant.'

She'd intended speaking to Rupert to find out if Giles Gargrave was Amabel Lyndhurst's cousin. Now she could do so and ask about the nature of Amabel Lyndhurst's death at the same time. That Rupert wasn't a policeman was immaterial. He would have gossip – and at Rupert's level it would be gossip that could be trusted. If Sir Monty Gargrave's niece had died of a drug overdose, then Rupert would know.

Still keeping as far apart as was possible on the High Street's relatively narrow pavements, they entered the first café they came to. Several heads turned in their direction. Deena wasn't surprised. Al Virtue didn't look the kind of man who frequented cafés, and he certainly didn't look at ease in one.

'What's it to be?' he asked her, seating a physique of solid bulked-up muscle on a chair that looked vulnerably fragile. 'Tea? Coffee?'

'Coffee,' she said, noticing he was wearing an ostentatious gold link bracelet as well as a gold Rolex. 'And a sandwich. Any kind of sandwich.'

Whilst he gave a simpering waitress their order, she took her mobile from her shoulder-bag and tapped in Rupert's number. Ideally, she had wanted to speak with Rupert face to face, but nothing was ideal at the moment and she didn't want to wait any longer for the information she was after.

It took several minutes for her to be connected to

Rupert's extension and by the time the common courtesies were over and she was stating her business, the coffee and sandwiches were on the table.

'Giles Gargrave,' she said, aware of Al Virtue's eyebrows flying high as, for the first time, he connected Giles' name with Sir Monty's. 'He's a student at Latimer. You wouldn't happen to know if he's related to Sir Monty Gargrave, would you, Rupert?'

There was a long drawn-out sigh from the other end of the telephone, almost as if it had been a question he had long been expecting. 'Yes,' he said. 'Yes, Giles is Sir Monty's youngest son. His mother is a Challoner. Your mother was very friendly with the Challoners back in the forties . . . They were all very good tennis players, I believe.'

'There's something else I need to know, Rupert,' she said, cutting him short before he proceeded to tell her in detail about the Challoner family's athletic ability and keeping her voice low, so as not to be heard over the general clatter of clinking teacups and chatting women. 'Is Sir Monty related to Nicholas Lyndhurst?'

'He is. One of Monty's sisters is Lady Lyndhurst. Their daughter died in tragic circumstances a few months ago.'

Deena steadied her breathing. 'So I understand. You couldn't tell me what the circumstances were, could you, Rupert? I know the official version, but I'm in Oxford trying to get a lead on where Hugh might be, and I keep hearing rumours. Rumours I'd like either confirmed or scotched.'

There was a pregnant pause from the other end of the phone and then he said, a note in his voice she couldn't quite place: 'Whatever *unofficial* version you have heard, it is, in fact, the correct one.'

'And the unofficial police investigation? Is it still ongoing or has it been satisfactorily concluded?'

'Ongoing, I believe. But then drug investigations always are, aren't they?'

'Yes,' she said, her mouth dry. 'Thank you, Rupert.'

She flicked the phone shut and looked across at her companion. 'Your bent copper is obviously highly placed. Giles Gargrave is Amabel Lyndhurst's cousin and Amabel is . . . was . . . Sir Nicholas Lyndhurst's daughter and Monty Gargrave's niece.'

'All of which I knew already.' Al bit into a generously filled ham roll. 'What I didn't know was that your son . . . my daughter's boyfriend . . . was a drug-dealer. And even if his dean has denied it and said he wasn't about to be rusty-whatever-it-is, there's no smoke without fire.'

'Let's get this straight!' She leaned forward. 'Any such accusations levelled against my son are *totally* without foundation. To imagine that Hugh would risk a first-class honours merely to make pin-money dealing dope is farcical. Hugh is fiercely ambitious. Picking up a police record would be as unthinkable to him as it is to me!'

Al put his half-eaten roll back down on his plate and began to give her a slow, sarcastic hand-clap.

Deena looked swiftly around, seeing with relief that nearly everyone who had been seated in the café when they had arrived had left. Only one couple, who had the look of American tourists, remained, and they were seated some distance away by the window.

She turned to him again. 'Your daughter is a far likelier candidate when it comes to drug peddling. She was Amabel's friend, she comes from an environment where drug money is no doubt regarded as daily currency, she's –'

He moved his chair back so swiftly she thought it

was going to be a re-enactment of the scene in Sheila Golightly's study, the difference being that this time his fist really was going to connect with her jaw.

'Christ but you are one vicious, ignorant bitch! You prosecuted my case! You know I've never dealt in drugs in any way, shape or form!'

'That was ten years ago! You could have been up to anything since you were released!'

The American couple rose hastily to their feet.

'Not drugs.' His eyes glittered as they held hers. 'My eldest nephew died after being hooked on crack cocaine. He was thirteen. *Thirteen!*'

The Americans beat a speedy retreat.

'Billy's death nearly killed my brother and his wife,' Al continued, oblivious. 'They're still not over it. They'll never get over it. *No one* in my family deals drugs.' He thought of Tommy, Zac and Clint and saw no reason to mention them. They simply weren't relevant. 'Fleur's friend may have OD'd, but Fleur doesn't share her habit and she sure as fuck wasn't her supplier!'

His phone rang.

He snatched it from out of his back pocket, checked the incoming number and jabbed the receive button.

Grateful for the interruption, Deena placed her hand against the coffee-pot, registered it was no longer hot, and looked for the waitress. Not too surprisingly, she'd emulated the Americans and done a disappearing act. To all intents and purposes they were on their own.

'No, Shar,' Al was saying tersely. 'I haven't a clue when I'll be back. If you want to go to Chinawhite with a friend, go.' He hit the end-call button, flipping the phone shut.

'Where's Hugh's father in all this?' he asked, taking her so much by surprise she nearly knocked the coffee-pot over. 'What does he think? Where the fuck is he?'

'Do you have to swear every other word?' She'd had enough experience of low-lifes to know it was an unfair criticism. Compared to most criminals, he swore very little. She'd needed to give herself a beat of time, though, and the remark had given her the necessary breathing-space.

'Hugh's father is dead,' she said when she had recovered her equilibrium. 'But I might ask the same with regard to Fleur's mother. I'm assuming she knows that Fleur is missing. What are her thoughts on where she might be?'

'Carol isn't dead, but as far as playing a part in Fleur's life is concerned, she might as well be. Understood?'

She'd believed herself to be beyond shock when it came to men of Al Virtue's ilk, but his hard indifference sent shockwaves rippling down her spine. 'She should know,' she said vehemently, wondering what kind of woman would marry such a man; wondering how the marriage had survived even for a short time. 'What about your second wife? What kind of relationship did Fleur have with her? Might she know where she is? Might she even be with her?'

'Fleur's relationship with Marsha ended when I went in the boob. No way was I going to spend seven years or more wondering what my wife was up to and who she was with. She didn't want a divorce, but I divorced her. From my point of view it was easiest.'

'If you're trying to make me feel guilty for your years of imprisonment, you're wasting your time! You were guilty. You were guilty of far more crimes than you ever stood trial for. Ten years was lenient.'

'Really? You think so?' His eyes narrowed. 'I never killed anyone. Never injured anyone. Paedophiles are in and out of nick like ping-pong balls, serving two- and three-year sentences. In my book, *that's* leniency!'

'And in my book that's your uneducated opinion and it has nothing to do with the matter in hand.' She wished to God the waitress would put in an appearance so they could order some more coffee. A phone rang. This time it was hers.

'Hi, darling. How are things?'

Benedict sounded sleepy. She glanced down at her watch. It was mid-afternoon.

'Shit awful,' she said, aware she was beginning to sound like one of The Maid's regulars.

'Oh!' Benedict was clearly taken aback by her language. 'I just thought things might have sorted themselves out by now . . . And I wanted to apologise again. I was out of order the other night and . . .'

'I'm with someone,' she said, having no intention of bringing Benedict up to date on what was happening with Al Virtue listening to every word. 'And I'm busy.'

'Ah,' he said uncertainly. 'OK then. It's just that . . .' He hesitated, clearly unsure whether to continue or not, then said with a rush: 'It's just I wondered what was happening tonight, because if you're not going to be back, or if you're going to be busy, I thought I'd go out clubbing. The 10 Room, L'Equipe, Chinawhite. Somewhere like that. I've gone stale on the Tin Man and need to blow some cobwebs away.'

'Fine. It's the last thing in the world I want to do at the moment.' Incensed at his indifference as to the present situation with regard to Hugh, she didn't bother to say goodbye. Flicking the phone shut, she dropped it back into her shoulder-bag.

'Right,' she said, once more giving Al Virtue all her attention. 'Now I know what the relationship was between Giles Gargrave and Amabel Lyndhurst, I want to speak with him again.' She glanced again at her watch. 'Let's try the Corn Dolly, shall we? Even at this time of the day, he's as likely to be there as he is in college.'

'So you've known all along that Hugh never intended going to Turkey – that he just wanted his mother to think he was so that he could drop out of sight to meet up with his old man,' Phil Swayles said crossly to Giles Gargarve, one arm resting high on the jukebox. 'And it didn't occur to you that it would have saved an awful lot of trouble all round if you'd bothered to tell us?'

'If I'd told you, when Admin questioned you about Hugh's whereabouts, you'd have passed the info on.'

'And would that have mattered?' Tim Grant asked bewilderedly. 'I thought after what happened with Amabel, you *wanted* to cause all the trouble possible for Hugh. He did supply her with the coke that killed her, didn't he?'

'Oh yes,' Giles said, his light-coloured eyes as hard as flint. 'He did indeed, Tim. And I *am* causing trouble for Hugh. Believe you me, I am.'

'By telling your father about Hugh's so-called Turkey trip?' Phil gave an uncomprehending lift of his shoulders. 'What good has it done? The police investigation is off. I don't understand why you seem so pleased about things, Giles.'

'I'm pleased because my father is going to make quite, quite sure that Hugh comes a cropper,' Giles said with a self-satisfied smile. 'How, I don't know. All I know is that Hugh's mother isn't to be told about Hugh meeting up with his father until she and Fleur's old man begin hunting in a pack.'

'And what about the blokes who sold Hugh the coke?' Tim asked, his bewilderment deepening. 'How is your father going to make sure that they take a fall? If the stuff they were selling was adulterated with crap, they're just as responsible for your cousin's death as Hugh is. Christ, they're *more* responsible.'

'Rest assured the London cowboys will be taking a very hard fall,' Giles said, reaching up to the top of the jukebox for his drink. His arm halted in mid-air. 'Well, well,' he said, looking towards the door. 'Talk of the devil and he appears.'

Phil and Tim looked. And blanched.

'Christ!' Phil said as Al Virtue, Deena behind him, began threading his way towards them. 'What line do you want us to take, Giles? What is it we're to say?'

Giles finished reaching for his glass. 'Leave it to me, Phyllis. Say nothing.'

'What *I'd* like to know,' Tim said to Phil, 'is where the nickname "cowboys" comes from.'

'You're pathetically dense at times, Tim,' Phil said as Deena and Al came to a halt only inches away. 'What else would you call a couple of berks with names like Zac and Clint?'

Chapter Fifteen

'I've sorted things and I can make it tonight, babe,' Sharlene said throatily, using the telephone in Ponderosa's kitchen. 'Chinawhite it is.'

'Well, at least we won't risk running into any of your boyfriend's cronies there,' Benedict replied as he sat cross-legged, bejeaned and barefoot on his studio floor. 'Prince Andrew, yes. South London villains, no.'

He was wrong, but Sharlene couldn't be bothered correcting him. All that mattered to her was that on this particular evening Al wouldn't be at Chinawhite and, as he'd given her the all-clear, even if someone he knew saw her there, the repercussions would be minimal. And best of all, if Prince Andrew *was* at Chinawhite, Benedict might very well be able to introduce her to him.

'You're a *viscount?*' she had said incredulously when he had casually mentioned his title. 'Then why aren't you wearing ermine and all that stuff? Why are you wearing *jeans?*'

He had laughed at her naivety and she had laughed with him. She hadn't been laughing inwardly, though. Inwardly, her mind had been racing. Where did a viscount fit in the nobility pecking order? Was it higher, or lower, than an Italian count? 'In England it's below an earl and above a baronet,' he had told her, amused. 'It's one of my father's lesser titles, which is why, as his eldest son, I've been given it.'

'His *lesser* titles?' she had asked, enraptured. 'So what's *his* title, sugar?'

When he had told her that his father was an earl she had nearly died and gone to heaven. Count Andreas d'Argenio had immediately been consigned to the position of also-ran. Benedict was a dream package. Young, handsome, stylish, talented, sexy – and now it turned out he was a viscount who would one day be an earl.

In a different way, he was almost as intrigued by her lifestyle. 'How did you get involved with a gangster in the first place, sweetheart?' he was asking her now. 'He's nearer to fifty than forty, isn't he?'

'He doesn't look it,' she said fairly, 'and he isn't a gangster. Gangsters hurt and terrorise people. Al is a thief. There's a world of difference.'

'Is there?' Benedict was nonplussed. 'Some thieves hurt and terrorise though, don't they? What about when they pour petrol over security guards' crotches and threaten to set light to them? That's pretty gangsterish, isn't it?'

'I guess.' Sharlene had never bothered to give it much thought. 'I doubt it's ever been Al's method of working, though. Mind you, if he wanted to be nasty, I'm sure he could be.'

Benedict felt the nape of his neck prickle. Christ Almighty – what was he doing? If Virtue found out he was shagging his live-in lady, he'd probably have him nailed to a cross on Clapham Common. His dick, as well as his neck, began to tingle. There was danger in barrowloads where continuing to see Sharlene was concerned, but it was the danger that gave the relationship such a buzz.

'Why are we waiting till late tonight to see each other?' he said, suddenly very, very eager to get her in his bed. 'Virtue's in Oxford, isn't he? Let's take advantage of it. Come round to the studio and I'll show you my Tin Man.'

'You can show me anything you like, sugar,' Sharlene

said with a husky giggle, 'especially if, like tin, it's hard and lasts a long time.'

Al and Deena stared across at each other like two punch-drunk fighters. How many more shocks were lying in wait?

'You said Hugh's father was dead.' They were facing each other in the busy Cornmarket. '*Dead.* Now why the fuck would you lie about a thing like that?'

As he waited for an answer his brain was teeming with the knowledge that Zac and Clint had been peddling drugs in Oxford. It was a can of worms nearly equal to the Lulu–Ritchie can of worms. Except that he was certain Ritchie hadn't killed Lulu, whereas two young London drug-dealers by the name of Zac and Clint could be none other than his step-nephews.

'I didn't lie. Not really . . .' She looked ill, her skin so pale against her blue-black hair, he thought she was going to pass out.

He caught hold of her arm and she near-collapsed against him. Swiftly he moved his arm so that it was around her waist and he was taking her weight. What now? Even if he could get her down the Corn Dolly's stairs, he'd no desire for another confrontation with Hugh King's friends. At least, not yet. And he sure as hell didn't want another long session in a café. What he wanted was to get back to London. He wanted to be on Zac and Clint's case – and Tommy's – and with a vengeance. Then he was going to tool up and have words with Ginny's former husband.

'Where are we going?' She was still leaning heavily against him as he headed towards the parked Shogun.

'Town.' He knew her car would be parked somewhere nearby, but he'd no intention of wasting time finding out where. He had business in London that wouldn't wait and, as she was in no condition to drive, he was going to load her into the Shogun and hare back down the motorway. She could come back by train tomorrow and pick up her car – or she could have it picked up and driven back to London for her. It wasn't as if she was short of a bob or two.

'We're driving back together,' he said, unlocking the Shogun's passenger-door with his free hand. 'And I want to know where your husband is – and why Hugh looking him up is such a big deal.'

He'd expected her to protest vehemently at the mere idea of returning to London with him, but she didn't. She didn't look as if she had the strength. She looked as wiped out as an accident victim.

He helped her up into the Shogun's high front seat and strode round to the driver's door. Zac and Clint's involvement in this mess was a mega pig's ear, but at least the scenario where Fleur was concerned was looking less sinister. She had either gone with Hugh to visit his old man because Hugh King owed drug money to the twins – and consequently to Fat Pat – and needed to lie low somewhere, or they were visiting him for the mere hell of it. Either way, all he had to do was to go and get her.

'So . . .' he said with what he thought was saintly patience as he slammed the Shogun into gear and drew away from the kerb. 'What about answering a few questions, *Miss* King. Why tell me Mr King is dead when he isn't? I take it the two of you are divorced and not on friendly terms? And do you have a phone number for him? Where does he live? How long will it take to get there?'

Deena felt so queasy she thought she was going to throw up. How much did she tell? How much of it was relevant? Hugh hadn't a valid passport. He *couldn't* have gone to visit Jimmy. But if Jimmy was in England . . . If Jimmy was in England where would he be? Oxford? London? And why had he contacted Hugh? It had to have been that way round. Hugh couldn't possibly have contacted him. He simply wouldn't have known where to start.

'When I said that Hugh's father was dead, I meant that he might as well be,' she said as they began speeding out to the city ring road.

Her mouth was so dry that speaking was difficult. 'Hugh doesn't know him. Jimmy and I . . . separated . . . before he was born.'

'And his phone number? Does this mean you don't have one?' The prospect of being reunited with Fleur within hours was fading fast. He overtook a bus, wondering why the hell things couldn't be simple just for once.

'No.' How had Jimmy known how to contact Hugh? Had he been keeping tabs on her all these years? As she, to a certain extent, had kept tabs on him?

'And no likely address either?'

She shot him a swift look, suddenly aware that if there had been one he would probably have driven straight there. 'No,' she said. 'No address. None whatsoever.'

He swung off a roundabout and on to dual carriageway.

'Then it's going to have to be the cozzers,' he said, not intending to go to them in a million years, but curious whether the prospect would jog her memory.

'No.' There was something odd in her voice. 'No. We can't do that.'

'Why?' he asked, suddenly as tense as he'd been in the Corn Dolly.

'Because . . .' She paused. It was a pause so deep the Eiffel Tower could have been dropped in it. 'Because I've told the police what I told you,' she said, beginning to have some idea of how her clients must feel under interrogation. 'I told them Hugh's father was dead.'

For the second time that week he nearly drove the Shogun off the road.

'You did *what*?' he swerved away from the pavement, missing the curb by a hair's breadth. 'How could you lie to the police? You're a silk, for Christ's sake! You're a fucking member of the fucking judiciary!'

'Silks are not members of the judiciary.' Lines of strain etched her mouth. 'Judiciary means pertaining to judgement: judges or courts of law. I'm a barrister. Barristers don't judge. They simply make a case so that others can make a judgement on it.'

'Don't come the high-handed school-teacher with me, lady! If you've *lied* to the *police,* you'd lie in the dock! Which means you're no better, and no different, than me and mine!'

Hardly able to believe the sheer, bloody hypocrisy of it, he took a corner so fast the tyres squealed.

'So what do we do?' he rasped when he'd straightened the jeep, knowing he had to curb his fury; knowing he had to focus on what really mattered. 'Ring every King in every phone-book there is?'

Aware that even if he did, it wouldn't help a jot, she didn't answer him. He, too, had been pole-axed with shock in the Corn Dolly – and she knew when the shock had hit him. It had been when the names of the two London drug-dealers had been mentioned.

'You know this Zac and Clint, don't you?' she asked, glad to be able to change the subject. 'Will you be able to track them down? Speak to them . . . ?' Unsaid was the thought that if Hugh had been buying drugs from them, he might still be in contact with them and they would know where he and Fleur were.

'Oh, I'll be able to track them down,' Al said with heavy irony. 'Believe you me, that's going to be no problem. And if you're thinking they may know where Hugh is, so am I – and I'll be finding out if they do or not, pretty damn quick.'

They fell silent, occupied with thoughts they weren't willing to share. Not until they were entering London did Deena say: 'I live in Bloomsbury, remember? This way is going to bring us out near the river.'

'Which is where we're going.' He glanced in the rear-view mirror, checking the traffic behind him before changing lanes. 'I haven't time to arse about dropping you off on your doorstep. We're going to my brother's.'

'Which one?' Deena's voice was acid enough to corrode paint. 'Stuart the gellyman? Kevin the heavy? Or Tommy the turd *par excellence*?'

'You've got a nasty mouth, anyone ever tell you?'

She was so pleased she'd got him on the raw, she almost smiled.

He headed for the City and Tower Bridge. She wondered what slovenly hell-hole they were making for. From what she'd seen of Tommy, it was quite possibly going to be a high-rise flat full of cigarette-smoke, cans of lager and Rottweilers. Well aware that she could simply demand he let her out then and there, she didn't. If he was able to track down the drug-dealers Hugh had had dealings with, then she was going to stick to him come hell or high water.

Doing so turned out to be harder than she had thought.

'My sister-in-law, Ginny,' he said, leading the way into

a spacious, pin-neat Edwardian terrace-house. 'Ginny – Deena.'

Ginny, who had caught a glimpse of Deena in The Drum, smiled welcomingly. No one had enlightened her as to who Deena was, whether she was a part of Al's business life or a new love interest. She was hoping she was the new love interest. In her book, Sharlene was far too young for a man in his mid-forties. Deena, who she judged to be in her early to mid-thirties, was a much more suitable age. She also oozed style. She didn't look well, though. She wondered whether Deena was in some kind of trouble and if Al was helping to get her out of it.

'Would you like a cup of tea?' she asked her, knowing she didn't need to bother asking Al. Al, like Stuart, was always ready for a cuppa.

As she went off to the kitchen and as Al followed her, Deena looked around the room. Apart from the oversized television it wasn't at all as she had expected. There were framed prints of ballet scenes on one wall, several well-filled bookshelves, and the dog that ran to greet them wasn't a Rottweiler. It was a Pekinese.

Nor was Ginny as she had imagined. Wearing an olive-green twinset and beige pleated skirt, she looked more like a respectable Women's Institute member than a woman married to a career criminal.

She crossed to the bookshelves, her attention caught by a photograph propped on them, not hearing Al say to Ginny: 'Where are Zac and Clint, Gin? I need to meet up with them sharpish.'

'They'll be with Tommy. They're always with Tommy these days. Deena looks nice, Al. She's a bit pale, though. Is she not very well?'

She was fishing to find out who Deena was, and he knew it. Now, though, was not the time to tell her. It would take too long to cope with her reaction. And as Stuart quite obviously hadn't yet told her the kind of errands Zac and Clint were running for her ex, he wasn't going to say anything about them, either. Not when Stuart wasn't there.

'Wherever Tommy and the boys are, they won't be at The Maid,' she said, not too put out by his ignoring her question. In Al's world there were often times when just who a person was, or what they did, was never fully stated. 'Not till this business about Lulu is sorted,' she added. 'You know Barney's been arrested, don't you? It's a wicked thing to say, but I can't help hoping it *was* Barney that killed her. That way the police won't be looking for someone else to pin it on. I'm terrified that once they know she was Ritchie's girlfriend they'll fit him up for it. And I just wish I'd *known* she was his girlfriend.'

She was obviously all set for a long heart-to-heart, but, with the best will in the world, he didn't have time to listen.

'No tea for me,' he said, resting a hand affectionately on her shoulder. 'I'm going to leave Deena here while I catch up with Zac and Clint. With luck, I won't be long.'

He left the house via the rear door. Ginny took a deep, steadying breath, too concerned as to what would happen to Ritchie if Barney was released without being charged, to wonder why Al wanted a word with the twins.

'Would you like a slice of cake, Deena?' she asked as she walked back into the sitting-room. 'There's banana-cake or walnut-cake. Or have we to forget about our figures and have both?' Seeing the photograph in Deena's hand, she smiled. 'That's Fleur. She's a pretty girl, isn't she? She lived here for a long time when she was younger and Al was away. She could be quite a little madam – being as stubborn as a mule is a Virtue trait – but she was such a winning little thing it was impossible to be cross with her for long.'

Looking down at the photograph, Deena could well imagine that Fleur Virtue had a strong will. It showed in the set of her chin and in her eyes. It was, though, a likeable face – and a beautiful one. With a tightening of her heart, she understood why Hugh had become infatuated with her.

'Al won't be long,' Ginny continued chattily. 'He's gone to have a word with the twins.'

'He's *what*?'

'He's gone to have a word with the twins,' Ginny repeated as Deena rushed out of the room, heading for the front door.

Seconds later she had yanked it open, just in time to see the Shogun surging away from the curb.

Her fury was so great it was all she could do to stop herself from swearing out loud. How *dare* he go off to track down the two London drug-dealers without her? It was *her* son they were alleged to have sold to! And he'd known she wanted to be with him when he found them!

She stormed back into the sitting-room. 'Who,' she demanded, 'are the twins?'

'My two boys from my first marriage.' Ginny was accustomed to rucks and scenes and was unperturbed by this one. 'Let's go into the kitchen for our tea and cake,' she said, leading the way from the room. 'I like a solid table to sit at. I hate balancing things on my knee. There's a photo of the twins on the fridge door. They're good-looking, but not in the way my other two boys are. Paulie and Ritchie are like all the Virtues. Tall, dark and with smiles to die for. The twins are stockier and much fairer.'

As she carried two steaming mugs of tea across to the kitchen table, Deena looked at the photograph in question. The twins were identical and their mother was right: they didn't have the head-turning good looks of the Virtues.

'Al's always spent a lot of time with all the boys,' Ginny said, 'When they were little he used to take them out on the Thames on their granddad's old sailing barge, *The Mallard*. Al has a *Mallard* of his own now, *The Mallard II*. It's the love of his life. He keeps it pretty much to himself, but when the twins were young he was always taking them – and Fleur too, of course – out on *The Mallard*. The twins had never known anything like it and they loved it, especially Zac.'

Deena put her mug down so sharply the tea slopped over the rim.

'Clint was never as keen on being on the water,' Ginny said, not noticing. 'What Clint loved was the time and attention Al gave him. He wasn't used to it, see? And it wasn't as if Al was his new stepdad. He was only his step-uncle, but treating my kids right from the off as if they were his own nephews is typical of Al. I'd become family and so my kids had become family as well.'

'Clint?' The blood thundered in Deena's ears. 'Did you say the twins' names are Zac and Clint?'

'Yes.' Ginny flashed her an engaging smile. 'I suppose you think their names are a bit naff. I was only seventeen, though, when I had them and at least I didn't call them Hoss or Trampas! Zac was named after Zachary Scott – my dad's favourite film-star cowboy, and Clint was named after Clint Eastwood. I used to be mad for Clint Eastwood's Westerns.'

She chuckled at the silliness of it, but Deena didn't chuckle with her. The breath was so tight in her chest she could scarcely breathe. No wonder Al had said he'd have no trouble in tracking the London cowboys down – and no wonder he hadn't taken her with him. They were his family, for Christ's sake!

She pressed her fingers to her temples, trying to think what this latest revelation could mean. Al hadn't known his step-nephews were part of Oxford's drug scene. However good an actor he might be, he wasn't that good. She'd seen his reaction when Giles Gargrave had proffered Zac and Clint's names, and his shock had been as deep as her own when Gargrave had told her that Hugh had been in contact with Jimmy.

So . . . now that he did know, at least he'd be able to find out if Hugh had bought drugs from them. Soft drugs, of course. Anything else was inconceivable. As inconceivable as his having been in any way involved in the tragedy of Amabel Lyndhurst's death. Whoever had sold Amabel the cocaine she had OD'd on, it hadn't been Hugh. It *couldn't* have been Hugh. It could, though, have been Zac and Clint.

That she would be giving their names to the police went without saying. She wasn't going to do so yet, however; not until she knew for sure that there was no risk to Hugh.

The thought that there might be was so horrendous she clamped down on it immediately. She had to look on the positive side. Hugh had to have vanished from sight because Jimmy had contacted him and suggested they spend some time together. It was a scenario almost impossible to believe, but at least it was preferable – just – to a scenario in which he was responsible for a girl's death.

At least there was one mercy to be grateful for. Hugh wasn't visiting Jimmy at his home. He couldn't be. Not when he wasn't in possession of an up-to-date passport. The realisation brought with it relief so intense she felt giddy. If there'd been any chance, any chance at all, that Hugh was visiting Jimmy in Colombia, then the situation would no longer be deeply disturbing; it would be a full-scale nightmare.

'*Out!*' Al bellowed at the half-dozen youths loitering around the pool-table Zac and Clint were playing on.

It wasn't a command he had to utter twice.

'Christ, Uncle Al! What's the matter?' Zac Docherty affected a nonchalant stance, but the nonchalance didn't extend to his eyes.

Al could see Zac knew what the matter was – and that Clint knew also.

'You two fuckers have been going behind my back – dealing drugs for your wanker of an old man!'

'No, we ain't.' Still with his pool cue in his hand, Clint was trying to sound off-hand about the allegation, and failing big-time. 'And if anyone's been saying we have, they're way out of order . . .'

'*Shut it!*' Al had no intention of arguing the toss or giving them a lesson – that was for later, when he had more time. What he wanted now was information – and he wanted it fast. 'You've been selling in Oxford,' he said, continuing to eyeball Zac. 'And I want some gen on one of your punters, Hugh King . . .'

'Punters don't give us their fucking names!' The speaker, as before, was Clint.

Al ignored him. 'Hugh King is missing and what I need to know from you is: did he owe you money, and were you on his case for it?'

Several reactions flashed through Zac's eyes. First was relief that his uncle's interest didn't seem to be so much in their drug-dealing as in who they'd been dealing drugs to. Second was bewilderment as to why Al should have any interest in their punters. Third was indecision about whether to keep him sweet or to stay shtum.

Al took a menacing step towards him and he decided to try and keep him sweet.

'I think I know the geezer you mean,' he said, trying to sound far cooler than he felt. 'He's a student. Looks a bit like a pikey. Dark hair, dark eyes. Thinks a lot of himself.'

That Hugh King could be mistaken for a gypsy was so surprising it almost put Al off his stroke. 'And what did he buy?' he asked, remembering how dark-haired Deena was. It didn't make her look like a pikey, though.

'Christ knows. Could have been marijuana and cocaine. Could have just been marijuana. All I know is, he doesn't owe for anything. Not like some of the dons . . .'

Al wasn't interested in the dons. If Hugh King didn't owe money, then that wasn't the reason he'd dropped from sight. He'd most likely simply gone to visit his dad. And his dad couldn't be that hard to find.

The temptation to head straight back to Bermondsey so that he could pick up Deena and start hunting her ex-husband down immediately was overpowering. He subdued it, though, aware there was still unfinished business.

'Amabel Lyndhurst,' he said. 'Was she buying off people you sold to, or was she buying off you direct?'

'Never heard of her.' It was Clint again, cocky as usual. 'But if she was Oxford and she had cocaine, it'd be our gear. Which should be no problem to you. We know how paranoid you are about drugs, so we don't push near home . . .'

Al was on him so fast Clint barely had time to register surprise – or fear.

'*I'll* tell you what it is to me – and what it's likely to be to you, you stupid fucker!'

He had Clint pinned across the pool-table, the pool cue hard across his throat.

'She OD'd and died! And the only reason you didn't read about it in the papers is because her dad's in the government and the investigation is undercover! How the fuck the cozzers haven't caught up with you two yet, beats me, but they will!'

Clint stopped struggling.

Zac said, 'It's a wind-up. It has to be. We'd have heard, and nothing's been said . . .'

Al eased his weight off Clint and brushed pool-chalk from his jacket sleeves. 'It isn't a wind-up,' he said, aware he should be thrashing the life out of both of them but he couldn't afford the time. 'You're in deep shit, both of you. And you soddin' well deserve to be.'

He turned away from them, sick to the stomach at their lack of loyalty and their total disregard as to their mother's feelings.

'But how did you get to know?' Zac was a judicious pace or two behind him. 'Why've you been in Oxford? Why are you interested in this Hugh geezer? I don't get it.'

Al paused at the open door leading from the pool-room, and turned to face him. 'Fleur's missing, remember? And as she goes to Oxford University she lives in Oxford, so that's where I've been. And Hugh King is her boyfriend!'

'Christ, Al!' Zac blanched. 'How were we to know? And what does he say about where Fleur might be? If he's her boyfriend he must . . .'

'He's missing as well.'

This time Zac didn't merely blanch. He went white. 'And you thought he might be missing because he owes

238

dosh to Fat Pat and we were on his case for it? Well, we ain't!'

'Good. I'm pleased to hear it.' He was, as well.

'The less trouble he's in, the less there'll be ricocheting on to Fleur,' he said, looking at them through narrowed eyes. 'You two, though . . . you two are in big trouble. Undercover investigations go on for months. You'd better warn your dad – and I don't mean your stepdad. I mean the wanker you rate higher than the bloke who's loved and cared for you since you were nippers.'

'Guilt trip. Guilt trip,' Clint said through his teeth and from what he judged to be a safe distance.

'You're wrong about Hugh King being clear of trouble.'

The speaker was Zac. Al had been walking away from him, but he stopped instantly. 'Just what,' he asked, spinning round to face him, 'do you fucking mean?'

Zac shrugged. 'He wanted a favour. Wanted the name of someone who could do something a bit specialised.'

'And you gave him a name?' Even as he asked the question, Al knew what the answer was going to be.

'Sure I did. For a consideration.' The gleam in Zac's eyes was malicious. 'I put him on to Tommy.'

The pulse at the corner of Al's jaw began to throb. 'And did Tommy tell you what the favour was?'

Zac grinned. 'Yeah, he did, as it goes. Fleur's bloke wanted a hookey passport. Christ knows why. It ain't as if he's an armed bank robber on the trot, is it?'

Chapter Sixteen

Deena paid off the cab that had brought her home, deeply grateful not to find Benedict on her door-step. She needed some time alone; some time in which to think.

There were six messages on her answerphone. She didn't play them back. They could wait. It was still only early evening, but it seemed an eternity since she had driven away that morning heading for Oxford, and she was bone-weary. What she needed was a cup of decent tea. She had drunk gallons of tea whilst at Ginny Virtue's, but it hadn't been Earl Grey.

She plugged the kettle in, refusing to allow herself to think, just yet, of the horror of Jimmy having contacted Hugh or, even worse, of Hugh not having told her that Jimmy had done so — and of his agreeing to meet with him. Other whys and wherefores came so thick and fast it took her all her considerable self-control not to begin dwelling on them then and there.

She scooped a caddy-spoon of tea into a warmed teapot and forced herself to think, instead, about the enigma that was Ginny Virtue.

She'd liked Ginny. There'd been something deeply genuine about her — especially in her concern for her family. As one hour had turned into two, and then three, and Al still hadn't returned, Ginny had confided her fears where her youngest son was concerned.

'We didn't even know Ritchie was seeing Lulu,' she'd said, making another two mugs of tea with tea-bags. 'That was on account of her dad, you see. Apparently she was terrified that if word got round she was seeing Ritchie, it would get back to her dad and then he'd have stopped her working at The Maid.' She'd shaken her head in genuine bewilderment. 'It's a shame, but you know how it is with families like ours. People get paranoid. Just because Ritchie's dad and uncles have a bit of form, people like Lulu's dad think we're a firm of gangsters. It's a liberty really . . .'

She'd been so taken aback at the rose-coloured view Ginny had of the family she'd married into – and at being spoken to as if she were part of that family – that she hadn't set her right. Only now, as she waited for the kettle to boil, did she realise why Ginny was speaking to her with such frankness. Ginny had assumed her to be one of Al's girlfriends.

The realisation was so preposterous she didn't know whether to laugh or to cry. It explained, though, why Ginny had confided in her with regard to Ritchie and Beryl Keene.

'She was found by the railway line the morning after Tommy's acquittal party,' Ginny had said with obvious distress. 'I'm surprised you haven't read about it in the paper, Deena. Of course, it didn't give her name as Lulu. It gave her proper name, Beryl. Beryl Keene. It said she'd been strangled, but we knew that anyway because one of the coppers who does favours for Al rang Max and told him so.'

Deena poured boiling water into the teapot. From the sound of it, the policeman in question wasn't as high-ranking as the Met officer who had confirmed for Al that Amabel Lyndhurst had died of a drug overdose.

That meant Al Virtue had at least two bent coppers in his pocket – and possibly more.

'It's all a lot of worry for Al, of course, as well as for us,' Ginny had said, 'because once the cozzers get to know Lulu was seeing Ritchie, they're bound to stitch him up for it . . . Which is just ridiculous, because my Ritchie is like his dad – he'd never lose his temper with a woman, not in a million years.'

The knowledge that the information Ginny was so artlessly giving her was information she would have to pass on to the police was not pleasant. It made her feel like a spy. It simply hadn't occurred to her that in not explaining to Ginny at the outset who she was and why she was with Al, an exploitative situation was being created.

She waited for the tea to infuse. If Ritchie was innocent of Beryl Keene's murder, with luck, no harm would come of his being questioned. His half-brothers, though, were a different matter. Once she was sure there would be no repercussions where Hugh was concerned, she was going to have to inform the Thames Valley Police about Zac and Clint's drug-dealing activities.

She poured the tea into a wafer-thin teacup and added a slice of lemon. It would be the end of any friendly relations between herself and Ginny, but then, what kind of future relations was she anticipating, for God's sake? It wasn't as if they would be regularly meeting for morning coffee at Harrods.

She carried her cup and saucer through into her sitting-room and pressed the play-back button on her answerphone.

'Mungo, here,' her Head of Chambers said in his dry, crackly voice. 'I understand you're going to be absent from chambers for several days – possibly longer. More details would be appreciated, Deena, if you please.'

'Cheryl,' Cheryl said crisply. 'I've passed all your messages on to Mr Deakin, but he doesn't seem too happy about things. Milton Darcus is covering for you on briefs outstanding, so there's no cause for panic. Hope all's well.'

'Inspector Rose, Ms King. I've received a report from Thames Valley Police and they deem there aren't enough suspicious circumstances connected with your son's disappearance to warrant a full-scale investigation. He will continue, of course, to be logged as a missing person, and we will keep you updated on any information that is received.'

'Hi, darling,' Benedict said, sounding suspiciously as if he'd been drinking. 'Just thought I'd leave a few welcoming words for when you potter back from Oxford. As I mentioned when we spoke earlier, I'm out on the town tonight. I'll see you some time tomorrow, though, to make up for these few days of not being together.'

'Hello, Deena,' Rupert said in mellifluous tones. 'I was wondering if you had any further news of Hugh? Please keep me informed as I am, of course, most concerned. If there's any way in which I can be of help, don't hesitate to let me know.'

'Al here. I've spoken to the London cowboys and Hugh was buying from them. He didn't owe, though. If he's a student, where did he get the money? Was it from you?'

It clicked off.

She stood for a few seconds, her eyes closed, her lips pressed tight. A few days ago, the idea of Hugh having dealings of any kind with members of Al Virtue's extended family – let alone criminal dealings – would have been enough to have given her a heart attack. Now, incredibly, it wasn't her main anxiety. Her main anxiety was the kind of drugs Hugh had bought from Al's step-nephews. Had it been cocaine? And had he then sold or given some of that cocaine to Amabel Lyndhurst?

The knowledge that if he had, Al Virtue's assumption was correct and he had done it with money she had provided, overwhelmed her.

Hugh was very money-conscious. No way would he have merely subsisted whilst at Oxford – and there had been no reason why he should have. She earned an astronomically high income and, as a single parent, her life revolved around Hugh. Naturally, she had provided him with money. Why shouldn't she, when she had never had the slightest reason to suspect that he had been spending a sizeable proportion of it on drugs?

She opened her eyes, feeling both sick and dizzy. Was his having bought drugs and Jimmy having contacted him for the first time ever just hideous coincidence? Whatever, it certainly wasn't an avenue of investigation she could hand to Rose or Fallon – nor could she speak of it to Rupert.

With legs like candyfloss she sat down. One thing was certain, the Foreign Office would be familiar with the name of one of Colombia's oldest and most influential families.

'The Noguerras are directly descended from Colombia's first wave of settlers,' Jimmy had often said to her with pride, showing her photographs of a *hacienda* of enormous proportions set against a background of jagged, smoke-blue mountains. 'We come from the Basque region of Spain. We were aristocrats when your father's family were Elizabethan peasants.'

She had been amused, only half believing him, not caring if what he said was true or not. It hadn't mattered to her what his family were. All that had mattered was that she loved him and always would.

It had mattered to Jimmy, though. It had mattered to Jimmy in ways she had never dreamt of.

'But of course I will marry my second cousin,' he had said quite matter-of-factly when she had told him that he couldn't, that she was expecting a baby – his baby. 'For over three hundred years my family have kept a pure Spanish bloodline. Do you know how few families in Colombia can claim that? None of them. But we Noguerras can, for if a Noguerra intermarried with an Indian, he was no longer regarded as a Noguerra. A line was scored through his name in the family bible and it was as if he had never existed. And so, my beautiful, most precious Deena, I love you with all my heart, but I will marry my cousin.'

It had all been so archaic that at first she hadn't believed him; she had actually laughed, thinking he was teasing her. He hadn't been teasing. And he hadn't completed his studies at Trinity. His father had died and he had returned to Colombia, vowing he would love her for ever.

Her hands clenched. She had been four months pregnant and he hadn't even written.

She'd managed. She'd changed her name by deed-poll, and as far as her parents – and anyone else – were concerned, she'd married whilst at college and, as it had been a mistake of monumental proportions, had been divorced almost immediately. She hadn't let Hugh's birth hinder the obtaining of her law degree. She'd had family money to cushion her in the early years and her own, more than adequate income, in later years.

She hadn't fallen in love again because she no longer believed in love. She'd enjoyed reasonably satisfying affairs and, when they had ceased to be reasonably satisfying, had terminated them without a second thought. Her affair with Benedict had lasted longer than most, but she knew by her indifference to his latest telephone message that it was fast heading for the rocks.

Alone – as in so many respects she had always been alone – she sat in her expensively furnished sitting-room and wondered why, after all these years, Jimmy had thrust himself into her life again. Her knuckles clenched even tighter. She was being grossly inaccurate. He hadn't thrust himself into her life. Why should he? He couldn't care less about her. It was Hugh's life he had thrust himself into. And Hugh had allowed it.

It didn't surprise her, of course, that Jimmy knew they'd had a son and that he had known where to contact him. With the kind of money Jimmy had at his command, keeping track of an illegitimate offspring was child's play.

And she had kept track of him, too. How could she not, when the name 'Noguerra' had become synonymous with that of Colombia's leading drug cartel?

That Hugh's father was one of the major wheelers and dealers behind his country's cocaine trade was a skeleton buried so deep in her cupboard she had scarcely acknowledged it even to herself. Certainly Hugh hadn't known. Hugh hadn't even known that his father was Colombian.

He would know now, though.

The thought was so appalling she began to tremble.

Was that why he hadn't contacted her and had drop-ped out of sight? She hugged her arms to her, trying to control her rising panic. Hugh had always been an undemonstrative child. He had always kept his thoughts and feelings to himself. Was he now going to cut himself off because the revelation of his Colombian paternity was so unacceptable to him it had catastrophically altered the way he felt about her? And if that was the case, what would be his reaction when he knew just what the name Noguerra signified?

She looked towards the telephone, wishing to God there was someone she could ring; someone she could confide in. There wasn't. Bearing in mind her social circle and her profession, there never would be. She simply didn't have friends so close that they would take such a revelation about Hugh's paternity in their stride. She didn't have friends – real friends – period. She hadn't had friends since Jimmy had destroyed her ability to trust people. All she had were acquaintances – and the occasional lover.

And Al Virtue.

She wondered how much she was going to tell Al Virtue.

She wondered why he hadn't returned to Ginny's after his meeting with the twins.

And she wondered where he was now.

Al shouldered his way into the crowded North London pub, certain he would find Tommy at the bar. Whether he would find Fat Pat with him, he didn't know, and didn't care.

It wasn't a pub he ever drank in, but that didn't bother him either. The people in it knew who he was – knew he and Tommy were brothers – and a fight between brothers wasn't a fight they would pitch in on. And there was going to be a fight. Of that he hadn't a minute's doubt.

'Play games somewhere else, short-arse,' someone said to someone else as he squeezed past them. 'I'm busy.'

'Make up your friggin' mind, gel!' someone was saying in exasperation to the woman they were with, a few feet further on.

There was laughter; thick cigarette-smoke; and Tommy seated at the bar. He was perched on a high stool, a jacket over his shoulder, a cigarette between his fingers.

As Al approached him and their eyes met, Tommy's

eyebrows lifted. 'Christ, Al! What are you doin' this side of the water?' He gave a lopsided grin. 'Have things got so tricky at The Maid that Max has shut up shop?'

There was no answering grin on Al's face. His eyes were like chips of ice. 'I know who you've been running with, you fucker,' he said through clenched teeth. 'Who you're still running with.'

The expression on Tommy's face changed instantly and Al knew that his brother had been anticipating this moment for days – possibly weeks.

'What is this? What the fuck are you on about?' Though he was trying to sound bewildered, there was no bewilderment in Tommy's eyes. That he knew the game was up was obvious. All he was doing was stalling for time.

'The lorry hijacks you were collared for were set up by Fat Pat Docherty, weren't they? Only it wasn't Fat Pat who got you off the hook for them, was it?' Al's eyes glittered with venom. '*I* was the mug who did that! If it wasn't for me, you'd be in the boob now, not sitting on a fucking bar-stool!'

Tommy shrugged, giving up any attempt to front it out, knowing that where he and Al were concerned, his number was up.

'So?' he said indifferently. 'What else did you expect me to do? You haven't sorted a job we could do as a family for months – and you haven't sorted a worthwhile job for years – not since you went down for handling. And how old was I then? I was a *kid*. I didn't even get a sniff of that job! You and Stuart and Kevin did all right out of it, but I bleedin' didn't! And neither did the twins! So, fuckin' right we're doin' business elsewhere – and if you have a problem with that, it's just too fucking bad.'

'Oh, I have a problem with it, all right.' Al moved so close to him that everyone standing nearby stepped back. 'And you and the twins are going to have a problem with it, as well.'

Tommy's eyes were instantly wary. 'Oh yeah? What kind of problem?'

'Lorry hijacks are the chicken-feed end of Fat Pat's interests, aren't they? Drugs are what Pat is about.' Al spat the words, not caring who was within ear-shot; knowing that as it was a villain's pub, it didn't matter. 'And even though you know how the rest of the family feel about drug-dealing, you're in there up to your neck, aren't you? And you haven't gone alone. You've taken the twins with you. How do you think Ginny's going to feel when she knows Zac and Clint are peddling? What do you think her reaction's going to be?'

He paused to give his next bombshell maximum effect.

'Especially now one of their punters in Oxford has OD'd,' he said, his lips thin against his teeth. 'Just as Billy OD'd.'

'Rubbish.' Tommy crushed his cigarette out. 'Anything like that, we'd have heard, and there hasn't been a whisper.'

'There hasn't been a whisper because the girl who died was the daughter of a government minister! There's an investigation going on, though. My guess is the cozzers have known for weeks where the cocaine came from that killed her and they haven't made a move because they want to nail people further up the chain. They don't just want petty buyers and the twins. They want Fat Pat. I'd put good money on the entire organisation being under observation right now – and that includes you, Tommy. Not a nice thought, is it? Especially as I

249

won't be doing my big-brother-riding-to-the-rescue act for you. What do you think you'll get if you take a fall for Amabel Lyndhurst's death? Eight years? Ten? A life sentence?'

'I don't fucking believe you!' Tommy was off his barstool now, his eyes on the half-open pub door as if he expected a squad of plain-clothes cozzers to come bursting through it at any minute.

'You'd better believe me – and you'd better give a straight answer to what I'm going to ask you.' The muscles in Al's arms and shoulders were tense as he fought the temptation to let rip at Tommy then and there. 'Zac and Clint sold to an undergraduate by the name of Hugh King,' he said, cobra-eyed. 'He wanted a favour. A hookey passport. And they put him on to you.'

There was a pause. A long pause.

'I want to know if you met up with him, Tommy. I want to know *why* he wanted a hookey passport. I want to know if you arranged one and, if you did, *I want to know the name he's now travelling under!*'

'And what will you do if I don't soddin' well choose to tell you?'

It was the petulant defiance of a kid brother to an older brother.

Al, mindful of how deeply Fleur could be embroiled in whatever it was Hugh King was up to, didn't hesitate.

He drove his right fist into Tommy's face, lifting his shoulder and all his weight into the blow.

As he had anticipated, no one came to Tommy's aid. The people who had been standing nearby and who had already stepped away from them once, simply moved sharpishly even further away.

Tommy held on to the bar, his hand trembling uncontrollably on his mouth, his eyes dilated with shock, his fingers shining with blood and bits of teeth.

'Now,' Al snarled. '*What name is Hugh King travelling under – and where has he gone, and why?*'

Chapter Seventeen

Deena was fresh out of the bath when the doorbell rang. Wearing a white towelling bathrobe and with her damp hair scooped high by a tortoisehell clutch-comb, she opened the door, half-expecting it to be Benedict. It wasn't. It was Al.

It was nine-thirty and dark and at first she didn't see the blood.

Not until he stepped into the light of the hallway did she realise the condition he was in. A deep bleeding gash ran from his left eyebrow to his cheekbone. The hand holding the blood-sodden bar-towel he was staunching it with was raked by what looked to be razor-cuts. Blood was dripping from his mouth on to his jacket. His upper lip and his right eye were swelling with almost visible speed.

'My God!' she gasped as he swayed unsteadily. 'What happened?'

He didn't answer. Appalled, realising he was even more hurt than he appeared to be, she took hold of his arm, intent on getting him to a chair before he fell.

'Who did this to you? Was it the twins? Should I call the police?'

'For fuck's sake, Deena . . .' His voice was thick as the blood continued to pump from the corner of his mouth; it was also utterly exasperated at the idiocy of her last question.

Later, she, too, realised something. She realised that it was then he began calling her by her Christian name.

'You need a doctor,' she said urgently as, en route to her living-room, he leaned heavily against the newel-post at the foot of her stairs. 'Those cuts need stitches. Can you hold on here while I go for my car? We can be at University College Hospital in five minutes, maybe less.'

'No.' He shook his head. 'I need a shower. Then we'll see.'

Something in his voice prevented her from arguing. He began climbing the stairs and she went with him, not letting go of his arm, giving him what support she could.

'Who did this?' she said again. 'I thought the twins were your *nephews,* for God's sake!'

'It wasn't the twins.' They were at the top of the stairs now and he rocked back on his heels. 'It was Tommy.'

She opened her bathroom door and in its clinically white interior and beneath its strip lighting, the blood on his face and hands and clothes looked more nightmarish than ever.

She didn't have to ask 'Tommy who?'

'But he's your brother!' She remembered the photographs that had been plastered in all the newspapers only a few short days ago. The ones of Al with his arm round Tommy's shoulder as they euphorically celebrated Tommy's acquittal.

'Yeah.' Al dropped the saturated bar-towel into the handbasin and, as blood still oozed and dripped, began easing his arms out of his jacket.

Deena turned the shower on, aware that her shower cubicle was soon going to resemble the one in Alfred Hitchcock's *Psycho.*

'The twins are peddling drugs for a bloke called Fat Pat,' he said as she lifted the jacket from his shoulders.

'And so is Tommy. He needed showing how I felt about that.' He pulled his black polo-neck sweater over his head and let it drop to the floor. 'And I did. One punch, but one that counted.'

He eased his feet out of his shoes and, sitting on the edge of the bath, took off his socks. Everything he touched, shoes, socks, the bath-edge, was smeared with blood from the cuts on his hands and the blood still dripping from his face.

'It was what he'd have expected from me and for what he'd done – is still doing – it was pretty small beer.'

He stood up. Now he was no longer holding a bar-towel to the wound slicing from eyebrow to cheekbone she could see just how deep and ugly it was. It needed stitching. It needed stitching fast.

'When I'd made my point, he gave me some info I was after. Then I turned my back on him and walked out of the pub. Or I was going to walk out of the pub . . .'

He leaned over the handbasin, spitting gobbets of blood from his split lip into the sink.

She stood, watching him, wishing to God he'd get under the shower so that he could see his injuries clearly and agree to her taking him to UCH Casualty. Broad-shouldered and muscular in his clothes, he looked even more impressively built without them, his skin lightly tanned, a dimple in both shoulders.

'He came for me.' As he stood up, looking into the mirror at the wound above his eye, there was incredulity in his voice and disbelief in his eyes. 'He came at me from the back with a razor.'

She said nothing. She couldn't. She felt too sick.

He turned away from the handbasin, his face once again granite-hard and expressionless.

'One thing you need to know,' he said as he began

unbuckling his trouser belt. 'Hugh did buy from the twins, but whether he bought cocaine as well as marijuana they weren't saying. He wasn't buying on credit, though. He doesn't owe money.'

He dropped his trousers to the floor and it occurred to her that if she wasn't to see him stark naked, she needed to make a speedy exit.

'Then Hugh isn't in hiding?' She moved towards the door, her relief that there was still a chance he'd had nothing to do with Class A drugs, enormous.

Al's boxer shorts dropped beside his trousers. 'He doesn't owe money for drugs,' he said, stepping into the shower cubicle, wincing as the jets of hot water hit his cut and gouged flesh. 'But that doesn't mean he isn't in hiding.'

She paused, staring at him, deeply impressed. Then she raised her eyes. 'Why not?'

'Because he asked the twins if they knew of someone who could do a favour for him. That's why I went to see Tommy. He was the one who obliged.'

His voice was now nearly as exhausted as his battered and bruised body.

She didn't care. 'What favour?' she asked, no longer aware of his nakedness; no longer caring that her bath-room looked as if someone had cut their throat in it.

'A hookey passport,' he said, lifting his face up to the shower-head as water, foaming and pink with blood, swirled around his feet. 'But Tommy didn't know why he'd want one. I can't fucking think of a reason – not one that's legit. So it's down to you. Where would he be going that he didn't want anyone to know about? And think hard, Deena. Because wherever it is, he's taken my daughter with him.'

*　　*　　*

Thanks to the shower-jets he neither saw, nor heard, her reaction. Somehow she propelled herself through the open door and down the stairs. Until now she had been certain that, no matter how bizarre Hugh's meeting with his father had been, at least he was still in the country.

But he wasn't.

He was in Colombia.

There could be no other explanation.

Her hand shook as she poured herself a drink, the decanter clattering against the rim of her glass. She should have realised, right from the beginning, that Jimmy would never risk his own security by travelling to Europe. He would be too vulnerable to arrest by any one of half a dozen international drug enforcement agencies.

Why, though, had Hugh travelled to meet him using a false passport? Had it been his idea, or had it been Jimmy's? Had Hugh hoped that, if he travelled under another name, she would never find out that he knew his father's identity and had been to Colombia to meet him? Or had Jimmy insisted on the precaution as some kind of protection for himself?

She took a swallow of whisky, every fresh thought worse than the previous one. If Jimmy had insisted on Hugh obtaining a false passport, what on earth had Hugh made of the request? Surely it would have set alarm bells ringing – and ringing deafeningly?

Other, more terrible thoughts came thick and fast. Had Jimmy indicated to Hugh what the name Noguerra signified?

And if he had? If he had – *and Hugh had still gone.*

She stifled a sob, knowing there was no one she could confide in nor go to for help. No one apart from Al. From upstairs the sound of the shower-jets ceased. He would be downstairs in a minute and she had to come to a major decision. Did she tell him the only reason she could think of as to why Hugh had wanted a false passport? Did she tell him about Jimmy?

She took another swig of whisky, her hand so unsteady the glass jarred against her teeth. She had to tell him, she had no moral option; not when his daughter was quite obviously with Hugh in Colombia – house guest of one of the biggest drug-barons in the world.

The door-bell rang and her nerves were so fraught she dropped the glass. As it rolled away from her, trickling liquid, she stepped over it, making a beeline for the door.

The caller was Benedict.

'Hi, sweetheart,' he said, making no move to enter the house, just as she made no move to encourage him to do so. 'I'm just off to hit the bright lights and thought I'd call by to see how you were – and to tell you I'm going to be away for a couple of days. An exhibition in Dublin that I don't want to miss.'

His eyes evaded hers. He wasn't a practised liar and was glad he wasn't standing in her well-lit hall. Not that he was lying *utterly*. 'I have to go to Dublin tomorrow, babe,' Sharlene had said less than an hour ago on one of their many telephone conversations. 'It's a modelling job I've had scheduled for weeks.'

He'd decided to go with her almost immediately.

'Fine, Benedict,' Deena was saying to him distractedly. 'Thank you for calling by and letting me know.'

She was so dazed and disorientated he assumed she'd been asleep.

'Did I wake you?' he asked, and then he saw the man walking downstairs into the hallway behind her. A man dripping wet and naked except for a bathrobe. His bathrobe. Despite the fact that the man was holding

257

a hand-towel to the left side of his face, he recognised him instantly. It would have been impossible not to.

His eyes widened and his jaw dropped.

If Deena was aware of his stupefaction, she gave no sign of it.

'Bye,' she said, closing the door on him as if he were a tradesman.

Benedict blinked, wondered whether he was awake or dreaming, and then, certain he was awake, felt an exceedingly odd kind of euphoria. Deena was two-timing him. In normal circumstances the knowledge would, he was sure, have devastated him. *But she was two-timing him with Al Virtue.*

Which meant Sharlene was off the hook where Virtue was concerned. She would no longer have to be afraid of his reaction if she were to tell him their relationship was over. And when he, Benedict, told her what he'd just seen, he was certain that the relationship *would* be over.

But *Deena* with *Al Virtue*? It was so bizarre as to be funny. Hell, it *was* funny. As he opened his car door he was grinning. You just never knew what people would do – even people you'd been close to.

'Who was that?' Al asked as the front door closed.

'That?' She was still distracted, her head so full of terrible possibilities she could barely think straight. 'It was no one that matters.'

As she followed him into the sitting-room she realised the truth of what she had just said. Whatever had existed between herself and Benedict was now well and truly over. She was in deep, deep distress and where was he? Out partying. In fairness, of course, he didn't know a smidgeon of what was going on, but that was because he hadn't put himself out to know – and because she hadn't turned to him and confided in him as she would have if their relationship had had real depth.

'So why has your son had need of a hookey passport?' Al asked abruptly, lifting the towel away from the deepest of his cuts to see how much blood was still running from it. 'And where is he likely to have gone?'

She sat down on the edge of the sofa. The gouge, that had it been a millimetre further to the right could well have robbed him of sight, was still bleeding darkly, but the journey to University College Hospital would have to wait a few minutes longer. Her legs were so shaky she barely trusted herself to stand on them, let alone drive.

'I don't know,' she lied, 'but there are some things that are relevant. Some things you should know.'

He sat down on the winged-chair opposite her, drops of water glistening on the hairs on his legs, the rapidly reddening towel again to the corner of his eye. 'Such as?' he said.

She took a steadying breath. What she was now going to do was enormously difficult for her. Stupendously difficult. She had never told anyone the truth about the circumstances of Hugh's birth. Not her parents – not Hugh – no one.

'Hugh is illegitimate,' she said, waiting for the world to cave in.

It didn't.

'And?' he said.

'And his father's name wasn't King. I changed my name to King by deed poll.'

He didn't let his stunned surprise show.

'So what *is* his father's name?' he asked, not knowing which was stupefying him most, the realisation that she lived under a near-as-dammit fake persona, or that she'd had a child out of wedlock.

She hesitated and then said: 'Noguerra.'

He looked blank – as she had half expected. Jimmy's name wasn't generally known. He was far too much of a Mr Big for that. His was a name known to governments and organisations such as America's Drug Enforcement Agency – not to the man in the street.

'What kind of a name is Noguerra?' He was frowning. 'Is it Greek? Spanish?'

'Spanish.'

There came the muted sound of a mobile phone ringing.

'It's mine,' he said. 'Get it for me, will you? It's in the bathroom. In my jacket pocket.'

Dry-mouthed she left the room, hurrying up the stairs in order reach it before the caller rang off.

'AV's phone,' she said a second or two later. 'Can I take a message?'

'Is AV there?' a voice she recognised, but couldn't place, asked guardedly.

'Yes.' Even as she spoke she was hurrying back downstairs. 'Just a minute . . .'

'Max?' Al said a few moments later. 'What is it? If it's about Tommy . . .' He broke off, listened, then said, 'OK. If there's another arrest, let me know pronto.' He clicked the phone shut.

'A barmaid at The Maid was murdered a couple of nights ago,' he said briefly. 'It could make things dicey for one of my nephews. Did Ginny tell you?'

She nodded.

He dropped the phone into the pocket of Benedict's bathrobe. 'The cozzers were questioning one of the regulars. That was Max ringing to say the bloke in question has just been released. Which means Ritchie could now be in the frame. Ginny will be frantic with worry.'

Feeling a stab of sympathy for Ginny, Deena rose to her feet. 'Get dressed,' she said decisively, not wanting the conversation to revert to Jimmy again. 'I'm taking you round to Casualty.'

Five minutes later, as they walked to her car, he said, 'No names, no pack-drill when we get there. It's standard procedure for Casualty staff to report fight injuries so that the cozzers can breeze round for a word. We're in and out, understand?'

She understood. What she hadn't fully taken on board was how much they looked to be a couple – though she did when, after he had given a false name, the nurse registering his arrival assumed her to be his wife and next of kin.

She was still fuming when he reappeared from behind the screens, a zig-zag tapestry of stitches decorating the left side of his face.

'Where do I take you?' she asked through gritted teeth.

'Christ knows.'

When they reached the car he sank down heavily in the passenger seat. It wasn't often he felt so knackered, but then, it wasn't often he felt so stressed. He didn't want to go back to Ponderosa. A fight with Sharlene about where he'd been for the last few days and why he hadn't been in touch, wasn't something he had the patience for. Over the last few days Sharlene had shown no concern about Fleur's disappearance and it was affecting the way he felt about her. If, of course, he still felt about her at all – and he wasn't sure that he did.

A return to Stuart and Ginny's place would mean hours of listening to Ginny agonising about what would happen to Ritchie if the cozzers cottoned to the fact that he'd been Lulu's boyfriend. A return to The Maid would mean hours of listening to Max agonising about the high level of police activity The Maid was receiving.

'Your place,' he said. 'We still have things to talk about – or we do when I've had a good kip.'

She put him in her rarely used guest bedroom. Whether he slept well, she didn't know. She certainly didn't sleep well. Possibility after possibility chased through her mind, all of them deeply disturbing.

Had Hugh travelled out to Colombia *knowing* that his father was a leading member of the country's largest drug cartel?

A week ago, she would have dismissed the idea as so ludicrous as to be laughable – but a week ago the idea of his buying drugs from Al Virtue's step-nephews would have also been laughable.

She turned over on to her stomach, pummelling her pillow in the darkness. Half the country smoked marijuana, of course, but Hugh had been buying from people who also peddled cocaine. What if he was also a cocaine user?

She rolled once again on to her back, staring up in the darkness towards the ceiling. Lots of otherwise respectable people were cocaine users. That Hugh was one of them wasn't the worst scenario in the world. What about the other scenario, though? Why was she finding it so easy to believe that, if Jimmy had contacted Hugh, Hugh would have responded? Was it because she knew that if Hugh had sensed that Jimmy had money – real money – he would have been immediately interested in meeting him? And Jaime Noguerra had always had real money.

His obvious wealth had set him apart when they were at Oxford. 'I think the Noguerras are near bloody royalty back home,' a fellow student at St Hilda's had said when she'd let slip how interested in him she was. 'It's the Patinos in Bolivia and the Noguerras in Colombia. Or is it the other way round? Anyway, one family has multi-millions from silver-mining and the other multi-millions from cattle-raising. Whichever it is, Jimmy Noguerra is loaded!'

It hadn't been his wealth, though, that had so attracted her. It had been his looks. Tall and slenderly built, he was olive-skinned and dark-haired with eyes the colour of amber. They were looks that Hugh had inherited – though because Hugh's hair was curly and because he wore it longer than Jimmy had ever worn his, there was a gypsyish aspect to Hugh's dark handsomeness – an aspect she knew he didn't like.

There were other differences, too, between Hugh and Jimmy. Though she was well aware that Hugh had inherited Jimmy's inability to feel deeply for anyone, Jimmy at least had charm. It had shown in his smile and in his engaging manner. Hugh, though he exuded self-confident good-breeding, was charmless. Why that was so had always been a mystery to her – as Hugh, himself, had been.

She turned over yet again, longing for sleep. Her clerk, Cheryl, had told her that children were a often total mystery. She didn't think Fleur was a mystery to Al, though – leastways, not in the way that Hugh was to her.

Thinking about Cheryl prompted thoughts about chambers. She hadn't as yet responded to the messages she had picked up that evening from Mungo Deakin and Cheryl, and she wondered if there were also e-mail messages awaiting her attention.

She got out of bed and padded downstairs to the sitting-room. Her laptop was on the coffee-table with her shoulder-bag. Seconds later she had logged on and was staring in disbelief at the screen. There was a message from Rupert. Her stomach muscles tightened. Why would Rupert be e-mailing her? He'd never done so before and, though he'd expressed concern about Hugh's disappearance, she'd assumed it to have been motivated only by politeness.

> *My dear Deena, If there is still no news of Hugh you must be very perturbed – as, of course, I am. Was there any joy at Oxford? Your intention was to speak to some of Hugh's friends. I must confess I was rather hoping that they would solve the mystery. Please keep me informed as to the present situation. The return e-mail address is absolutely private so no worries on that score. With much affection, Rupert.*

As she double-clicked on the reply button there was a lump in her throat. Rupert was such a dry old stick that it had never occurred to her his affection for her ran deep.

'*Contrary to what we thought, it does look as if Hugh may be abroad,*' she tapped in, responding with uncharacteristic frankness, '*and I will most certainly keep you up to date with things. Love, Deena.*'

When she had sent the message and logged off she knew why she had replied as she had. His message had touched a chord. For a brief few moments it had been as if her father had been alive and showing concern for her. That, she knew, was a pipe-dream. Even if he had been alive, her father wouldn't have been showing concern – nor affection. His lack of warmth towards her had been total – and not compensated for by her mother.

As a child her home life had been cushioned by material comforts -- a good education, riding lessons, tennis lessons, music lessons – but had been devoid of joy. She hadn't been a wanted child and had been made to know it. Then she had met Jimmy and at long last had believed herself to be loved. Only she hadn't been, and the realisation had been painful; so painful she had never fully got over it.

Bleakly she rose to her feet. Thinking about the past was not going to help her to get to sleep. She would take comfort from the fact that her father's old friend had her in his thoughts and, until the morning, she would somehow block Jimmy from her mind.

'So . . .' Al said three hours later as they sat like a married couple over toast and coffee. 'Hugh's father contacted him out of the blue. Hugh told his friend that he was going to meet up with him, taking Fleur along. And his father is Spanish and you don't have his Spanish address. Is that right?'

'Yes,' she said, her head averted from his as she poured herself a second cup of coffee. It wasn't a lie. She didn't have a Spanish address for Jimmy for the simple reason that there wasn't one.

'What's this bloke's full name? If he was living in England when you met him, he must have friends here. Someone must have a contact number for him, even if it's an out-of-date one.'

He was still wearing Benedict's burgundy bathrobe; his suit and polo-neck sweater were too blood-stained to be wearable. More clothes were on the way to him. Phoning Paulie and organising him to bring a suit and shirt over to the house had been the first telephone call he had made that morning. Another one had been to Stuart.

She had been standing over the toaster when that particular call had been made. Until then, though she'd been shocked by the viciousness of Tommy's attack on him, she hadn't realised how deeply shocked Al himself was. She'd assumed that such behaviour was par for the course where the Virtues were concerned.

His phone call to Stuart left her in no doubt that she'd been way out in her assumptions. 'It's over as far as me and him go,' he'd said, his voice raw with bitterness and something else – something very like grief. 'By running with Fat Pat and taking the twins with him, he's broken family unity for good.'

There'd been silence then from him as he'd listened to Stuart for a minute or so.

'Yeah,' he'd said at last. 'I feel the same way. We've run our course and if the only business now worth a beat is Fat Pat's kind, it's time we called it a day. If you and Ginny join the old man on the Costa del Crime, it could be a good thing out of a bad. The old man'll be pleased as punch at having you out there, and it's what Ginny's always wanted, isn't it?'

That had been half an hour ago and she had been left to make of it what she would.

Now she said: 'Hugh's father's full name is Jaime Noguerra. At Oxford he was always known as Jimmy.'

'Then we go to Spain and start looking through phone directories.' He helped himself to another slice of toast. 'Do you have any Spanish?'

She assumed he was wearing boxer shorts beneath the bathrobe, but he certainly wasn't wearing anything else – apart from a gold chain around his neck. In her book, gold chains on men were in the same category as gold ear-rings: they proclaimed the wearer to be excruciatingly vulgar. Even as she wrestled with the problem of how to tell Al that going to Spain wouldn't advance their search for Jimmy – and Hugh and Fleur – one iota, she found herself registering that, on a chest as broad as Al's, a gold chain looked surprisingly good.

'I do have some Spanish, but . . .'

His mobile rang again. He swallowed a mouthful of toast, checked the incoming number and, after a few seconds of listening to his caller, said: 'I know I didn't make the meet, but everything we agreed about the re-fit is still on. At the moment she's berthed in Marseilles. Yes. Fine. Keep in touch.'

He clicked the phone off and flicked it shut.

'Was that about *The Mallard II*?' she said, remembering her conversation with Ginny.

An expression she couldn't quite decipher flashed through his eyes. 'Who told you about *The Mallard II*? Ginny?'

'Yes. It isn't a problem, is it?'

'No,' he said, as she registered that his eyes weren't a hard granite-grey, as she had always believed. They were blue. The blue of Cornish slate. 'Except that *The Mallard II* is pretty private territory.'

There came a distinctive knock at the door.

'That's Paulie,' he said, rising to his feet. 'You haven't met him yet, have you? Not properly.'

'No,' she said, grateful that the interruptions to their original conversation were continuing. As far as she was concerned, the delay in returning to the subject of Spain and what steps they could take in Spain to find Jaime Noguerra, couldn't be long enough.

Al walked out into the hall, opening the door to Paulie as if the place was his own.

'This is a nice gaff.' As he strolled into the sitting-room, Paulie looked around appreciatively. 'I saw it from the outside a couple of nights ago,' he said to Deena as Al took the suit, shirt and tie he had brought and disappeared upstairs with them. 'I thought then that it looked pretty swish.'

Deena frowned, trying to remember when he could possibly mean – then realisation came. He had obviously been with Al the night he had made a forcible entry into the house, terrifying her out of her wits. So much had happened since then that the incident seemed weeks ago rather than days.

Paulie, too, was frowning slightly. He'd seen Deena King since then, of course – and had got a very good look at her in The Drum, but he'd seen her somewhere else too – somewhere when Al hadn't been looking for her, and she hadn't been looking for Al. As she asked him if he'd like a coffee, it suddenly clicked as to where and when it had been. She had been the dark-haired, good-looking woman Al had nearly mown down as they'd driven through the centre of Oxford towards St Hilda's, the one he'd then recognised in the Kidlington cop-shop.

'No,' he said, amused at the realisation, wondering what Al would say when he told him. 'Thanks all the same, but I need to get back to The Maid.'

He broke off as Al strode into the room.

'There's ructions on,' he said to him. 'Uncle Kevin's done a runner with Marilyn. According to Auntie Lol, the two of them have done a trot to Marbella to stay with Granddad. Lol's throwing a right wobbly over it. She says it's all Max's fault. That if Max had been more of a man, Marilyn wouldn't have left him for Kevin in the first place. Mum's trying to calm her down, but she's not having much success. The atmosphere ain't nice, that's for sure.'

Despite his bruises and his stitches and his swollen lip, in a knife-sharp suit and ice-white shirt, Al still looked remarkably presentable. In fact, he looked more than presentable. She'd always been aware of how attractive he was, of course, but previously it had been an attractiveness it had never occurred to her to respond to. Now, though, she knew she was feeling differently. It was a hell of a realisation – and a hell of time to realise it.

'And Max doesn't help,' Paulie continued. 'He's such an old woman – he's driving Dad round the bend.'

He grinned across at Deena and she knew that he, too, thought that she and his uncle were an item. 'I had to borrow his car to get over here, and you'll never guess what I found in the glove compartment – pair of sky-blue washing-up gloves! He hadn't been using them for an oil change, either. More like gardening, from the look of them.'

Al made a noise in his throat that could have meant anything and Deena knew that he was anxious for Paulie to be on his way so that their discussion about Jimmy could continue.

As Al led the way back out into the hall, Paulie said, no longer amused: 'It's common knowledge what happened between you and the twins and Tommy, Uncle Al. Dad's sick about it. Real cut up. What with Kevin having done a bunk to Spain, it's as if the family's crashing apart.'

Deena could tell from the way he said it that he was expecting Al to rubbish the idea. Instead, as he opened the door, Al said, 'Yeah, it's beginning to look that way, Paulie. Perhaps a bit of sun and sangria would be the ticket for you and Ritchie as well. It's what your mum wants, so think about it.'

Paulie stared at him, all Jack-the-Lad cockiness gone. 'Christ, Al! You can't be serious . . .'

Al's mobile rang and as he retrieved the phone from an inner jacket pocket, Deena said impulsively to Paulie:

'Give your mother my best, Paulie. I know she has a lot of worries. Tell her I'm thinking about her.'

Appreciative electric-blue eyes met hers. 'Thanks, Dee. Will do.' He glanced towards his uncle again, saw his attention was now entirely focused on the call he was taking, and with a 'See ya' he turned away and jog-trotted back to the car parked at the kerb.

As she remained standing at Al's side while Paulie drove away it occurred to her, wryly, that it was almost as if they were family. Certainly no one had ever called her Dee before.

'*What?*' Al was saying explosively, the mobile to his ear. 'Are you *sure* of that? Why the *fuck* didn't you say so earlier?'

Assuming he was again talking to either Stuart or Max, she walked back into the house, knowing that the discussion Paulie's arrival had interrupted would soon be under way again.

'Does anyone else know?' she heard Al shouting into the phone as the front door slammed shut and he marched down the hallway after her. 'And you're *certain* he took Fleur with him?'

She'd just stepped into the kitchen, intending to make a pot of fresh coffee. It was an intention never fulfilled. The instant she heard Fleur's name – the instant she knew that his telephone call was nothing to do with the goings-on at The Maid but was to do with Fleur and Hugh, she froze, her heart jarring against her breastbone.

The next second he had hold of her arm and was spinning her around to face him. 'That was Giles Gargrave!' he spat, eyes blazing. 'He knows damn well where Hugh's gone! He's known all along!'

'Where . . . ? What . . . ?' She knew what was coming;

knew, and would have done anything in the world to have prevented it.

His grip on her arm was bruisingly savage; his free hand bunched into a white-knuckled fist. 'Your precious son isn't having a harmless meet with his dad! He's trying to get into the drug-game big-time! He's gone to Colombia, for Christ's sake! He's trying to muscle in on the action at the sharp end – not knowing just how fucking sharp it is – *and he's taken my daughter with him!*'

It was the very worst of the many bad moments she had lived through over the last week, yet, strangely enough, she felt no panic. Instead, she felt an almost icy calm. Everything was out in the open now. All the cards were on the table – and she still had an ace in her hand.

She knew exactly where Hugh and Fleur would be in Colombia. They would be at the Noguerra family home, high in the mountains. And though no one else – not even Al – would have been able to gain access to it, she knew that she could. Jimmy wouldn't refuse to see her. Especially not now, when he wanted to build a relationship with their son.

'He hasn't gone to Colombia to traffic in drugs,' she said, surprised at how calm and matter-of-fact her voice was. 'He's gone to meet Jimmy.'

'How's he going to do that?' He threw her away from him with such force she went crashing into a bank of wall units. 'He isn't in Spain, for Christ's sake!'

She flattened her hands against the units, steadying herself, all icy calm gone. 'I know!' she shouted back at him. 'Hugh's in Colombia because Jimmy's Colombian!

Chapter Eighteen

There was a moment's pause as he registered the enormity of the information she had been keeping to herself; the depth of her duplicity. And then he did what he'd have given thousands of pounds to have done when, years ago, they'd faced each other across a courtroom. He slapped her back-handedly across the face with such force that she reeled the full length of the units.

'You bloody knew!' he bellowed as, gasping and fighting down sobs of shock and outrage, she struggled to maintain her balance. 'You've known where Fleur's been all along!'

'No, I haven't!' Her fury was incandescent. 'Before I knew about the fraudulent passport I assumed she and Hugh were somewhere in England!'

'You've known about his hookey passport ever since I told you about it last night!' he thundered, hardly knowing how to contain his fury . . . and his fears.

If she'd been a man, he would simply have weighed in with fists and feet. As it was, slaps weren't enough to relieve his feelings and, aware that the one he had delivered hadn't given him an iota of pleasure, he raised his arm and violently cleared the nearest shelf of its contents. A gold-edged soup tureen and plates, a tea service and a collection of cut-glass milk jugs crashed to the tiled floor, smashing into shards.

'You could have told me then what the bottom line was!' he raged as she pushed her tumbled hair away from her face. 'But you didn't! And if Garside, or Gargrave, or whatever his name is, hadn't thrown Colombia into the equation, you never would have come clean about it, would you?'

'On a need-to-know basis, I didn't think you needed to know!'

It wasn't true. Morally, he'd had every right – and she'd known it. To have admitted it, though, would have been to admit that she'd acted in a way that had been far from open and honest.

'And did this need-to-know basis of yours take into account the fact that my daughter's life and liberty could well be at risk?' The tendons in his neck stood out like cords. 'You expect me to believe that Hugh would travel to Colombia to meet his father and, once there, he wouldn't try his hand at a bit of drug trafficking? Bearing in mind that he's already been questioned by the police over possession and peddling?'

'Hugh didn't peddle!' she shouted back at him. 'Your nephews said he didn't!'

Al was just about to respond that nothing Zac and Clint said could be trusted when there came hard knocking on the front door. Certain that someone was calling with news of Hugh, Deena pushed past Al, stepping over shards of crockery as she made for the hallway and rushed towards the door.

'Yes?' she said, attempting to wipe away the runnels of mascara and tears that streamed her cheeks, disorientated to find herself speaking not to a police officer, as she had expected, but to one of her neighbours.

'I'm very sorry to have to ask this of you, Ms King, but would you please keep the noise down?'

'Would I *what?*' It was so unexpected, she wasn't sure if she had heard correctly.

Al strode up beside her, still breathing heavily.

'Would you and your . . . *partner,*' her neighbour said scathingly, 'please keep the noise down? Otherwise I shall have to inform the police that a domestic disturbance is taking place.'

'Fine. Do that,' Al said and, before Deena could stop him, slammed the door in her neighbour's face.

In the muted light of the hallway they looked at each other, their chests still heaving from the exertion of their ruckus, both of them aware that it had achieved nothing.

'If Fleur's in Colombia,' he said flatly. 'I'm going to get her.'

'If she and Hugh are with Jimmy, you'll need me with you in order to make contact.'

'Then pack a bag. We need to leave now. Today.'

She turned away from him, having already come to a similar conclusion. 'Ring Heathrow,' she said as she made for the stairs. 'See when the next flight is and if there's availability on it.'

'That isn't the way to do it.'

She was already on the third tread of the stairs and she turned, looking down at him.

'Never travel direct from one destination to another,' he said, taking his mobile out of his jacket pocket. 'We'll take the train to Paris and fly from Charles de Gaulle to New York or Boston. Then we'll fly from there on a plane that's via Bogotá to somewhere else in South America. Anywhere, just as long as the final destination on our ticket isn't the place we're going.'

'Why?' She stood with one foot on the next step, her stance unknowingly provocative, her skirt pulled tight across her hips. 'We're not on the run. Why do we need to be so careful?'

He scrolled through his mobile's address list, found the number he wanted, and hit it. 'Hasn't it occurred to you,' he said, 'that this whole scenario stinks to high heaven? Initially Thames Valley Police suspect Hugh of having supplied cocaine to a girl who has OD'd and died. Then, not only is the investigation dropped, but Hugh's dean is told it isn't to be mentioned.'

The number he was calling was engaged.

'But that's obviously because Hugh didn't supply cocaine to her – or to anyone else! If he did buy from the twins, all he was buying was marijuana . . .'

'And yet he wasn't prosecuted for possession? More to the point, why weren't Zac and Clint picked up? It's *four months* since the Lyndhurst girl died. Thames Valley may be cack-handed at times, but they're not completely dozy. And why didn't they tell you Hugh had been recently questioned when you went to them and reported him as a missing person? You're a barrister, you must have realised by now there's something way out of kilter in their handling of this.'

She didn't answer him. She didn't need to. What she needed to do was to tell him the significance of the name 'Noguerra'. If she did, though, she knew he would no longer believe that Hugh's trip to meet his father was just that and nothing more. He would believe that somehow there was a drugs connection. That perhaps Hugh intended buying drugs in Colombia and smuggling them back into Britain, or that it was Jimmy's intention to dupe Hugh and Fleur into carrying drugs back into Britain without their knowledge.

The last hypothesis was, of course, ridiculous. Jimmy was a trafficker on an international scale and international traffickers didn't need to use family members – or family member's girlfriends – to act as mules. In the mood he was in, though, she doubted if she would be able to convince Al of that.

Instead of saying what she knew she should say, she said, 'I'm going to pack a bag. It won't take me long. Ten minutes, perhaps less.'

Once in her bedroom she moved fast. Her always pre-packed toilet-bag was already in her Louis Vuitton travel-bag. Opening drawers, she scooped up a handful of knickers, some bras, a half-dozen T-shirts, two pairs of jeans, a blouse, a skirt, a pair of wedge-heeled sandals and a denim jacket.

Then she pulled a chair across to her wardrobe and, standing on it, searched through the score or so of spiral-bound diaries that lay on top, hidden from view by a rim of ornamental carving.

The diary she was looking for was thick with dust. She blew the dust off, opened it at the back page to make sure that her memory had not deceived her, and then jumped from the chair. Seconds later the diary was packed in her travel-bag with her clothes. Her passport and credit cards were to one side, ready to be put in her shoulder-bag.

When she left the room it was to find him still at the foot of the stairs; still on his mobile.

'We're on the six o'clock flight to New York from Paris this evening,' he said, flicking the phone shut. 'Until then there's no point in wasting time. I've arranged a meet with the geezer who's running the twins – and Tommy. I don't like unfinished business, and not only do I have a lot of unfinished business with Fat Pat Docherty, but where responsibility for the Lyndhurst girl's death is concerned, he's the likeliest candidate. And if he is, I'd like to know.'

'So would I,' she said with deep feeling, sliding her passport and credit-card wallet into an inner pocket of her shoulder-bag.

He watched her, noticing that her mascara was still smudged. It didn't affect her beauty; he didn't think anything could.

'Have you any phone calls to make to explain your absence from home?' he asked as she hooked the strap of her bag over her shoulder and picked up the leather-trimmed travel-bag. 'Your boyfriend, for instance?'

'I need to phone Mungo Deakin.'

They were outside the house now and she was double-locking the front door.

'Is he the boyfriend?'

'He's my Head of Chambers. He's sixty, looks seventy and acts as if he's eighty,' she said, dropping her key-ring into her bag.

His relief was vast. He didn't have to ask himself why. Where self-knowledge was concerned, he'd always scored high.

'No cars,' he said, making no move towards his parked Shogun. 'From now on we take cabs.'

She nodded acquiescence.

'If you're about to make your call to Mungo Deakin, don't tell him you're leaving the country,' he said, waving down an approaching black cab as she reached in her bag for her mobile. 'Tell him you're going to Scotland or Wales.'

Perversely, once they were seated in the cab and she was connected to Mungo, she said: 'I'm going to be in Cornwall and out of touch for a couple of weeks, Mungo. It's a family matter and . . .'

Al could hear a dry, stick-like voice rise dangerously high.

'I'm sorry you're finding my behaviour unprofessional, Mungo,' she said, not sounding sorry at all. 'But my family has precedence over chambers and . . .'

There came two minutes of even higher pitched remonstrance.

'If you wish to review my position in chambers, then by all means do so,' she snapped as Mungo finally paused for breath. 'It makes absolutely no difference to my decision. I shall be accepting no briefs for at least two weeks . . . possibly longer.'

'Disgraceful behaviour . . . unethical . . . unprofessional . . . untenable' were just a few of the remarks Al overheard before Deena severed the connection and flipped the phone shut.

'I suspect,' she said as the cab cruised over Blackfriars Bridge, 'that I no longer have a set of chambers to practise from.'

'Does it matter?'

They were seated hip to hip and thigh to thigh on the cracked leather seating.

'No,' she said, catching sight of herself in the driver's mirror and reaching in her bag for a tissue. 'It would have once, but now all that matters is Hugh.'

'I know the feeling,' he said as she wiped the mascara smudges away. 'A few days ago I had all sorts of plans on the boil. But not now. Now I couldn't care less.'

He thought back to his breakfast meeting with his Swiss banking friend. The bonds theft he'd had in mind then was a theft he knew he would now never carry out. It would have needed every member of the family in on it, with all of them acting in complete unity. With Kevin now in Spain and Tommy and the twins running with Fat Pat, any such heist was a complete impossibility.

Plus, over the last few days, he'd lost the taste for his old way of life. Stuart had been right when he'd said that where crime was concerned they'd become a couple of dinosaurs. The heyday they'd enjoyed was well and truly over and it was time to move on – and he knew exactly where. Once Fleur was safely back at Oxford he was going to say goodbye to London and everything in London – including Sharlene – and live aboard *The Mallard II*. He'd sail her down to the south of Spain and hang out with the old man in Marbella for a few months. Then . . . who knew? He'd poodle off to Corsica perhaps. Or the Greek islands . . .

'Is this the club you're after, mate?' the cabbie asked, breaking in on his thoughts. 'It's a bit early in the day fer a drinking club, ain't it? Are yer sure it'll be open?'

'Positive.' Al retrieved a bundle of notes from a back pocket and peeled off a couple. 'This is for now. We'll be half an hour or so. Then we'll want taking to another address in south-east London and then to Waterloo.'

As they walked across the pavement towards the uncompromisingly plain door, she said: 'What's the other address we're going to?'

'A greasy spoon on the Old Kent Road. I phoned Stuart from your place and he's picking up a passport for me and a bag of clothes. By the time we're finished here, he'll be at the cafe with them, waiting. It'll just be an in-and-out collection job.'

He cupped her elbow with his hand. 'Whichever way the conversation goes in here, don't create. If you do, we'll learn nothing. Understand?'

'You mean if Hugh is mentioned?'

He took the travel-bag from out of her hand and pushed open the door. 'Yeah,' he said drily. 'And he will be, Deena. Any indignation, leave till later, OK?'

'OK,' she said, knowing that he was right and that any questions or comments from her would not go down well in the sort of company they were about to keep.

*   *   *

The club was empty, except for a mammoth figure seated on a bar-stool and a powerfully built young man lounging against the back of the bar.

'I take it this ain't a friendly call?' Fat Pat wheezed as they walked up to him. 'And who's the bird?' He ran his eyes over her dark suit and high-heeled court shoes. 'She your silk, is she?'

'Nope. But where I go, she goes. So no remarks.'

Fat Pat grunted and nodded towards his fit-looking back-up. 'What's it to be?' he said as the young man pushed himself away from the cold-shelves in order to serve drinks.

'Two whiskys and two coffees,' Al said, not even turning towards Deena to ask her.

She didn't mind. He'd got it right.

'So . . .' Fat Pat said as his walking-door set about delivering service. 'What's your beef, AV? The twins or Tommy?'

'A couple of days ago it'd have been all three. Now I don't give a shit about any of them. What I do give a shit about, though, is my daughter. And the people my daughter mixes with.'

'Oh yeah?' Fat Pat's piggy eyes were suddenly wary. 'And who might they be?'

The walking-door pushed two glasses of whisky in Al and Deena's direction. Al picked up his glass and took a swallow of its contents.

'A girl called Amabel Lyndhurst and a young bloke by the name of Hugh King. The twins say King was a regular buyer from them, though they conveniently don't remember just what it was he bought. Amabel Lyndhurst OD'd on cocaine and the cozzers, suspecting King had been her supplier, pulled him in for questioning. Then he was released. And it was put about that Amabel had actually died as the result of an asthma attack, so no more was said. Which is all very odd. So odd that I'd be very worried if I was you, Pat. From where I'm sitting, I'd say the Other Firm are doing a bit of watching and waiting, wouldn't you?'

Fat Pat took a cigar out of an inner jacket pocket. 'You're not warning me about the drug enforcement boys out of loving concern, AV. What is it you're after?'

'I've told you. Information about the people my daughter's been mixing with. I reckon the Lyndhurst girl died because the cocaine she was supplied with was cut with trash – and I'd like to know who last cut it before she was supplied with it. Was it Hugh King? Was it the twins? Was it you?'

'I ain't got a clue about the King kid – maybe he did buy off the twins, maybe he didn't,' Fat Pat said as the walking-door unceremoniously pushed a cup of coffee across the top of the bar in Deena's direction. 'But remember that, even if he didn't, it don't mean to say he didn't buy elsewhere. Where the twins are concerned, they know better than to mess with anything they get from me. And where I'm concerned, I ain't into cutting with trash.'

'Then if it wasn't you, perhaps you should be finding out who it was, so that you don't end up carrying the can for it. Who else does your wholesaler supply?'

'Leave off, AV. I *am* the wholesaler! I don't see everyone who deals from me, though. I have a warehouse man. He takes a heap, breaks it up into tens or fives or whatever, and does the deliveries for me. Didn't work that way with the twins, of course, but that's because they're my kids. They wanted some piss-easy money and I dropped them as much gear as they could shift. So even if my warehouse man was doing some hookey cutting – and he fucking well ain't – the gear the twins have shifted wouldn't have been affected.'

'What about further up the line? Who's your importer?'

'Like, if I knew, I'd tell you?!' Fat Pat gave a bark of derisive laughter. 'Do me a favour, AV. Christmas ain't for another two months!'

He pushed an empty glass towards the walking-door and, whilst it was being topped up, said: 'One thing I will tell you. The gear I get is high-grade Colombian, 33 per cent pure, which is a pretty high ratio. By the time it goes on the streets it's usually down to 12.5 per cent – but it's still safe. You think I'd have my own flesh and blood peddle something that wasn't?'

Al made a noise in his throat that could have meant anything. Deena finished her coffee.

'Beats me why the Other Firm put so much effort into trying to collar petty street dealers, when they never get their acts together to get the real Mr Bigs,' Fat Pat said, becoming almost chummy now he sensed there was going to be no big ruckus over the twins and Tommy. 'Those blokes in the producing countries, they're kings, believe you me. If they bombed a couple of sites in Bolivia and Colombia, the war on drugs'd be over in a flash.'

'Yeah, well, it's a pity they don't.' Al drained his glass and pushed it back across the bar in a manner that said he was about to leave.

'Those blokes don't even have to keep their identities secret,' Fat Pat said enviously, easing his vast bulk off the bar-stool. 'That's because they're not sought on their home ground. Their governments love 'em because of the back-handers. And we're talking *real* back-handers,' he continued as he walked them towards the door. 'Housing projects, hospitals, schools. You name it and cocaine supplies it. My importer says that in Colombia, Jaime Noguerra funds the water and electricity supplies to half the bleedin' country. Think about it. The man's practically a national hero!'

'Noguerra?'

Deena stumbled and Al whipped an arm around her waist, holding her upright against him.

'Jimmy Noguerra?'

'Jimmy, Jaime, what does it matter?' Fat Pat gave a shrug that sent mounds of fat rippling and quivering. 'He's a real Mr Big. *The* Mr Big. And do the Colombian government care? Course they don't. They probably make noises about caring to the Americans, but when it comes down to it, they do sweet fuck all. Why kill a goose that lays so many golden eggs? I just wish the Customs and Excise boys would see me in the same light, but the bastards don't. There's no fucking justice in the world. Not a fucking ounce.'

Al's teeth were clenched and the pulse at the corner of his jaw was pounding as he strode out of the club and manhandled Deena into the rear seat of the waiting cab.

'Why?' he demanded as the cab pulled away from the kerb, 'Why am I not fucking surprised? Why do I get the feeling that you've known about Hugh's father's little business interest all along? And why am I not strangling the fucking life out of you?'

'Because it isn't connected.' Her voice was cracked and on the verge of breaking. The effort she was making to ensure that it didn't, was colossal. 'What Jimmy is has nothing to do with Hugh flying out to meet with him.'

'Christ Almighty! Wise up, Deena! There's a connection, all right! I just can't work out what the fuck it is!'

She looked out of the window, unable to face his rage and anxiety. If he was right, then so was the instinct she'd had the first day she'd realised that Hugh was missing. He was in trouble. Big trouble. And if he'd dragged Fleur into that trouble with him . . . ?

She agonised over the probability in silence all the way to the café and then remained in the cab whilst he strode across the pavement, returning seconds later with a travel-bag.

'Waterloo International,' he said to the cabbie, slinging the bag to the floor and again sitting beside her.

Not until they were walking across to the Eurostar ticket office did he speak again.

'Have you been to Colombia?' he asked abruptly. 'Did Jimmy take you there? When we get there, do you know where to find him?'

'No, I've never been,' she said, wondering if it might be safest to take the diary out of the travel-bag and put it in her shoulder-bag. 'And yes, I do know where to find him.'

'Thank Christ,' he said with genuine depth of feeling, stepping away from her and up to the ticket booth.

A woman walking away from it eyed him appreciatively.

Deena noted the look and understood it. Even with stitches slicing down through his eyebrow, he was still a head-turning package.

Watching him, she wondered when would be the best time to break the news that, knowing where to find Jimmy and actually finding him were going to be two very different things. Jimmy's description of his family home hadn't been of a house conveniently sited in a residential street in Bogotá. It had been of a *hacienda* so big as to be almost a village – a village high in the mountains, forbiddingly difficult to reach.

Once they were seated on the train she took in a deep,

steadying breath. 'Al,' she said purposefully, 'about the address I have . . .'

His mobile rang.

He took it out of his pocket, checked the incoming number and said: 'Yes, Paulie. What is it?'

A beat later he was sucking in his breath, rigid with tension. She heard Paulie say the words 'Ritchie' and 'charged', and then Al was saying fraughtly: 'Tell your dad to ring Brian Vault. *Vault.* No one else. Have you got that?'

He clicked the phone shut, looking across at her, saying succinctly: 'Ritchie's about to be charged with Lulu's murder. If I'm to be of any use to him, I need to get off this train.'

At the thought of being left to travel to Colombia and meet with Jimmy on her own, something very like panic surged into her throat.

'No!' It was all she could do not to grab hold of his arm. 'The next few days aren't going to make any dramatic difference to Ritchie's situation, but they might very well make a huge difference to Fleur and Hugh. Let Vault take care of things for Ritchie. There'll be time enough for you to do whatever needs doing when you get back from Colombia with Fleur.'

As the train started to move she saw the agonised indecision on his face and knew she had to engage his full attention if he wasn't to leave her the second they drew into Ashford.

'Tell me about Lulu,' she said, just as if he were a client or a briefing solicitor. 'Tell me everything you know about her. How long she'd worked at The Maid. What kind of girl she was – was she an extrovert or an introvert? Did she come across as being sexually experienced or inexperienced? Who did she talk to? Who showed an interest in her? Ninety per cent of murders are committed by family members or people known to the victims. If you're right in believing that Ritchie didn't kill Lulu, someone else who knew her probably did. Let's try and work out who.'

'So everything is working out as the profile planners at the DEA had hoped?' Rupert said, looking down over Whitehall, his back to his visitor.

'So it would seem.' Sir Monty Gargrave checked his watch. 'They're aboard the Eurostar as we speak, heading for Paris.'

'Perhaps they intend travelling no further.' Rupert said, his attention apparently still on the view from his massive window. 'Perhaps they are simply going for a romantic weekend away.'

'Wilfred Frensham's daughter and a convicted bank robber? I don't believe that for one moment, Rupert, and neither do you. Credit has to be given to the Americans, though, doesn't it? No one this side of the Atlantic would have thought of trying to put this scenario in place. And if it comes off as predicted . . .'

'If it comes off as predicted, is Wilfred's daughter's safety guaranteed?' Rupert asked, turning away from the window.

'Of course.' Sir Monty rose to his feet. 'That is the whole point of the exercise, isn't it? The safe retrieval of a kidnapped British citizen?'

'But not citizens? Not Hugh? And not Al Virtue and his daughter?'

'I'm sure the Americans will do their best where the girl is concerned.' The tone of his voice indicated that whether they did or didn't was of little interest to him. 'Where Virtue is concerned, our Customs and Excise people would prefer him alive and in court, facing charges of drug trafficking so mammoth he'll be put away for the rest of his natural – and giving them a great deal of kudos into the bargain, of course. However, in any commando-style hostage-retrieval attack, very little can be guaranteed and it may well be that Customs and Excise will be disappointed. As for Hugh King – or, as I would prefer to dub him, Hugh Noguerra . . .'

Sir Monty's mouth tightened into a thin white line.

'. . . We both know the part he played in my niece's death. Hugh Noguerra is expendable. *Exceedingly* expendable. I thought you understood that from the outset, Rupert?'

Not trusting himself to speak, Rupert merely nodded, walking around the corner of his desk to escort his visitor from the room. What he understood was that the Americans – not for the first time – had taken advantage of them. They had manipulated a scenario that would enable them to bring pressure to bear on the Colombian Government – pressure that would mean the storming of the Noguerra enclave and an end to Jimmy Noguerra.

What the British would get out of the operation – Al Virtue being finally nailed – was, in his opinion, very small beer. True, Sir Nicholas Lyndhurst would get satisfaction where Hugh was concerned. Instead of gaining retribution through the courts – which would entail making public that his daughter had been a drug user – Hugh would simply be declared a 'casualty' when the Americans went in, guns blazing.

Assuming, of course, that Deena gained access to the Noguerra mountain retreat.

And there was another 'if', one Sir Monty and his American colleagues appeared not to have given much consideration to. What if, when the raid was over, Deena refused to go along with the myth that she had been at the enclave against her will? What if she refused to act out the part that the Americans expected her to after the event, when provided with a doctored explanation? Would she, too, then be expendable?

And if she was?

A tic began flickering in his left eyelid.

If she was, he would be partly responsible.

Her blood would be on his hands.

Chapter Nineteen

'In fifteen minutes, we shall be landing at Bogotá,' a heavily accented voice informed Flight AA915's passengers. 'Will passengers continuing on to Rio de Janeiro please remain seated.'

Deena looked across at Al. The flight from New York had taken a little under six hours, but they had had a wait of several hours at JFK and it had now been nineteen hours since they'd left London. It was a long time to have spent in each other's company without other distractions, and they had put the time to good use.

'Tell me about Lulu,' she had said as their train had left Waterloo Station. Then, when he had done so and they were speeding down through Kent towards the coast, she had said: 'So it was Max who employed her? I don't quite understand about Max, Al. He just doesn't seem to fit in.'

He'd explained how Max fitted in – how having a friend who was straight and had no criminal record was exceedingly useful. 'And when it comes down to it, when this business with Fleur is sorted, Max is the one I'm going to feel bad about,' he'd said.

She'd raised her eyebrows, mystified. He'd shot her one of his rare smiles. 'When Fleur is back at college I'm going to do what I've always wanted to do. I'm going to leave London and sail *The Mallard II* around the Med. The way things are, Max is the only one it's really going to affect. Stuart and Ginny have already decided to up sticks and move down to Marbella to be near the old man. Paulie is likely to go with them. Kevin's already down there with Max's ex-girlfriend, Marilyn. Tommy and the twins I no longer give a toss about.'

'How long will it take you to sail the Mediterranean?' she'd asked, bemused.

He'd given a slight shrug. 'Who knows? It depends where I anchor, how much I like a place. I should think five years would be a likely guess.'

'And then? What will you do then?'

'You mean what will I do for the rest of my life?' His smile had deepened. 'That's easy, Deena. For the rest of my life, there's the rest of the world.'

Not until they were on the other side of the Channel, speeding through the flatness of northern France, did the subject return to Ritchie. 'Phone your tame Met officer,' she'd said. 'The highly placed one. Ask him if he can find out what the evidence is against Ritchie.'

When, an hour later, Sid Ashworth rang back with the required information, Al's reaction was extreme.

'Christ!' he'd kept saying. '*Christ!* That can't be, Sid! It just can't be!'

They'd been sitting in a snack bar in the Gare du Nord and by the time he'd clicked his phone shut and looked across at her, she'd known the news was very bad. 'It's his car,' he'd said grimly. 'There's evidence of a body having been carried in the boot. Once Forensics have done their stuff, there's not much doubt that Ritchie will be charged.'

'And you're still sure he couldn't have done it?'

He'd shaken his head, not a second's worth of doubt in his eyes. 'No,' he'd said tautly. 'It doesn't fit. Ritchie doesn't have a temper and doesn't hold grudges. He isn't the jealous type. He isn't sexually inadequate. He isn't a nutter.'

From then on, all the way to Charles de Gaulle and whilst checking in and waiting for their flight to New York to be called, they'd gone over and over the little they knew about Lulu. The fact that her father disliked her working at The Maid; that she hadn't told him Ritchie was her boyfriend because she'd known how angry he would be; that she'd still been at The Maid when, on the night of her death, Al had left Tommy's homecoming party and driven out to the Woolwich Flood Barrier to meet Sid.

'According to Ritchie, he and she had already had their barney by the time I left,' he'd said to her as they approached passport-control. 'But she seemed OK. The only person having a problem was Max.'

'Why was that?' she'd asked, her thoughts on other things. The cars that had been parked in The Maid's car park that evening, and the easy way the Virtue family borrowed each other's cars.

He'd told her about the Max/Marilyn/Kevin scenario; the way Max's inability to keep a girlfriend for any length of time was such that his frustration where Marilyn was concerned was understandable.

'He just doesn't try for the right kind of girl,' he'd said as they began walking to their departure gate. 'Most of the girls who go in The Maid are gangster-groupies. They latch on to Max as a way of spending time around the twins and Tommy, and the twins' and Tommy's friends.' He gave another almost Gallic shoulder shrug. 'Natch, they never stay with him for long. Max needs a nice respectable girl, but he never looks for one. Instead he wants a fast, glamorous tart on his arm and fast, glamorous tarts need a little more in the bed department than Max seems able to supply. He bores them. He certainly bored Marilyn. The instant she was able to get Kevin interested in her, she was off without a backward glance.'

They'd boarded the plane and her thoughts had reverted to Hugh. Al hadn't referred again to Fat Pat Docherty's comment that even if Hugh hadn't bought cocaine off the twins it didn't mean to say he hadn't bought it elsewhere, but she'd been unable to stop thinking about it.

She'd thought about it nearly all the way across the Atlantic. Then, an hour or so before touch-down, she'd fallen asleep, waking to find her head resting against Al's shoulder.

It had been an intimacy she'd been untroubled by; an intimacy she was beginning to find oddly comforting.

When they'd landed in New York it had still been night-time and they'd had a meal as they'd waited for their Bogotá flight.

'Will your girlfriend be happy about your plans to sail the Mediterranean?' she'd asked, not knowing whether he had a girlfriend or not, simply assuming.

'Sharlene?' Again his shoulders had lifted beneath his close-fitting jacket. 'Sharlene Diss wouldn't step aboard *The Mallard II* even if she was paid to. Only gold-tap luxury complete with uniformed crew would entice Sharlene afloat – and *The Mallard II* is a fifty-footer needing no more than a crew of two.'

It hadn't been a subject he'd pursued and she hadn't asked any more questions. On the long flight south she'd slept again, his shoulder once more serving as her pillow.

Now, as she looked down at the rugged landscape visible through the low cloud cover, he said: 'Have you put your watch to the right time?'

She hadn't and, as the drone of the engines changed pitch in preparation for landing, she did so.

'We'll have currency to sort out immediately we land,' she said as the 'fasten seatbelts' sign flicked on.

'And a phone call to make.'

That the telephone number written in the back of her 1979 diary was now massively out of date and useless was a fear neither of them had put into words.

'You have a number for him?' he had erupted when they'd been sitting out the wait for their Bogotá flight at JFK and she had told him about the information in her college diary. 'You have a *number* for him and you haven't rung it? Christ Almighty, Deena! One phone call and we'd *know* if Fleur and Hugh are with him!'

'He could lie,' she had said. 'And we wouldn't be in Colombia, practically on his doorstep. This way is best, Al. Trust me. I *know* this way is best.'

Whatever his thoughts on her reasoning, he'd kept them to himself. Now, as the wheels of the plane touched down and there was an outbreak of clapping from the Colombians aboard, he said: 'Are you going to try the number from the airport, or are you going to wait until we check into a hotel?'

'The airport. It may make a difference whether we need a hotel at all.'

Heat and brightness hit them with the force of a physical blow as they stepped from the plane and made the short journey across to the arrivals hall. The noise, once inside, was chaotic. Having hand luggage only, they were able to give the mayhem at the baggage carousels a miss, but the obtaining of currency took an eternity. Only as it was being handed across the counter to them with their passports did she see, with a stab of shock, that the name he had travelled under wasn't his own.

She hadn't wasted time commenting. She'd been too busy heading for the nearest public phone.

'*No conozco tal hombre – no conozco tal hombre,*' Al could hear someone saying over a cacophony of static when Deena finally got an answer on the number she was ringing.

Not having a word of Spanish, he hadn't a clue what was being said, but Deena's reactions made the gist of it clear. The speaker was refusing to admit he even knew a Jaime Noguerra, much less that the number was Jaime Noguerra's.

'*Soy* Deena King!' Owing to the hubbub going on all around them she had to shout to make herself heard. '*Soy* Deena King! Deena Frensham. *Si, soy inglesa.*'

'*Cómo? Cómo?*' came from the other end of the phone line and then the connection was abruptly severed.

'Don't ask,' she said to him as she turned away from the telephone booth, exhausted from the long hours of travelling and the anti-climax of the call. 'It may be the right number, it may not. Let's book into a hotel and try it again from a hotel phone. Without the background noise it may be easier.'

If there was a queue for the taxi-cabs, they couldn't see one. Like everything else so far, it was a mad scramble; a case of every man for himself.

Al put his impressive shoulders to good use, bundling her into a cab ahead of the throng.

'The Hilton,' he said peremptorily to the driver and then, to Deena, 'There must be one. There's one everywhere.'

'This address you have for Jimmy,' he said a little while later as they sat in an almighty traffic jam, looking out at a hillside sporting a poverty-stricken shanty town. 'How difficult do you think it's going to be to get to it?'

'On a scale of one to ten? Ten plus.'

The traffic began to move again and little by little they edged into the city proper. The noise and chaos at the airport paled into insignificance as their driver negotiated streets thick with careless pedestrians, stall-holders, Maseratis and mules.

'I never believed the day would come when I'd be grateful for a Hilton Hotel,' Deena said wearily as they finally drew up outside a modern glass and steel façade, 'But at least the bathrooms will be clean and the water hot.'

At reception Al booked a twin room.

'Don't worry,' he said as she started to object. 'I'm not going to jump you. All we need is somewhere to shower, have coffee and a sandwich and make phone calls. With luck, by this evening we'll be out of here.'

The room they were taken to by a bell-boy was so standardised it was hard to believe they weren't still in London. 'I'm getting straight in the shower,' he said as she took off her jacket and eased her feet out of her shoes. 'If you have any joy, give me a shout.'

The knots of nervous tension in her stomach as she sat down on the edge of the bed and reached for the phone were crippling. Without Jimmy's assistance, travelling deep into the mountains was going to be incredibly difficult. There were no trains and the roads would, she knew, beggar description. That was if there were roads. She didn't know much about Colombia, but she did know that mountains and ravines and jungle made it a country of nightmare terrain where guerrilla groups thrived and kidnappings were frequent. Without help, reaching the Noguerra family home could prove an impossible nightmare.

After an interminable delay she got an outside line,

rang the number Jimmy had given her two decades ago and sucked in a deep, steadying breath.

'Señor Jaime Noguerra, *por favor*,' she said as there came the sound of the shower being turned on in the en-suite bathroom. '*Soy* Deena King, née Frensham.'

'Deena?' The answering voice ripped wide the years. 'It's me, Jimmy. I was told you tried to contact me half an hour or so ago and I've been sitting near the phone, waiting for you to ring back. Where are you? Oxford? London?' There was a slight pause. 'Bogotá?'

The shock of having made contact with him was so intense she was robbed of speech.

'I've been expecting you to call,' he said, his voice as unperturbed as it had been when he had told her he wasn't going to marry her.

'Hugh,' she managed to say at last. 'Is Hugh with you, Jimmy? And Fleur Virtue?'

There was the sound of a low voice in the background, a young woman's voice, then he said smoothly: 'Yes. Hugh and Fleur are with me. At the moment Hugh is out riding . . .'

'I'm at the Hilton in Bogotá,' she said, cutting across him, her voice strident with urgency. 'Can he meet me here? I have to see him, Jimmy. I have to speak to him.'

'It's easier for you to come out to the *hacienda* than it is for Hugh to travel in to Bogotá. I'll send a car . . .'

'You've got through to him?'

Stark naked and dripping wet, Al snatched the phone from her hand.

'Put Fleur on the line!' he thundered to Jimmy.

There was another fractional pause and then Deena heard Jimmy say: 'And you are?'

'Al Virtue! And I want to speak to my daughter!'

Deena's head was so close to Al's that she heard the

girl in the background give a gasp and heard Jimmy say to her: 'You'd better speak to him, *querida*.'

'Dad?' The voice that came on the line was tremulous. 'Dad, I'm sorry if you've been worried . . .'

'Fleur?' Al's voice was raw with relief. 'Christ, Fleur! Of course I've been worried! Are you all right, sweetheart? Are you safe?'

'Yes . . . there's nothing to worry about, Dad . . . truly . . .'

There came a rush of static that made anything else unintelligible, and then Jimmy's voice was back on the line, saying assertively: 'Deena? Are you still there? A car will be with you within a few hours.'

The static came again – and then the line was lost amidst high-pitched screeching.

Deena put the phone down, her hand shaking. 'Thank God,' she said unsteadily, her relief so vast she didn't know how to give expression to it. 'I've been so terrified that they wouldn't be there . . . that something terrible had happened to them . . .'

He sat down on the bed beside her and slid his dripping arm around her shoulders. 'There's still the mystery of why they haven't been in contact with us,' he said grimly. 'I'm so goddamn angry with Fleur I could throttle her.'

'But you won't.' Emotionally exhausted, she leaned against him, knowing his feelings were the same as hers. There would be anger for the anxiety his child had put him through, but not until after he had been reunited with her and hugged her tight. As he was hugging her tight now.

His mouth was brushing her hairline, his state of arousal impressive. Apart from her shoes, she was still fully dressed. All she had to do to put a stop to things was to stand up, move away from the bed, begin talking about the probable length of the journey to the *haci-enda* . . .

She didn't. Ever since she had first seen him she had wondered what it would be like to be made love to by him – and now all she had to do to find out was to turn towards him.

With slow deliberation, she turned.

Time wavered and halted, so charged with sexual tension she could barely breathe.

His arm slid from her shoulders to her waist, draw-ing her even closer against the damp nakedness of his chest, his eyes so dark with desire they were almost black.

Her own desire was at fever-pitch. She was confounded by it – utterly consumed. Even before his mouth closed on hers, her lips had parted, and his hair was coarse beneath her fingers.

He bent her back upon the bed with a forcefulness she couldn't have fought even if she had wanted to, all the barriers between them tumbling into non-existence.

'Do it, do it, *do it!*' she panted in deep need as, breathing hard, he pulled her blouse from the waistband of her skirt, pushing her skirt high, his hands sliding up over her suspendered-stockinged legs.

Silk tore as he tugged the dark triangle of her panties aside, pinioning her beneath him.

There was no tenderness as he entered her – neither of them had time for tenderness. Raising her legs high, crossing them over the middle of his back, she moved in exquisite tightness with him, reaching a point she'd only rarely reached with previous lovers and then being carried far, far beyond it.

With his hands and mouth on her breasts, she was brought to near insensibility, their bodies fusing together in a rocking, shattering, ferocious climax that took them in a tangle of sheets from the bed to the floor.

Later – much later – after she had showered and was rifling through her bag for a clean change of clothes, he said with wry amusement: 'Do you think it was the ten-year build-up that made that so earth-moving, or will it be the same the second time around?'

He was towelling his hair dry, his trousers low and snug on his hips, his chest and feet bare.

She dragged a white, pencil-straight skirt from her bag and stepped into it. 'There's only one way to find out,' she said, fighting the temptation to meet his eyes, knowing what would happen if she did, 'but there's a car on its way, so it will have to wait.'

A chuckle rumbled up from his chest and it took all of her willpower to continue putting clothes on, instead of taking them off.

'I've been thinking about Ritchie,' she said, pulling a red silk blouse from her bag.

It was a lie. She hadn't thought about Ritchie since their last conversation about him, on the plane. If they were talking about Ritchie, though, they wouldn't be talking about what had just happened between them – and her emotions were in such chaos, she couldn't talk about what had happened. She couldn't even begin to think about it, or analyse it, nor did she truly know how she felt about it happening again.

It wasn't, after all, a relationship that could have a future. Deena King, QC, and Al Virtue, villain, was not a pairing that would be socially acceptable – in her world, or in his.

'Ritchie,' he said, the amusement in his eyes vanishing. 'What about him?'

Deena began buttoning her blouse. 'He left his car in The Maid's car park the night of Lulu's murder, right?'

'Right.'

'So anyone could have borrowed it to transport Lulu's body from The Maid to the railway embankment.'

'They could if she'd been killed in The Maid, but she wasn't.' He slid his feet into Gucci loafers and reached for his shirt. 'Max says she left on her own. If someone had been lying in wait for her in the car park and attacked her there, Max would have known. He lives on the premises. Nothing goes on at The Maid that he doesn't know about.'

She took a pair of white, wedge-heeled sandals from her bag and sat down on the edge of the bed to put them on.

'When I said I'd been thinking about Ritchie, I really meant I'd been thinking about Max in relation to Ritchie,' she said, wondering just how he would take her little hypothesis. Max was his friend. It wouldn't be a hypothesis he would like, but the more she thought about it, the more of a possibility it seemed.

'Max is a failure with women, or at least he's a failure with the type of women he fancies,' she continued, speculating aloud. 'His last girlfriend publicly humiliated him by dumping him for Kevin. You said yourself that he was seriously unhappy the night of the party.'

With the top two buttons of his shirt still undone, Al reached for his tie. 'And?' he said.

Deena stuffed the clothes and shoes she had travelled in into the Louis Vuitton bag and zipped it up. 'So . . . what if he had chanced his arm with young Lulu and been rejected there as well? It may very well have been a rejection too far. OK, so she left The Maid and, because of the squabble she'd had with Ritchie, did so unaccompanied. But what if she returned? You said Barney had been making a nuisance of himself where Lulu was concerned. What if, aware of her fall-out with Ritchie, he'd lain in wait for her?'

Al slid the knot of his tie towards the buttons undone on his shirt, and no further. 'And what if he hadn't? You're making suppositions out of thin air.'

'Not complete thin air.' With her bag packed and waiting only for the phone call to say that their car had arrived, she rose to her feet. 'If Ritchie didn't use his car that night, returning it to The Maid's car park after he had dumped Lulu's body, then someone else did. Someone who, I suspect, used rubber gloves whilst handling Lulu's body. The same kind of rubber gloves that Paulie found in Max's glove compartment.'

'For Christ's sake . . .' Until now he'd been paying her no serious heed. Now he was.

'And yes, of course you're right when you say it's all complete guesswork, but it's the kind of guesswork that could bear a little police scrutiny. If I were you, I'd give your friend Ashworth a ring. He's in a position to drop a word to whoever is in charge of the investigation. And I'd do it fast, before Ritchie is formally charged.'

His face had become a shuttered mask.

She looked away from him. Substituting his friend as a suspect for Lulu's murder in place of his nephew hadn't been much of a favour. But, if her hunch proved correct, Ginny would be grateful to her.

The bedside phone rang and she crossed the room to answer it, seeing, as she did so, that Al had taken his mobile from his jacket pocket and was flicking it open.

'*El coche?*' she said as Al began stabbing in a long series of numbers. '*El coche blanco? Bueno. Gracias.*'

She put the receiver down. 'The car has arrived,' she

said as he waited to be connected to Sid Ashworth. 'I'll go down to the desk, settle up whatever we owe and wait for you there.'

He nodded, his mouth the thin hard line it had been before the days of their easy familiarity.

Turning her back on the tumbled bed, well aware of the hateful position her hunch had put him in, she left the room.

The car was a white Maserati. For a long time, as it negotiated the chaotic streets and finally emerged in the city's sprawling outskirts, they sat hip to hip on the rear seat, saying nothing.

Finally, as they hit a road that shelved off at the verges into unkempt fields, he said: 'I've spoken to Sid. If you're right . . .' His hands were clenched as they rested on his knees.

She said nothing. If she was right then Ritchie would be released and Ginny would have one thing less to grieve over. Al, though, would have a shattered friendship to come to terms with . . . and possibly a great deal more.

There were no shanty-towns now, only clusters of shacks intermittently strung out along the road's dusty verges. The desperate poverty was cloaked in beauty. Searing magenta-coloured bougainvillaea climbed doorways and lay in thick drifts on tin roofs. Canna lilies threw up stately heads. Orchids gleamed wax-white.

Soon the land on either side of them began to rise with increasing sharpness. Foothills covered in dense vegetation soared high, gashed by perilous-looking ravines. The air in the back of the car was heavy, thick with dust and strange scents and heat. Deena laid her head against soft leather and closed her eyes. When the journey was over, she would be reunited with Hugh – and then there would be explanations and apologies and total, blissful relief.

She woke with a start as the Maserati swerved to a halt. Eagerly she leaned forward, looking out of the windows, certain she was going to see the Noguerra *hacienda*. All that met her eyes was a gigantic hangar-like building on the edge of a runway. And mountains – great, soaring mountains.

'From here, apparently, we fly,' Al said drily, opening the door at his side of the car as the driver strode to open hers.

There was a cluster of helicopters on the runway, and a small plane.

As she stepped out of the car, desperate for the journey to be over, she wondered whether they would be flying by plane or helicopter, and then she saw him and all inconsequential thoughts were driven from her mind.

He had been standing in the doorway of the building. Now, as Al walked round the car towards her, he stepped from its shade, strolling forward to greet them.

The years had been kind to him. He was still darkly handsome. Though slenderly built, he still had the whippy, tough look about him that Hugh had inherited. And he still had charm.

'Welcome to Colombia, Deena,' said Jaime Noguerra, prime mover and shaker of his country's most infamous drug cartel, opening his arms towards her. 'Welcome to my world, *querida*.'

Chapter Twenty

'Fuck the welcomes!' Al snarled, uncaring of the heavily armed bodyguards who had stepped out of the long, low building in Jimmy's wake. 'Where's my daughter, Noguerra? Why isn't she with you? What the fuck is going on?'

Deena still hadn't spoken. Jimmy held her by the shoulders as he kissed her lightly on both cheeks, and she stood as immobile as a statue, so overcome by the past that she could barely breathe.

'Fleur is waiting for you at the hacienda,' Jimmy said, turning towards Al, giving him every atom of his attention. 'It's a pleasure to meet you, AV. I've heard a lot about you.'

'Cut the crap,' Al said, grim-faced. 'All I want from you is a ride to wherever the fuck my daughter is.'

'And Hugh,' Deena said, a light breeze blowing hair around a face that was as pale as a carved cameo.

'Ah, yes.' Jimmy's eyes returned to hers. 'Hugh.'

He was still smiling, but it wasn't a smile that reached his eyes. There was speculation there. And something else. The anxiety that had near pulverised her for days and that had only eased when she had known for certain where Hugh was, returned in full force.

Now, though, wasn't the time for more questions; not when she knew they wouldn't be answered. All that mattered now was being reunited with Hugh.

He turned towards the bodyguard standing nearest

him, saying, as if having read her thoughts: 'Vamos, Arturo. Let's go.'

As the black T-shirted and be-jeaned Arturo led the other bodyguards towards a helicopter standing a short distance away, Jimmy cupped her arm, walking her towards the helicopter nearest to them.

'Wear these,' he said when they were all aboard, handing them ear-defenders with a mike attached. 'We'll still be able to hear and talk to each other. The journey is about an hour. Enjoy it, Deena. You'll be flying over some of the most perilous terrain in the world.'

There was no pilot. As she and Al seated themselves and strapped themselves in, Jimmy took the controls.

With his attention now firmly focused on the instrument panel, Deena took the opportunity of looking across at him, knowing his eyes were unlikely to suddenly meet hers. He was still as slim and supple and as handsome as ever – and still as smooth and as glib and as totally untrustworthy.

She could smell the untrustworthiness. It emanated from him in waves, just as it had always done. Now, though, there was another, far more dominant aura about him. For years she had known that he had become a very dangerous man. Considering the position he held in the cartel, how could he be anything else? Yet knowing in theory and being faced with reality were two very different things – and the fear she had been living with, barely even acknowledging, was how she would respond to that reality when she met him.

The rotor-blades whirred deafeningly as the helicopter surged forward, up and off the ground.

She was aware of a vast feeling of relief – not because they were again on their way, but because, though she had loved Jimmy once, she knew with overwhelming certainty that she did so no longer. For twenty years he'd exerted a hold over her so strong all subsequent relationships had paled into insignificance – yet when he had held her again, and kissed her, she had been completely unmoved. The past had become as dust in the wind and her sensation of freedom was euphoric.

For half an hour they travelled in silence and then Jimmy said, raising his voice over the noise of the rotors. 'I know all about you, AV. The bank raids in the eighties. The bullion job ten years ago. The days of such crimes are over now, eh? Now you have to change direction. And for those that do, this country – my country – is a country made in heaven.'

They were flying head-on towards a rain-forested crag, soaring up and over its lip at what seemed to be the last split-second possible.

He flashed Al a dazzling smile. 'And all major crime in Colombia is controlled by *la compañía,* the company I, and a handful of others, preside over. Which is very interesting to you, eh?'

Deena looked swiftly towards Al, a new terror seizing hold of her. The company Jimmy was talking about so nonchalantly was the cartel. And it was beginning to sound very much as if Jimmy was leading up to making Al a criminal job offer to end all criminal job offers.

If Al was thinking the same thing, his face gave no indication of it. Its strong-boned hardness was impassive. She felt a glimmer of relief, knowing why. All Al was interested in was Fleur's safety – and not until he was reunited with her would he show a flicker of interest in anything else.

'Down there, in the forest, I have hundreds of air-strips such as the one we have just flown from, and though my major laboratory is deep in the south of the country, there are laboratories here, too,' Jimmy continued, as chattily informative as if he were talking about clothing or glass manufacture, not the manufacturing of cocaine. '*La compañía* is a mammoth operation,' he added unnecessarily as they swooped down into a high-sided ravine, 'far bigger than anything a Londoner can imagine.'

The vastness of the rain-forest they were flying over was so awe-inspiring Deena didn't doubt for a moment it could conceal all that he said it could. Terrain so treacherous would be impossible to police.

The helicopter veered, tip-tilting, skimming down low.

'We're nearly there.' Jimmy's gleaming smile flashed again. 'Be warned, Deena, that when people visit my home, they seldom want to leave it.'

His voice was light, with no undercurrents, but all her apprehensions returned in full force. Was he preparing her for the fact that Hugh didn't want to leave it? Or that Fleur didn't? She remembered the endearment she had heard over the phone when he had been speaking in an aside to Fleur. It had been the same endearment he had used to her just a short time ago: *querida*. Darling.

It had mystified her. Some Londoners, of course, called everyone darling, but Jimmy wasn't a Londoner. She pressed her nails deep into her palms, yearning for the journey to be over and for explanations to be made.

'Of course, this is not my only home,' Jimmy was saying as a massive hillside came into view and they swooped down towards its lower slopes. 'I have homes in Brazil and the Bahamas. Here, in Colombia, my main home is a *finca* in the north. But a *finca* is accessible. It has to be. You cannot breed horses without accessible terrain. Here –' the helicopter wheeled towards a complex of white-walled buildings nestling on the flank of the hill, a complex so vast it looked to be a village – 'no one can come, unless by air.'

Buildings that looked almost to be barracks were set at a distance from a magnificent looking, many-verandah'd house. It faced an enormous courtyard and it was towards the courtyard that they were heading. As they dipped down to land, Deena could see a girl shielding her eyes as she looked upwards. A fair-haired girl, unmistakably European. And then she saw Hugh and her heart began slamming like a piston.

'Keep your head down when you get out, Deena!' she heard Al shout and then the helicopter doors slid back and both he and she were scrambling out, stooping as they ran clear of the still whirring rotor-blades.

Within the beat of a second Al was beyond her, sprinting across the sun-baked earth towards his child. Deena saw Fleur race towards him; saw her enter his arms like a rocket.

Hugh, though, didn't move.

'Hi, Mum,' was all he said laconically as, with tears of emotion streaking her face, she hurtled up to him, throwing her arms around him. 'Welcome to *Hacienda Noguerra.*'

'Let's go inside,' Jimmy was saying, a few feet away from them. 'Fleur, take your father into the *salon.* Hugh, your mother has come a long way. A little more emotion would be in order.'

Deena felt as if ice-cold water had been hurled in her face. The last time she had been with Hugh, he hadn't even known Jimmy's name. Now, suddenly, Jimmy was admonishing him as to how he should be treating her. It was as if he and Jimmy were bonded inseparably and she was the parent he'd never known; as if this *hacienda,* deep in the Colombian mountains, was Hugh's home.

'What's going on?' she said tautly, overcome by feelings of bewilderment and crushing disappointment. 'How *dare* you leave England in a way that meant I had no idea where you were? I've been out of my mind with worry! I called the police! I reported you as a missing person! I went to Rupert for help . . .'

'Rupert Pembury-Smythe?' Jimmy said suddenly, looking across her to Hugh. 'He's Foreign Office, isn't he?'

Hugh nodded. 'And an old family friend. It isn't sinister.'

Suddenly, from behind them, Fleur cried out in a wail: 'I *can't* explain everything to you in a few words, Dad! It's just too difficult! Too complicated!'

All the while, they had been walking towards the house. They were inside it now and, as the member of his entourage who had flown the second helicopter hovered nearby, Jimmy said authoritatively: 'I don't know how many hours you and Deena have been travelling, AV, but you must both be exhausted. Can I suggest we put the inquisition on hold till you've had a chance to rest? We'll eat dinner tonight at the Look-out and then, afterwards, there will be explanations.'

'The Look-out?' It sounded like a restaurant, and Deena's weary reaction was that, if it was, it was also a lengthy helicopter-ride away.

'The Look-out is a bungalow half a mile distant, hidden from view from the air in a way the *hacienda* is not.' The explanation came not from Jimmy, but from Hugh. 'It's where my father goes when he wants to be private. It's ideal for the kind of family conference we'll be having. You'll like it. It's on even higher ground than the *hacienda* and the views are staggering.'

Deena heard Al suck his breath in. She didn't blame him. Hugh's carelessly indifferent attitude was flagrantly provocative. 'I don't give a . . .' she began, about to say that she didn't give a flying fuck about the views.

Al laid a hand on her shoulder. 'Leave it, Deena,' he said tightly, his eyes holding Jimmy's. 'Let's go along with this until this evening.'

With a flicker of his eyelid Jimmy acknowledged the message Al was silently sending him; that he wanted to speak to him immediately and alone. 'Show your mother to one of the guest rooms,' he said peremptorily to Hugh. 'Fleur – you look as if you need rest, too. We'll have dinner at seven o'clock at the Look-out. Far too early for an evening meal in Colombia, of course, but adaptability is one of my strengths.'

Hugh began walking from the room and, in the seconds before she followed him, Al gave Deena's shoulders a squeeze she was deeply grateful for; a squeeze conveying far more than anyone witnessing it could possibly imagine.

The room Hugh led her to was a distance away along a corridor floored in cool blue and white tiles. Indian carvings and intricate embroideries decorated dazzling white walls. Balconies looked out over rain-forested ravines and distant mountains, their peaks gleaming like silver in the late afternoon sun. It was, as Jimmy had told her all those years ago as they had strolled, hand in hand, along the banks of the Cherwell, a house that was almost totally inaccessible.

Remembering, it occurred to her for the first time that Jimmy hadn't simply *become* one of the most wanted men in the world; it had been a mantle he had inherited. The house had been built by his father and, for him to have chosen to build such an enclave, in such a position, he, too, must have led a life way outside the confines of the law.

Hugh led the way into a cool, airy room. The bed was a vast four-poster, swagged and swathed in muslin. 'There's something you need to know before you begin reading the riot act,' he said, closing the door behind him and leaning against it. 'I'm not returning with you to London. My father's legitimate son – his only other son – was killed in an air crash six months ago. That's why he made contact with me. I'm staying here, in Colombia, as his acknowledged son and heir.'

The room was very still, the only sound that of distant voices far below them in the courtyard. Somewhere else along the long corridor they had just walked down, a door opened and was quietly closed. She stood, looking at him, knowing that the most terrible thing about the moment she was now living through was that nothing he was saying came as a surprise to her. In a corner of her subconscious, she had known all along that the outcome would be something like this.

'The man whose heir you're so eager to become is one of the biggest drug-traffickers in the world,' she said, her voice perfectly steady. 'But then, you know that, Hugh, don't you? That's the attraction, isn't it? Money beyond the dreams of avarice.'

She turned away from him, walking across to one of the windows, looking out over the glistening white buildings of the enclave. 'He's a killer, too, Hugh. It's part of the job description. Anyone who stands in his way is always removed. All over Colombia and America – and Europe – murders of judges and lawyers and other honest, honourable men are carried out at the behest of the cartel.'

She sensed, rather than saw, the indifferent shrug he gave and knew that she was wasting her time; nothing she could say would make the slightest difference to the choice he had made. She had a question to ask, though, before what was probably going to be their last private conversation was over.

Pushing her hair away from her face, she turned towards him. 'Tell me about Oxford,' she said abruptly. 'Tell me about Amabel Lyndhurst. Did you supply her with cocaine?'

For a split-second his eyes widened and she knew it had never occurred to him that she would know about Amabel Lyndhurst's death, or of his possible connection with it. It was a stab of shock he quelled almost immediately.

'Sometimes,' he said, his indifference never wavering.

He was still standing with his back against the door, his thumbs hooked in the front pockets of his jeans, a wing of sleek black hair falling low across his forehead. Her son. Her beloved son.

Once.

Looking at him, seeing only a clone of his father, she knew he was her beloved son no longer. In his place was a stranger she found it impossible to relate to. In some ways, of course, he had always been a stranger. Even as a small child he had always held himself apart from her, been distant. And now the distance was unbridgeable.

'And did you buy from the twins?'

This time his shock was obvious. 'How the *fuck* do you know about the twins?'

'They're Al's nephews. It's a small world, Hugh. Or hadn't you noticed?'

He gave a short, mirthless laugh. 'Christ, but I never thought you and Fleur's old man would join forces! That must have been the hardest thing you've ever done –

voluntarily putting yourself in the company of such a piece of scum.'

She tilted her head slightly, regarding him with almost academic interest, as if he were an exhibit in a zoo. 'Scum? Al Virtue? On the Richter scale of the world's scum, Hugh, Al Virtue doesn't even register. You register, though. You register high. Almost as high as your father.'

His face tightened as if she had slapped him. 'So he's made a favourable impression, has he?' he said nastily. 'It isn't one that will last. My father is going to make him an offer he won't turn down. When you return to London, you'll be returning on your own.'

'You're wrong,' she said, praying to God that she was right; thinking of *The Mallard II* awaiting Al in Marseilles. 'When I return, both Al and Fleur will be with me.'

He smiled and, as she saw that there was amusement even in his eyes, her stomach muscles clenched in a spasm of fear.

'Fleur won't be travelling with you, or anyone else,' he said, his pleasure at the blow he was about to deliver obvious. 'There's been a little rearrangement of relationships whilst we've been out here. It's now Fleur and my father who are an item, not Fleur and myself. That's the reason she kept stalling about phoning home. She knew that once she did, he'd come out here after her.'

Deena reached out to one of the heavily carved bed-posts, curving her arm around it, holding on to it for support. '*Querida*', she had heard Jimmy say to Fleur when she had telephoned him from Bogotá, and she had known then that nothing was going to be simple when they arrived.

She'd had intimations. Some corner of her mind had

313

been prepared. Al wouldn't be prepared, though. As she thought of the pain and devastating disillusionment Al was going to suffer, her throat tightened so that she could barely breathe.

'Get out of my room,' she whispered to the son she had travelled thousands of miles to find. '*Get out of my sight!*'

'Before we talk about Fleur, let's talk about business,' Jimmy said to Al as, accompanied by Arturo, he led the way across the courtyard to one of the white-walled, barrack-like buildings. 'There are several facets to *la compañia*. Security, transportation, distribution. One of them will, I am sure, be of interest to you.'

Arturo stepped ahead of them, opening the door into the building.

'One of the biggest tasks is the obtaining of all the raw materials cocaine production needs,' Jimmy said as he and Al entered a room banked with sophisticated computer and radio equipment. 'Getting hold of enough ethyl ether is always . . . how do you say in English? A bug-bear. Under US pressure, the government has placed strict controls on its import. We have to bring it into the country illegally and, as the few manufacturers are either American or German, it isn't always easy.'

Al could well believe it, but it wasn't the problem of obtaining ethyl ether that was holding his interest, it was the Planned Position Indicator.

'And then, of course it has to be ferried to the laboratories,' Jimmy continued as Al crossed to the PPI screen to take a closer look, 'and not all the laboratories are in Colombia.'

'So this is how you keep track of your helicopters and planes when they're airborne,' Al said, standing behind

314

the member of Jimmy's entourage who was seated in front of the radar monitor. 'How is it done? Where's the satellite dish?'

Jimmy perched on the corner of a computer-laden table, one leg swinging free. 'I have a British Army 4 Mark 6 scanning radar system. It's situated up by the Look-out. It has a range of a hundred miles. Anything unfriendly approaching and I'd know at least thirty minutes in advance.'

'And if it did? What then?'

'If it was a serious raid . . . a hit-squad . . . I'd be away.'

Al quirked an eyebrow.

'The Look-out has a camouflaged air-strip and a couple of helicopters are always on standby. If the worst should ever come to the worst . . .' He opened his arms wide, palms upwards, looking beyond Al to make eye contact with Arturo. 'We would wait until the incoming task force had landed, wouldn't we, Arturo? And then, whilst they ram-raided their way through the enclave, we would soar away from above, out of their clutches.'

The young, impassive-faced Arturo, nodded.

'You sound as if it's an event you're looking forward to.'

Jimmy rose to his feet. 'It will happen and so it is best to be philosophical about it. Left to itself, of course, the government would leave me alone. The Treasury needs me too urgently, and I am too generous to it, to be dispensable. Washington, however, feels differently. The Drug Enforcement Agency want me badly, dead or alive. Preferably dead.'

He flashed Al another of the down-slanting smiles that never reached his eyes. 'The Americans like playing games, AV. And sometimes they play them with British co-operation. Which is why I found Deena's mention of Rupert Pembury-Smythe so intriguing. Pembury-Smythe is a highly placed Foreign Office official – and a Foreign Official taking an interest in Hugh's present whereabouts is not a comfortable thought. It deepens suspicions already aroused.'

'What kind of suspicions?' Al's eyes had narrowed. 'We weren't followed, if that's what you're thinking. We didn't fly from London, we flew from Paris. And we didn't fly from Paris to Bogotá. We flew in to JFK and then bought tickets for Rio and caught a Rio via Bogotá flight.'

Jimmy slid his hands into his trouser pockets. 'Very careful – which is what I would expect of you, AV. The thing is, you wouldn't have had to be followed if it was known, from the instant you left London, that this was to be your eventual destination. This enclave isn't a secret, AV. The problem for the DEA isn't in their finding it, or finding me in it. Their problem is that they can't persuade my government to storm it and arrest me. Not that my being arrested would satisfy them. There are too many loopholes in Colombia between arrest and conviction. What would satisfy them, however, is a raid on the enclave in the course of which I might accidentally be shot very, very dead.'

'And how would our being here help them achieve that?' Al could feel all the tensions that had eased when his arms had closed around Fleur and he had known her to be safe, returning.

'Hugh's mother is a British subject. If, encouraged by the Americans, the British made representations to our government that they believed she was being held here against her will . . .' He shrugged. 'It would serve as an excuse to send a rescue task force in.'

Al gave a mirthless laugh, his tension immediately

316

ebbing. 'No one could possibly have known that Deena would come out here. She didn't know Hugh was here until forty-eight hours ago and, once she knew, the only person she told was me. She isn't here as part of a set-up. Yes, if the DEA had known she was coming here, they might well have tried to capitalise on the situation, but they didn't know. And even if they had, they'd only have known for the last twenty-four hours or so. That's not long enough for them to have plotted to suggest a false kidnapping scenario to your government!'

'Ah! You're wrong in thinking there has been so little time for a plan to be put into place.' Jimmy's chipped-ice eyes were almost amused. 'When Hugh arrived here, he told me how well-timed my invitation to him had been. The Thames Valley Police were interested in him with regard to a drugs offence. He didn't know then, of course, that his name was logged on the Narcotics and Dangerous Drugs Summary files, and he was oblivious of just how excessive the police interest would have been – or that, had I known about it, I would most definitely have postponed his visit.'

He began to lead the way back towards the door. 'Deena may be under the impression that, as my name is not on Hugh's birth certificate, there isn't a bureaucrat in the world who knows that I am Hugh's father, but she's wrong. The NADDIS files are a computerised summary of *all* knowledge about trafficking and traffickers. That Hugh is my son was logged in those files the day he was born.'

Arturo opened the door for them and they stepped out into the moist heat of late afternoon. 'As a consequence, an eye has always been kept on Deena. The minute I realised Hugh had brought himself to the attention of Drugs Intelligence, I knew that eyes would be on him as well, and that his joining me in Colombia would have been noted. You believe that you weren't followed here and that no one knows the two of you have come here. I don't believe that for one minute, AV. And neither do I believe that the situation is one that won't be taken advantage of.'

'Then why the fuck bring us out here?' They were crossing the football-pitch-sized courtyard towards the *hacienda's* main verandah.

'Because I, too, like to play games. This enclave was built by my father. He had a real use for it. I do not. The main production plant is in the south of the country. It's there that the leaves are brought in from Bolivia and turned first into paste, then base, and finally cocaine hycrochloride. The Americans think I run things from here – and I've encouraged them to think that. In reality there is nothing here, not even paperwork. The only building still serving any real purpose is the communications room we have just left.'

Al came to an abrupt halt. 'Christ Almighty,' he said softly, comprehension dawning. 'You *want* them to attack!' It was a statement, not a question. 'They'll raze the place, believing that a great step towards destroying you has been taken. Your government will have been seen to have co-operated with the Americans, so the Americans will be off Colombia's back for a while. Your national drugs squad will be off your back, and the cosy understanding you have with the government will continue as before. You'll pour money into the Treasury, prop up the economy, and be left alone.'

Jimmy nodded. 'Yes,' he said, 'that is, I think, a fair summation of what a raid would achieve.'

'And if you get your wish, you get it because you're using Deena and my daughter as bait!'

'Not Fleur,' Jimmy said. 'Never Fleur. Fleur, I'm going to marry.'

Every one of Jimmy's black T-shirted bodyguards was conspicuously and heavily armed and Arturo, only feet away from them, was no exception. Al was uncaring. Moving with lightning speed he delivered a pile-driving upper-cut to Jimmy's gut, lifting him off his feet, sending him hurtling backwards to skid, half-senseless, in the dust.

Chapter Twenty-one

When the knock came on her door only minutes after Hugh had left, Deena was sure it was Al. Numbed by a feeling of loss so akin to bereavement as to be indistinguishable, she swung the door wide, dreading telling him what had happened between herself and Hugh – knowing she would also have to tell him about Jimmy and Fleur.

The person who had knocked wasn't Al.

It was Fleur.

'May I come in?' She was wearing beige linen slacks and a black T-shirt not unlike those worn by Jimmy's bodyguards. 'I know Hugh has been talking to you,' she said, her face pale with stress as Deena motioned her inside the room. 'I know he's told you about . . . about Jimmy and me. You were in love with Jimmy once. I'm hoping you'll understand. That you'll help me explain things to Dad.'

'Dear Christ,' Deena said devoutly, knowing her own deep distress was going to have to be put on hold. 'You don't want much, child, do you?'

A ghost of a smile touched Fleur's strained face. 'It does seem like a massive cheek, doesn't it? And under any other circumstances I suppose it would be. I leave England with your son . . . fall in love with his father . . . It's an awful lot for you to have to accept.'

Deena closed the door, wryly aware that where she and Al were concerned, Fleur, too, was going to have quite a bit of accepting to do.

'I know it must seem to Dad that I've behaved scummily this last few weeks, not letting him know where I was or what was happening, but how could I?' She sat down on the edge of the bed. 'When I came out here with Hugh, it was just something a little crazy to do in the summer break. I told Dad I was going to Turkey because he'd have gone haywire if I'd told him I was travelling to Colombia with someone he'd never even met . . . And I couldn't introduce him to Hugh because of you being Hugh's mother. God, if you knew how crazy things have been . . .'

'I've a good idea,' Deena said drily. 'Look, before we carry on any further with this conversation, I think we both need a stiff drink. Is there any in the room, do you know?'

'There's a mini-bar in the wardrobe. You're being very nice about everything, Mrs King. From what Hugh said about you, I thought you'd be . . . well, I thought you'd be different.'

'It's Ms King,' Deena said, opening a small fridge, seeing with relief that it was well stocked with minia- tures and mixers. 'But call me Deena. Under the present circumstances anything else would be bizarre.'

'It *is* bizarre,' Fleur concurred, not knowing the half of it. 'When Jimmy first contacted Hugh, inviting him out here, Hugh didn't have a clue that Jimmy was a *dueño de cupo*. He knew he was wealthy, of course. Jimmy mentioned the houses in Brazil and the Bahamas, and Hugh couldn't wait to check everything out . . .'

Deena opened two miniatures, pouring the contents into glasses that were already frosting in the fridge, well able to imagine Hugh's reaction when he'd realised how wealthy Jimmy was. 'What's a *dueño de cupo*?' she asked, handing Fleur one of the glasses.

'The Mr Bigs who preside over the cartel produce coca paste not only for themselves but for scores of smaller groups,' she said, as if explaining a knitting pattern or a cookery recipe. 'Because they control it and allot it, they're known as *los dueños del cupo* – the holders of the quota. When Hugh realised just what position Jimmy held . . . and when Jimmy told him he wanted to acknowledge him as his son . . .' She lifted slender shoulders expressively. 'It wasn't an offer Hugh even had to think about. Nothing on earth would have made him turn it down.'

'And what about the offer Jimmy then made to you,' Deena said, one arm across her waist as she stood nursing her drink. 'Your friends in Oxford assumed you were in love with Hugh. They obviously assumed wrongly.'

'Yes,' Fleur said, meeting Deena's eyes unflinchingly. 'They did.'

Her face wasn't classically beautiful, but it was intriguing; a face which, once seen, would not easily be forgotten. Her features were too fine-boned for her to bear a marked resemblance to her father, but there was something more than a little familiar about the obstinacy in her chin and the firm set of her mouth. It was the face of a girl who would allow nothing to stand in her way once her heart was set upon something – and by her own admission it was set upon Jaime Noguerra.

Deena took a deep breath, knowing that, for Al's sake, she had to do her best to make his daughter see sense. 'No way will I help you square things with your father where Jimmy is concerned,' she said baldly. 'You may believe that Jimmy is in love with you, but he isn't. He isn't capable of loving anyone. He abandoned me when I was pregnant with Hugh, and before long he'll abandon you. Try and imagine what your father's feelings will be if you force him to return to London without you. It will destroy him.'

'But that isn't how it will be!' Fleur jumped up from the bed in a fever of enthusiasm. 'Dad won't be returning to London – Jimmy is going to give him a position of control in whatever aspect of the cartel's operation most appeals to him. I've explained to Jimmy that Dad is paranoid about drugs, but this level of drug-dealing is so mega mega, no one could turn down the chance of being involved. I just don't want Dad's immediate reaction, when Jimmy tells him we're in love with each other, to spoil anything. I thought that perhaps if you had a word with him first . . .'

'Not till hell freezes over!' Deena exploded, hardly able to believe Fleur's naivety. 'Have you any idea of the realities of Jaime Noguerra's world? Of the fear and misery he's responsible for? The deaths? Have you even an iota of an understanding of the kind of man he is?'

'Yes!' Now she knew that Deena wouldn't do her the favour asked, Fleur's reaction was defensively angry. 'Yes, I have! And I know something else! I know why you're talking to me like this. You're jealous. You thought that when Jimmy met you again everything would be as it had been twenty years ago. Well, it isn't. He loves me now and –'

The sound of a gun-shot, coming from the courtyard, cracked across whatever it was she had been going to say. Amid frenzied shouting could be heard a voice instantly recognisable to them both.

Fleur rushed for the door but Deena reached it first, yanking it open, hurling herself out on to the verandah.

Down in the courtyard, Jimmy's distinctive white-suited figure was sprawled in the dust and dirt. Two of his bodyguards had hold of Al whilst a third was holding a gun to Al's head.

A fourth bodyguard, the one who had flown the second helicopter into the enclave, was shouting what sounded to be words of restraint, the gun he had warningly fired still held skywards.

'Oh my God!' Deena gasped. 'Oh my *dear* God!'

She began to run. She ran along the length of the verandah. She ran down the wide, shallow steps at the verandah's end. She ran and she ran and she ran. She ran over marbled flooring, out into the courtyard and across it, the blood pounding in her ears, her heart slamming as if it were going to burst.

Jimmy was on his feet now, brushing dust from his suit with one hand, holding up the other towards the man pressing the gun to Al's head, saying emphatically as he did so: 'No! *Bastante!*'

People were running from other directions, too. Fleur was only feet behind Deena. Hugh and another member of the black T-shirted brigade were sprinting from the barrack-like building that lay nearest the house.

Deena rushed up to Al as Fleur, hesitating only minimally between her father and her lover, opted for her lover and rushed towards him, throwing her arms around him, sobbing hysterically as she did so: 'I love Jimmy, Dad! Please try and understand! You have to understand!'

'Never!' Al's hands were still bunched into white-knuckled fists and it was obvious that the only thing preventing him from laying into Jimmy again was the gun being held to his head. 'He's nearly as old as I am, for Christ's sake! No way am I going to let you stay here with him!'

'It isn't a situation you have any say in, AV.' Jimmy's arm was around Fleur's waist and though what he was

324

saying was provocative, his voice was matter-of-fact as he tried to defuse the situation. 'All you need to know is that I'll never let any harm come to Fleur, and that there's a place waiting for you within the cartel . . .' He broke off as the bodyguard racing pell-mell towards him began shouting as he ran.

Hugh, too, was shouting.

'It's happening!' Deena heard him yell as he sprinted hard in the bodyguard's wake. 'The radar's picked up a whole squad of helicopters!' Seconds later, as a cacophony of frenzied Spanish was let loose and all attention was drawn from Al, Hugh and the Colombian came to a breathless, floundering stop in front of Jimmy. 'They'll be here in twenty minutes, maybe less!' Hugh gasped, panting hard. 'What's the drill? What do you want me to do?'

'Help the men get the jeeps out of the hangar and into the courtyard.' Jimmy said tersely. He turned to Al. 'Arturo will drive you and Fleur to the Look-out's air-strip. Hugh will go in one of the jeeps taking my men. I'll follow with Deena.'

'What's happening?' Deena looked from Jimmy to Al and back again, her bewilderment total. 'Who's coming? Where are we going? Why is everyone so panicked?'

With a gun no longer at his head and with the body-guards who'd had hold of him now running towards a hangar and the jeeps, Al put his arm around her shoulders. There was nothing casual about the gesture. If Fleur had seen it – if she hadn't been intent on listening to what Jimmy was now saying to her – her eyes would have been on stalks.

'There isn't time for explanations,' he said grimly. 'All you need to know is that Jimmy believes the Colombian authorities are about to make an armed raid and that, in case he's right, we're getting the hell out.'

325

'We need to leave now,' Jimmy said as the first jeep to be driven from the hangar screeched to a halt beside them, Arturo at the wheel. 'Immediately.'

Fleur was clinging to him as if she would never let go and he gently removed her hands from around his neck. 'You and your father will be at the air-strip within minutes,' he said, lifting her into the jeep. 'And the rest of us are going to be right behind you. There's nothing to worry about, I promise.'

Another open-topped jeep slewed to a halt alongside them, and then another. Al, aware that Arturo was waiting for him, brought his mouth down on Deena's in swift, urgent contact. Seconds later, uncaring of the stunned expression on Fleur's face, he'd vaulted into the seat beside her and all that could be seen was a cloud of dust as Arturo drove out of the courtyard at high speed.

Without speaking to her or looking towards her, Hugh scrambled into the next jeep with three of the body-guards. More bodyguards scrambled into the remaining jeep and then both vehicles sped from the courtyard in Arturo's wake.

'We're going by Land-Rover,' Jimmy said, glancing down at his watch. 'We're not quite as short of time as I made out. There's still a few minutes before we need to be on our way. Have you got your shoulder-bag with you? Your passport?'

'No,' she snapped, mentally reeling from the speed with which one critical situation had catapulted into another. 'Does it look as if I have?' She was still wearing the red silk blouse and white linen skirt she'd changed into at the hotel room in Bogotá, and was obviously purseless.

He grinned. 'You're as sharp-tongued as ever, aren't you? You haven't changed in other ways, either. You're still dark-eyed, dark-haired and dazzling. I know you won't believe me, but I missed you with real pain when I first came back to Colombia.'

'You're right,' she said, totally impervious to the charm that had once held her in such thrall. 'I don't believe you.'

This time he laughed, his amusement genuine.

'What is going on, Jimmy?' she asked bluntly as a Land-Rover nosed its way from out of the distant hangar. 'We arrive and in little more than a couple of hours you have everyone high-tailing it out of here as if the place is about to be bombed into obliteration.'

Jimmy took a cigarette-case from his jacket pocket and removed a cigarette from it, his movements as unhurried as if the urgency of a few minutes ago had never taken place.

'Your coming here has, I think, been fortuitous to certain people.' He paused, lighting his cigarette. The T-shirted youth driving the Land-Rover slid it to a halt a half-dozen yards away. 'The US Drug Enforcement Agency seem to think I am personally responsible for all the tons of cocaine that finds its way into Florida and, as a consequence, they would like to see me arrested or dead. Your coming here has given them a new card to play in achieving that end.'

'Explain,' she said.

He took a deep draw on his cigarette, exhaling smoke through his nose. 'Kidnapping is rife in Colombia and, if foreign nationals are involved, the government reacts with commendable efficiency. If the British Government claimed that you were a kidnap victim, any request they might make for a rescue raid would be a request it would be hard for the Colombian Government to refuse – and I think it is safe to say that the raid would be one I wouldn't be allowed to survive.'

'And how,' she asked, fiercely logical, 'would they know I was here? No one knows of my connection to you. The helicopters on their way here aren't a spurious rescue bid! They're probably just fellow cartel members calling in for tea!'

'Time will tell,' Jimmy said easily, glancing down at his watch. 'But you're wrong if you think it isn't known that Hugh is my son. That has been known to the drugs intelligence services ever since he was born.'

He saw he had shocked her and decided to shock her some more. 'When I invited Hugh out here, I intended that his visit should escape the DEA's attention. Unknown to me, however, Hugh, was already of interest to the drugs intelligence services. I don't know whether you are aware of it, but Hugh was recently questioned with regard to a drugs death in Oxford. He foolishly told the cousin of the girl who had died that he intended travelling to Colombia to meet with me. The cousin informed his father – who is a power in the Foreign Office. From then on, I gather Hugh's movements have been followed – and I also think that since then plans have been in place in the hope that you, too, would come here.'

He flashed her the down-slanting smile that had once so mesmerised her, his teeth very white against his olive skin. 'All of which I can put to my advantage. A raid such as this, as long as it is abortive, means the government will have been seen to have been co-operative in the international war against drugs and that it won't, where I am concerned, have to bow again to American pressure for quite some time. There may even be doubts as to whether or not I have survived. So, no worries, eh, Deena? Go get your passport and we'll be on our way.'

Aware there was little alternative, she turned on her heel, running back towards the now empty hacienda.

The sound of her feet as she ran up the short flight of stairs echoed hollowly and the light flooding the shaded verandah was smoked with the blue of dusk. Aware that it would soon be dark, she ran breathlessly into her room, seizing hold of her shoulder-bag. As she did so, she heard the noise of an engine.

It wasn't that of a helicopter.

It was a vehicle.

A Land-Rover.

She whirled out of the room and on to the balcony. He was at the wheel of the Land-Rover, the bodyguard who had been driving it now in the passenger seat beside him. He was driving fast, heading out of the courtyard, dust bellowing in clouds behind him.

'No!' she howled, running like a wild thing towards the stairs. 'No! No! NO!'

By the time she'd hurtled again into the courtyard he was long gone.

He'd left her, just as he'd left her twenty years ago – and she knew that, just as he hadn't returned for her then, so he wouldn't be returning for her now. The only way she featured in his plans was in her being successfully 'rescued' in order that his government could be seen to have taken decisive action against him.

With her heart still slamming against her breastbone, she stood in the deserted courtyard, struggling to come to terms with her abandonment, wondering what would happen when the Colombians arrived. Would they be army? Police? National drugs squad men? Presumably she would be flown to Bogotá and then escorted straight to the British Embassy. She wondered how long it would be before they arrived, assuming from the urgency with which Jimmy had evacuated the enclave that it would be about fifteen minutes, maybe less.

It was very still and very quiet. From where she was standing she could see high peaks shimmering silver-grey and tawny in the deepening dusk. She knew that the mighty Cordillera de los Andes ran the length of South America and that, on reaching Colombia, it split into three massive ranges. Which of those ranges she was now looking at, she had no idea. Her interest in the country, so fierce when she had first fallen in love with Jimmy, had died a savage death when he had returned to it without her.

She strained her eyes in the direction from which she and Al had flown into the compound, certain it would be the direction the squad of helicopters, now on its way, would also come. There was nothing. Only a great bird, wheeling as it searched for prey.

She watched it for as long as it was visible, grievingly aware that when she returned home, she, too, would be doing so alone. Whether Hugh had known that Jimmy hadn't any intention of flying her out with the rest of them, she had no way of telling. If he had, then his not even glancing towards her as he'd left for the air-strip was a hurt so deep she didn't know how she would come to terms with it.

Another thought edged into her mind.

Al.

Had Al known, too? She thought of the way he had kissed her before vaulting into the jeep beside his daughter. Whether or not he had intended it as a kiss of goodbye, that was, in effect, what it had been. Even before Fleur had told her so explicitly of Jimmy's plans for Al, they had been plans that Jimmy had made obvious. He was going to offer Al an entrée into the biggest criminal organisation in the world; the biggest in history.

It was, as Fleur had so starkly pointed out, an offer

that would bring in its wake money so 'mega mega', so stupendously unbelievable, that no criminal – not even one with Al's deep aversion to drug-trafficking – was likely to turn it down.

As she thought of how he'd been about to utterly change his lifestyle, giving up on a world of crime that had, in many ways, given up on him, settling instead for sailing the Mediterranean aboard the boat he'd named after his father's old Thames barge, she felt as if her heart were being squeezed into extinction. It was all such a tragedy. Such a waste.

A butterfly danced close by, its wings a deep metallic blue. As she watched it hovering over a clump of white impatiens growing close to the hacienda's walls, she wondered what Al's reaction had been when Jimmy had arrived at the Look-out's air-strip without her. Had he, perhaps, been relieved that she would so soon be on her way back to Bogotá and a return flight to London? And, whether he had been relieved or not, would he miss her as she knew she was going to miss him?

In the distance, what she had at first thought were a cluster of birds, took on clearer, harder outlines. They were helicopters, a whole squad of them, coming fast into the valley that led up to the enclave.

They were still too far away to be heard, but she could make out the sound of an approaching engine. It was coming from the section of wooded hillside that the jeeps leaving for the air-strip had disappeared into.

Knowing instantly that if anyone was coming back for her it wasn't Jimmy but Al, she began to walk towards the courtyard's wide entrance, and then, as the jeep sped out of cover of the trees, to run towards it.

The same bodyguard who had driven Al and Fleur out of the enclave was at the wheel, Al beside him. Well before she had covered the distance to the entrance, the jeep was bucketing off the rough track and between the open gates.

Arturo didn't pull to a halt beside her as she had expected him to, and neither did Al leap out of the jeep. Instead, as Arturo slowed down, swerving in a dust-fumed curve around her to face the way he had come, Al flung his door open, stretching an arm towards her, yelling: 'Come on, Deena! We need to get the hell out of here!'

A second later her hand was in his and, even as he was hauling her into the jeep beside him, Arturo was picking up speed.

'But we'd have been taken straight back to Bogotá if we'd stayed,' she gasped, falling against him as they bowled out of the courtyard and on to the track leading into the woods. 'Surely that would be easiest? Jimmy doesn't want me flying off anywhere with him. It doesn't fit into his plans.'

'I know all about Jimmy's plans,' Al's voice was hard and abrupt. 'And I know what would happen if Colombia's national drugs squad evacuated me from the hide-out of the country's biggest drug-baron. They'd deposit me straight at the British Embassy and I'd be charged with drug-trafficking offences so gross I'd never see the light of day again.'

They were under the thick canopy of the trees now, and gaining speed.

'Arturo is going to fly us back to the air-strip we flew from this morning,' he continued as the beat of approaching rotor-blades began to be heard. 'You're right in thinking that the last thing Jimmy wants is for you to be joining him, but once he knew I was coming back for you he had – for Fleur's sake – to make some arrangement to get both of us away. Arturo's instructions are to drive us back to

Bogotá. He'll take you to the Embassy, me to the airport.'

'You're not staying with Jimmy?' She was dizzy with relief. 'You're not accepting the offer he's made you?'

'No,' he said, as they rocketed into a small clearing. 'And if you thought I would, you still don't know me very well.'

She wanted to say that, if she didn't, it was a situation she very much wanted to put right, but the noise of the helicopters was now too loud for her to make herself easily heard.

In the middle of the clearing was the Look-out. An overhang of rock hid it from view from the air and a lip of land fronting it gave staggering views of the enclave and the valley beyond.

The helicopters were now almost on top of the enclave, though showing no signs of landing. Arturo veered to a stop, the engine still running. '*Veamos*,' he said to Deena. 'Let's see. Let's see what they will do.'

What they did was to let loose from the air such a barrage of fire-power that no one in the hacienda's courtyard could have survived it.

As they watched, glazed-eyed in horror, acrid smoke rose in plumes. A fire started on the hacienda's verandah and quickly began to spread as the helicopters wheeled over the enclave, heavy machine-gun fire spraying down in round after ceaseless round.

'Je-sus!' Al said on a long drawn-out breath of disbelief. 'What kind of a brief were these fuckers given? This isn't a rescue raid! It's a mass assassination squad!'

'He knew.' As gunfire tore up the ground where, until a few minutes ago, she had been standing, Deena was white to the lips. 'Jimmy knew this was going to happen – or at least that it might happen. And he left me there. He left me there on my own.'

As smoke plumed up towards them and the noise of the beating rotor-blades became deafening, she began to shake, overcome by the realisation that Jimmy hadn't cared whether she had lived or died; that in coming back for her, Al had saved her life.

His arm tightened around her shoulders as he hugged her close.

'Let's go,' he said savagely to Arturo. 'We've seen enough. Let's get the hell out while we can.'

Chapter Twenty-two

'It's a most extraordinary story, Ms King.'

'That one of my son's father's cohorts should have flown me to safety when, if he had not done so, I would most certainly have been killed in an attack carried out by the Colombian authorities with both British and American blessing?'

The room she was seated in looked out over an immaculately manicured lawn. Though the British Embassy was situated centrally in Bogotá, its ambience was entirely English and there had been times over the last three days when she had found it hard to believe that she wasn't in an Edwardian house in the Home Counties.

The Foreign Office official she was now facing had been flown out specially from London and, a clone of Rupert Pembury-Smythe, was not endearing himself to her.

'This is ground that has been covered before, Ms King, in your interviews with the Detective Inspector who accompanied me from London, and with British Customs and Excise officials.' Sir Edward Tyler's voice was wearily reproving. 'There has never been, at any time, a situation in which your life has been knowingly put in danger.'

It wasn't true, and both of them knew it.

'And my son?' Deena persisted. 'What outcome was envisaged where Hugh was concerned? From the moment it was known he intended meeting up with his father, you viewed his life as expendable.'

Seated at the British Ambassador's desk, Sir Edward rested his elbows on its polished surface and steepled his fingers. 'Believe me, Ms King, that has not been the situation – though by allying himself with his father, your son has regrettably placed himself in a position where the risks to his life are the same as those to Jaime Noguerra's; they are many and come from a whole variety of sources.'

Deena's hands tightened in her lap. Her scarlet blouse and white skirt had been laundered and ironed, her white peep-toed sandals cleaned. Her legs were swivelled to one side, neatly crossed at the ankles; her hair was brushed to a high gloss, held away from her face by two tortoiseshell combs. Despite Bogotá's clammy heat, she looked both cool and composed. Inwardly she was seething.

'That wouldn't be the case if steps had been taken to prevent him from leaving England,' she retaliated, her voice dripping ice. 'Thames Valley Police knew he'd been buying drugs – and who from. I find your information that not only have Zac and Clint Docherty been arrested on drugs charges, but also their father and Tommy Virtue, extremely interesting. No doubt if Al Virtue had been arrested at the Noguerra *hacienda*, every link in that particular drugs chain would have appeared to be very conveniently in place.'

She regarded Sir Edward with contempt.

'The delay in their arrest was because of the decision to co-operate with the Americans, wasn't it? Instead of my son being arrested and charged – and remaining safely in Britain, once it was known his father had made contact with him, he was, instead, followed. A situation that should never have been exploited was exploited with murderous ruthlessness.'

'No one coerced Hugh into supplying Amabel Lyndhurst

with cocaine,' Sir Edward said coolly. 'Had he not done so he would never have come to police attention when she died – and if he hadn't come to police attention, no interest would have been taken in his travelling to Colombia, because the connection – that he was Noguerra's son – simply wouldn't have been made.'

'But when it was made – and when you knew his father had contacted him, you passed the information on to the DEA so that NADDIS files could be updated.'

'Of course. Not to have done so would have been criminally negligent.'

'And the Americans came back with the idea that if I were to follow Hugh to his father's mountain retreat, the resulting scenario would be one that could be taken advantage of?'

'I think the word you are looking for, Ms King, is monitor. For your own safety, it was decided that, if such a situation arose, it was one that would need careful monitoring.'

Deena rose to her feet, knowing that the truth of the situation – and the truth about the nature of the raid – was never going to be acknowledged. If, as had been expected, she had been killed along with Jimmy and everyone else who had been at the *hacienda,* then it would have been docketed and filed as a failed rescue mission – a rescue mission in which one of the world's biggest drugs-traffickers had conveniently died.

Jimmy's reading of how the DEA, with British co-operation, would take advantage of her being at the *hacienda* had been spot-on, as had been Al's certainty that, when it was known he had survived the raid, he'd have been accused of drug-dealing on an international scale and immediately arrested.

'And one of Noguerra's men flew both yourself and Al

Virtue away from the *hacienda* to a clandestine air-strip a couple of hours' away, and, from there, drove you back to Bogotá?' the Detective Inspector had asked her, steely-eyed.

'Yes,' she had said, as Al had agreed she should.

'Keep to the truth,' he had said. 'It's simpler. I didn't fly into Bogotá as Al Virtue and I'm not going to be flying out as Al Virtue. They may think they'll pick me up easily enough at Heathrow or Gatwick, but they won't. And they won't pick me up at any of my usual haunts, either. I'll be in London just long enough to drive down to Ponderosa and pick up Blitz, then it'll be straight through the Chunnel and down to Marseilles. Blitz likes sailing. He's going to be well happy aboard *The Mallard II*.'

'And the man in question – Arturo, I believe you said his name was – dropped the two of you off at a junction close to the Embassy?' the Detective Inspector had continued.

'Yes,' she had said.

'And Al Virtue then announced he was making straight for the airport.'

'Yes,' she had said.

There had been many moments of decision, and that had been the final decision.

She could have gone with him.

And she had chosen not to.

How could she have gone? He was a villain – now an ex-villain – who had long intended slipping off to sail the world and who, if he was to avoid trumped-up charges of international drug-trafficking, now had very little choice in the matter. She was a highly respected barrister with an exceedingly well-regulated lifestyle.

Or she had been a highly respected barrister.

As she turned her back on Sir Edward Tyler and walked from the room, she wondered how much of what had happened would now be in the public domain. If it became public knowledge that her son's father was Jaime Noguerra – and that Hugh, far from being censorious of his father, had joined him in the family business in Colombia – then her professional reputation would be bound to suffer. She would be asked to find another set of chambers from which to practise. And, under the circumstances, doing so would be difficult.

Wondering whether she cared, she walked out of the Embassy and stepped into the car that was waiting to take her to the airport.

The answer, as the car eased away from the Embassy and out into Bogotá's wide boulevards, was that she didn't care a jot. She had become a barrister because it had given her the kind of self-esteem she had so badly needed after Jimmy had rejected her. She'd always known that he would keep tabs on her and Hugh. That knowledge had been one of the reasons she had worked so hard at becoming a silk. She had known that when she became one of the country's youngest QCs, Jimmy would know.

She leaned her head back against soft leather as the car purred its way towards the airport, knowing she'd been mad to have cared for so long about what he would think of her, how he would view her.

That she didn't care any longer was the only blessing to have been gained from the traumatic hours at the *hacienda*. There were no other advantages. Hugh was lost to her as completely as if he had died. The pain that had been a part of her ever since he had told her that he was staying in Colombia with Jimmy knifed through her with fresh intensity. Without Hugh, she had, in effect, no family.

The departure hall, when she entered it, was nearly as

chaotic as the arrivals hall had been. She was booked on an Avianca flight to New York, with a connection onward to London. As she waited for her gate number to be called she bought a sheaf of newspapers, both British and Colombian. There was nothing on any of the front pages about the raid on the *hacienda*. She quelled any premature relief, reminding herself that it had only taken place three days ago and that there was still time for a highly doctored account of it to be released to the press.

Once on board the aircraft she read the British newspapers more closely. Nothing world-shaking had happened in her absence. There had been floods in Devon and Manchester United had trounced Juventus in Rome.

As the engines revved and the plane began trundling down the runway, she turned to an inside page of the *Daily Mail*.

A story near the bottom of the page was headed 'Publican charged with barmaid's murder'.

The names Beryl Keene and Richard Virtue leapt out at her.

Richard Virtue, a member of a south-east London family with a notorious criminal history, was today released from police custody shortly after Max Collett, landlord of The Maid, was charged with the murder of Virtue's girlfriend, Beryl Keene.

The satisfaction she felt was intense. Her assumption had been right after all. Sid Ashworth had quite obviously done his stuff after Al's phone call to him, and the police hadn't wasted time. Ginny would be a happy woman again and, with a bit of luck, Ritchie would go with her and Stuart when they left London for Marbella.

There was another familiar name on the next page of the newspaper – and a photograph to go with it. 'Earl's son to marry top model, Sharlene Diss' was the heading over a photograph of Benedict, leaving a nightclub with his arm around a stunningly beautiful black girl.

A wry smile touched her mouth. There was only one stunningly beautiful Sharlene Diss, and that was the Sharlene who, until Al had forgotten her existence, had been Al's live-in lady. Had that been who Benedict had been with when she'd phoned him on his mobile at the Sugar Club? Whether it had or not, it was certainly who he was with now. She wished him well. Whatever her muddled thoughts as to her own future, he hadn't featured in them. The two of them had run their course a long time ago and he was now a part of her past – just as Jimmy was.

The plane had reached cruising height and she looked down on thick cloud-cover, wondering how difficult resuming her old way of life was going to be. She had never been wildly in love with Benedict, but for a couple of years he had given a certain framework to her life. And there had always been Hugh. Now there was no one.

She declined the meal a flight attendant was proffering, trying to think of something she could look forward to once she was back home. It was impossible, because all she could see in her mind's eye, whenever she allowed her thoughts to drift, was Al. Al, naked in the shower, dimples in his broad shoulders, his hair curling tightly in the nape of his neck. Al, reaching out to haul her aboard the jeep as the helicopters flew in. Al, turning his back on the fortune Jimmy had offered him, returning to Europe to sail *The Mallard II* around the Mediterranean.

The bleakness she felt was so bone-deep that, rather than suffer it any longer, she closed her eyes, willing herself to sleep.

When she woke, they were coming into JFK and sleet was driving against the aircraft's windows.

'You're travelling on to London, too, aren't you?' the woman who was seated next to her said. 'Re-acclimatising to British weather isn't going to be easy, is it?'

'No.' Deena gave her a polite smile, very aware that she had no coat or jacket and that, when she left the aircraft, she was going to freeze.

The transfer from the plane to the airport building was mercifully swift, but she was still frozen to near-ice by the time she reached the transit lounge. Hugging her arms for warmth she looked up at the departures screen. The flight to London wasn't scheduled to leave for another forty minutes.

Her eyes scanned the flights listed above it. There were eight of them, but only one interested her. It interested her so much that, looking at it, she knew she would never be able to re-acclimatise herself to London; that she had no intention of re-acclimatising herself to London; that nothing on God's earth would persuade her to give it even the teeniest of tries.

'Where's the Air France ticket desk?' she asked an airport attendant. 'I need to find it! I need to find it fast!'

Chapter Twenty-three

Though it was late October, the weather in Marseilles was mild. The sun was shining as she paid off the cab driver at the side of the vast harbour where the smaller boats were berthed.

Her one fear, as she turned away from the cab to begin her search, was that she wouldn't be able to find him; that he would have already sailed.

The quayside was cobbled and walking wasn't easy. Wearing the red blouse and white skirt that were now her entire wardrobe, she scanned prow after prow and name after name: *La Petite Fleur, Jezebel, Queen of the Seas, Marie-Claire, Pierre-Jacques.* Berthed together, as close as peas in a pod, there were so many small yachts – scores of them, possibly hundreds – that panic fizzed in her throat. Even if he were still here, it was possible she might not find him. She might not find him again – ever.

The panic grew worse, nearly over-powering her, and then she saw the dog. He was big and black and was standing four square on the prow of a yacht whose name she couldn't see.

She didn't need to see it, though. She knew.

'Blitz!' she shouted, running heedlessly towards the yacht's gangplank. 'Blitz!'

As the dog began racing up and down frantically, barking at full throttle, Al stepped up from the companionway and on to the deck. He was wearing a turtleneck sweater, jeans and rope-soled loafers, and her first reaction, as he shouted to Blitz to be quiet, was that he looked unutterably weary; as weary as she had felt on the flight from Bogotá to JFK.

She knew why. Just as on that flight she'd had to come to terms with having lost Hugh from her life, so Al was having to come to terms with no longer having Fleur in his.

They could have each other, though.

That was the simple truth that had been borne in on her as she had stood before the departures screen at JFK.

They could have each other – if they still wanted each other.

'Al! *Al!*'

He looked in her direction – saw her – and a brilliant, blinding smile spread across his face, the weariness vanishing as if it had never been.

As she reached the foot of the gangplank, he was at its top.

'I want to sail the Mediterranean!' she shouted to him as he closed the gap between them, knowing it was going to be all right; knowing that he did still want her; that he would always want her.

'And after the Mediterranean?' he asked, his arms closing around her.

It was the question she had once asked him.

'And then the rest of the world,' she said, secure in the knowledge, as his mouth came down hard and sweet on hers, that the rest of the world would take the rest of their lives.

344